WAY
UPTOWN
IN
ANOTHER
WORLD

SHANE STEVENS

By Shane Stevens:

GO DOWN DEAD
WAY UPTOWN IN ANOTHER WORLD

WAY UPTOWN IN ANOTHER WORLD

• • • • • •

G. P. Putnam's Sons
New York

This is a novel. But no names have been changed to protect the innocent. They're as guilty as the guilty.

FOR CINDY STEVENS
May you live forever

I never expected to live to see my new novel published. Violence is exploding all around me and I have too often been too close to its heart. Yet I am here to marvel still at the beauty of life. I have seen death and so I stand before life—all life—in wonder and awe; yes, and reverence.

There are those who have helped me stay alive. Some are themselves still among the living. Others, too many of them, are unimaginably distant; preparing for childhood's end. Among the dead I note, with respect, Allah, Malcolm X, Charles Joseph, James Chaney, Dorothy Arrington and her daughter Liza and her son Clifton.

And among the living, Emby Wyckoff, who believed.

SHANE STEVENS
New York, 1971

Part One

Part One

If Harlem is one big playground
like the motherfuck whites say it is,
how come they ain't up here playing with us?

   —An old Harlem blues line every kid knows

1.

ON the night I was born they put the tar and feathers to my uncle Ben. They chained him on the ground and packed tar all over him and wrapped him in white pillow feathers. Then they poured the gasoline over everything and burnt him alive.

He had killed a white man in a fight over a trick baby whore.

My mother didn't know about it till next day 'cause she was too busy with me. When they told her, she carried on so bad I spent my first few days sucking air. He was her last brother and the only first-blood kin she had left 'cept for a sister. She never got over him being killed like that, she usta tell all us kids growing up how the white man murdered our uncle Ben. By time I was four I knew so much 'bout it same as if I been there.

Missippi is where it was. Where I was born. Down in the Delta back of the Pearl River. In a three-room elbow house with a porch and a outhouse. A road run close by, and the cotton fields stretched every which way all 'round. There was six of us lived in that house 'cluding us four kids. Rosa and Sally, then me, and Little Ben he come last. My mother called him after her brother when she have him.

Pa did roadwork sometimes and other times everybody was choppin' cotton for the white man. The thing about it was there wasn't never enough to eat. I was always running growl hungry, that's what I remember most 'bout that place in Missippi.

When I was six my pa got run over by a white man. On the road, where he was goin' to the cotton field. It was still dark out and the white man said he didn't see anything. Day after we buried him the white man come 'round the house. He said he was sorry 'bout the accident but he was hurtin' too 'cause his car goin' cost a lotta money to fix up. When he leave he put a ten-dollar bill on the table. My mother asked him what for and he told her it's for what happened. "I hope this makes up for your loss" is what he said to her. She let it set there two days 'fore she picked it up to buy food for us kids.

I can't ever disremember that. My pa was worth ten dollars to the Missippi white man. He worked hard all his life, learned to say yassuh and nawsuh and was the father of four children. And he was worth just 'bout ten dollars.

I told that to Tiger one time and all he said was "Shit, you mama lucky that whitefucker didn't charge her for to get his car fixed up." But I didn't laugh 'cause I knew he was right.

After that we moved outta Missippi. One day my mother got a letter from her sister in South Carolina tellin' us to come over there. Inside a month we left Missippi for good. On the last day people come over and there was crying and all that woman stuff. Somebody asked my mother what she gonna do in So'Lina. "I don't know," she said, "and I don't care. I drug my children through the cotton fields long enough. Ain't goin' that road no more."

Aunt Joe was a big woman, big all 'round. And she was older'n my mother. All her children were growed up and on their own. Her husband worked in town, in a factory where they made cloth. He didn't say too much 'cept when he got drunk, then he made all kinda noise. But he was good to us kids and I think he liked having us around. He told us all to call him Hannibal.

They lived in a big old house with five rooms and a lotta trees and a well, so we didn't hafta fetch water from far 'way like back in Missippi. And they had a mule and a cow and some pigs and chickens. Even a garden nearby the house. Right from the start we were eating better'n we ever done. I ate everything they put in front of me but after a while I couldn' eat no more chicken. That's 'cause I never seen them killed 'fore that. But there in So'Lina I watched Hannibal kill them chickens for eating. He'd take his big knife and grab one of them by the neck and hold it down and just chop its head off. Wonk. The head would roll on the ground and he'd let it go and the chicken'd still be runnin' around the yard for a few minutes. First time I seen that, I begun dreaming 'bout chickens with no heads running after me. I never liked any kinda bird after that and I'd never eat chicken again. Not even now, never touch it.

My mother got a job cleaning for white folks in town, and every day Hannibal'd drive her over on his way to work and pick her up at night. During the day Aunt Joe looked after us kids. By the next year we were all in school 'cept for Little Ben. I learned reading right quick but I didn't care 'bout numbers. All them examples they give us—if you on a train goin' so fast and you got to go so far, how long will it take?—they all made no sense. I never been on a train.

The teachers didn't like me much 'cause I only did what I wanted. And maybe I talked a lot, they don't like when you do that. But mostly I just didn't care for all that sittin' around when I coulda been out doing things.

And when I was in third grade some dumb-fool teacher tried to put this dress on me so's I could be a girl in a school play. I kicked him least ten times 'fore he give up on me.

That was about the time Sally die. She was always smiling and happy and nobody ever heard her talk crossways 'bout anyone. She was smart too. One time she was gonna be something at a meetin' in town and she hadda learn near half a book by heart so she could talk it in front of people. And she done it too. Then she got to feelin' poor and she got even more skinny. Something was all bad in her blood and she just watered down to nothing. Inside a year she was dead.

Sally was fourteen when she go. She looked like a doll layin' in that coffin. Everybody come 'round to share the misery with my mother and Aunt Joe.

"She was so good the Lord done took her right off."

"She in heaven now with the baby Jesus."

"She lookin' down at us from in heaven."

13

Aunt Joe was all wet with tears the whole time. And Hannibal quiet like ever, but you could see in his eyes how bad he felt. I think he liked Sally the most. Rosa was all growed up and she helped what she could.

My mother sat in front the coffin that whole time. Every little while she'd get up and go stand by it and look down at Sally and she'd say, "I brung you into the world and you was too good for it, and that's the God truth." Then she'd sit down again. She had a little praybook she held tight in her hands but she never opened it that I seen. Just kept on squeezing it.

When Sally was buried my mother screamed a few times, scared everybody to death, then she jumped in the grave right on top the coffin. Took plenty to pull her outta there. Then she didn't say nothing else the whole day.

Aunt Joe was always big on religion. After Sally die my mother took it up too. Sometime I'd go with her to the Calvary Baptist Church but I never could get into all the hootin' and howlin' that went by in that church. I just didn't have no religion, I guess it was. But all the kids hung 'round there, so little by little everybody'd join up. The thing of it was where I grew up those years, everybody believed if you died before you were 'bout eleven you'd go right to heaven. After that you hadda save youself or you'd go to hellfire. So people were always coming 'round with their kids to get saved when they were eleven.

When my time come, I listened to the preacher talk about that hellfire but I knew I didn't do nothing so I didn't see what from I hadda be saved. Then he asked all us kids to come up to him and shuck hands. That meant you was ready for the waters, ready to be baptized and saved. I was one of the last to go on up, I knew I was goin' but I waited till the end. When I shuck the preacher's hand my mother jumped straight up in the air 'cause she was so happy. Couple days after that, I was baptized in somebody's stream and I got the religion.

But I never really lost it 'cause I never rightly had it. Later on when I got my age, I come to know about that white man's religion, that Christianity. What it is is death to the black man. Same as in that *Snow White* picture I seen once, the church is

14

the wicked witch that does evil and Jesus is the poison apple that makes the black man sleep just like he was drugged. Which he is.

Christianity is just the snow-white man's religion is all it is.

The next year after I got saved I got laid. Down the road from where we lived was the Petersons and they had two little girls, Daisy and Sue. I remember this one night we were all playing down there, and I was pushing them on a rope swing tied to a tree. We got tired of that and played hideout, me and Sue hiding in some bushes while Daisy tried to find us. We got real tight together and we started in touching each other. Sue was thirteen and she already had little jugs. I put my hand inside her dress 'cross both of them, the nipples tickled my skin and we laughed. That's how Daisy knew where we were.

"Do that to me too," she said when she found us.

She took off her blouse and got down on the other side of me and I put my other hand 'cross her jugs. They were a lot bigger'n Sue's 'cause she was least a year older. There I was kneeling down on the grass with my hands on their jugs. It felt good and we stayed like that for a while.

"Lemme see your thing," Daisy said to me, and 'fore I could do anything, she had it out my pants and was squeezin' it. Then Sue was squeezin' it too.

"Did you ever stick it in?" Daisy asked me.

"Sure. What you think?"

She squeezed it too tight and I yelped. "You is a liar, Marcus Black."

"How you know that?"

" 'Cause you ain't got a white spot on it, that's how I know."

I looked at it. "What white spot?"

"The white spot you get every time you sticks it in."

Sue looked at it. "I don't see no white spot."

"That's 'cause he ain't stuck it in yet," Daisy said.

"How you know 'bout this white spot?" I asked her.

She smiled with her nose in the air. "I just know."

"Bet you don't either," I said to her. "How would you know anyway?"

That got her mad. "I know 'cause a boy told me 'bout it after I let him stick it in." And she stuck her tongue out at me.

Sue jabbed her in the arm. "You mean some boy put it inside you?" She didn't believe her sister.

Daisy turned on her. "That's what I said, ain't I?"

"Well, what it feel like?"

"Felt good."

"Who was it stuck you? I bet I know. Lonnie Hart."

Daisy had her nose up in the air again. "Don't matter none to you who it was."

I kept after her about the white spot. "And he told you it gets a white spot on it every time?"

"That's what he said. Every time you stick it in you get a tiny white dot somewhere on it. And if you do it enough, someday it turns all white."

"Whooeee."

"So that's how I know you ain't never stuck it in."

"How 'bout who was with you?" I asked her. "Did he get the white spot on it?"

"I don't rightly know."

"What you mean? Didn't you look?"

"I looked awright but I couldn' see nothing 'cause all of it was white."

Sue jumped halfway up. "You let a white boy do it to you?" She was shocked.

"Well, it's all the same, ain't it? I mean, they's all got the same thing. And if you shut your eyes, they all black."

Nobody said nothin' for a while, we all just lay on the grass there. I was thinkin' mostly 'bout the white spot. I didn't know if I wanted to have white spots all over it. Which besides, how come the whites didn't get little black spots on theirs? It didn't seem fair to me.

After a while we took off our clothes. Sue pulled down my pants and my thing jumped straight out at her. She giggled and pushed it down. It jumped back like a rubber band. She giggled some more.

16

Daisy got on the ground and I kneeled between her legs and she pushed her little ass up along me and guided my thing inside. I let her do everything 'cause she was the only one knew what she was doing. I laid down on top of her and started moving like she told me, soon I felt all tight inside and I was thinkin' 'bout a lotta things and then I wasn't thinkin' about nothing and I felt real good.

When I got up something happened to my thing and it wasn't a rubber band no more. Daisy wiped it off with Sue's dress, then she put her face to it and licked it like it was candy. And soon it was snapping again and I started moving on top of Sue but she wasn't like Daisy. Every time I moved she'd moan and throw her ass all 'round. Daisy told me to get off and when I did there was blood on everything. I got scared but Daisy just laughed. "That's only 'cause you ain't had a boy inside you 'fore this," she told Sue. And Sue started laughing, so I started laughing too.

Soon everybody was laughing and I'm laying there with blood on me and Sue's laying there with blood on her. When I got on top of her again she didn't move her ass so much but she still kept making all them moanin' sounds like she was feeling it deep inside. It sounded like she was in that church gettin' saved 'stead of out here on the grass gettin' laid. Then I got that same good feel like before, only even better.

Now my thing was soft again and I'm just laying there and the two of them are licking it and then Daisy puts it in her mouth and everything gets warm and I'm feeling better'n I ever done in my whole life. And I didn't say one word when the two of 'em took turns licking and sucking on it like it was a ice cream stick. Or even when they'd do it together.

We played hideout a lotta times after that, me and Daisy and Sue. But not for the next few days. I was too busy looking for that damn white spot. I looked 'bout every ten minutes for days and days.

But it never come.

That was the same year Mr. Coles said he'd give me a dollar

if I'd go to bed with him. Mr. Coles was the teacher I had that year. He was old and he talked so low you couldn' hardly hear him.

One day I was sitting on a bench by the school and Mr. Coles come over and sat down next to me. "A beautiful day, Marcus. God has made a beautiful day for us."

"Yessir, Mr. Coles. Sure is."

"Umm. And here we sit, you and me," he said. "The young and the old, ready to help each other." He looked close at me. "I been watchin' you in class, Marcus, and what I'm seeing is a very restless boy. Very restless. But you a big boy for your age and I can see the girls already after you. Like the bee to the flower, they smell you have what they need." He smiled down at me. "Do you have what they need, Marcus?"

"I guess I do, Mr. Coles." And I give a short laugh.

"Good boy." He patted my leg. "Now, how'd you like to make yourself a dollar, boy?"

He put his hand in his pocket and took out a dollar bill, it sure was a pile of money and I just kept looking at it. He held the bill in his hand while he told me if I come to his house, it was mine. All I'd hafta do is suck him. Only he said it with other words but I knew that's what he was saying. He'd keep asking me if I understood him and I'd keep saying, "Yessir, Mr. Coles." And he'd keep saying, "Good boy."

But I was thinking he must be crazy. Girls suck the boys and I ain't no girl. If he wants that, how come he don't give the dollar to Daisy or Sue or any girl who'd do it? That's what I was thinkin' about. That maybe he's even more crazy'n everybody knew he was.

"I gotta go home now, Mr. Coles," I said to him.

He didn't like I said that but he got up from the bench. "That's too bad, Marcus. I was hoping we'd be friends." While he said that he put the dollar back in his pocket.

"Oh, we friends awright," I told him, "just I gotta go on home."

He looked down at me. He had big fat glasses that covered half his face, I didn't see how he could see with them on. "You

18

go on home, boy, and we forget all about we have this little talk. Ain't that right?" He was holding my arm, tight.

"Sure thing, Mr. Coles, anything you say."

He let go my arm and I walked fast away. Never even looked back till I got all the way home.

Next day I told Billy Stubbs 'bout Mr. Coles. He said Mr. Coles wanted to give him the dollar for the same thing couple months 'fore me.

That's when I knew what was wrong with Mr. Coles. With them big fat glasses he was always wearing, he just couldn' tell the boys from the girls.

I sure felt sorry for him.

Year after that, Rosa got herself married off to somebody lived in town. She was twenty and so quiet you'd hardly know she was there. She was kinda plain and skinny and a lotta boys just passed their eyes over her and went right on by, so when she married up like that my mother was real happy. She made clothes for Rosa, and Aunt Joe got her linens, and everybody come 'round that day and had a good time. They got married in town and went right to live in a two-room house he got for 'em. It had a yard and somebody give them chickens and a pig. Litte Ben ate too much and he got sick as a hound dog.

Five months later Hannibal was dead. Shot down as he got out his car on the road somewhere 'tween town and where we lived. He was at a lodge meetin' after work that day and when he was goin' home it was late at night. His body was laying next to the car when they found him. Nobody knew who done it, and they never got no one for it.

"It was the white mens, I just know it," Aunt Joe said the next day. "They was after him 'cause he was always talkin' up for them school people."

What she meant was the kids goin' to that college in Orangeburg, which was over a good piece from where we was. When they wasn't in school, some of them went 'round to the towns and talked to factory men 'bout better work and more money and all that.

Hannibal listened to them right off 'cause he liked what they said. When they come to town he got some of the black men to hear 'em. But the whites didn't like that, they was madder'n a hen in heat. Least three times some of them come all the way out from town just to pass the house, shouting and cussing Hannibal.

"They is what done it," Aunt Joe said.

The coffin was closed the whole time for the service 'cause he been shot so many times they didn't want nobody see him. 'Tween the service and putting him in the ground, Aunt Joe fainted dead away a half-dozen times. My mother was crying too, and so was Rosa. Me and Little Ben stood 'round, trying to help best we could.

Hannibal was always good to me, all them years in that house, and I was real sorry 'bout that he was dead. I was way past thirteen and I didn't believe no more that when you die you go somewhere in the sky where everybody is happy and singing all the time. Shit. If there was a place like that, the whites already done took it over and made it for whites only. And if they done that, it can't be such a much.

After Hannibal go, wasn't nothin' the same no more. Aunt Joe got real quiet and took to her bed a lot. My mother couldn' do no work in town 'cause Hannibal wasn't there to drive the car. She'd fool with the garden and sit out there most the day. Sometimes her and Aunt Joe'd just set 'round for hours and not say nothing. At night they mostly went to church.

Then one day my mother said we were moving. They couldn't keep the house without no money and which besides, they were sick of the South. It done killed off all their men folk and they were solid fed up. That's just what my mother said. Rosa was gonna stay 'cause she was set but we all were goin' move far 'way.

"Where we goin' live?" I asked my mother.

"Harlem" was all she said. "We goin' live up North in Harlem."

One day in school I asked Mr. Stark to tell me 'bout this Harlem we goin' to. Mr. Stark was my teacher that year. He didn't wear big fat glasses so I figured he must know something. Least he be able to tell the North from the South.

Mr. Stark looked at me real serious. He grumped in his throat and wiped his nose on his sleeve.

"Harlem is the work of the devil," he said. "Its streets are paved with sin, its women are painted whores. Whisky comes outta the taps 'stead of water. And on every block there's a barn where young boys and girls are forced to do sex acts with everybody standing 'round watching."

Sounds to me what some of us been doing right around here.

"The schools teach only how to cheat and kill, and the churches teach there is no God. The people wear masks whenever they go outside, and when they die their body is fed into a great big machine that crushes it into dog food for the wild animals that guard the gates of Harlem." He blew his nose on a scratch of paper.

"The houses are made of glass and they have no windows. It rains every day and the sun shines only at night. And after you live there awhile your blood runs right outta your skin." He picked his nose with a broken pencil.

I'm standing there thinkin' I never wanna go nowhere like that. "How long you live in that Harlem?" I asked Mr. Stark.

His nose begun to bleed. "I never been there," he said, holding the eraser under his nose to catch the blood. "But I'm a teacher, ain't I, boy?"

So that's how come I didn't learn 'bout Harlem from that Mr. Stark. But it didn't matter none 'cause right after that, Aunt Joe and my mother and me and Little Ben just got on that bus easy as you please and went way up North to Harlem.

I was almos' fourteen and I was big and strong for my age and as I sat in the back of that bus I was saying to myself, "Look out, Harlem, here come Marcus Garvey Black."

2.

I NEVER seen snow before. That's the first thing I remember about Harlem. Snow. Everything was white so much I knew we were in the wrong place. Little Ben saw that snow and he bust out crying, he was so scared. He was nine years old but he was crying 'cause there was snow over everything. I got a little shook up myself when I seen all that white coming down from the sky. It looked like the end of the world, like white pieces of skin were gonna cover us and make us all white men. That made me feel bad. But I was thirteen goin' on fourteen and I didn't cry for nothin'.

My mother and Aunt Joe got this place had four rooms but it was in a great big house where other people lived. 'Bout a million of them. Felt funny livin' with all them other people. Everybody had doors in their kitchens and that's how they got in and out. But it was always cold in that house. And everything always smelled bad in the halls and the streets were full of garbage all the time and 'stead of chickens there was rats.

Took me a long time to get the right feel about Harlem and I never really did get it when I was a kid. Most nobody does 'cause you still too strong when you young like that.

Me and Little Ben went to this school right off and Aunt Joe took care of the house 'cause she was sick. My mother got a job making dresses where she worked all day, and at night Aunt Joe'd make tomcat stew and maybe a hoecake of corn bread, and then for a little while it was like we were all back home with Rosa and Sally and Hannibal and all the dogs and a big yard and old Mr. Coles who couldn' tell the boys from the girls. But then I'd go to bed and lay there in the cold and listen to the rats running 'round and even in the dark I knew where I was.

I didn't like school at all. That school was so old the first floor was called the second floor 'cause the real first floor was in the basement by time I got there. You walk in that school and up a couple steps and first thing you know, you on the second floor. You ask someone where's the first floor and they say, "In the basement, where else it be?" Soon the third floor goin' be on the first floor and the real first floor gonna be even more down. Then they hafta call it something else 'cause the second floor be in the basement. Maybe they call it the roof. Someone ask where is the first floor and they say, "Down in the roof."

Everything in that whole school was broke. The walls were broke, the seats were broke, the windows were all broke. Even the blackboard was broke. Only thing wasn't broke was the teachers. Sometimes they'd tell us about a big party they been to or about their big house or their big car. Everybody listened to them 'cause it was better'n when they'd tell us about the things they were gettin' all that money for. There was one teacher, Mr. Jordan, he'd come in sometimes in one of them black suits with the black bow tie and the fancy white shirt. And he'd spend the whole time tellin' us about the party he been to all night, and how he never even was home to change his clothes. Everybody was waitin' for him to go to a fuck party so we could see what he'd wear. But he never did, not in his clothes anyway.

Most of the teachers were young and they didn't like the school. They all said so. One time somebody was mad and told the teacher to go to hell and the teacher said, "I'm in it now, with you little bastards." So right away we knew he didn't like us.

The old teachers were even worse. They just sat up there and talked low so we could hardly hear 'em. They didn't care about us at all. Least the young teachers hated us but the old teachers didn't even see us no more.

23

When I was there maybe a year one teacher went crazy, even more'n the others. Mr. Marvin was his name but all the kids called him Old Shithead. He liked to read the paper in class while we just sat there. There was this one kid, Concho, who kept shooting things at the paper with a rubber band. Mr. Marvin liked to hold the paper up on the desk while he sat behind it picking his nose so we couldn' see him. But Concho kept hitting the paper from his seat. And Mr. Marvin kept throwing him outta class. But he kept coming back.

One day Mr. Marvin come to school with a box. First time Concho hit his paper Mr. Marvin told him to come up to the desk. Soon's he got there, Mr. Marvin opened the box and quick put this piece of pipe around Concho's neck. It was just a pipe with heavy string on the ends. But there was a little battery and some other things you could see inside the pipe. Mr. Marvin told Concho it was a bomb that was gonna blow him up in a half hour, and if he moved at all or touched the bomb it would blow right away. Then Mr. Marvin said good-by to Concho and he walked out the door. Just like that. We all knew he wasn't coming back 'cause he took his newspaper with him.

Ten seconds later that room was empty. 'Cept for Concho.

The po-lice come and they got everybody out the building. Then the bomb men come and they got Concho out the building. They put him in a special truck. "Why they do that?" I asked one of the teachers. "That way, if the bomb goes off, nobody gets hurt." That's just what he said.

But the bomb didn't go off 'cause it wasn't no bomb. It was just a pipe and heavy string and a battery and some pieces of wood. All the kids were sorry, 'cept for Concho. He was scared. He was sweatin' so much his rubber band melted right in his hand. Took 'em two hours to scrape all the rubber off his skin. After that everybody called him Old Rubberhand.

They got Mr. Marvin and put him in jail a few days for scaring a minor. Then he went to some other school with his newspaper and pipe. "He was just a old shithead," Old Rubberhand said when he was gone, "and we got plenty more 'round here like that. This shithouse full of 'em."

I never had no white teachers 'fore that. Never even seen none. First day I walked into the room and seen that white teacher I didn't know what to do. So I figured I'd watch the other kids and see what they do. By the first week I knew everything to do. We were all doing the same thing. Badmouthing the teachers, breaking the desks, fucking the fox, shouting and screaming. And that's how it went on in that crazy school till I quit. Nobody learned nothin' 'cause the teachers didn't care. So nobody done nothin'.

But I was lucky 'cause I knew how to read and write real good. I could read a whole book if I wanted, and write just 'bout anything. I figured I could always get a job.

The kids in Harlem were not the same as back home in the country. They hung out in gangs and a lotta them shot up on dope and got in all kinda trouble. The streets were always full and you hadda fight for everything. Even the games we played were fights. There was one game we played called Last Across. You wait for a car to come down the block and then you run in front of it. Everybody do. And whoever runs last 'cross the front is the winner. Sometimes kids try so hard to win they lose a leg. A few I knew got hit so bad they died.

There was a lotta games like that. Like stealing a car at night and driving it on the highway the wrong way. And jumping 'cross the rooftops of houses. Nobody wanted to get themselfs killed in the games but it was just something to do.

Same with the gangs. When one gang goes down on another nobody's lookin' to get knocked off, but like any army they gotta fight for what's theirs. And some of them go down dead. I had two friends die like that, in gang wars. What they were fighting for was the right to walk down a stinking block that was half junkyards with nothin' but bricks and garbage, and half junk houses with nothin' but old people and babies.

I run with the gangs a couple years when I was still in school. But I never went in heavy 'cause it didn't make that much sense to me. I mean, it was good to have friends awright, but where I come from I seen a lotta land and I wasn't gonna get

25

myself wasted for no little strip of shit with cement on top of it. These North niggers was crazy.

But Little Ben, he was younger and he really liked the gangs. They were a family to him. He grew up with them and when he was sixteen he was a leader of the Egyptian Kings, one of the best gangs ever come outta Harlem. Little Ben was always small for his age but he had heart.

Dope was another thing I didn't get into heavy. I could see pushin' it to make the money but to be a junkie made no sense to me. If you strong you fight, if you weak you cop out. And then the strong live on you. I was strong and I didn't mind livin' off the weak. By the time I was sixteen I was all set for pushing and pimping. I figured I knew enough about both to make myself some real bread. I been in Harlem two years and I learned a lifetime of things. And what I learned most was that money talks best. Even when it whispers, everybody listens.

I wasn't gonna be worth just ten dollars like my pa was. No, and I never won't.

One day I just come home and told my mother I was gonna quit that fool school. She got all upset. She wanted me to get the paper from the school that means I got outta there. I told her I don't need the paper 'cause I goin' get outta there anyway. She was all set to bruise my soul. She woulda too, 'cept I was bigger'n she was.

"Why you wanna quit?" she asked me. "Just tell me that."

" 'Cause I'm not learning nothin' and 'cause I'm wasting my time and 'cause if I got the paper I'm still a nigger and will always get a nigger job which ain't good as a white job. That's all why."

"If you wants a white job so bad, why don't you stay in school and get the ed'cation what you need?"

She didn't understand but I told her anyway. "I am getting a ed'cation. Why should I go to school to interrupt it?"

Right after that I quit school. I had two sixteen-year-old whores humping for me and a local supply man who was gonna let me push for him. I was on my way to money and power and I was the big black beautiful boy from Harlem outta So'Lina

26

outta Missippi outta a ten-dollar father and I had everything goin' for me and then everything fell apart for me and I was just outta luck. One of my whores was stole by a chili pimp, wearing green alligator shoes, the first week I'm in business. And the other one, Nancy, I'm bangin' so much she ain't got nothing left for her work. I begun to see that my heart wasn't in my head when it come to the pimp game and maybe I ain't cut for it.

Two weeks later my supply man was outta business 'cause of a death in the family. Him. And I was outta the junkie game.

I decided to go straight and give the world a break. I needed money so I went to where they give you jobs. New York State Employment Agency. I was part of New York and I wanted a job. I went in and filled a card with writing, then another card, then I waited with all the others. Most of them looked older'n sixteen, some of 'em looked dead. When my turn come the man asked me what I been doing. I didn't know what he'd think about pimping and pushing so I told him I was just outta school.

He looked serious. Sittin' there behind his desk very serious and he asked me what I'd like to do. I still didn't know what he'd think about pimping and pushing so I told him I'd do most anything that pays money. That's when he put on his glasses. They were big fat glasses that covered half his face. He put them on and looked close at me, half his face under glass, and he asked me if I was interested in housework.

"Sure ain't," I said, gettin' up from the chair next to his desk. "If I was, I wouldn' be here. I'd be home." And I walked on out.

All them old men that wear them big fat glasses, they just can't tell the boys from the girls nohow.

I looked for a job 'round where I lived. There was plenty of things open but I already figured I wasn't cut out to be a pimp. Then I got lucky again. One of them hot chicken stores needed a delivery man at night. Toasty Tasty Chicken. I got the job 'cause I told them how much I hated chicken. They hated chicken. Anybody works in those places hates chicken. They figured if I hate chicken enough when I start, I wouldn' quit when I got to hate it even more later on.

I worked four nights a week. I took baskets of toasty tasty chicken to sick people, drunks, stoned heads, old ladies, grifters, grabbers and chink laundrymen. Everybody loved that chicken.

"Ain't nothin' like a good hunka chicken meat, boy."

"Where the chicken heads? I gives the chicken heads to my cat."

"I like to suck on the legs, you know what I mean?"

"Where you been, little miss chicken man?"

"How'd you like a breast of chicken, honey boy? I mean a real live chicken."

The work was hard, climbing all them stairs. And the baskets were heavy. I begun dreaming about chickens chasing me. Some had heads, some just come after me with their necks. But I was making good money in tips, that's what kept me working there. Plus I was selling chickens on the side, whenever I could get some out the door that they didn't see me. If I couldn' run whores, least I could run chickens.

One night I took a dozen chicken dinners to a hotel. That's a real heavy order and I just 'bout made it there. I get to the room and I bang on the door. No one comes. I bang again. Hard.

The door opened.

"What you want here, boy?"

"I'm the chicken man."

"The what?"

"I got your chicken here."

"And I got your balls here if you don't get your ass moving."

Someone called a name and I heard talking. I wasn't gonna move 'cause this was the room number they give me.

The door opened a little more and someone was lookin' at me but I couldn' see his face. Too dark.

"I got a basket of chicken for somebody here," I said.

"Come on in, Little Red Riding Hood."

All the lights were out. It was so dark I shut my eyes to make sure I had them open. Somebody took hold of my arm and I almos' dropped my basket. I got pulled along till we went through this door and next thing I know there's a light on. I'm in a big room with couches and soft chairs and even a piano. Biggest room I ever seen in a house, it was so big there was steps in the middle of it. I was wondering if maybe half the floor fell down like in that fool school.

A big black man was standing over by the door I just come through. "I'll take the basket."

"First I get the money, that's what they told me."

He took out a roll and peeled off a bill. "You keep the change," he said. And he put the bill in my jacket pocket, but not before I seen it was a twenty.

My ears opened 'long with my eyes.

"How old are you, boy?"

"Sixteen."

"How'd you like to make yourself some easy money?"

"How easy?"

He took out the roll again. "Hundred dollars easy."

And he put fifty dollars in my hand 'fore I said a word. It felt hot. I closed my fist over it. That felt hot too.

"We're putting on a show for some people in that room we just was in, a private show just for very important friends. We got the two girls and one of the studs but the other one didn't show." He smiled with a lotta teeth. "Think you can handle it?"

"What I gotta do with them?"

"Just the normal things. Fuck-suck, rimming, chipping, 'round the world. You know, things like that. They got an act all set up so they'll tell you what to do."

What he's talkin' about is whore theater. I heard of them but I never seen one. They go 'round and put these shows on for money, just like the stage shows at the Apollo. Only they do other things.

"Who all goin' be out there? I mean, they ain't from around here?"

29

He made a face. " 'Course not. They all white folks. Business-men and women, shit like that."

I made up my mind. "I do it awright. When I goin' get the rest of my money?"

"When it's over, when else?"

We went into this other room, a bedroom. I looked at the two whores. The white whore was Mindy. She had short blond hair and nothing on and I could see she was a real blonde all the way down. The black fox was called Girl Girl. That's what she said. "Just call me Girl Girl." She was big and laughed a lot. I think they both was my age 'fore I was even born. The stud was white but he was hung heavy, like maybe this was his main job. His name was Chris and he told me about the act and what I do. Mostly what they tell me. "And if you feel you're gonna come, just fake it till you're okay again 'cause we gotta have it hard all the time we're out there." I was wondering how you fake a fake but I didn't say nothing.

"What kinda people watch your act?" I asked him.

Everybody laughed. "The horny kind," Girl Girl said.

Chris looked serious. "Sick people watch it mostly. The child rapers, the incest burners, the men who can't get it up and the women who can't get it in. The ones that hurt and the ones that need to be hurt. Like I say, just nice ordinary, everyday people."

"Yeah," Mindy said. "They're so ordinary, everyday sick they can't give themselves to anybody. They're loners, jackoff artists. By the time we finish the act, most of 'em have jacked off right in their seats."

"Or feel they have," Girl Girl added.

"Same thing. The women love to suck but can't stand to have it inside them. And the men want to come but can't stand to put it inside anyone. They're all sick, crazy sick. You know what I mean?"

"If you don't like it so much, why you do it?"

"Who says I don't like it?" Girl Girl asked me. "I like it fine. It pays good, better'n tricking. I was always meant for the stage anyway." She laughed.

30

"This ain't no real show place," I said looking around. "This just somebody's room."

Mindy give me a dirty look. "Don't be a snob, you don't know enough yet. This beats tricking a mile. And I don't hafta take no shit, and lay under some dope moanin' my head off that I feel good when I really wanna scream in his ugly face."

"What 'bout the people out there?" I asked.

"We're actors," Chris said. "They're just the audience. When we finish the show, we go. What they do with each other is their business but nobody touches us."

I was beginning to think maybe I'd be a actor. Easy money and free fucking. Sure beats walking 'round with no-neck chickens for a living.

"Just remember one thing," Mindy said to me when we all set to go on, "don't come inside me. My husband don't mind I get fucked 'cause I'm an actress but he don't want nobody's juice inside of me. This is just acting we do so don't get carried away. You follow?"

"Yes, ma'am," I said.

We walked back into the dark room and there's a little stage with some lights 'round it over against a wall. I could feel a lotta eyes on me but I couldn' see nobody. But when we got on the stage I seen it was a big room, like one of them lodge meetin' rooms Hannibal took me to when I was a kid. Easy fit sixty people in this room.

There was a blanket on the floor of the stage and Mindy laid down and jackknifed her legs wide open with her cat to the people. Girl Girl kneeled over her and started tongue-lashing her cat. Mindy begun saying "Fuck" over and over. Very slow, like she was prayin' in church. After a while Mindy took hold of Girl Girl's jugs and pulled her down on top and they were eating each other. They rolled over a few times, still eating and making loud noises.

Then Girl Girl got a banana from on the blanket next to her and put it in Mindy's cat and moved it up and down. She put Mindy's legs on her shoulders and stood up so Mindy was upside down with her head on the blanket and the banana sticking

Couple months later my aunt Joe die. She'd been in bed most the time with her legs all fat from water inside them. The rest of her was skinny, not big like she usta be. My mother helped her best she could but we all knew she was gonna die.

She go in her sleep, real easy. One morning my mother said to me, "Aunt Joe's dead." I felt bad 'cause she was good to me, just like Hannibal. But I was gettin' used to death.

When we buried her a lotta people come to the service, mostly women from her church. Everybody was praying and singing and I couldn' help thinking I was on the stage again. And somebody was gonna get in the coffin with Aunt Joe and soon everybody'd be suck-fucking and having a good time. For a couple minutes there I wasn't sure what was real and not real.

That's when I decided I wasn't gonna go into show business. I had a hard enough time as a nigger living a fake life in the white man's real world without having to live my real life in the fake stage world. I just couldn' handle it. No way.

By then I was outta the chicken business too. They started checkin' the chicken and found I was delivering 'bout twice as much as they got orders for. They called me a chicken stealer. That got me mad and I called them all chickenfuckers. That got them mad and they called the po-lice. That's when I called it quits.

"You can't quit," they said. "We got to fire you."

So I stayed there while they fired me and took away my white apron. Then the po-lice come. They were so mad 'bout being called just for a chicken stealer that they stole two big chickens on the way out. "And if you chickenfuckers call us again," one of 'em said, "we'll come down here and beat the chickenshit outta you."

I coulda told them not to call the po-lice. Pigs don't like no bird. They eat it but they don't like it.

By the time Aunt Joe die like that, I was really hurtin' for money. My mother was still working but there never was nothing much exter, so me and Little Ben hadda scratch around best we could. When Doublehead told me I'd make some money just by helping him out, I said sure thing. He had this

34

big case of watches, all kinda watches. I knew they were stole from somewhere but I didn't care. All we hadda do was sell 'em. Ten dollars each, and I got half.

Easy money.

Next day I took the subway down to Forty-second Street by that park they got with all the stores 'cross the street and I sold six watches just like that. How you do it is you go up to someone standing by a store looking in the window, and you got the watch in your palm. You quick say something to them and you flash the watch. You tell them it's hundred-dollar watch they can have for fifteen. Soon's they hear that, they know it's stole and most of 'em walk away. But the greedy ones, they stay and listen to you. You flash it again and it looks real good in the soft case and you tell them shit like they never get a deal like this again. Sometimes they say ten dollars, and that's it. If they don't, you do. You tell 'em you gotta hurry somewhere and they can have it for ten, yes or no. First day I sold one to a man was wearing a watch on each arm. He showed 'em to me, then he took the one I had. I'm thinkin' maybe they were all stole from him and he was buying 'em back the hard way.

That night I went home with thirty dollars for myself. Easy money. The next couple days I done even better. I found my life work as a con man and I was on my way to be a big shot in the hustle game. I moved on over to Fifth Avenue but up more. The stores were bigger and I smelled more money. First day I'm there, I flashed it on this dude lookin' in a shoe store and he listened so I figured I got him hooked. But when I finished he said he was the po-lice and he flashed the buzzer. His buzzer beat my watch. I ended up in jail for selling watches on Fifth Avenue without a license. When he took me in, he said to me, "We don't want you 'round here, nigger boy. Next time you keep your black nigger ass over on Eighth Avenue where it belongs."

If I was thinking right that day I woulda seen he was the po-lice 'cause he was lookin' in a women shoe store. That or a drag fag.

The judge knew the watch was stole, besides which I had five

35

others on me. But I wouldn' tell where I got them or nothing like that. He was mad but he couldn' do nothing to me 'cause I was a minor. I was only half past sixteen. But he give me what he could, six months in jail for being black on white Fifth Avenue.

I was in trouble a few times 'fore that. For fighting and a gang bang and once for joyriding in a car we just took. But I never done no time. I was in school and they musta figured that was jail enough. Then I wasn't in school no more and the watches I was selling made me a public enemy.

My mother was sorry but I was glad 'cause it told me that Mister Whiteface was gonna treat me like a man from now on. Not really a man, they never do that, but a adult. Anything I did he was gonna slam me down so I hadda be quicker and better to beat him. Shit. I was big enough to fuck his daughter. His wife too. He was scared of me now.

I done my time in the city workhouse easy as rolling off a whore. And I learned some swift things too. I met a few good hustle men and I listened close to them. I come out knowing things worth least three high school diplomas. I was seventeen and wise, and any bad in me was there from living in a enemy country and tryin' to stay living. That was clear to me as black and white.

3.

THAT year I was seventeen, that changed many things for me. I come outta jail after six months and I was a yardbird with a record. I knew I had to hustle for my life and I figured I knew it all. The kid days were all gone behind me. Little Ben was only thirteen and still in school, running with the gangs and the girls. My mother was gettin' wore down from a lifetime of misery and it was my turn to pick up the slack. That next year I spent in one hustle after another.

First thing I did when I got out was to hook up with this crazy whiteface I met in jail. He'd been a con artist all his life and he always had something goin' for him. What he had at that time was a machine that stretched dudes who were too short to become po-lice. They all were mean enough but they were just too short to pass the exam. You hadda be least five feet seven to pass and some of them poor fuckers were so short they were midgets. But Al'd tell 'em all the same thing. For a hundred dollars he'd stretch them till they were tall enough. He didn't care how small they were, long's they were big enough to have the hundred dollars.

What the machine was, was a long wood table they laid on, and it had a lotta wheels and shit like that. It looked like nothin' nobody ever seen before. I'd tie their hands above their heads and then I'd tie their feet down the other end. When everything was ready Al would turn a crank and you'd hear the bones stretching. And Al would say things like, "How's he doing, doctor?" That was me. I was a doctor and Al was a doctor. We wore white doctor coats like they do on TV for all them ads.

I'd say to him, "I think a little more, doctor," or "His legs are starting to grow, doctor." Sometimes I'd just say, "He's fainted, Al." Then he'd turn the crank the other way till the poor bastard woke up again.

Al had a mirra, a big floor mirra that was 'bout six foot high. He done something to it so anyone lookin' into it was taller'n they really were. I don't know what he done but it worked. I was just about tall as the mirra but when I looked into it, my head was over the top. When we were stretching somebody we hadda be careful not to walk in front of the mirra. But when the sucker looked in, he'd be taller.

Al stretched them just once for the hundred but if it didn't work he'd give 'em another stretch free. If they ever found us again.

'Course nobody was ever stretched enough to get on the

po-lice so we hadda keep moving around. In three months we musta been in ten places. But while it lasted they were sure coming 'round. I was getting thirty dollars a stretch and sometimes we had five and six a day. A lotta them were PR's. Many of 'em are mostly too short and the motherfuck po-lice kept the rule about how high you gotta be just so the PR's couldn' get on. So in a way me and Al were helping the po-lice. But they never thanked us.

Then one day a sucker got back to us with a gun and Al hadda give him back the hundred. Far as I could see, our pig-stretching days were over.

But that didn't stop Al. He was a con man all his life, and a good one. He just painted the whole machine black and put black leather everywhere he could on it. Then he rented a showy place in one of them doorman buildings and put the machine in there. We were now in the leather for kicks business. Inside a week we had a hundred dudes begging to be hurt on the new black leather stretcher.

Al hurt them awright. He got a hundred and twenty dollars for one hour's pain. And they loved every two-dollar minute of it. I was gettin' forty dollars a pain and my pockets were full up. Then Al got us two black leather monkey suits and he started having parties, sometimes two and three a week. They were all the same. Everybody was dressed in leather. Dresses, gowns, boots, pants, jackets, everything was black leather.

One of the bedrooms had a black leather door. When someone was in it a little black light would go on over the door, and when it was empty a white light'd be on. Al paid a young whore and a stud to work the parties. Anything anybody wanted, they'd do. In the bedroom. And it was free. The black light was always on.

The machine was in the middle of the big room. After a while everybody'd be around it and Al would put some dude on it for a minute for free. His cries'd get everyone hot. Soon they'd all want to get on it, the fox as much as the dudes. And Al would give them all a sample, then he'd make a date for them for the next day or the day after. Sometimes he was booked up a week ahead. At a hundred and twenty dollars a hour.

Those were the days of wine and leather awright. I wasn't nowhere near eighteen and I had more money'n I ever seen. Had all the fox I could handle too. 'Cept most of them smelled like cows. From all that leather. I had fox that when we went to bed they pulled off leather panties. I even had one rich fox who had soft leather dipsticks made for when she was bleeding. When one was full up she'd just shove another leather in. Musta cost her fifty dollars every month just to bleed. I told her for fifty dollars she could put a leather zipper on it. And she asked me where.

After a while I got tired of all that leather. It just got to my nose, I guess. But I made out real good in that con game so I can't badmouth it. I was black on black. When I had my black leather suit on and my black leather boots on and my black leather face on, every fox in the place creamed in their black leather G strings. Half the dudes too. After all, they were just white on black but I was the real thing.

We were on the way to big money but then Al got too smart. He wanted to make it last and he put a camera and one of them tape machines in the bedroom. Only he had them hid so no one knew but us. Cost him plenty.

At the next party this young blond fox took the stud we had working into the bedroom. Then she took the whore into the bedroom. Everybody was pissed off at her 'cause they wanted some but nobody said nothing. She was like the biggest thing there 'cause she was a Senator's kid.

The next day we looked at the film. Unfucking-believable. I never seen nothin' like it and I mean there wasn't much I missed growing up. This fox, this little Miss Whiteass America was a asshole artist like I never expect to see again. She'd make French love turn Greek overnight. If she was in that whore theater I was in that time I was the chicken man, they'd be fucking on Broadway by now.

Even Al was impressed. "Well, well," he kept saying, "now who'd believe that? And she looks so sweet and innocent."

39

He ran it a second time. "What you think, Marcus?"

I told him. "I think she makes them other nuts we got coming 'round here look like a ad for mental health."

He smiled at me. "No, no, I mean the film. What about the film?"

"Burn it."

He wasn't smiling no more. "Why you say that?"

Al was a good con man awright, maybe even a great one. But like all good con men who start conning themselfs, he was missing something. Common sense. I tried to warn him. "It's trouble, Al. Big trouble. You got a good setup here. Why blow it?"

But he didn't understand. "This film should be worth at least fifty grand to her old man. Fifty grand. That's a lotta money, Marcus, my boy. And you get some of it."

"I don't want none of it, Al. You keep it all," I said to him. And I walked out. I didn't plan to come back either. Even left my black leather monkey suit there.

I knew what would happen. He'd call the kid's old man that same day. The old man'd call somebody who'd call somebody else. Then a couple shooters'd call on Al. They'd get the film from him, make sure there was no dupes, and then tell him to leave town right away. He wasn't worth killing, just scaring away for good.

I knew once they got the film they wouldn't bother with me. To them I was just the nigger houseboy.

And that's just about what musta happened 'cause I never seen Al again.

But the money I seen for a little while longer. I got myself clothes enough for a horse and things for my mother and Little Ben. Even sent Rosa and her kids some presents down in So'-Lina. We ate real good for a while too. Meat every night. Not that fatback or tomcat stew but real steak. And when Rosa got sick I sent my mother down there to stay with her a spell. Paid for everything. She stayed for two months and I took care of everything. Then when she come back I went 'way for a couple weeks myself. Down to Florida. I went on one of them jets. I'm

40

passing a sign one day and it says, JET AWAY TO FLORIDA AND LEARN WHAT LIFE IS ALL ABOUT. That sounded good to me. I wanted to learn about life. I'm just a high school dropout plus I'm a coal-black nigger with a jail record at seventeen. So I gotta learn about life awright.

I put on my best threads and I went out to meet life. In this travel place called American Express. I was in the American Express office on that same Fifth Avenue where I got busted that time for selling watches.

I walked in and a dude behind the desk looked out the window for the po-lice. I was a nigger. I quick took out a roll of bills and he quick looked like he was just watchin' a elephant pass down the street. I was a nigger with money. That made me half white.

"Yes, sir. May I help you?"

I put the roll away. If I saw him looking out the window again I could pull it out again. "I wanna jet away to Florida and learn what life is all about."

He coughed.

I didn't know what that meant so I coughed too. He wasn't gonna catch this boy sleeping.

"Yes, sir. Is there any special way you'd like to go?"

"I wanna fly."

"Of course, but is there any, ahh, particular airline you care to fly?"

Now he had me. How many motherfuck airplanes they got flying to that Florida?

I took a chance. "One of them planes with the wings and all that. You know, man."

He coughed again. I coughed again. Must be some kinda signal these fuckers use 'round here.

"Yes, of course. Now, ahh, when would you like to go?"

"Tomorrow. I wanna go tomorrow."

"Any special time?"

I hadda think that one over. Maybe he's seeing if I know what I'm talkin' about. "Whenever the airplane goes," I said.

41

He looked a little red 'round the edges. Then he looked in a little book. If he looked out the window again I was gonna give up. "There's an Eastern flight at 11 A.M. How's that, sir?"

"Is that in the morning or night?"

"Uhh, that's at eleven in the morning, yes, sir."

"That sounds good. I take that."

He almos' smiled when I said that. I'm standing there thinkin' maybe he don't get too much business if he gotta look in a book just to see when a plane goes to Florida. Then he did a lotta paperwork all the whites love to do so much.

"Your name, please?"

I looked at him, trying to see why he wanted my name. Maybe he was gonna call one of his kids after me.

"What is your name, please?"

I didn't know what to do but fuck him, if he wanted it I wasn't gonna give it. "White," I said. "My name is Mr. White."

He smiled. I smiled. Then he asked a couple more questions and did more paperwork. When I handed him the money he handed me some of the paper. I didn't like that too much.

"That's about it, Mr. White. You have all you need right there." And he told me all these things 'bout how long it takes the plane to fly to Florida and how to get to the airport and what to do when I'm ready to fly back. I listened to him, nodding here and there just like I knew what the hell he was talkin' about.

When I stepped away from the desk to go out the door, I seen this little nameplate on the end of the desk. I looked at it. Mr. Green. That was the name on it.

"Have a pleasant journey, Mr. White. And thanks for thinking of American Express."

He smiled big. He was standing there lookin' right at me 'stead of out the window. He made money on me so he was real friendly. All the whites are like that. They all got them fake faces.

"That's awright," I said to him. "Anytime."

"So long, Mr. White."

"So long, Mr. Green."

42

Next day I was in Florida. In Miami. I got up in the morning in that stinkin' dark room with Little Ben sleeping next to me in that stinkin' dark Harlem and I said good-by to my mother and walked out that stinkin' dark building and got on a subway and got on a bus and got on a plane and in a couple hours I was in that stinkin' dark Miami. Yeah. It was raining so hard everything was black like at night. It was so black the plane couldn' find the airport till they called it up on the phone. A voice kept saying, "We are in contact with the airport and should arrive on time."

And we had these belts on so we don't dirty the back of the next seat if we hit it with our head. The plane kept jumping up and down and the fox that worked in the plane kept walking up and down and the dude sittin' next to me said, "Are you scared?"

I looked over at him. He didn't look like no po-lice. I'm high in the sky goin' away and there ain't a pig on the plane. What the hell I gotta be scared about? I leaned over and I said to him, "Man, I'm so scared I gonna get me one of them par'chute things and jump out the window and go for help."

That shut him up the rest of the way.

When we got to the airport they had a boat waitin' to take us inside. Then I stayed 'round there most that first day till the rain was over 'cause I didn't know where to go. It's a big long building with a lotta stores in it. I passed this one store and it had a bus in the window. It was a Greyhound bus only it was small like a toy. But it give me a idea. I went inside and asked the man if he worked for the Greyhound bus.

"Do I look like I work for Greyhound?"

I looked him over. He was too small to work for Greyhound. "You too small to work for Greyhound," I told him.

He pushed his glasses up his nose. "And you are too big to be askin' silly questions. Now is there somethin' I can do for you, boy?"

I smiled him down. "Now that's what I call a silly question awright, and you is just small enough to be askin' them silly questions." I cut the smile. "There's only one thing you can do

43

for me, white man, and I figure you already know what that is."
And I walked out that store.

But I still had the idea. Which was to see some of that Florida on the Greyhound bus. That was the only thing I knew about in Miami. Every nigger knows about Greyhound. When you growin' up, by your bed you say, "God bless Mama and Aunt Joe and the Greyhound bus." That's 'cause whenever a black man gotta go anywhere fast, he goes Greyhound. That's the poor man's airplane. Someone don't see you, then they see you and they say, "How you get here?" and you say, "I fly Greyhound." But if they black they know how you get there. Then someone says, "That Greyhound. It's the only way to fly."

Goddam right. One time I read 'bout this mob in Missippi was gonna lynch a black man. But he was a little 'head of them and he got hisself a ticket and got on the Greyhound bus. The mob come up and they all set to lynch him right there. But the bus driver said no good. He told 'em the nigger is on the bus with his ticket all paid for and he's under the protection of the Greyhound bus people. And he told them if there was gonna be any lynchin' done, they better lynch that whole motherfuckin' Greyhound bus 'cause they ain't gettin' the nigger off it. That mob was madder'n a cow's tit on a cold day but there wasn't nothin' they could do. They just slunk away.

So what I was gonna do was get my ass on the bus and go 'round a little, learning about life and like that. By the time it got night dark 'stead of day dark outside, the rain was over. I went out the big building by the plane and I seen these cars. They looked just like cars only they were long as two of 'em. Right away I seen that I said to myself, "Sonovabitch, Al is down here with his stretching machine stretchin' cars now." But then I knew it couldn' be his work 'cause they woulda shrunk long ago.

I got in one of them but up near the front, just in case. Soon the car filled up and this old man pulled away with it and a little while later we were in Miami. I told him the Greyhound bus. He told me that was his last stop. Then we were all told out. I think I had too much suntan for him.

He parked in front of this big hotel. Didn't look like no bus station to me. I told him that. He told me that's 'cause the bus station is 'round the corner. But I didn't give him no tip. That told him off.

I walked 'round to the bus station, but it sure wasn't such a much. Not big like in New York or nothing. I went up to this one man to talk with him, coming on with my best smile. "I'm off duty," he said. And he walked away like he was really off duty.

I moved over to the next window and waited. After a long time someone come over and said, "This window's closed." And he walked away.

I just stood there for a minute. You don't live long as a nigger 'less you got a long trigger. If you show mad, someone goin' beat you all the time. You gotta be an easy rider.

I'm an easy rider. I just walked on over to the next window. A man looked up at me and said, "You'll hafta wait your turn."

That was fair. I counted the people in front of me, slow and easylike. There wasn't nobody. "How long 'fore it's my turn?" I asked him.

"Can't tell," he said. "Got a lotta paperwork here."

Soon's he said that paperwork I knew it'd be too long. I stepped outta line and went over to get some milk and figure out how to get around these motherfuck crackers.

I'm drinking and thinking and when the milk's all gone, I'm gone. Back in line with something I wrote on a paper napkin. There was still nobody in front of me so I knew it wasn't my turn yet.

"Here's some more paperwork for you," I said to the man. And handed him my napkin. He didn't wanna touch it but he couldn' get past the word paper. If it's paper it must be awright. So he took it and read it and then he looked at me again and then he read it again.

"Yes, sir, young man. Can we help you?" And his eyes smiled and his face smiled and his nose smiled. It was my turn. I sure got to be first fast.

"I wanna go somewheres 'round here on the bus. What have you got where I can go?"

And for ten minutes he told me where I can go. Trying to help me out 'cause we were good friends. He said Panama City was real nice. I looked at it on the map he had. It was so nigger nice it was almos' in Alabam'. "The other way," I said to my friend. "I'm just now learning 'bout life. Ain't no use leaving it yet."

The other way was all these little islands called Keys. There was Key Lock and Key Chain and Key this and Key that. The last island was Key West. It was so south you couldn' go south no more. That's why it was called Key West.

"That's where I wanna go," I told my friend.

He got me the ticket and I give him the money. I turned to go. "How about the others?" he asked me. "Won't they be goin' with you?"

"No," I said to him. "They all goin' stay right around here watchin' out for things till I get back." And I walked on out the door.

He didn't like that nohow. He was hoping to get all of us far 'way from his bus station. He didn't know there was no other us, that there was just me. 'Cause on the paper napkin I give him I wrote, "I'm from New York up North. The others are waiting outside."

This was 'bout twelve years ago, and people down South were gettin' touchy 'bout us Yankees coming down and making trouble for them. 'Specially on the Greyhound bus.

I hadda wait till early next morning to get the next bus down to this Key West. But it was warm out. Everything was wet but it was a warm wet and it all smelled good. I walked some. Stopped in a place and got burgers and milk. Looked in store windows. By midnight I was back in the bus station, only it was closed so you couldn' sleep in it.

I walked 'round the corner to the big hotel where I got out from that car. The street in front of it was the biggest street I ever seen in my life. It had trees in the middle of it, that's how big it was. And on the other side was more trees, looked like a park. Two men were standing on the hotel steps and I asked them what was 'cross the street. "That's the ocean," one of 'em said, "the Atlantic Ocean." The other man laughed. "Well, sort of more like the bay," he said.

The ocean. That meant there was water. I was thinking maybe the water in Florida was better'n the water in Harlem. Couldn' be no worse.

I crossed the street. Trees were everywhere. There was a little building, like a house. And more trees and grass and benches all over. Then I got to the end and there was the water right in front of me. It smelled so good I shut my eyes and just smelled that water and I never ever smelled nothing so good as that. Never.

I sat on the last bench near the water and I kept my eyes shut and I just sat there for hours. I don't know what all was goin' through my mind but it was a powerful lot. I was thinkin' mostly 'bout how I grew up black in Missippi and So'Lina and then Harlem, and all the shit I seen. I never knew there was no place like this. I was thinking how my uncle Ben got hisself burnt up the night I was born. And my pa gettin' run over by a white man and how he was worth just ten dollars. And Sally dead and Aunt Joe dead and Hannibal dead and my mother having the misery all her life. Then I seen myself being so sad 'cause I was all alone that I walked in the water till it got over my head and I kept walking and walking.

That scared me so I started thinking other things, like about Daisy and Sue back home and how we played hideout all them times. And all the fox I been with since then. And 'bout when I was the chicken man and that night in the whore theater with Girl Girl and Mindy and Chris. Never knew what happened to them, never know what happen to nobody after they leave or you leave.

I got so tired of thinking I laid down on the bench and went to sleep and then I was dreaming 'bout sitting there on that bench in Florida and thinking about my whole life. And then I got so tired of thinking I laid down on the bench and went to sleep, and that's when I woke up.

47

I looked at my watch. It was after five but it was still dark. I walked over to the bus station. Still closed. When I got back to the park there was a woman sitting on my bench so I sat down on the next one. After a while she got up and went to the water and stared at it a long time, then she turned 'round and saw me. "Beautiful, isn't it?" she said to me.

It was a funny thing. The benches were so far apart I couldn' see her face too good but I could hear her voice plain as anything. She didn't even talk loud but I heard her.

"Sure is," I said.

Then we said nothing for a long time. She was a white woman and I wasn't in this town for no trouble, had plenty of that back home. I just sat there lookin' out at the water.

When she come on down I kept saying to myself, "Walk on by, white woman, walk on by." But she come over and sat down on the bench and I wasn't gonna get up and go.

"Are you waiting for the sunrise?" she asked me.

She was maybe forty and too heavy but she looked like she took care of herself awright. And she had a real nice voice. I smelled at her. "Yes," I said, "I'm waitin' for the sunrise."

She smiled back. "I come out here every morning to watch it. It's the most beautiful thing I've ever seen." She give a big sigh like she was feelin' good. "Are you from Miami?"

"New York."

"Oh. I've never been there but I hear tell it's lovely this time of year." Silence. "I'm from Nebraska. Lincoln, Nebraska. Have you heard of it?"

I shook my head.

She laughed. "Not everyone has, I'm afraid. It's not like New York. Wherever you go, people have heard of New York and I imagine there's always something to talk about."

I listened to her voice. It was like the water, soft and peaceful. "You live here now?" I asked her.

"Oh, no. But I wish I were." Her throat giggled. "My husband and I are here on a business trip for his company. We're staying in the hotel across the street, and every morning while

48

he's still asleep, I sneak out here to watch the sunrise. He doesn't think it's anything."

She was a schoolteacher in this place she lived in. She liked kids, had some of her own. She was very interested in what was happening in America but her husband didn't care too much. And she was a little scared 'bout some of the things goin' on, 'specially the race thing. What got her most scared was this test she give her kids in school. She divided them into kids with brown eyes and kids with blue eyes. For two days she let the brown eyes be right in everything and she give them power over the blue eyes and exter things like time off and no homework. Then the next two days she done the same for the kids with blue eyes. They got the power and all the exter things.

"I was sick by that Friday," she said to me. "The youngsters acted just the way many adults do. The superior group acted like tyrants on their days, and the other group hated them so much there almost was violence. And these youngsters were just ten years old. In most of them I saw anger and despair I never would have believed possible."

I was sitting there listening to her and I was thinking how little some people know who are s'pose to know so much.

"That Friday I asked them all to write down their feelings, and do you know," she asked me, "do you know that half of them wanted to quit school and at least a third of them thought of killing their classmates with different-colored eyes?"

"If I told you I knew, you wouldn' believe me," I said to her.

She stopped. And her eyes got a little watery. She had green eyes, sea green. "Yes, yes I would," she said to me very soft, "I would believe you, and I do."

We didn't say much after that. We just sat there and watched the sunrise. She was right. It was the most beautiful thing I ever seen.

When it was light out she went back to the hotel, to her husband who didn't care too much about what was happening in America, and who didn't think a sunrise was anything.

"Goodby," she said to me, "and good luck."

I wished her the same. Goodby and good luck.

I was the first one on the bus. I didn't even hafta hand the bus driver a paper napkin, just the ticket. He didn't care who got on first, all he cared 'bout was who got off last. Him.

In a while we were on this road that was just one lane and another one goin' back. We went over so many bridges I couldn't count 'em all. One bridge was so long it musta been the longest in the world. And it was right down on the water too. The water was green mostly and sometimes it was blue. I never seen so much water, it was all 'round us. Didn't matter where the bus went, the water'd be right there. I kept thinking if the green water set itself up as the power, it would make slaves of the blue water. And then the blue water would wanna kill it.

I fell asleep thinking like that.

"Key West, last stop. Watch your step, please."

That was the first thing I heard when I woke up. I grabbed my gym bag and got off the bus and I was in Key West. In a parking lot. I followed some people through this little alley with houses on the side and I come out on a street. The sun was hot and everything looked so light it hurt my eyes. I walked down to the corner. Duval Street. That was the name of the street. There was stores everywhere and a movie and a lotta bars. Looked just like Harlem 'cept for everything being so motherfuckin' light. I didn't think it ever got dark on that street.

I asked somebody where the water was and they pointed both ways and walked on by. Didn't say a word. So I walked the other way. All the houses and stores were small, no big buildings like in New York. And this bus come up past me and a fox was driving it. Remind me of a picture I seen once where the whole town was nothing but foxes and they hadda fuck each other 'cause there wasn't nothin' else around.

A little ways down I begun hearing spic music. Made me feel good 'cause I sure wasn't seeing nothin' black in this town. But if there's PR's around, least that's halfway to home. And there was a lotta them too. Some even smiled at me so right away I

50

knew they must be some special kinda PR. They don't do that too much back home.

When I was almos' to the end of that Duval Street I got to the corner and I started 'cross the street and I heard this funny noise. I turned around and my eyeballs jumped straight out my head. I looked 'round and I'm gettin' run over by a train. This flipflop motherfuck train is coming down the middle of that street just like it was a truck or something. It's a train but it thinks it's a truck. That motherfuck is trucking on down the street at me, there are no tracks or nothing but it don't care. It just comes down at me making noises and I quick get my ass off the tracks that look like a street. There are people on the train and they laugh when they see me jump like that.

"Lookit that coon go."

"Just lik' a rabbit."

"He run like the wind, that boy."

"Never seen a nigra that couldn'."

The train passed and I picked myself up real quick, case it come back to get me on this track that looks like a sidewalk. But I'm mad. What the hell is that little train doing in the middle of the street like that? If that train was in New York they'd give it a ticket for blocking traffic even when it was moving. I quick shout after the train, "You ain't no truck, you motherfuck."

The train said nothing. Just kept trucking on down the track.

Another two blocks past some motels and I was in the water. On this long pier in the water. I sat down on the end of it and I was by myself for a long time with the water lapping all 'round me. I shut my eyes and laid down on that pier with my legs half up like the whores do and I went to sleep.

I was God and I was sittin' on a bench and I was lonely. So I decided to make some people and I went up to the stars at night when it was dark and I got a pail full of darkness and I come back. Then I made the people and I painted them all over with the darkness from the pail so the sun wouldn' hurt them. The more people I painted, the lighter dark they got

51

'cause the pail was gettin' empty. I kept on painting till there was no more darkness in the pail and I told all the people left that they hadda live without the darkness. They didn't like it 'cause they knew the darker you were, the better you were, and they knew that someday the sun would drive them crazy. But the pail was empty. And so they became the slaves of the people who were painted with darkness.

The sun was still out when I woke up and my coal-black body was full of sweat. I took off my shirt and went over to the beach next to the pier. It was just a little bit of sand with a lotta stones and wood in it. But it was warm. I put my hand in the water and that was warm too. Then I put my shirt back on and walked over to this eating place, it was like a shack right on the beach and it had a porch with tables and chairs.

I sat on the porch. At the last table over by the rail was this dude with a funny hat on and his feet sticking out over the side of the rail. He was wearing shades and lookin' out at the water. "What you see out there?" I asked him. Just being friendly.

"Nothing," he said. And he turned to me. "But I'm lookin' for Cuba."

"Is that out there?"

"Ninety miles," he said to me. "Just ninety miles away is all."

Ninety miles? If he wanted me to think he can see ninety miles with them shades he was a bigger con man than Al. But maybe they got 'em even down here.

"You're from New York."

Must be a con man awright 'cause he's plenty sharp. "How'd you know that?"

"From your walk. I was watching you come off the pier. New Yorkers walk like a cat, always ready to run."

"Where you from?" I asked him. From his hat I figured he just come from the moon. But from how he was sittin' there I was thinking Missippi. All them crackers sit funny like that. And if he was a cracker con man, I was headin' for the moon myself.

"New York," he said. "Same as you."

I stuck my feet half over the rail and we talked 'bout New York. He was a teacher and he lived downtown somewhere. Only he didn't like to teach so he just did it one month a year to keep the paper that said he could do what he didn't like to do. Rest of the time he did what he really liked to do. Drive trucks and work on the docks, things like that. He didn't need a paper to do that, so he could do it all the rest of the year. "Work with your hands, and your head works with you." He said a lotta funny things like that made me laugh. Make anybody laugh. He told me his name was Jim Southernmost.

"I'm the last of the Southernmosts," he said.

"And I'm just 'bout the last of the Blacks." Which was true. 'Cept for Little Ben, I was the last Black man.

We talked right into dark, sittin' there on that porch. Mostly he talked and I listened. I could see he didn't like to listen, maybe he couldn' hear too good. Whenever I said something he just talked louder and went right on. After a while my ears hurt from all that talking I didn't do.

"People are all the same" was one of the things he said. "No matter where you go, people are all the same all over." He shook his head. "Rotten. Rotten clear through."

I told him I seen the sunrise in the morning and now the sunset, both on the same day. He wasn't impressed. "Happens every day," he said. "Been going on like that for years."

"Yeah, but—"

"Someday," he said, talking louder, "someday the day will come when the day won't."

If he keep on talkin' like that, someday goin' come for him a lot sooner'n for the rest of us. That's sure as shit.

When the place was closing and no one left on the beach, me and Jim walked like two cats back up that Duval Street and 'cross the train tracks. He was gonna see some friends in a bar way the hell up the other end of the street. They were all staying in this house somewheres 'round there and he said I could stay with 'em. Which was good with me.

The bar was called Captain Tony's. It was real dark inside and it had fishnets and all kinda crazy things hangin' all over.

Looked like a jungle is what it was. We went on over to these two friends of his and we all sat around drinking the whisky. I'm big for my age so I'm okay. And besides, the motherfuck whites don't never look close enough at a black man to tell how old he is.

These two dudes he was with were bartenders in New York, downtown where they lived. They were in Key West doing fishing and shit like that. I figured if they friends of Jim Southernmost they must really be teachers who just like to be bartenders, like some people wanna drive trucks and work on the docks. But I didn't say nothing.

When they heard I been busted already, they come on real friendly 'cause they both done time in the slammer. Some more people come in later and everybody got stoned and Jim Southernmost was sitting there tellin' everyone he was the last of the Southernmosts. Somebody said, "Good," and ten people drunk to that. Then this one bartender got up and said that ain't true 'cause *he* was the last of the Southernmosts, and everybody cheered. And the other bartender got up and said they both liars 'cause *he* was the last of the Southernmosts, and everybody cheered again. I figured what the hell, so I got up and I said any fool with eyes could see I'm the most Southernmost of all, so that makes *me* the last, and a sailor in a sailor suit said, "Get that nigger."

My friends were gonna make *him* the most Southernmost of all anybody could be that night, but Captain Tony's people threw him out fast.

And a stranger come up to us and said, "One of you shoulda hit that guy. Anybody calls my friend a nigger is a nigger." Then I didn't know who to hit.

At the end of the night only me and the two bartenders was left so we went to other bars drinking. In this one place we walked in, the fat man behind the bar said, "We don't serve Negroes here."

The two of them went right up to him and one said real soft, "Listen, fat man, we don't *want* a Negro." And the other said, "Whisky. All we want is whisky."

And that fat motherfuck backed up three feet and we got all the whisky we wanted. Right when we wanted it too.

I stayed with Jim Southernmost and all them New York dudes for 'bout ten days. I was down the beach in the day and the bars most the night. And the money run down fast. When it was all gone I got that bus back over the water and all them bridges to Miami. And I got that long car back to the airport. When I left Miami the sun was shining and everything was clean and smelled good. I got on a plane and got on a bus and got on a subway and in a couple hours I was in that stinkin' dark Harlem. Nothin' was changed.

All the money was gone so I started hustling again. First thing I did was team up with this stud who had a jackoff machine. It looked like one of them kid toys that come in a big box at Christmas. There was two rubber belts that you put 'round your waist and ass, and a big battery pack that rested up against your back. An arm come outta the pack and 'round your waist. It was in the shape of Mary Fist and it had a glove on to make it soft. All you hadda do was slip your rig in the fist and start the arm goin'.

It cost the stud ten dollars to make one and we sold it for fifty. I went to some big stores askin' if they wanted to stock it but they didn't have the balls for it. But I sold least ten to their salesmen for home. I sold it to fags in bars on the East Side and to business types on Wall Street. I even put ads in the sex papers as a home relax machine. It was strictly a downtown item, I couldn' sell any in Harlem for nothing. Jacking off is a middle-class thing, the uptown stud comes by his balls the hard way and he ain't gonna let 'em kick off so easy.

We were making money and I was rolling again. But you always gotta count on everything goin' wrong, that way you already know what's gonna happen 'fore it happens. What's gonna happen is everything's gonna go wrong.

The machines didn't work right. The stud couldn' set the arm to work at all kinda speeds so it was too slow for some and too fast for some. And the arm'd jam a lot and then the battery'd go dead. Nobody come back for a second one. "It needs

55

more work," one dude told me. Till then, he was gonna go back to his hand, or someone's hand. "Been tested and proved," he said, "over a whole lotta years."

After that it was all downhill. I sold bottles of spring water for a sawbuck each 'cause they'd give you a stiff rig for a week at a time, didn't matter what you did with it or how many times you did it. I sold shares in a bowling alley that was gonna be built on top the Washington Bridge. I even sold metal coffins that kept dead people dead till they could be made live again when a cure was found for whatever they were dead from.

I stayed on the job, hustling my ass off making a dollar. Then I was eighteen and it didn't look like I was doing too good. I wasn't sure where I was goin'. Six weeks later I knew where I was goin'. To prison. I just didn't know for how long.

4.

THE early spring morning was a woman laying on the bed next to you, soft and warm and waiting. The street was still asleep, and the cars stretched out along the curb were slowly turning to gold in the sunlight. We sat on the stoop and listened to old man Mose beat the shit outta his wife.

"Goddam it, woman, I'se gonna whup yo' ass good this time."

I was eighteen and restin' easy and not thinkin' at all where my next hustle was coming from.

"Who the fuckin' hell you think you is but a nigger woman?"

Wallace laughed, a short slobby laugh that started somewheres in his nose and pushed itself on out.

"You is shit, you is less'n the dog shit out on that street."

He poked Leroy in the ribs and made a sign with his hand. Old man Mose was one crazy old man.

*"When I says something 'round this house you listen, you
hears me?"*

We tossed the softball around, sitting there on a spring morning with nothin' to do but toss a softball around.

"Sure wish something'd happen 'round here."

"You ain't the only one, man."

"We could go jumpin' the cars."

"Fuck that, man. I got my good pants on."

"Shiiit, man, them's you only pants."

"Who say so?"

"I know so, man. Everybody know that."

"Shiiit."

The softball bounced off the stoop and ran down to the
gutter.

"Go get it, man."

"Shit, man, you dropped it, you get it."

"You throwed it."

"But I throwed it to you."

"Marcus?"

"Yeah, man."

"How you think this nigger ass got hisself so lazy?"

"Who's that, man?"

"That lazy ass nigger sittin' right there next to you, thas
who."

"Ain't no nigger sittin' there, man. He just got hisself too
much sunburn is all."

A rat come up outta the cellar and stopped in front the garbage piled up 'gainst the building. He looked scared 'cause he
was in the sun.

"What the hell that rat doing here?"

"What you mean what that rat doing here? He live in the
building, don't he?"

"Shit, man, that rat so small if'n I catched him I'd throw him
back."

"Oh, man, if you catched that rat you'd take him home to
your mama so's you'd all have somethin' to eat tonight."

"Old woman, I'se tell you for the last time. Any money

57

'round this house belong to me, and that go for everything else too. Now feed my dogs, goddam it."

Old man Mose lived on the first floor with two great big dogs and his wife. She was a nice yella woman that always smiled at everybody.

"He goin' kill her one of these days, sure as shit."

"She kill him first, man."

"What you talkin' about?"

"Every time when he beat up on her then he fucks her, don't he?"

"Yeah?"

"So if he fucks her enough times, with his old heart he ain't goin' last much longer."

"Not the way he beat up on her he ain't."

"Maybe he don't know that."

"Don't matter none. Long's she know it."

I walked out to the curb and picked up the softball. It was all dirty from the water and shit in the gutter.

"What kinda money you got on you, Leroy?"

"I'm tapped out, man."

"What 'bout you, Wallace? What you got?"

"Same here, man. I ain't got spit."

"I got three dollars. Ain't enough."

"Ain't enough for what?"

Somebody threw a dead rat out one of the windows in the house next door. It broke all open on the sidewalk.

"Ain't enough for nothin'. Shit, man, all the money I had down in that Florida."

"Where'd it go?"

"Where'd it go is gone, man. All gone."

"That the way it go awright. Slippin' out even when you sleepin'."

A car passed with the radio blasting away.

"Man, things too quiet 'round here. This keep up I'm goin' back to that motherfuckin' school."

"What you goin' do there?"

"I ain't goin' *be* there, man, but if'n I stay out when I *s'pose*

58

be there least I feel like I'm doing somethin'. This way I ain't doing nothin'.''

"Wallace, man, you is crazy, you know that?"

"Ain't I right, Marcus? Tell this dumb nigger I'm right."

"How the hell would I know, man? I quit when I was sixteen same as you."

Leroy grabbed Wallace's baseball glove off the stoop.

"Where you goin' with my glove, motherfucker?"

"I'm just gonna dip it in this rat shit, man."

Wallace jumped up quick.

"Leroy, I'm goin' bust you ass if you don't gimme my glove."

Old man Mose stuck his head out the window.

"Shut up out there when I'se sleepin'."

"Fuck you, man."

"Who say that?"

"I say it, man."

"Me too."

"We all say it, man."

"Go and beat up on you woman some more."

"Yeah, you old fuck. You be lucky we don't get the po-lice on you."

"Niggers."

The window slammed down.

"Why he always call us niggers? Like he ain't black as rat shit hisself."

"That's 'cause he thinks he a white man. In the head, you know?"

"He white in the head awright. Crazy white is what he is."

I picked up the bat and started walking.

"C'mon."

"Where you goin', man?"

"Let's go play some ball."

"Where at?"

"Them fields they got over by the highway there."

"Shit, man, thas too motherfuckin' far," said Wallace, throwing his glove up in the air.

"How you make that far, man? It's only a few blocks over."

59

"More'n ten blocks easy."

"Well, what 'bout it, man? You got feet, ain't you?"

"Them ain't feet what he got. Them's tanks."

"C'mon, man."

"My feet is sore and I ain't goin'," said Wallace.

"Now ain't that some shit? C'mon, let's go without him," said Leroy.

The two of us walked up the block, me with the bat and Leroy holding the ball and his glove.

"Hey, you motherfucks."

We turned 'round and here come Wallace runnin' after us.

"What's this, man? We heard you was gonna stay off your feet."

"Yeah, but I wasn't goin' stay offa them all 'lone."

"Is you scared of the light, you little black bush head?"

"Fuck you, man."

We crossed the street and a truck almos' hit Leroy.

"Goddam."

"Man, you sure can move your ass."

"Just like one of them rockets goin' off. Zoom."

Leroy laughed.

"Man, that wasn't nothin'. I'm so fast, man, I'm so fast I gotta run backwards so's the cars can catch up to me."

"I bet you so fast if someone shoot at you, the bullet turn right around just from the wind from where you was."

"Shiiit."

"Hey, here come Ophelia."

"Oh, man, that funky bitch is so bad she give you the clap just lookin' at you."

"You know, one time I had her down on me and my meat's right in her mouth and she tryin' to talk like wasn't nothin' happening."

"I know, man, I been there."

"Everybody been there."

"Goddam right."

Ophelia seen us and went into her whore walk.

"Uh-uh, she seen us."

60

"Here she come."

"I feel the clap oozin' out already."

"How you men?"

"In a hurry," said Wallace, pulling at us.

"What's goin' on?"

"Usses, thas what. C'mon."

"How you mama, Ophelia?"

"She's workin' Lenox Avenue now."

"Yeah, well, thas a good street awright."

"She do good enough for a old whore. Hey, you men got time I take on all of you."

"Ain't got no time now," said Leroy.

"No time for nothin'," said Wallace.

"We see you some other time, Ophelia."

"Anytime, you men know me."

We all laughed and moved on down the block.

Leroy shook his head.

"Jesus, she sure is ugly," he said.

"And she ain't got no tits at all, only the nipples."

"Yeah, and her ass so fat it got waves in it."

"And her cat got worms in it."

"And her mouth got evil teeth in it."

"And her head got bugs in it."

"And her one eye got blood in it."

"Jesus, she sure is ugly."

We got to Broadway and crossed it 'gainst the light, jumpin' the cars like we always done. The last car got so scared it stopped dead and the man come runnin' out.

"You crazy sonovabitchin' kid, you trying to kill yourself?"

"Ain't no sweat off your balls, man. Just go right on by," Wallace said.

"Listen, jigaboo, I oughta break your ass for you."

Me and Leroy moved in closer to Wallace and the white man.

"What's the trouble here, man?"

"This motherfucker is goin' break asses is what he said."

"Uh-huh. Yeah, well, we stay 'round for that awright."

"Wouldn' miss it for nothin'."

The white man started to say something, then he looked at me and Leroy and then at Wallace and he stopped. He got into his car and took off without sayin' another word.

"Chickenshit," said Wallace.

"Birdfuckers, all of 'em," said Leroy.

"Chickenshit birdfuckers," I said.

We passed one of them store clubs with a couple dudes sittin' outside. They looked like they might be worth a few bucks on a quick hustle.

"Hey, my man, I got three dollars here says I'm so fast I could stand right next to you and you never touch me once."

"How's that again?"

There was a newspaper laying on a empty chair by the club door.

"On that newspaper. I'll stand on one end of it and you stand on the other. I got three dollars says you can't touch me."

They looked at each other. Sucker money. One took out a roll and peeled off three singles. I give him mine and he put them all on the chair.

"Okay, Charlie, take the man's money."

Charlie was big awright and I was glad I wasn't gonna be feelin' his punch. I took the paper and I put it on the step under the door, half on each side. Then I stood outside on my half of it.

"Awright, man, you go inside on your end and if you can touch me you got youself a sucker."

Charlie walked inside the club to get on his half of the paper but I could see he knew he been took. I quick shut the door. He was gonna hafta put his fist right through it to touch me. I waited.

In a minute he opened the door and walked out past me.

"Pick up the money," he said very soft.

I folded the bills and put them away.

"We wouldn' wanna see you 'round here again."

"Yeah, nigger, take a walk and don't come back, hear?"

"Yassuh," I said in my best shuck voice.

Me and Leroy and Wallace moved on.

"Smart nigger," Charlie said to my back.

"Goddam smart nigger."

It was still a couple blocks to the ball fields and we laughed all the way there.

"Whooeee."

"Did you catch the look on that dude's face when Marcus shoved the paper under the door?"

"And then shut the door?"

"He looked like he was goin' die."

"Whooeee."

It was a early spring morning, that morning I was just eighteen, and we were gonna play some ball and have a good time.

We got to the ball field.

"Let's go way over by the highway."

"What's the matter with right here, man?"

"Nothin' the matter, 'cept the diamond's over there."

"Well, we ain't playing no big league game, is we?"

"Man, you just gotta be the laziest nigger I ever come 'cross."

"Ain't lazy, motherfucker. I'm just careful 'bout how I move myself," Wallace said.

"You be any more careful you don't goin' be moving at all."

We walked on to the last softball diamond right by the highway.

"This look good right here."

"What if a whole team come by?"

"There's a diamond over there ain't used, they could play on that."

"Not too many studs out here today, man."

"Too early still."

Wallace picked something up from the ground.

"What's that, man?"

"A dollar bill," Wallace said. "All crumpled up and dirty from all the dust 'round here."

"Lemme see that."

"This my lucky day, sure enough."

"Sure look old awright."

63

"That's 'cause it been here so long."

"How long you think, man?"

"Can't tell, maybe years and years," I said.

"This my lucky day, I know it," Wallace said.

We were by home plate, standing under the big curved fence. I begun swingin' the bat.

"I'll hit some out first."

"Then me."

"No, me."

"Don't matter. Everybody gets a turn."

Wallace run out almos' to where the outfield was. Leroy stopped by the infield. I hit the ball high in the air and Leroy missed it when it come down.

"Hit one out here," Wallace yelled.

I hit about ten and I was tired already.

"C'mon in, man. Your turn."

Leroy walked on in and threw me the glove.

"I hit better'n I can catch," he said.

"That's good," I told him, "or we be here all day."

After Leroy, Wallace got up and then me again and we went around three or four times like that. Then we laid down in the grass in back of the fence.

"Man, I'm so tired I feel the bones under my skin."

"Shit, man, that ain't nothin'. I'm so tired every hair on my head is sleeping."

"What you talkin' about? That nappy hair you got curl up no matter what."

"You men don't know what tired is. I'm sittin' here talkin' to you and I been sleeping for ten minutes already."

"You call that tired? Shit, I'm so tired when I sleep I'm gonna be dreaming 'bout how tired I am."

We were stretched out facing the highway.

"Man, them cars are comin' close by."

"Too close."

"Where all them cars goin', you s'pose?"

"All crazy places."

"Then tomorrow they turn right around and go back."

"Make no sense."

A big black Caddy went on by.

"Umm-huh, thas for me."

"Piece a shit, man."

"Listen to this nigger talk. Man, you ain't got two nickels makin' noise and you say a Caddy's shit."

"Shit is shit, man."

"Nigger, you brains is leaking through all them holes in your hair."

"Easy, man, Wallace don't like no one talk 'bout his hair."

"Shiiit. His hair so nappy he could put a pencil in that hair and it'd stay there through a fuckin' hurr'cane."

"Whooeee."

We laid there all silent for a long time, warm on the grass. The sun was right over us and a whole mess of dark clouds was passing the time of day up ahead. It felt like maybe it would rain.

One of them copters come chopping out of the sky, lookin' like a big evil spider.

"I wouldn' wanna be up there, man."

"Fuck, no."

"Motherfucker ain't even got no wings."

"Don't need none, it got them things that go 'round."

"Looks like it beatin' its meat up there."

"Yeah, and if it stop it goin' shoot up all over the ground."

We watched the spider spin away, smaller and smaller till it was gone. We were gonna play some more and I went over by the fence to get the bat. That's when I first seen 'em. They come roaring off the highway and onto the little dirt road by the ball field. There was three of them.

"Over there, man."

"I see 'em."

Their cycles were the real big kind, all black. But the handlebars were way high up 'round their heads. Looked like great big birds zoomin' down for the kill.

"What the hell they want here?"

"They ain't no ball players, thas for sure."

65

"Maybe they just out for a ride," Wallace said.

"More like they out for blood," I told him.

"This don't look too good, man."

We watched them come closer.

"Wish we had a couple more bats, just in case."

They were white studs but all dressed in black. Black cycle jackets and pants and big black boots. Black gloves too. And they had big chains all tight 'round them.

"This is trouble, man. I can smell it."

"Yeah, me too."

It was time for lunch and hardly nobody was around.

"Most everybody gone," I said.

"Time we was goin' too."

"Too late now."

They stopped in front of us on the dirt road. My ears jumped from all the noise. Then there was no more noise and they got off the cycles.

"What you niggers doing here?"

I looked him over. He was big awright and mean like a motherfucker, I could see that. I gripped the bat tighter.

Nobody said nothin'.

"Ain't you got ears, nigger boy? What you doing over this way?"

He was talkin' to Leroy.

"Just playin' some ball, white boy."

He turned to me, looked me up easylike. But he didn't like what I said. His eyes rested on the bat I was holding.

"Hey, Dago, you hear this nigger boy? You hear his punk mouth?"

"Yeah, punk mouth."

He moved closer to me. His hands were swingin' like a monkey, ready for anything. Dago and the third white boy moved along the side.

"I don't like punk mouths, 'specially from nigger boys."

"Why don't you ride on, man. You ain't waitin' on us."

He spit.

"I'm waitin' on you, nigger. I'm waitin' for you to tell me

66

why a shitass jigaboo like you ain't back in fuckin' Africa with the elephants."

Dago laughed. The other one laughed.

"Dago and Billy laugh at everything. Last week they chopped up some joker's face and they were laughin' the whole time."

"Maybe they just sick."

"You hear what the nigger says, Dago? You and Billy are sick."

"Yeah, sick."

"Dago don't talk much. But he's good with a blade, know what I mean? Very good."

"What you want with us, man?"

He smiled. With his teeth out like that, he looked just like old man Mose dogs.

"I want you to get your nigger ass back to that nigger town you live in. You crossed the border into white country and we don't like it. We don't want no niggers comin' 'round here."

"We got a right to be here same's anybody else."

He spit again.

"You ain't got no rights. That's the trouble with you sonova-bitchin' niggers, you think you got rights. So we gonna help you remember you got nothin'." He opened the chains from 'round his body. "We gonna beat you niggers down to nothin'. That's all we can do for you."

My face got hard like rock.

"Motherfucker, all you can do for me is die."

I slammed the bat into his guts and he went down. I heard the thunnk of the blade opening and I quick got behind Dago and cracked him on the head 'fore he could stick Wallace. I turned and I seen Leroy kick Billy in the balls.

Bang.

Wallace was standing right next to me. I watched him fall as the blood rushed outta the hole in his face.

"He got a gun," Leroy shouted.

I just stood there. I couldn' move and I watched him point the gun at me. Then Leroy jumped him, grabbing for the gun.

"I'll kill you, nigger."

Bang.

Leroy was holding him and then I seen Leroy's fingers slowly slip down till they wasn't holding nothin' no more.

I ran up and hit him with the bat on the arm and the gun flew outta his hand onto the grass. He made a dive for it and I kicked him in the head. Then I went over and picked up the gun.

"Don't shoot, man. Easy."

I looked all around. Dago was still out where I hit him. Billy was doubled up in pain from where Leroy kicked him in the balls but he was watchin' me with the gun.

I bent over Leroy. He was dead. Blood was all over the front of his T-shirt and drippin' down into the grass, turning it red.

I walked over to Wallace. He was dead too. I didn't need to bend down to see that.

The gun was in my hand. It was a small gun, all black. I kept staring at it 'cause it was hard to believe this little thing killed my two best friends.

I put my finger around the trigger.

When I turned to him, he knew.

"Don't kill me, I didn't mean to do it. Don't kill me, please."

He was scared and he started to shake, kneeling there on the ground begging me like that.

"Please, mister, don't kill me. I'm sorry. Please."

I put the gun against the side of his head and I pulled the trigger. The gun jumped in my hand. And his whole head blew open.

There was nothing more to do. I sat on the grass with the gun in my hand and waited for the po-lice. Billy watched me with dead eyes, piss runnin' down his pants leg from being scared that I was gonna kill him too.

When the po-lice come I told them everything just like it happened.

Over the next couple months I told the same thing to all kinda people. It was a warm spring morning and we went to the park to play ball and these three white boys on cycles

68

started a fight with us and one of them pulled a gun and killed my two best friends and so I killed him.

Billy told something else. That they just wanted to play ball with us and I hit one of them first and the gun was pulled in self-defense.

Some people made a lotta noise 'cause I killed him after the fighting was over, but that meant nothing to me. If he had the gun he woulda killed me. It was simple as that.

The people helping me said I was crazy at the time. I told them they were crazy all the time if they think that.

They told me to shut up.

That's what they said about me to the judge. That I was crazy at the time for those few minutes 'cause my friends were killed like that.

I got four years in prison for manslaughter. I was a couple months past eighteen when it happened so I was a adult. My mother was with the misery for me and Little Ben was a big shot in his gang 'cause his brother was in prison. A killer. That was a big thing.

We got to the prison in a funny kinda bus. All the way there I was thinkin' about myself. I been through Missippi and So'Lina and Harlem, through the gangs and the streets. I been hustlin' all my life just to stay alive. I never stole from nobody and never hurt nobody on purpose. Mostly I just wanted to be left alone. And there I was riding in a bus goin' to prison. The only thing I could figure I done wrong was to get born black. And I sure didn't ask for it.

First thing we done when we got to the prison was shower up so we could put on the prison clothes they give you. There was this white dude right behind me. When we got in there he said to the guard, "I ain't gonna shower with this nigger."

Then I knew inside wasn't goin' be nothin' but the same as outside. And I knew I'd be able to take it.

5.

THERE is white man's time and there's black man's time. Even in prison. That's 'cause black man's time is about twice as long. It's hard time is what it is. The hours may be the same but hours don't have nothing to do with it. A black man gets the worse jobs and takes the most shit. In summer, his part of the yard is always in the sun. In winter, his cellblock is always the coldest. In any time he is a nigger who don't cross the line. Even when he's in the hole with just his shorts on, he don't get a blanket like the whites do. And if he ever bitch about it, he be one dead nigger.

When I done my hard time in prison I was almos' a dead nigger a few times. First thing was I couldn' cotton to doing everything at the same time every day. Didn't make no sense to me. On the streets when I was hustlin' my ass off, the only time that counted was street time. You be there when the time was to con somebody or rip off something for youself. But the motherfuck pigpen I was in was run on the clock, on white man's time running 'round the clock. Every day at the same time I done this, then this, then this. Everybody did. It was crazy.

The food was nigger food. Made you fat and that's all. Anybody walk outta any prison and they weigh less'n they did when they went in, you know there's somethin' big wrong with them and they be dead inside six months. I put on near twenty pounds in that motherfuckin' rat's ass pigpen I was in for them three years. And three months sixteen days.

70

I musta done almos' half my first year in the hellhole, seemed like it anyway. That's where they keep you all locked up by youself, and they take 'way just 'bout all your clothes. It's just a tiny bare-ass room with a paper mattress and a pan to piss in. The mattress got bugs in it and the pan stinks worse'n a skunk in heat. The only place to sit is a piece of rough cement that's built right into the floor. There's never no heat, no passing air, no window. It's a stove in the summer and a icebox in the winter and the walls are always wet. The only light comes from a big Judas-hole in the door.

Anyone in the hole lives like a animal. When I was first in there, it was so bad I wanted to die right there but I didn't have no way to kill myself. After a while I wanted to stay alive just to fuck 'em up.

And I wasn't even there 'cause I done anything wrong. Minute I walked in that pigpen, I was already playing their game. Yassuh, nawsuh, doing my shuck sweet as sugar tits. I mean, I can do anybody's number if I gotta. If it's kiss ass time, I kiss ass. And if it's kill whitey time, I can play that game too, good as anybody.

It was kiss ass time in the pigpen and that's just what I done. Wasn't lookin' for no trouble from nobody. But I was eighteen and I was a nigger. So they figured they better break me a little. Which is why I got the hole so much, that and 'cause I kept mostly to myself and didn't have people lookin' out for me. But the more they broke me, the madder I got. I was mad till the day I got out, then I was glad. When I was leaving, one of the screws said to me, "See you again." Just being friendly.

"Not on your wind-sucking grandmammy's stiff cat," I told him. Under my breath. And I meant it. Anybody been in a big-time slammer and then goes back to it just ain't made for this world. And if they a nigger, they ain't made for any world.

Besides always being cooped up like some fuckin' bird, and the beatings and badmouthings and bad sleep and nothing to do and crazies running around and shit food and ice showers and everything stole or took away from you, the sex thing was the big hangup. It was bad enough not having a fox to bang

71

away on, but the fag gangs made it ten times worse. Not the real freak fags, anybody could get them for the price of a smoke. But the fake fag gangs that went 'round raping everything young they could get their hands on. They were mostly the hard cons, older and tougher. A lotta them were lifers. On the outside they woulda been straight studs but this wasn't the outside and they got into anything they could.

My first week inside I got these two packs of smokes from somebody. I don't use them but I took 'em and traded for other things, why not? Then I begun getting candy bars and socks and shit like that. I was thinking maybe I was the head screw's bastard son or something, and I was waitin' for some good threads and maybe a car to drive 'round the yard. Then after I'm through my first solo stretch and I'm let loose on the other cons, this funky dude with hair all over him and eyes like shit comes up to me and says, "Pay back or fuck." Just like that.

I told him what he could do. He wasn't mad or nothing. He just smiled nice and easy and said, "Then I'm gonna rape you." And he walked away, still full of smiles.

My cell partner told me the facts of life. I was young and thin and I looked good and if I didn't take on one dude to bang me, whole gangs were gonna go for the rape. And once that happened I'd be marked a punk boy and open to anybody. When I asked him how to beat it, he told me there was only one way. "You gotta be tougher'n they are."

I wasn't gonna let nothin' like that happen to me but I needed an angle. So I got me a single-edge blade and I hacked about a third off it, then I took the piece and put tape 'round the sides a few times. My cell partner told me the hairy dude and his friends'd come after me in the morning when the cells are open and he's working in the laundry.

"How you know it'll be tomorrow?"

"They can't wait no more. By next day another gang be after you."

Early the next morning I fixed myself up and just stood there waiting. I couldn' sit down or nothing. About ten thirty, sure enough, here come Shit Eyes and three other dudes. They quick walked in the cell. Shit Eyes told me to get down on the floor or they'd beat up on me and then rape me. "Either way you gonna get it, boy."

"I don't want no trouble," I said to him. And I took down my pants and laid face down on the floor and spread my legs apart and old Shit Eyes is grinning and laughing with his friends and tellin' them who's next and he pushes my face down and mounts me with his hands flat down one on each side of me and his legs spread outside of mine and his dick is big and hard and he's singing "Home on the Range" and he jams it into my asshole and his singing turns into the biggest motherfuckin' scream I ever heard in my life. That scream was so loud it knocked off two cups on the shelf and almos' blew out the window bars.

Shit Eyes rolled offa me onto the floor. He was bleeding like a pig. The piece of razor I stuck up my ass cut right down the middle of his dick and sliced the head of it almos' off. He was never goin' be a man again, that was for certain sure, 'less they had magic dick stitches. It wasn't even sure he was gonna live.

I jumped up quick. "Awright, you motherfucker father-rapers. Who's turn now?"

They were standing there, too scared to move. They were all lookin' at Shit Eyes bleeding to death on the floor. He was very quiet.

"C'mon, you shit eaters. You fuckin' fags. You fuckin' fag fuckers. You dick-sucking ass-fucking chicken-stealing sonfuckers." And I spit at them.

I was a little mad.

"If I ever even see your cunt-clap dip-shit faces anywhere 'round me again, I'll split your dicks so far down you be comin' and goin' at the same time."

Then the screws come.

They took one look at Shit Eyes and couldn' decide to call the doctor or the carpenter. "Better call the doc," one of them said, "you know how he likes to look at blood."

I told them what happened but they could see what happened. I took the piece of razor outta my asshole. They stared at it but they wouldn' touch it.

73

By that afternoon I was in to see the head screw. He couldn'
help smiling when he asked me 'bout things he already knew.
"You're a smart sonovabitch," he said. "You'll go far, just make
sure it's up and not down." And he told me he'll see I get some
kinda prison job that's smart as me.

Then I got thirty days in the hole.

When I got out and come back to my cell, I was a hero. The
whole prison knew about me, everywhere I went dudes talked
to me. Even the screws were better to me. Every time they'd put
me in the hole for something they'd tell me how sorry they
were. Then they slammed the door shut.

All those three years in that pigpen I never was bothered no
more for sex. I had a rep and everybody respected it. That's the
way it is with a rep. They coulda stuck me with blades a hundred times or ganged up on me, but nobody did nothing 'cause
my rep was too big.

I even got a new name. Razor Ass. They'd all say, "Here
comes Razor Ass." I'd walk in the yard and they'd say, "What's
up, Razor Ass?" And I'd say, "Nothin' right now, man." Then
everybody'd laugh. And when I'd leave, they'd say, "Don't mess
with him, man. He's a cold ass killer."

Shit Eyes didn't die. Somehow they put his dick back together and give him blood and all like that. He was in the hospital three, four months, then they took him away to some
other prison. But he couldn' never been no good after that.

Some men seen him just 'fore he left the prison. He was shaking and he lost a lotta that hair was all over him and he looked
like death come 'round again is what they told me. That's just
what they said. "He ain't worth a pound of piss no more."

Served the nigger right.

But not everybody was sharp as me. I seen and heard plenty
when I was in that motherfuck pigpen. Everybody ever done
time knows so many stories they could talk for a year and not
even scratch paint on what they seen and heard. And no yardbird ever forgets a minute of it neither. Anyone tells you he's a
yardbird and he don't know a thousand stories of what goes on,

74

then he's just one of them ghosts who nobody ever seen no matter where they say they been.

I remember when I was there 'bout six months, this young stud come in and he was small and very soft. Soon's I seen him, I knew there was gonna be trouble. Everybody knew it. He wasn't a fag or nothing, just that he looked too much like a fox. The third day he was in, they ganged him. About a dozen of 'em. They went crazy over him, taking turns. Even after they all come they still kept on jumpin' in. The kid was bleeding from the ass long 'fore they finished on him. A dude I knew was watching from another cell.

They fucked the kid dead. That's just what happened. After they left he stayed on that floor just laying there. By the time the screws come 'round he was dead. Something broke inside. They didn't want no trouble so they said he fell off his bunk. A accident.

Everybody knew what was goin' on that day but nobody said nothing then or later. Never deal youself into another man's hand 'cause you might get hurt bad. That's rule one in any slammer. Anywhere.

Gang banging like that went on all the time day and night. Once they made somebody a punk boy, they'd be after him every time they needed to get their rocks off. The kids who were gettin' it up the ass never said nothin' to the big shots 'cause they were scared of the gangs. And of the screws too. The screws didn't like nobody making waves. Long's nothin' was said, they didn't much care what went on.

I knew one kid who was gang banged so much he turned freak. He figured he'd never be able to make it with a fox no more so he went all the way and made hisself into one of the girls. A lotta them did that. Then they'd get one stud taking care of them and they wouldn' hafta worry 'bout the gangs no more. Or they'd run with the freak crowd and take on anybody.

Some of 'em did the whole number with the clothes and makeup and everything. And they'd look good too 'cause they were mostly small and soft. Everybody knew least one kid who come in a straight stud and walked out a drag fag.

75

But there was some who went the other way. They couldn' handle that they been raped. One stud was doing ten years. For rape. When they ganged him, it blew his mind. He'd go 'round saying things like "I'm the one does the raping, not the one gets raped." Crazy things like that. He got so strange after a while even the gangs left him alone.

Another one poured hot lead from the machine shop up his ass so they couldn' bother him no more. Least three of them killed themselfs that I know of while I was there. One wrote on the floor of his cell, FUCK ME NOW. In his own blood. And some kid did it while one of the gang was inside him. Got a blade somehow and held it handle up on the floor and sunk hisself onto it. Done it so quiet the dude jumping him never knew he was fucking the dead till it was over. Then nobody talked to the dude no more 'cause he was a cold-cock fucker and ain't nobody got use for that.

All of them were accidents on the prison records. Those things are always accidents. But when a kid knocked off somebody else stead of hisself, then it wasn't no accident and most times even the head screws couldn' make it look like one. I mean, anybody could walk into a cell and fall on a blade that was standing straight up on the floor. But it's goddam hard to make a accident out of a stud staying up all night cutting somebody into six pieces and laying each piece neat on a blanket by the cell door and then in the morning shouting, "I did it, I did it," and standing there with the big knife in his hand and blood and everything else hangin' off the walls.

That's just what one kid did while I was there. Some poor sonovabitch jumped him one night without the rest of the gang around, and he got chopped up into corn bread.

They took the kid away. Said he was sick.

Somebody else did it in the machine shop. Got behind his man and shoved him into the metal-cutting machine. Took his head clean off. The screws couldn't call it accident 'cause a dozen men seen it. And four of 'em were screws. It was just too much to keep down so they said the kid who done it was sick in the head. They took him away too.

There was this one stud I knew good enough to talk with a few times. Earl come in when I was there maybe a year. He was my age but he looked like a baby and he was skinny and scared of everything. The second day he was there a gang got to him and did their number on him. Maybe a half dozen took turns. Then every couple days after that, they'd grab him. He told me all this when I got to know him.

"And you know something, I could almos' take it," he'd say to me, "if it wasn't for that motherfuck Jackson."

This great big black stud named Jackson liked to stick his dick in Earl's mouth and get a suck job. And he'd say, "If you bite it, I'll kill you." He'd keep saying that. "If you bite it, I'll kill you."

This went on for a couple months and every time I'd see Earl he'd say to me, "I ain't taking no more. I'm gonna kill him 'fore he kills me." But I didn't pay him no mind 'cause he was so scared of everything. Then one day he told me he had a dream that Jackson was gonna burn in hellfire. And a few days later he lit the match.

What happened was Jackson come to his cell one day and Earl musta somchow knocked him out. He dragged Jackson over to the bars and then he poured gasoline that he got from somewhere on Jackson's head. Just his head. And then he fired it up.

By time the screws got there Jackson's head was just a skull. I didn't see it but a lotta others did, and everybody talked about it for months. The screws quick put out the fire and there on the floor is this skull set on top of this big naked body that didn't have a mark on it. 'Cept for one thing.

Jackson's dick was bit in two.

Nobody in that pigpen ever seen Earl again. We heard they sent him to that prison where they got all the crazy people. Even more crazy than in any other prison.

When somebody got killed or messed up bad, things got tight for a few days. Then most everybody jumped right back on the sex wagon. There was so much sex goin' on inside where I was that if the vice po-lice ever raided the place, they'd hafta lock

77

everybody up all over again, 'cluding half the screws. But it was all one-hand sex, there wasn't a fox in the whole motherfuck place. 'Cept for the bakery.

I worked in the bakeshop. When the head screw told me he was gonna get me a job smart as me, that's what he got me. In his little white mind maybe he figured a baker works with clean things like bread, and clean means smart like white. So I was a baker. Which was fine with me 'cause I got to be with the only foxes in the whole prison. Blond, red, brown, black, any color you wanted. Great bodies too, the best you could think of. And every one of them was snow white and a virgin.

Every day we baked the bread. And every day before we baked the bread, we jacked off. Into the bread. Then we baked it.

Before we baked the bread and before we jacked off into the bread, we made the dough into these great foxes. The dough felt like soft flesh and looked like soft flesh. All we did was make it look like a fox, with great big tits and a soft cat hole that we made by shoving the rolling pin through it. Then we backed off and jacked off into the hole. With my eyes closed, I was banging every movie star I ever seen. Every day another one. And when I had my hand on them tits and I felt all that soft flesh and I put my dick in the dough, yeah, man, I was shootin' up into the greatest cat in the world. I went through so many movie stars I started fucking fox I'd fucked for real. And some of them were better the second time around. One time I even got to where I was fucking ugly clapsy Ophelia from 'round the old block. Then I knew was time my mind moved on and I started thinking of fox I seen in school or just on the street. After a while I even run through them and went back to the movie stars.

One thing about that bread, it not only had all them vitamins in it but it was so full of the juice of life it coulda turned rotten eggs into fat hens and kept a dead man alive for a hundred years. It was super dynamite wonder bread is just what it was awright.

Only thing is I never ate any bread while I was there. The

78

whole time I was in that prison from the day I was a baker, I never ate a slice of bread. At every meal the bread was passed around and at every meal I passed it right on by.

Why eat what you've already fucked?

I was a baker for about a year and a half. Then my fucking baking days were over. Some of the men I worked with finished up their time and I didn't like what come in after them. I wanted out but the screws said no, so one day I started throwing the dough around. By time I was through, that room looked like a atom bomb hit it. Musta took 'em a week to clean it up.

I got thirty days in the hole. When I come out, they give me a job in the library, which was just a little room with some books in it. It was a nothing job but I liked working there 'cause it was quiet. There was just this other dude and me. He was a teacher in some high school and he raped one of the foxes in his class.

We'd sit there playing cards and he'd tell me how this one little bitch who was fifteen kept shaking her ass at him and staying after school leaning over his desk talkin' to him with her big jugs staring him in the face. One time she told him she burnt herself and she took out one of her jugs to show him. She just reached in and took it out and made him feel the burn right near the nipple. And another time after school she told him some boy beat up on her and 'fore he could stop her, she pulled down her jeans to show him. It was way below her belly button but he couldn' see it 'cause he was too busy lookin' at all that fine fox hair she had down there.

He was the mouse kind and he was 'bout forty-five at the time and the kid was really givin' him the business. He never had a woman of his own, just maybe a whore once in a while in the summer when he'd go 'way somewhere, and he wasn't gettin' no sex nohow. The day he raped her, he was doing some of that paperwork shit all the whites do, and she just hung 'round till it got real late and then she come up where he was and sat on the desk next to him. It was cold in the room and they talked 'bout that, and then she took his hand and put it under

79

her dress right on her cat and she told him that'd keep it warm for him.

He went ape. He grabbed her and pushed her on the floor and just ripped off her panties. By this time the kid was crying scared 'cause she was just a little cunt getting some kicks jazzing a old man. Only now the old man was a wild animal on top of her. He jammed his iron dick into her and she screamed and he didn't care. He kept pumping into her and she kept crying, and then he exploded inside her and that little cunt didn't know what was goin' on. She musta been thinkin' she was dying.

When he come the ape went. He seen what he done to her and it was his turn to die inside. There was blood all 'round her cat and blood on his dick. She was a virgin. The little bitch that liked to get old men all hot up was a stupid fuckin' virgin that didn't know the first thing about sex.

She was so bad off she just laid on that floor. He went to a phone in the office and called the po-lice. Right from the school. They put her in the hospital a few days. Then she was awright and ready to jazz some more old men. They put him in prison for fifteen years. He never was awright again. He felt he had killed her somehow and he hated hisself for what he done. After a while he just lived for hating hisself.

Sometimes I tried to get him back to the real. But it was no good 'cause I was just a young stud who didn't even finish high school and he was a teacher who finished everything.

I kept that library job the rest of the time I was there. After 'bout six months they made the teacher head of the hospital office, so I was by myself most of the time. Some of the men liked to read and they'd take books out and bring them back. I read a lotta those books 'fore I left there. I read so much in that pigpen, I read everything from travel books to how to build a boat. We had plenty of them how to do it books. We had so many I kept lookin' for one on how to break outta prison, but there wasn't none. I even read the dictionary. Only thing I never read was the lawbooks, they'd give me a head pain 'cause they used words even the dictionary didn't have the balls to put in. But a few men kept reading the lawbooks. One time I asked

80

this dude why he read them and he told me he was gonna get hisself outta prison.

"Just by reading all them books?"

"Damn right," he said. "If you know the law you can do anything."

Maybe he was right but I knew one thing he couldn' do. He couldn' find a book on how to break outta prison 'cause I already looked. He was just fooling hisself. 'Bout the only thing he could do with them lawbooks was pile 'em up one on top the other next to the wall and try to jump over.

When I left he was still reading law. But he wasn't in no hurry 'cause he was a lifer.

The one thing bad with that library job was the no sex. There was no dough to turn into foxes and stick your dick in. I mean, you can fuck a bread but you can't fuck a book. And there I was, fucked up at twenty. Full of juice and no fox to fuck with, not even no more bread to roll with. I was in bad shape.

Then I traded something for one of them little motors you hold in your hand and it got a rubber tip on it with all tiny rubber teeth. When you plug it in, it shakes and you run it over your head. Makes your whole head feel like it's crawlin'. On the motor it says, "Good for your scalp." Which was a lotta shit 'less it's good for your scalp if it crawls. But maybe it works better on white scalps. They know all about things that crawl anyway.

But what it really was good for was to jack off. I'd turn on that motor and run it up and down my dick a few times and then go slow over the watchtower and the dick'd jump up snapping. Then I'd put it tight on the rim right under the head where the juicer is, and that motor'd start talkin' to my dick just like a fox. And the dick'd start talkin' to the balls and they'd start talkin' to each other and my mind'd be talkin' to some boss fox and soon everything's talkin' and it's all quiet and then the time for talk is over and it's war fight kill burn and all the bad shit that's in me making me tight making me hate comes oozing out. Ooooooommmmm. Uhmm. Uhm.

81

And then I'd feel okay again. And after a long time I'd open my eyes and the fox in my hand is just a little motor with a rubber tip on it with all tiny rubber teeth. Till next time.

Goin' into my third year in prison Little Ben got killed. He was only sixteen. He was still runnin' with the gangs and one night him and a couple friends stole a car and the po-lice shot him dead. They were just out joyriding, like after they finished they'd put the car back. Most gangs did that, mostly 'cause it was something to do. Joyriding. But to the pig that shot him three times, it was the crime of the year.

This pig, this rat's ass pigfucker who got on the po-lice 'cause he didn't have the balls to be a real shooter on his own and he needed the badge to hide behind. This motherfuck pig pulled his gun and shot my brother in the back and then run up to him and shot him two times in the head 'cause he was still moving stumbling coughing up his own blood on that street trying to get away from a madman.

His name was Gilligan. A young punk pig named Gilligan. The kind that'd go to a bar owner and graft him for money and when he got ten or twenty in his pig paw would say it ain't enough. Nothing's ever enough for a pig like that long's it's still alive.

I stopped hating all whites or all po-lice or all anything a long time ago 'cause I seen how it rips up people's guts. But I never stopped hating pigs like Gilligan, don't matter what color they are or what they do. Even after all this time I hate a Gilligan. Not to hate pigs like that would be a sure sign that you goin' crazy for real.

My mother took Little Ben's dying very hard. 'Specially the way he die, in the street like that. She done her best for all of us but she mostly took favor to Little Ben 'cause he was the baby. When he go, she just got the misery so bad she near die herself. She was living all 'lone after that. Rosa was in So'Lina and I was in prison. It was a bad time.

Nine months later my bad time was up. Three years, three months and sixteen days. I was half past twenty-one. The day I walked outta that pigpen, they give me the gray suit and double sawbuck everybody gets. State-0 and 0-20. The suit was too big and the twenty dollars was too small but I wasn't gonna hang around for a better fit.

When I got to the bus station I went right to the dude behind the counter. He knew what I was, where I was, and where I was going. "Next bus to New York City be in two hours" was all he said. The only thing he didn't know was when I'd be back.

I wanted to tell him I'd never be back, never in a thousand years. But I didn't say a word. I just walked on out and waited for the bus in the rain. It beat down on my black skin head and I never felt nothin' so good in all my life.

6.

THE day I got outta prison it rained so hard all the junkies in New York were doing the junkie rock. When it rains like that, they get a trapped feeling 'cause nobody's on the streets and they can't even find their dealer. Then they start to shake and if the rain goes on another day they get in a real bad way. That's the junkie rock.

I bused into the Port Authority and subwayed uptown. When I got home my mother was waitin' on me. She had one of them small apple pies on the table and she just sat there looking at me while I ate that whole pie. Then she begun to cry.

"I told myself I wasn't gonna do no more cryin'," she said as the water rolled down her big black face. "I'se too old a woman for all that now."

Nine months 'fore I come home, she cried herself out over Little Ben when he got shot down. It was the worse thing could ever happen to her and she looked twenty years older than when I went away.

"Everything goin' be awright," I said to her. And we sat there and I tried to make her laugh with funny stories about prison life. It was a hard job makin' em up.

I took Little Ben's room and the next day I looked for work. I was goin' on twenty-two and I was a yardbird and a high school dropout and a nigger. Not too many big jobs waiting for me. The best I could do was a porter or a dishwasher. No money that meant anything but good scraps of food. That's just what one peckerwood said to me in some hotel. Good scraps of food. I didn't know if I should bark or bite him, so I just walked away.

I couldn' get a license to drive a truck 'cause I been in prison. Even if I knew how to do anything I couldn' get a license for it. I tried some bakeshops but all I could make was bread 'cause that's all we ever made inside and that wasn't good enough outside. I went to the big library and when I told them I worked in a prison library, they all laughed like it was a big joke. So I laughed too, all the way out the door. Till I saw the sign, THIS IS YOUR LIBRARY. Then I stopped laughing.

I went downtown to some of them employment places where you pay to get a job. They didn't go too wild over me, more like they kept lookin' over my shoulder at the next card sittin' on the bench. After the first couple, I didn't tell them I been in prison. But it was the same thing, still nothing. Then I got smart and I put down on the card that I got outta high school. Still the same. So I said I been to college. Nothing. That's when I got mad and the last place I went I told them I got outta three colleges and I was a doctor and a lawyer but I wanna do something else. Didn't move 'em at all.

Then I seen the number. The only way I'd ever get a job through them was if I come in with a whitewash. That's what was fuckin' me up all the time. They just didn't like my paint job. But if I come in whiteface, I could be a yardbird and never get outta school and I'd still get something.

There was one more place to go 'round where I was downtown and I walked in and right away I said, "I got a very heavy suntan from the beach but I come back next month when I got

84

my pure white body like you." And I marched right on outta there.

I was feelin' so good I got outside and I seen the po-lice on the corner and I went straight up to them. They were standing next to this big table with a sign on it that said, COME ALONG WITH US. It was for taking a test to be on the po-lice.

"I wanna come along with you," I said to them.

That didn't bother them, they meet a lotta nuts in their job. They talked nice to me about all the great things happen to you when you the po-lice. Like you don't ever get busted and you keep all you can graft and you can scare poor people with your gun and shit like that. They didn't say that but I knew better'n them what it means to be the po-lice. I'm black and they are just that other no-color color.

I'm doing this whole jive number on them and after they all done tellin' me what all I get, I asked them what it took, and they read off some things. One of them was no record.

"Uh-uh, that ain't too good," I said to them.

"What's that?"

"I been busted."

"Well, if it's just an overnight thing for having one drink too many, maybe that can be cleared," one of them said.

"Ain't that."

"Ain't what?"

"Ain't overnight."

"Well, how long ain't it, is it?"

"Three years."

"How long?"

"Three years, three months and sixteen days. Matter a fact, I just got outta prison last week."

They were nice about it. They didn't shoot me right there in front of Macy's window where we were talking. They just kinda got by themselfs and I was by myself. But I knew they didn't want me to come along with them no more. But just in case, I put back all the papers they give me so's they couldn' say I stole 'em and *take* me along with them.

By the next week I was back hustling. I was doing good but

85

not too good. I sold magazines that there wasn't none of, and sex films with no sex in them and suits that shrunk first time you sweat and radios that worked for ten minutes after I got the money for them. I went through a lotta shit like that but it was all just chump change.

Then I hit the big time again, just like when I was seventeen with Al and his black leather stretching machine. Only this time it was even better. No machine. It was parties I was pushing, very special parties called love-ins. I set them up and got everything needed for them, 'cluding the people.

That was the big year of black and white forever together, the year of that integration. At least in bed. All the big people in New York wanted to have parties with blacks around, and many of the rich fox wanted to get black balled. Only trouble was they didn't know anybody black 'cept their maids.

That's where I did my thing. I put it all together and made sure they had just what they were paying for. Which was always more'n enough. At that time, whites were thinkin' black is beautiful. 'Course it didn't last too long, just one of them crazy things that sometimes hits everybody, like the flu. But I didn't care nothin' about black is beautiful long's they didn't think it was cheap.

At a love-in, candles and incense sticks burn all the time, no electric lights. The only music is whole soul blues. Not Chicago blues or Kansas City blues or New Orleans blues. Just Lightnin' Hopkins and John Lee Hooker and a few others. Played soft over and over till it soaks into the skin. There's no furniture in the big room at all. Just wall-to-wall mattress and a lotta pillows, all kinds. In the center of the room is a big smoker with a dozen long pipes all 'round it. Everybody gets stoned together. There's no whisky. But there is rice wine, which is the only thing to drink with hash. And there's whole soul food, served in wood bowls. Everybody eats and drinks and smokes. And begins to take off their clothes. Clothes ain't needed at a love-in 'cause all the senses are gettin' switched in to the head. Everybody's beautiful. People begin to see hear smell taste touch the beauty in someone else. They make love. Everybody makes love. Soon everybody is together making love and it's all one body with a lotta arms and legs. It's a love-in.

I not only got all the stuff for these parties but I got half the people. The black half. Studs for the women, fox for the men. Plus furniture movers and a cook and a server and like that. Everybody made something. The blacks got paid, the whites got laid. And I got mine.

In a couple months I had a bankroll and people were calling me weeks ahead to set up a love-in for them. I got into some goddam big Park Avenue homes doing that. I'd sweet-talk to them bitches and I'd shuck and jive and rap. Not scaring them with the King Kong bit, but just giving 'em enough nigger so's they'd think they were gettin' their money's worth. That's what they wanted. A wild nigger in bed and a dark white man in public. With talk to match.

I hadda lay that on most of the studs that were gigging for me. The heavy spade rap, the made in Harlem and paid in blood real nigger talk was only for the bedroom. That's where the white fox wanted to hear it so she could get the thrill of thinkin' she's being fucked by a ape who talks ape talk. And when the ape is grunting on top of her, she's laying there thinking if only her father could see her now or if only her husband could see her now. She's with a ape and it's outasight. Then if the ape says some secret ape words like bitch and motherfucker and funky, that turns the funky motherfucker bitch on so much she goes ape herself.

But outside the bedroom door it's straight white weak talk. And for any of the blood, it's shuck time, jive time, rapping 'way from home time. And he stands there smiling and shucking away with white fuckers all 'round him and they keep wishing he'd turn into a ape and he keeps wishing they'd turn to salt.

'Bout four months after I come home, my mother got bad sick and went in Harlem Hospital for a couple months. I was making money on the love-ins and I paid all the bills. When she come out, I took her down to live with Rosa in So'Lina. At first she didn't wanna go but Rosa said there was room and they wanted her to come. Then her one good friend died and she was almos' mugged on the church steps goin' to the service one night. That done it. When I told her I was gonna save some money and maybe later move on down, she decided to go back home to where she felt better.

Rosa was waitin' at the bus station. She had four kids and they all looked like her. Everybody was happy, 'specially my mother 'cause she'd have kids 'round her again. There was nothin' no more for her in Harlem. Little Ben was dead. She was too sick to work and wasn't nobody she cared about 'cept me and I was always runnin' around somewhere. She'd just be sittin' at the window all the time, lookin' out at the garbage street and the dirt buildings and the dark sky. Wasn't no life for a beat-down woman who done her best. Least with Rosa, she had people 'round her and the sun drying up her bones and some good country food again 'stead of all that shit soul food they sell in those big supermarkets.

I give Rosa seven hundred dollars and I told her to use it takin' care of everybody. And I give my mother some money and said I'd come see her when I could. Then I took the Greyhound flyer back to New York.

I hustled the love-ins a while longer but my heart wasn't in it no more. That kinda life was gettin' to be a drag. One thing was I was lonely. I was glad my mother went down there with Rosa 'cause that was best for her. But I didn't like it by myself and I didn't like any fox enough to put up with the shit they give you.

Another thing was I was restless. Since I quit school when I was sixteen, I been hustling for myself. Which is awright and you gotta do it 'cause ain't no one else goin' do it for you. But things were starting to pop in the black-white world and I was feelin' the pull. I done a lotta reading in that prison library and learned things I never knew about. Plus which, I come through so much death and misery 'cause of the motherfuck whites that if I hated them it would be only right.

But I didn't hate them all, I just felt sorry for them. I saved my hate for those who crisscrossed me myself. But I had this feel to do something to move the black fight out front. Not as a leader or nothing like that. I ain't all hyped up on one thing, don't matter what it is, 'cause I look out only for myself. I didn't know what I wanted to do but I knew it wasn't what I was doing.

Then a couple studs I met told me about some kids from New York goin' down South to help the blacks down there. White and black kids goin' down there together.

"Where they all goin'?" I asked.

"All over, but most of 'em goin' to Missippi."

"Man, I was born there. They must be crazy."

But I kept thinkin' about it. I was restless and it'd be something new. And I didn't remember much of Missippi. And I had enough money in my pocket for a while. But most of all I was restless.

I knew I was crazy but one day I told some people I wanna go down to Missippi to help out. So that's what I done. I said goodby to the love-ins and the rich white bitches and the whole scene. It was a good hustle but I knew it'd be over soon anyway. Soon's the apes got to talkin' strong outside the bedroom like they do inside.

I went down to Jackson and other places and helped out on some sit-ins at dime stores and offices. When we got busted, my years in prison come in handy. All pigpens are the same, some are just more of the same than others.

Whenever we got outta jail we'd have marches and church-hymn singing, all grassroots stuff 'cause the brothers down there were earth people. I was hip to their style but I seen I wasn't really one of them no more. I lived too long in that rat's ass Harlem and my head had too many things in it to ever go home again.

After a while other kids come down from up North and I moved on. By then I just about played out my string. I was tired and I figured I done my bit. When I got up to Greenwood they were gettin' set for some big marches and I helped on that, then I was gonna head back to New York.

The marches went on for days, and a lotta big names were

89

there. On the second day I got busted along with many others. The darker you were, the longer they give you. I was coal dark. So they give me long. And I was from New York. So they give me longer.

I done my time the hard way. There wasn't nothin' but hard time for a nigger in the Greenwood, Missippi, jail.

When I left Missippi, it was for the second time. On the bus goin' into Tennessee, I was thinking there wasn't gonna be no third time.

7.

SIX years now. Been six years since Ginny die like that. She was twenty-three when she go.

I still get the nightmares sometimes, watching her fall, falling. I reach out to her but I can't save her. My hands turn into tree trunks, all twisted and held down under the ground. I pull at them, pulling them out like roots, and they turn to stone. I'm standing there and I can't move and my hands turn to stone. Water's rolling down my face and I can see her out there somewhere in front of me, always falling but always there in front of me. I force my mouth open and I scream but nothing comes out and I don't know what it is I'm screaming or even what I want to say.

The nightmares are always the same, not the same but only the small things change. Sometimes I'm wearing rings on my fingers, and my hands are like burning swords 'stead of stone. But she's always somewhere in front of me, falling, and I can't never get to her. And sometime I wake up quick and the tears are real and I catch myself saying, "Don't leave me." That's always the same. Don't leave me. Like I could do anything about it after all this time.

90

Six years since she go. A fine high-yella woman with a soft body and these great long legs she'd always be throwing out like a purebreed pony when she walked down the street. She was always laughin' and she had the only smile you could hear. First time I seen her, I knew that woman was for me.

I just come out the Greenwood, Missipi, jail and was moving on up North to home. Was a lotta dudes from New York down there and some of us stopped off in Memphis just for a goof. Back then everybody from up North who come down to help was a hero, and that first night we blew into town some Snick people had a party for us. I was still tight from that jail. I been in the slam enough times and I always get this tight feel in my chest when I come out, so I wasn't having no wild time for myself at the party. I remember I walked on out to the kitchen for something and I seen this outasight fox over by the sink. She was washing dishes. Soft creamy-yella skin, almos' like a trick baby. But I could see she was full-blooded awright. She was into a skirt and a little red-checked blouse, and she had on this blue and white apron. I kept lookin' at it 'cause she sure didn't look like no maid.

"I like to keep busy," she said.

She turned me on right away with her smile, like it was there just for me.

"I like to keep busy myself," I said to her. And I quick picked up a dish towel. "How come you not out there with evcrybody?"

"Too much noise. I get a headache."

"Me too," I said, drying off a cup. "You from 'round here?"

" 'Bout fifty miles. You?"

"New York. I come all the way from there to this here kitchen." And I laughed. But I seen her eyes light up when I said New York.

"New York must be nice." She sat down at the kitchen table. "I hear it's big as anything."

I sat next to her. "Bigger. Ain't you never been there?"

"Not yet I ain't. But I get there someday."

"What's your name?"

"Ginny." She looked at me again with the smile. "What they call you?"

I turned on my own smile. Wasn't nothin' like hers with all my crooked teeth, but it was all I got. "Oh, they call me a lotta things," I said to her. "If I told you half what all I been called, your beautiful nappy hair'd turn straight."

She laughed. Like a cat, a fine cat laugh that made me feel good. "I don't mean that. I mean what's your name."

"My name's Marcus."

"Marcus? That's a funny name." She put her hand over her mouth. "Ooh, I shouldn' said that. Just that we ain't got too many Marcus 'round here."

"Now you got one," I said to her. And I'm sittin' there at the kitchen table thinkin' I'm glad I come to Memphis.

That's how we first come together. At a Snick party after I got throwed out of a Missippi pigpen. She come to Memphis from her hometown to get a job. All her folks was dead, and she was working as a waitress in a white rest'rant. "But just for now," she said to me. "Just till I see what I goin' do."

Later on, I told her I'd only be in town a few days and I wanted to see her again. But she was going 'round with some dude and she wasn't sure. I give her the address of where we all staying with this minister in his house. "When you get sure," I said to her, "come 'round there. I be waiting, but only a couple days. Then I'm long gone."

That was a Saturday night, the night of the party. We were blowin' town on Tuesday. Monday night I was all jumpy. I forgot 'bout her but I kept thinking 'bout her too. But I didn't expect nothin' to happen. Everybody was out that last night and I'm upstairs in that big house all by myself and I'm thinking it don't matter none. Then I hear the doorbell and I run down the stairs three at a time and I open the door all outta breath.

It was Ginny .

She stood there all hung together and she looked just great.

"Do you remember me?" she whispered. "The party Saturday night? You told me to come here if I'm sure." She give a short laugh. "I guess that means I'm sure."

92

"I knew you'd come by," I lied. "I was waitin' for you. We s'pose to leave tomorrow."

"I know."

"Maybe you be leaving too."

"That would be real nice," Ginny said, smiling up at me.

"Is that what you want?" I asked her.

"Yes, I'd like that," she said, putting her hand in mine. "I'd like that a lot."

Wasn't nothin' else to say. I knew this was something special, I just felt it. Ginny felt it too, I could tell that. Goin' back up the stairs, I kept thinking this was gonna change my luck. Goddam, I was tired of being alone all the time.

In the room I watched Ginny take off her clothes. I'd been with a lotta fox but right from the start there was something diff'rent 'bout Ginny, like I had this feel that I needed her. More'n anything, I needed her. When she had nothing on no more, she come over and laid down on the bed next to me and curled up on her side tight up against me. It was like she was a little girl that was lost and needed somebody to protect her.

I put my arm under her and kissed her jugs, sucking on the nipples and snaking my tongue down her body. She shivered and I opened her legs wide and played with her soft woman cat. After a while I got on top of her. Her eyes were all cloudy and her mouth was half open and breathing soft and I pushed myself inside, slow, feeling the warm flesh. She squeaked a few times and pressed me deeper inside her. Soon the little lost girl was all gone and I was with fire. And then I was fire too, and I didn't ever wanna come back to anything else.

For a long time we laid together in the dark. It was church quiet in the minister's house that Monday night while everybody was away. Me and Ginny, we laid there in the dark holding each other tight, and I was feeling better'n I ever done in my whole life.

"Was I awright?" Ginny asked. "Marcus, was I good for you?"

I told her the truth. "You were the best," I said. "For me, you were the best."

93

And which she was.

The next day the men went on to New York and we stayed behind and got a place in a rooming house. By day I worked in a cannery. At night I'd lay in that bed with Ginny next to me and I'd be thinking at last I got me somebody. A couple weeks later we had us enough money to move on North. We bused all the way into New York and got married. We were home.

It was cold when we hit New York, colder'n Memphis ever seen. Ginny never got used to it. She'd just sit around the house shivering all the time, and when she got knocked up it was even worse. I got us a place in central Harlem and then the next year we moved into a project. Three rooms for eighty dollars a month, and lucky to get it.

But we never had the money for everything. Ginny got sick from the cold and couldn' work and I couldn' get nothin' decent 'cause I done time and was a nigger and had no schoolin'. I tried a dozen diff'rent hustles but didn't nothing catch on. Then the baby come, and it got real bad. Ginny got evil sick with woman troubles and she hadda get a operation. She was in Harlem Hospital charity ward, but something went wrong and when she come home, she was always bleeding and feelin' tired.

By the time Debbie was two months old, there was something wrong with her blood and she was just a little thing that was crying all the time 'cause she had a lotta fevers and she wasn't eating right. She had scabs all over her head and her belly was too fat. I didn't know what to do, I couldn' get nothing with big money. And Ginny couldn' get on the welfare 'cause I was living home and the woman didn't get nothing if her man was still there, didn't matter none if she was starving. Which besides, she didn't understand all that paper stuff and she was scared of strangers coming 'round.

Everybody kept saying if Debbie make it past the first year she be awright. If she can get strong enough 'fore it tear her down, she goin' live to be a whole hundred.

But Debbie didn't make it. When she was almos' one, she got the fever exter bad and one night she just go in her sleep. She

94

had small little feet you could put in one hand and I usta play with them and then just like that, she wasn't there no more.

Ginny didn't cry. She didn't do nothin', just set there the whole time. It was like she was in shock, was what somebody said. Only she didn't come out of it. She'd cook or clean or talk to you but you'd know she wasn't really there. I got some people to talk with her but nothing helped. Her being sick like that and then Debbie up and dying was just too much for her, I guess.

I was feeling it myself. What it was, I was losing my push. It come on slow but after three, four months I was hittin' into the bottle real hard. Just 'bout everything was goin' wrong and I didn't care about things no more. Feeling sorry for myself, you know. And one day I just walked away from the house and went on a wine drunk that lasted more'n a week. I fell apart is what it was, I was so whacked out it was worse'n prison.

Then one night some hawks tried to steal my shoes in a alley on 115th Street and I beat one of 'em half dead. To the judge it was just one nigger bum hittin' on another, and he give me fifteen days. I was too shamed to let Ginny know.

By time I got outta jail my head was back on, and I was goin' home and try to get things lined up again. I wasn't gonna do no more gettin' shot down on the wine. Later for that.

I got off the subway at 135th Street. It was good to be back, even if it was Harlem. A half-dozen blocks and I was at the project. I walked in the entrance near to my building and I seen this crowd standing over by the other side, some po-lice were there too. I walked on over. On the ground was a sheet covering something. Right away I seen that I knew what it was. But it wasn't none of my business and I turned away to go upstairs.

"Ain't you Marcus Black?"

I looked 'round. It was the old woman lived one floor down.

"How you?" I said to her like I was in a hurry.

She started to cry. I figured maybe it was somebody she knew under the sheet. But when a old woman got the cries, best to leave 'em alone. I turned back to the building.

95

"If there's anything I can do to help."

That's all she said. But it was how she said it. I knew that tone voice, I'd heard it many times around death, and used it myself to people with the misery. It always means only one thing.

I stopped dead. My skin got all cold and the building waved in my eyes and everything's goin' through my head. It was a mistake is all. This crazy old woman was crazy as a hoot owl, everybody know she's crazy. After I see Ginny, I goin' come down and laugh in her face. Why they let a crazy old woman run 'round like that anyway?

I didn't say a word to her, didn't turn around. Just forced myself to walk up the four steps and into the building and I pressed the button for the tiny elevator. I'm doing nothing, thinking nothing, feeling nothing, and then the elevator comes down and this old man I know and his wife get out and they look at me and I see he wants to say something to me but she sets her face hard and pulls him on out the door.

The elevator went up very slow. Slowest elevator in the world, I told myself, and I was goin' up thinking 'bout all the elevators I been on but not too many, and the one I worked in that hospital which was slow as this but much bigger 'cause doctors got on with dead people taking them down to the basement where they cut 'em all up.

The elevator stopped.

I knocked on my door. I was goin' kiss Ginny and tell her I'm sorry but a man just do these things sometime. And I was goin' try make her feel good and get her outta the misery.

The door opened and a great big whiteface po-lice stood there. "Yeah? What you want?"

I couldn' talk. My mouth was open but nothing come out.

He looked at me. "You. What you want here?"

Somebody called out behind him. "Why don't you go on inside, Dempsey? I'll look out here."

The big po-lice grunted and moved out the doorway and back past the living room. He stepped on Debbie's toy dog and kicked it outta the way.

96

"Don't pay no mind to that rockhead," the voice said, "he's just too dumb to count."

It was a young black po-lice talking to me. I just stared at him.

"Is there anything I can help you with?" he asked. His voice was soft and his eyes told me he already knew who I was.

"I live here," I whispered.

"You're Marcus Black."

I nodded. My eyes told him I already knew what happened. There was nothing to say.

"Please come in, Mr. Black." He led me by the arm over to the couch, the one Ginny liked so much 'cause it had flowers all over it. "I'm real sorry about this."

I sat down. He sat next to me, waiting.

A sergeant come in and seen me. "This the husband?" He come over. "I'm sorry, Black, but I'm gonna hafta ask you a few questions. What time you leave the house today?"

It was my voice but it sounded like it was far away. "I ain't been home in a couple weeks. I been in jail."

"When'd you get out?"

"This morning. I just got out this morning."

The sergeant sat down next to me. "I know this is painful for you, Black, but was your wife depressed or anything like that? She may have told you or wrote you."

I raised my head and looked around the room at the little furniture we had, at Debbie's toy dog broke on the floor, at the cold walls and the cold floors. Was Ginny ever depressed? Wasn't everybody depressed? I looked at the po-lice. "She didn't know where I was," I told them. "She been depressed ever since the baby die, and maybe long 'fore that. She wasn't no diff'rent from anybody else 'round here."

A siren come closer. The amb'lance for Ginny.

I wasn't crying. I was a nigger and we couldn' afford to cry 'cause if we ever started, we'd be crying for a thousand years.

The funeral service was in a chapel over on 131st Street. Then she was buried in Frederick Douglass Cem'tery, right near Debbie.

Dust to dust is what they said over the grave.

Ginny never really had a chance. The sick got her and the misery got her and then the dead got her. She didn't know anybody much and she was scared of all the paper stuff and she was too proud to ask other people for help. She was a Southern girl who didn't understand the strange and easy ways of the North, and she never got used to the cold.

8.

NIGGER POWER.

That's what the sign said when we got there. A great big sign that said NIGGER POWER in great big letters. And under that was a great big picture of some dude trying to look like he was Nigger Power hisself.

Only thing was he was white.

His name was Abner Goldstein and he was some Jew writer who wrote something called the *White Niggers* and he was gonna do his nigger thing at the Harlem Ballroom where I was lookin' at that great big NIGGER POWER sign. This was 'bout five years 'go and that sign was really outasight hanging up there. I just kept staring at it. Then I seen what was wrong. NIGGER POWER. All the great big letters were in whiteface too.

"Let's go on in," Barbra said.

Back that time, Barbra worked in the library up here, and one day she laid something on me that the dude wrote 'bout how being just black or white wasn't enough no more. That it's a revolution of life styles goin' on and the real war is between the young and the old, 'tween those got nothing and those got everything. And that makes the white kids just the same as the black kids. They all get treated like niggers always been treated. Like shit. They no diff'rent no more. Hippies, college kids, poor kids, they all get banged over the head and kicked in the balls. They all white niggers. That's what the dude was saying. That the white niggers and the black niggers are together. And that the black boogies, the Negro, is really with the whites who own everything. The war is on and it ain't skin that counts no more, it's the life style and what you got and don't got that counts.

Soon's I read that, I called Barbra up. She was a little mad 'cause of what time it was. "What in the flaming fucking hell are you doing callin' me up this time of night?"

"I just read what you give me."

"Well, what about it, man?"

"It knocked me on my ass, that what about it. Who is this nigger, how come I don't know 'bout him?"

"He is a white nigger is what he is, and how I know what you don't know 'bout? Now don't bother me no more when I'm sleeping." And she banged up the phone.

A white nigger. What in the flaming fucking hell is that. Only white niggers I know about are those passing for white, and they sure as hell don't call themselfs nigger. I'm laying in bed thinking like that. This was least five years ago when everybody was still playing the Georgia skin game, and whatever color you was that was the side you were on. Things were still real simple back that time.

Next day I checked 'round and, sure thing, people up here knew about him. Besides the *White Niggers,* he had this book all about some war and how much fun it was. Yeah, that's just what somebody told me. I didn't read it myself 'cause I don't like fairy tales. But that's when I begun thinkin' serious about this white nigger business. 'Bout time we got some help. Spread the head around and maybe we don't get it busted so much.

But that part about the boogies. Right on, man. They so white they piss milk and shit snow. They get two dollars back to back and they wanna live next door to the white man. What's so good about that? With all the deodorant and shit they use all the time, they smell bad. Everybody know that. And they so busy taking showers all day, they never take a bath

99

to clean themselfs off. They not only smell bad but they always so dirty. Shit, no, I don't want them living next door to me. But the boogies, they do anything to live with the white man. They are Negroes is just what they are. The white man could beat them blind, he could say to them, "Nigger, I goin' kill you right now." Yeah. And all they'd say is, "Kill me and eat me, boss, just don't call me nigger is all."

The Negro is a white man who just come out the wrong color.

Like one time I was with this Negro from Alabam'. From Birmingham. He was tellin' me how good he got it down there. How he got a house and a car and all good clothes. And how he works with whitey in a big office and living in whitetown and they all call him Mister. That was the big thing for him, that they call him Mister. I told him if he ever step outta line, that Mister goin' change back to nigger quicker'n he can.

That's when I knew I was right 'bout not making it in the white world. I'd hafta be a Oreo cookie like that cracker.

But that's how I first heard 'bout the white nigger dude, from Barbra. But I'd never seen him so when Barbra asked if I wanted to meet him, I said sure. "At a party after he do his number," she told me. "Everybody be there."

The Harlem Ballroom was on 138th Street. When we got there a big crowd was out front and I seen some of the brothers I knew. Ben Pride was there with his men, and Oginga Kush was there looking real Africa. And a lotta white people. Plenty of pig power too. Looked like a small army huffing and puffing away in front the place.

When we got inside I could see everything was full up. The first thing I flashed on was the money, all seats a buck. I asked Barbra who got it but she didn't know. She didn't think it was important. "Goddam right it's important," I told her.

The show started with somebody introducing a lotta big shots, like anyone cared. Then when they got all done, this tall skinny hipster dude come on stage walking like a prizefighter in tight pants and one of them turtleneck sweaters. There's some kinda stand in the middle and he leaned on it and the light's right on him. Shit, he didn't look like no white nigger to me. Looked just like one of them Jews. We got plenty of 'em in Harlem 'cause they own all the stores and all the money too. And they all got that same kinda face that always looks worried 'bout everything, like they thinkin' deep. They all got them trick faces, all them Jews.

The dude fucked with the mike for a minute and then he said, "All the money from tonight's ticket sale is going to the Black Defense Fund right here in Harlem." That was the first thing he said. I quick looked all 'round to see if the seats were bugged. I gotta watch this man, I told myself.

The hall got real quiet. "What I'd like to talk about tonight," he begun, "are the white niggers of this generation. The white niggers have been in this country for many years, only they didn't know they were niggers. They thought they were just poor, oppressed, exploited, beaten, starved and neglected white folks. They didn't have dark skin and so they never thought of themselves as niggers. But we know better today. We know that anyone poor in this country is treated like a nigger. And anyone who rebels against the system is treated like a nigger. And so, because respectability comes with size— and as we all know, millions of people in America today are poor and rebelling against the status quo—the word 'nigger' has become respectable. Not to the middle class, the white and black bourgeois. And not to the power people, the big-shot businessmen and politicians.

"Well, then, to whom has the word 'nigger' become respectable? To us niggers. That's right. To you and me, to black niggers and to white niggers. We're all niggers if we don't go along with racist laws. We're all niggers if we don't go along with starving children to death. We're all niggers if we don't believe in this country right or wrong, and if we're not willing to be beaten, jailed, tortured and killed for the glory of free enterprise.

"So get used to the word 'nigger.' Use it. It's a weapon, use it like a weapon. Fuck the guns. That's the enemy's game, violence. Use the weapons you got. Show people they're being

101

treated like niggers. If half the people have everything, they've got to be living off the other half who have nothing or next to nothing. Show them where it's at. If everyone who was being treated like a nigger knew about it, you'd have half the people on your side. Show them, tell them. Live your life style as a nigger.

"If you ain't got enough to eat, you're a nigger. If you ain't got a decent place to live, you're a nigger. If you ain't got a good job, you're a nigger. If you ain't got the proceeds of your own work, you're a nigger. If you have to fight other people's wars, you're a nigger. If you have to live with someone's foot in your ass, you're a nigger. If you don't have power over your own life, you're a nigger.

"We're all niggers. If everybody knew it, we'd have a country where nobody would be dirt poor. We'd have a country where love could live instead of hate. We'd have a country where everybody would be safe because nobody would want. And we'd have a country where you'd be free to live as you please. But we don't have any of that because people don't know what they are. Now say it after me. I'm a nigger. I'm a nigger. I'm a nigger. Say it loud. Say it louder. I'm a nigger. I'm a nigger. I'm a nigger. *Say it.*"

Man, now I seen everything. Everybody in that whole hall jumped up screaming and shouting. I did it myself. Took us five minutes to get quiet. I was so shook up I sat my nigger ass back in that nigger seat and pulled out a nigger cigar and went to light it with a nigger match when that sneaky nigger usher come over and told me no nigger smoking in this nigger hall. "Nigger you," I said to him and I took that nigger cigar and that nigger match and threw them right on that nigger floor. Nigger it.

Too bad that white boy on the stage up there ain't no nigger.

"All right now, all right," he said when everybody hushed. "The schmucks in this country run everything and they wanna keep it that way. They all live in big houses and got big cars and big boats and big women. And them old people who ain't got all that, they ain't old. They just look old is all. What they

102

really are, they're young just like us 'cause if you ain't got anything you're young. But them old people who got everything, they don't wanna move over. They like what they got. They like keeping us slaves so they can get richer. They like killing us off so their stocks go up. They like using our bodies and our minds so they can still feel alive. But what they like most of all is treating us like niggers. That's how they get their rocks off. Yeah, they're sick. All they think about is killing and destroying. They wanna kill anybody who's peaceful, like us. Kill the niggers is what they wanna do. But we ain't gonna let 'em. We ain't gonna let 'em so much we're gonna wipe 'em out. That's right. The old gotta die, baby, and we're gonna help them. We're gonna worry them, scare them, screw them right into their graves. Yes, and if we have to raise a few of the dead, we're gonna do that too."

"Tell it, man."

"Sock soul to 'em."

"Tell it like it gonna be."

"Once we know that the word 'nigger' is a weapon, a weapon that means life instead of death, love instead of hate, and create instead of destroy, once we know that, then we got power that can do anything, get anything. Then we got Nigger Power. *Nigger Power!* Right here, right now, we got power can beat anybody. Power that can help the old to die and the young to live. Power that can make the straight world hip. Nigger Power is what does it all, because it is with this generation—our generation—that white niggers and black niggers are coming together once and for all. This is the Nigger Generation is just what it is. We're thinking young, and we're scaring the piss outta the white shitheads that run the game.

"Nigger Power. There's nothing can't be done 'cause Nigger Power's gonna do it. Up to now the Old Man of the white has had his way in this country. He stole it from the Indians and used it for himself. Now we're gonna steal it from him. But I mean this time we're gonna *do* it! I know that some people, good people, been trying for the last four hundred years, and that's a long mothertime to be in enemy land. But nothing

103

worked 'cause wasn't nothing to work with. Only Nigger Power can get what we need. Only Nigger Power can get what we want. Now that we've got Nigger Power, we're not gonna stand around in idle chitchat. We're gonna go out preaching and reaching and speeching. We're gonna move and groove with Nigger Power, and we're gonna *take care of business*."

"We hear you, niggerman."

"Shout it out."

"And the first business we're gonna take care of is this revolution jive everybody's talkin' about. Revolution this, revolution that, soon there'll be a revolution doll for little kids that fucks with a battery in its cat. Yes, and a revolution candy bar that comes in your mouth. Something's wrong here.

"What's wrong is that the old people been ripping off everything for themselves. What's wrong is that they hate us white and black niggers. And what's worse is that they won't give us anything they got. They take our revolution and makes games out of it. And we let 'em! We let 'em buy off our leaders. We let 'em drown our organizations in publicity. We let 'em turn our life styles into a money machine.

"We gotta stop this. We gotta stop selling our youth and our lives. This revolution's got nothing to do with fuckin' dolls and candy bars and sweat shirts and buttons and shit like that. And revolution's got nothing to do with leaders or organizations or schools or slogans. The only real revolution is the individual and what he does to fuck up the enemy. Don't talk revolution, live it! Don't wait for revolution, dig it! The revolution is here, right now, right here. The revolution is you! The revolution is us!"

Hot damn! This boy is good. Remind me of this big supply man I usta know years 'go, fattest man I ever seen. Everybody in Harlem knew him, everybody called him Dealer 'cause he was dealing the shit at the time. That Dealer was so smooth he could talk a snake outta skin. When you was with him you always kept one hand on your pants and the other 'round your money. The Dealer is dead now, killed few years back by a sec'-

tary he had that cut him all up and down into little pieces. Nobody ever know why.

"We are the first generation in this country to get together, I mean really get together—black and white—and make our own way. It's never been done before and that's why the old schmucks hate us. We ain't growing up like them. We're growing up so different it's a revolution. And they're scared. They're scared because they see that for the first time we got a weapon. Nigger Power. And they know we're gonna use it. There's millions of young people not here tonight who are part of Nigger Power. There's young people sitting in their homes tonight waiting for Nigger Power to help them. There's young people walking the New York streets tonight waiting for Nigger Power to help them. Young people whose bones need mending, whose troubles need fixing, whose spirits need lifting. Nigger Power is what we're talking about. If you got Nigger Power, you don't need anything else. If you got Nigger Power, you don't want anything else. If you got Nigger Power, you don't get anything else."

"Right on that."

"If we got Nigger Power we got the game."

"That the truth."

"We're gonna wipe out the enemy."

"Nigger Power do it."

"We're gonna take over the country."

"Nigger Power do it."

"We're gonna get what's ours."

"Nigger Power do it."

"We're gonna get more than ours."

"Nigger Power do it."

"Big houses."

"Nigger Power."

"Big cars."

"Nigger Power."

"Big money."

"Nigger Power."

"Big everything."

"Nigger Power."

"Okay, so we're all niggers, black and white. So it's all up to us niggers, black and white. This country's up for grabs and if we can pull it off, we got a good thing going."

He stopped to take some water and I looked over at Barbra. Her eyes were like two hot nuts. If he said the word, she woulda run up there and give him a suck job right there on that motherfuckin' stage front of everybody. And she don't go outta her way for no white man never. I'm sittin' there wondering if he likes the dark meat 'cause if he do, he must be gettin' it morning, noon and all night awright. Then I'm thinking maybe that's why he's turning this whole white nigger trick. But shit, I got a nasty mind that don't trust nobody. I don't trust nobody so much I hide my money in a diff'rent place every time I go to bed so I can't get up at night and steal myself blind.

"When you ain't got the rent money, trust in Nigger Power. When you ain't got a job, trust in Nigger Power. When you ain't got anything, trust in Nigger Power. 'Cause it's Nigger Power gonna get things for you. Now I know there's some people sitting here tonight who don't believe in Nigger Power, who don't think it'll work. But they're wrong. It's working already. All over this colorless country black kids and white kids are getting together, fucking, making babies. That's Nigger Power. If we all fuck enough, when the old die there won't be nothing left but us niggers."

I was sitting there listening real close. The dude was gettin' to me, I hadda admit it. 'Specially with all the fuck talk.

"When I look at all of you tonight, I see a lot of Nigger Power right here in this hall, just watching, waiting. I feel it all around me. And it feels good like a good woman. And strong like a strong man. And beautiful like a beautiful high. That's Nigger Power. I get high just from thinking about it. Now repeat after me. Nigger Power's good."

"Nigger Power's good."

"Nigger Power's strong."

106

"Nigger Power's strong."

"Nigger Power's beautiful."

"Nigger Power's beautiful."

"Louder."

"Nigger Power's beautiful."

"Uh-huh. Now you got the power. Now you got Nigger Power in you. If you got Nigger Power you're gonna feel better. If you trust Nigger Power you're gonna do better. If you believe in Nigger Power you're gonna be better. All power to the niggers. That's us. All the black and white kids gotta get together, spread the color around. These are the niggers I celebrate. These are the niggers"—for a minute I thought he was gonna say, "These are *my* niggers," and blow his whole game— "who will put the lie to this insane country. They gotta do it. We gotta do it."

"We know what to do, man."

"Do it."

"And when we do it, white America's gonna turn colors. Only Nigger Power can do it. Nothing's too big for Nigger Power. Nothing's too small for Nigger Power. If you're afraid of Nigger Power, don't be afraid. That's what I said. Don't be afraid. Be a nigger."

I quick turned to Barbra. "You hear that, you hear what that man's saying? He goin' get his ass in a sling talkin' like that in this country."

She looked at me funny. "Yeah," she said, "he keep talkin' like that he goin' fuck himself right into the grave." And she turned back to him and opened her legs a little more. I looked all 'round me. Every fox in the place got their mouths hung open. And all their legs are wide-open too. He's up there rapping and swinging with Nigger Power working in him and white power working for him and he's got all these cats warming up, and I'm here with nothin' between my legs but cold turkey. And I'm thinking maybe I'm too old already. I mean, maybe he's talking about me.

I sat there wondering if that white nigger comes with black juice or if it's just white like for the rest of us black niggers.

"Now listen to what I say. We can fight the schmuckheads and maybe get ourselves killed off. Or we can just lay back and fuck while they die out. And then we take over and run it the way we want. All we have to do until then is get our own shit together, get strong together, white and black. Get so tight together that we create a new color: blite. Right. Then when we're on top, there'll be no more race hatred and no more race war 'cause there won't be any more race. Just us.

"You dig? The message is kiss instead of kill. Fuck instead of fight. The only weapon you need is your body. Turn it on. We're all niggers, let's fuck like niggers. Instead of the Big Bomb, let's have a Big Bang. Instead of Cataclysm, let's have Orgasm. Dig it. Fuck fighting. Don't fight fucking. Fuck on the beaches, in the streets, in the homes. Anywhere and everywhere. Flood this country with blite babies, thousands and millions of them. Flood the welfare agencies with them, drown the country's economy with them. Don't deal in birth control. Let the enemy do that, he's got more than we got right now. We need babies, blite babies. We need so many of them that one day, maybe when we're old, there'll be nothing around but our kind. And when anybody asks what race you are, you'll say the human race, brother, that's all we got here."

I just know it sure as I'm sittin' here. This white-black black-white blite motherfuck rainbow nigger is gonna be President someday. He can't miss. If they start fighting he'll fuck 'em to death. He's putting together a party of young people that's gonna get him anything he wants. Now how's the Democrat Party ever goin' beat a Fuck Party?

"Live your life style as a nigger. If you're white, get black. If you're black, get white. Then get laid. Right now we're the first black-and-white nigger generation. If we fuck things up enough, maybe tomorrow we won't be the last."

"We know what to do."

"Fuck it."

Man, I'm sitting there sweating black, smelling white and seeing red. It's that motherfuck white deodorant I put on 'fore

108

I come here. The more you sweat, the worse you smell. Make anybody mad. Just another one of the white man's trick bags.

"Well, what you think of him now?" Barbra asked me.

"I wonder what kinda deodorant he uses."

I looked at her. She had her mouth open. Then she shut it. Then she opened it again. "Marcus, you are one crazy nigger sometime, you know that?"

Then her mouth shut again. Tight.

Everybody was moving out. In the lobby I seen Arab Ahmed rapping with the news people. They like him 'cause he's always good for pictures. He wears a funny hat and he carries a long sword everywhere he goes. One time some dude come at him with a blade and Arab Ahmed shoved that sword right through him. Come clean out the other side. The po-lice wanted to know why anyone'd be crazy enough to try a fool trick like that. Arab Ahmed said nothing. The dude had a blade in his hand and a sword in his chest. Wasn't nothin' else to say.

The gig was on Seventy-second Street in a big-money place by the Harlem River. Only there it's called the East River, that way the landlord gets more money. But it didn't fool me none, I knew it was the same river minute I smelled it.

We walked into this big lobby, the doorman holding a glass door open for us. Right away I seen he ain't no white nigger. I always feel okay with anyone hates me. It's the ones don't know how they feel that I watch out for. He followed us all the way back to the elevators, past the glass mirras and carpets on the floor.

When we got out the elevator way high up, this very tall dude was standing by a big door. "Hello, I'm your host," he said. He shuck hands with us and it was like he was 'specially glad we come. I watched him out the back of my head all the way till we got inside.

Barbra went to the sandbox to powder her ass and I walked on over to the bar. I ordered a shooter but the choc'late skin didn't know how to make it, he was playing white on white. I downed a bourbon, he knew what that was, and moved on.

There was some show biz faces I seen on TV and a few Harlem politicians I seen in nightmares. A lotta high priced ass was floatin' around too, most of it white. I wondered if maybe it was here free for the taking. But then I figured nobody could let that kinda stuff run loose, somebody's gotta end up paying for it and all I had was my black balls and a weekend job and a few bucks in my pocket. Nothing they'd want. These babes are color-blind as you can get, all they can see is green. If you got green they don't care if your rig is purple and strapped to your ankle. And if you don't got green, the rest of you could be purple for all they care.

"Marcus, Marcus Black."

I didn't hafta turn to see who it was. I knew the voice, low, deadly. Ben Pride, head of the Black Freedom Fighters.

"How you, Ben?"

"Fine, Marcus. I ain't seen you for a while. What you been up to?"

"Well, you know, man, still trying to make a living."

Minute I said it I knew it was the wrong thing. "We have to do more than just make a living, Marcus. We have to fight for what's ours. If we don't fight, we'll never have anything."

"I know that, Ben. I just meant I'm busy tryin' to stay alive."

"That's right. That's just what the fight's all about. Staying alive." He smiled at me. "What you think of tonight's little talk?"

"Well, he got some good ideas there—"

"He got shit. Shit is all he got there. He got white shit and he got black shit and he wants to put them together. Can't be done. You know what you get when you put black shit together with white shit? You know what you gonna get, Marcus?" I'm looking at him looking at me but somehow I don't think he wants a answer. "What you get is just a little lighter shade of black shit. What you get is black shit that ain't as strong as it was. Black shit that's lost its character, its identity, its power. That's what you get."

If I tell him shit is shit he'll just say I'm full of shit so I don't say nothin'.

"This motherfuck Jew intellectual is trying to destroy our blackness. He's trying to make us lose our heritage and forget who we are. If we listen to him, one day there won't be any more black man. Just a lotta yella shit runnin' around. You see, Marcus, he's trying to quick trick us out of our black skin."

"But he's saying the same thing to the whites, ain't he?"

"Fuck the whites. They deserve to lose their identity. They deserve to lose everything, including their stupid fuckin' heads. But by fighting, not fucking. Hitler had the right idea. Kill 'em all, 'specially them fuckin' Jews. Don't let them pollute our race. The black race is superior and will last a million years if only the devil whites are killed off. But this motherfucker is talkin' about getting blacks and whites together so much, they'll soon destroy the pure black man. He's talking genocide, that's just what he's doing." He looked around the room. "See all these white bitches here? They're here for just one thing, to pollute your pure black blood. Don't let 'em do it, Marcus."

I'm standing there shaking my head no and hoping yes. Man, I'd just love to get polluted by that high-tail bitch over by the window. Yeah, she could pollute me till I turn pure white. And I'd never even say a word.

Some people called him over and I quick moved away. I mean, Ben Pride makes a black man feel good 'cause he tells you how good you are. But he's all strung out on the color thing. He thinks the black world is all black and the white world's all white. He don't understand there ain't nobody who's all one thing. Pure blood. That's a lotta shit, and it don't matter what color it is neither. With all the fucking been goin' on all these years, ain't nobody got pure anything. I'm all for killing off whitey but there's a awful lotta niggers 'round here I'd knock off just as easy, and never even give it a second think. Pure blood, my black ass.

Barbra slipped up beside me. "I had two drinks already," she said to me, "and I'd like another, please."

That's the way it went for the next couple hours. We'd drink and talk and drift and meet and drink and talk some more. Like at any gig. Between drinks and drifts I met a po-lice from somewhere who liked grass so much he quit the pig patrol. Then I met this crazyass white dude with a pointed head who kept calling me a melonderm, something like that. I was all set to bust him right in his big watermelon mouth when he told me that this melonderm means black. So I shouted at him, "You mean black like nigger?" And everybody looked mad at the dude 'cause they figured he was calling me names. Which he was. Who the hell would call somebody a melonderm? He's lucky I didn't call him a turdhead.

I sent him on over to Ben Pride. Let Ben do it.

The blast was okay for what it was. Whisky, women, soul food, rapping. And everything black and white. I could see this white-black nigger fuck was serious business 'round here. Whoever was pulling the strings got a black mine goin' here, if they played it right. And I had a feel they were gonna play it right.

Some white stud was walkin' around wearing a button that said, NOT WITH MY WIFE YOU DON'T. Walking with a little black dude. I went up to the stud and asked, "Don't what?" and pointed to the button. "Fuck," he said. I was gettin' stoned and I figured he meant me so I said, "But you ain't even kissed me yet." That's when he showed some real nice teeth. "I'm ready any time you are, love."

I mean, how the fuck was I to know his wife was the little black dude next to him?

I weaved into another room and there was Barbra jamming with Abner Goldstein. This was my big chance. A lotta people were standing 'round gettin' him to sign books but I elbowed my way over and she introduced me. "Abner Goldstein, Marcus Garvey Black."

We mumbled some shit and shuck hands. I just kept lookin' at that trick Jew face and thinkin' about all that white-nigger black-nigger jive. There was a lot I wanted to know but I didn't have the time, so I tried to do the whole number in one question. "Abner, tell me something"—his red misery eyes were looking right at me when I give it to him—"what kind of deodorant do you use?"

112

Barbra fainted, two black niggers turned white for the night, and that sonovabitch Abner Goldstein kept his eyes straight on me as he said, "I use King Solomon spray deodorant. It's made by a black-owned business, and it's a good one." And he smiled at me.

That's when I knew for sure that he was mad as a melon-derm.

Barbra went home with somebody else ten minutes later. But I didn't care. I was gonna stick around a while 'cause the whisky was good, and there wasn't nothing wrong with these white bitches neither.

But deep down in my black nigger soul I knew the rest of the night was all gonna be downhill.

9.

WHEN my mother died, the last thing she told me was not to feel bad. "Everything be awright," she said. "I'se just goin' on home." Then she smiled, "I done talked to God so much He don't have to ask my name."

She held my hand in hers, it was bone thin and I bent down to kiss it. When I looked up at my mother again, she was sleeping. I called to her but she didn't hear me. I kept calling her.

"Mother's dead, Marcus."

I looked at Rosa. She was standing on the other side of the bed, crying. I was still holding my mother's hand and I put it against my face. "Now you'll be free," I said to her staring eyes.

Rosa sent one of the kids for the doctor and we sat there till he come and gone. Then we sat up all night with the body. The next day everybody come to give respect 'cause they all liked her. And her church did right nice for the funeral with singing and church music. Rosa's husband took care of gettin' the cars for all them goin' to the cem'tery, which was most the black people living 'round there. Some people cried and everybody prayed. Then it was all over. My mother was gone and I had nobody left 'cept for my sister Rosa, and she had her own family. Dust to dust is what they said, just like when Ginny died. I was only twenty-five and all my family had turned to dust.

At that time I was working as a bartender on Lenox Avenue. First real job I ever had. After Ginny gone, I tried a few hustles but I couldn' get my head into it no more. All the things I been through and what all I seen, I just seen too much to go around like the world was a big fat egg and I was the eggsucker. I didn't wanna take from nobody no more.

I got a friend to let me work in his bar. In the day he showed me all 'bout the diff'rent drinks and what to do. After a few weeks I got the feel and I took over at night. Me and this other stud, Lester. He was about ten feet high and there wasn't much trouble when Lester was around.

Like one time some fuckhead come in the bar and he was gonna blast everyone into their graves. That's just what he said. Lester walked 'round from behind the bar and put out his big ham hand and he said, "You don't wanna shoot nobody, man. Now just gimme the gun." And he's talkin' low and easy to the gun, moving in all the time. The fuckhead's just standing there lookin' at him moving up.

I'm behind the bar and it's like every second is a million years and I'm saying to myself, "This ain't happening." And my asshole's tighter'n a nun's cat.

Lester takes one step more and I hear the click of the gun. Loudest fuckin' noise I ever heard in my life. Now I know Lester's dead but he's still moving. The fuckhead pulls the trigger again and nothin' happens again and then Lester's got him and he knocks the gun to the ground and he picks up the fuckhead and throws him clear 'cross the bar. Took six men to pull Lester off 'cause he was gonna kill him. Almos' did too. When the po-lice come they took a look and quick called for the amb'lance.

114

Then one of the po-lice said to Lester, "You were wrong to go after him, that's our job. Next time just call us." Like a dude with a gun is gonna wait while we make a call.

Lester was so mad he wanted to throw that po-lice fuckhead clear 'cross the bar. Only thing stopped him was he knew the po-lice gun wouldn' jam.

But nobody come in lookin' for big trouble after that.

When my bus got to Orangeburg, Rosa's husband was waitin' on me with a car 'cause I called her from New York 'fore I left. Right off I asked him how bad my mother was.

"Bad" was all he said.

When we got there Rosa told me she was sleeping but I should go in anyway and sit there till she wakes up.

"Will she be awright?" I asked Rosa.

"She gonna die, Marcus. Then she be awright."

Two days later my mother was dead. Before she go I told her I was sorry I never been no good to her.

"Don't you go talkin' such nonsense," she said to me. "You been the best son God ever done give a mother."

I was sitting there wishing it was me gonna die 'stead of her. It ain't fair, I kept tellin' myself. But I knew it wasn't really s'pose to be fair.

I stayed with Rosa a few days after the funeral, then it was time to go on back. The thing was I wanted to get away from there 'cause it made me feel bad to be there now my mother was gone. I told Rosa I'd come see her again when I get a chance but she knew I wouldn' no more. She give me a big hug. "You always welcome here, Marcus." And she got all the kids to give me kisses and wave goodby.

When I left, Junior run out into the road after me. "Come back and see me, Uncle Marcus." Junior was the oldest boy and he liked me 'cause I was his big-shot uncle from up North in New York.

Rosa's husband took me back to Orangeburg. "You a good man, Fred," I told him on the way there. "You take care of Rosa, hear?"

Fred pulled out the pipe from his mouth where it always was.

115

"Rosa's a mighty fine woman" was all he said. Then the pipe went back in. But that was good enough for me, I trusted Fred to do right by his family.

He let me off at the bus station. The bus wasn't due in for a hour so I got me a paper and sat down to wait.

"What them niggers up to now?"

"I dunno, but if they come over my way I'm gonna get me a dead nigger sure as shootin'."

"I hope they shoot that Cleveland Waters. He's the one behind all this nigger noise."

"Yeah, he's the biggest nigger in the crowd."

"And a Commanist too, is what he is."

The two crackers were sitting the other way, right behind me. They were talkin' about Cleveland Waters that I met once when I was a kid living down here. I looked in the paper and goddam, there he was. A picture of him with a big story 'bout how the po-lice busted him for messing up one of them and for riot and a hundred other things like picking his nose in public and pissing without a license. He was with a lotta other brothers pushing for their rights. That shook everybody up 'cause the niggers was fightin' back. Nobody ever seen nothin' like that 'round here before.

Man, these crackers are crazy in the South. Shiiit. It's like they got a Kill-A-Nigger Club that you can't join 'less you get your share.

Then I think about a club I'm gonna start up just for bloods. Kill a White Tonight and Feel Better Tomorrow.

Even better. Kill a Gray Today and Feel Better Tonight.

That make me feel good right away and I turn to the paper and read what Cleveland Waters said. "We have the civil rights act of 1957, the civil rights act of 1960, the civil rights act of 1964 and the civil rights act of 1966. Now we got all these civil rights but the right to live. Are we civils or are we slaves? Something's wrong here."

Then I read 'bout somebody who claims the South really won the Civil War but the niggers kept the news from the whites through voodoo.

116

I close my eyes to get away from this madness. I wanna tell Cleveland to get out while he's still living but he wouldn't do it. I know these Southern niggers, I was one myself. They love the land even if they gotta fight it to death. But they ready to fight anybody tells 'em to move on.

Something hits my shoe and I open my eyes.

"You leaving town, boy?"

It's the po-lice hisself, all snip-snap.

"Yeah," I say, "I'm leaving town."

"Lemme see your ticket."

I give it to him.

"New York, eh?"

"That's what it say."

"You a New York boy?"

"I'm a New York man."

"What you doing here?"

I don't answer.

"I'm talkin' to you, boy. I asked you what you was doing here."

"Minding my own business." And I look right at him.

"You wasn't down here to make no trouble, was you?"

"No."

"Then why'd you come here?"

It was either tell him or kill him. I told him. "I come here to bury my mother." And I give him my name and where Rosa lives and all that.

"You leaving on the next bus?"

"Yeah."

"See that you do," he said and walked away.

"Fuck you, pigfucker," I said to him. When he was far 'way and couldn' hear me.

The two crackers behind me seen the whole thing. I knew they were mad 'cause I was still alive. I quick turned 'round to them. "Things ain't what they was, eh?" Out loud I said it.

They got up and left. Didn't have their guns with them, I s'pose.

117

I got up and drunk a dark Coke outta a white paper cup. Nobody said nothing about it.

When the bus left, I knew I wasn't ever gonna come back. Wasn't no reason to. I mean, if I had my way I'd kill off every last whitefucker in the South, maybe every white everywhere. Man, woman, dog, anything that even looked white, right down to the babies. That's the way I feel, the way every black man feels. But at the same time there's a part of me don't wanna kill nothing. I just like to live and be let alone. That's another thing every black man gotta put up with. There's like two people in us all the time. One says kill and one says live. If the white man hadda handle somethin' like that, they'd all been crazy mad long ago for sure. Even more'n they already are.

After my mother go, it took a long time to get my head together again. It hit me hard 'cause I felt so all alone. I freaked out on so much shit I didn't know where I was half the time, it was like I got lost somewheres down in hell and I couldn' find the key to get out. Only the hell was inside my own skull and nobody was gonna open the door for me. I was goin' crazy is what it was. Seeing things and hearing things, and the worst was the shakes I'd get when I wasn't stoned on something. I couldn' even hold the job no more. I had no family and no future and I was running shit scared for the first time in my life.

I kept tellin' myself that I goin' be awright, that I was just junking it through.

This went on five, six months. Then one day I come up against this giant motherfuck dragon. I'm standing there and it comes screaming down on me and it's got a big glass eye and inside the dragon's eye is a man. He's trapped in the dragon's eye. I quick pull out my sword and I'm gonna shove it right in that ugly fucker's evil eye and save the dude what's in there. But 'fore I can get set, the dragon goes right on by me and slows down and stops. I'm lookin' at it and it got glass all 'long its body and then the glass opens up. I'm standing there watching the dragon and the glass opens and I jump back five feet and shut my eyes and open 'em again.

It's a subway train is all. The fucking 125th Street subway

118

and I'm standing there on the platform with one of them long breads in my hand. I was gonna shove my bread in the glass window to save the shithead driving the subway. Then I got real scared and I start shaking and I quick run up the stairs and on outta there.

When I'm on the street, I'm shaking so much I get mad so I ain't scared no more. The sonovabitchin' motherfuck whitefuckers, they are what's doing it to me. I'm so mad I start running up the street. This white dude comes out from a store and I bust him right in the face. I don't say a word. I keep on running and I see a white kid and I bust him same thing. I musta hit on least a half dozen whites 'fore I turned down a corner and got the hell away from there. I was crazy 'cause I didn't know what I was doing and I couldn' stop myself.

That's when I got my asshole together. Man, look out. One more scene like that and I was goin' to the animal farm. I stayed in my room almos' a week drying myself out best I could. Then I said adios to Harlem and just moved on down the line and *went*. I mean I didn't care where. All I know was I needed a diff'rent movie for a while 'cause I wasn't staying 'round to see the end of this one.

I had five bills in my pocket and the East Village on my mind. Stayed down 'round there most of a year. And up by Columbia too. But first it was the East Village. I got a room on Avenue C, the scene was good there and I begun to feel better. The place was full of kids with long hair and walking 'round with no shoes. White kids. And everybody was turning on. Not the Harlem hard stuff but what they called the love drugs. When you took 'em, you right away loved everybody. Which was fine with me. I didn't mind a little loving long's I got a lotta fucking. And there was plenty of it, more'n anyone could handle. I missed a big three years of it in that rat's ass prison so I was getting my share and a couple more too. I had so many fox jumpin' in and outta bed I was thinking of workin' the pimp hustle. But it was no go 'cause everybody was giving it away free.

I had this one blond fox, Marcy. She was so out of it she

119

musta been from some other world. She was seventeen and she loved everybody. All she talked about was love. Everybody was good and kind and full of love if they were only treated nice. She walked around giving people flowers and everything she had. I tried to tell her that a whole lotta people were out front evil. But she just laughed. "People are just people, Marcus. They wanna love and be loved but they're all afraid," she'd say to me.

"This is a fuckin' jungle," I kept tellin' her. "Maybe someday things be like you want, but right now the animals are waiting to chop you up into little pieces."

"Oh, Marcus," she'd laugh. "You have to learn to trust people before they'll give you their love."

Marcy was so far into the love bag it closed over her head. One night she got so stoned she trusted some punks to go joyriding and they took her to some punk park and raped the ass off her and then dumped her down a hill. She laid there all night bleeding inside from the fall and by the time somebody come, she was dead.

That kinda thing happened a lot the year I was in the East Village. Cars'd go along the streets moving slow, lookin' for long-haired fox that didn't wear no bra. They'd be mostly from outta town. Punk kids or jocks or fuckin' businessmen who changed into lover boys after five. It was one big show and everybody was playing a game. Everybody but the love kids who just wanted to be let alone and who already dropped outta the stupid games.

That was the flip side of the scene. The nightmare side. That and the killer pigs.

They hated us from the git go. They couldn' take the idea that anybody was free, it just blew their minds. It you wasn't pushing your nose up a mountain like everyone else there hadda be somethin' wrong with you. A nigger was bad enough. But white kids who dropped out! Jesus Christ, what's the fuckin' world coming to? They'd ride around in their plastic wagons dressed in their plastic suits and that big cock gun strapped to their plastic belts and they'd be King Shit.

120

Then they'd see some fresh young thing walkin' down the block giving off love rays and they'd think of their plastic old ladies at home that couldn' fuck, wouldn' suck and didn't even like 'em to begin with. And they'd get their rocks off by messing up the kid's mind with their plastic death breath.

"Where you goin', girlie?"

"Your mother know you walk around like that?"

"You got any panties on under them pants?"

"Lemme see your ID."

"Who you fuckin' for? Some nigger Commie dope addict?"

Laughs all around, 'cept from the kid who stands there with love on her face, scared.

"You know you can make some money sellin' it. Why you give it away free?"

"Yeah. If you was to turn pro we wouldn' bother you, we'd even help you."

"Sure thing. You take care of us, we'd take care of you."

More laughs.

"Why you shakin' like that? You one of them dope fiends?"

"Maybe we should take her in just to make sure."

"Naw, I'd fuck her so much I'd never get home and my kid's got a birthday party tonight."

"Awright, girlie, we'll give you a break this time. But we don't like to see your kind walkin' our streets."

"Yeah, it makes us mad. Next time we see you we gonna pull you in."

"Then you can get fucked by some real men, not them long-hair faggots you got now."

And they drive away. Always on duty protecting the people.

The kid stands there crying to herself 'cause she's scared and she don't know what she done for them to hate her like that.

She don't know she ain't one of the people 'cause she dresses funny and she don't work in the straight world and she don't take money for her body and she don't hate everybody like she s'pose to. She just don't know.

That was the other thing I tried to tell some of them. That the pigs would bust ass 'cause they were scared of anybody who

121

wasn't scared of them. They had a license to kill and the gun to do it. They were killers, all of them. But not honest killers, like the shooters who do it as a business thing and that's all. The pigs did it 'cause they liked it. The straight world was so fucked up they hadda hire these kill crazy assholes to protect them from themselfs.

How does a pig become a pig? If he's born a killer but he ain't got the guts to stand on his own, he joins the pigs.

You can't be a nigger in America and be burnt all the time and not know that.

But it took the love kids a long time to find that out. They were white and they mostly come from good homes with some money and they never had no trouble with the pigs back home. They figured nothin' was diff'rent. I told them everything was diff'rent. When they jumped off the go-round, that blew it for them. They were outlaws with no cover and no rights and no lefts. Everything they did was wrong and anything they did was bad. What they was, was niggers. Just that they had white skin. White niggers. Same thing.

There was this one kid who called hisself Saint John. He was about nineteen and drug thin and his hair was way over his shoulders. He was always going 'round giving everybody whatever shit he was scoring. All he wanted was to see people happy 'cause he felt sorry for them. "They're in pain," he usta say, "but they don't know what to do about it. We gotta help them." And he'd lay one of the acids on them, or speed or weed or whatever he was holding.

Saint John had the idea that if the whole world got stoned there'd be no more wars. Nobody'd wanna kill nobody.

He was in a crash pad when the pigs got to him. They musta heard he didn't like wars and he was preaching a new kinda religion of love. They took him away somewhere and beat up on him. The more he talked love to them, the more they hated him. When he told them he was doing God's work, they got so mad they swung him high in the air and let him drop. He was in the hospital for maybe a month with everything broke in-

122

side. He kept asking us why the pigs done that to him. "All I did was tell 'em that God is love."

He didn't know the pigs got a diff'rent God.

"That's where you fucked up," I told him one time.

"How's that?"

"You didn't know the pig God got nothin' to do with love."

Saint John never did learn that neither. Before the summer was up, he was dead. Run over on a highway outside of town, stoned outta his mind. Only thing was nobody could figure out how he got to the highway. Somebody hadda take him, somebody that could make him get in the car and then push him out.

I stayed in the East Village the rest of that year 'fore I moved on up to Columbia. By then the scene was a drag, with bad heads crawlin' all over the place. But while I was there I dipped into the love drugs myself. First time I tripped out was with a fox who wanted to save my soul. I told her if she wasn't stone blind she'd see I'm so black I got plenty of soul. "Don't matter," she said. "This'll grow soul on your soul. And besides that," she whispered, "it'll make you holy."

She had two caps. One for one. And then just like that, I dropped some acid. LSD. I sat back and waited for the trip into somewhere else. I was tough, I was hard, I could take anything. I seen too much and I been behind it all. Most my people were dead and inside I hated everything so much I needed to punch out, rip up, kill off. Behind my laugh and easy ways was hate on hate. But I was trying to work it out, like anybody else.

What's acid like? It's a trip and a half, and there's just no way to tell anybody what it's like. No way. All you can say is once you drop acid, you know everything is part of the same thing. One Truth Beauty Love. You wanna tell everybody to stop playing the games, stop hating, stop fighting. The only thing that counts is to be honest. Every minute is like a hundred years and a whole lifetime is just a second and there's even spaces in the spaces in your mind.

It scared the shit outta me. I mean, what's the good of living

123

if you can't go 'round hating all the people who screw you down? Without that hate, you got no cover, no protection. And if everybody's the same and you ain't better'n nobody, how can you feel like a man? That's the games everybody plays, but without them all you got is love and beauty everywhere.

Which is a groove 'cept for one thing. Everybody don't feel the same. If the whole world tripped out on acid all at the same time, then everything'd be everything. But long's that don't happen, it just don't make sense to run mind naked in a pack of hungry dogs. They gonna eat you dead 'fore you can love 'em alive.

That's prob'ly what kept me from freaking out all the way. I already been down so much pain nothin' could save me for love. I was so tough I just wasn't gonna give up the one big game I had left, which was fighting to stay alive so I could keep fighting. I wasn't gonna spend my life lookin' to get people to see that love is what it's all about. Once I took the acid I knew that, but that's all I cared about. I was a nigger and I been fucked with too long to care 'bout anything else.

After that first time, I took acid maybe once a week while I was in the East Village. It was the wildest time I ever had in my life and some of the things I flashed on were so fan-fuckingtastic I knew I was goin' crazy. But I always snapped back.

Just about the time I was ready to move on, Super Spade come on the scene. By then the freaks were coming outta the walls. The pigs were bustin' loose and the drugs were gettin' tight. Super Spade was a big dealer and he come in dealing left and right. Didn't matter what you'd want, he had it. And if he didn't had it, you didn't want it.

I think he was a big head hisself. One time I seen him at this party and he come in and told everybody he got a new game for us to play and he pulled out a little bag full of caps and pills. All diff'rent kinds. There was LSD and DMT and STP and speed and downs, he had 'em all.

"This here thing is called *Waitin' for the Train,*" he said. Then he made everybody get in a big circle on the floor and he turned out the lights and dumped the bag of pills in the middle of the circle. Everyone reached out in the dark and downed the first thing they picked up. After that we just sat back in the dark and waited for the train to hit. It was wild. Nobody knew where they were goin'. But soon you'd hear some outasight sounds.

I asked Super Spade once if the whole love-drug thing was gonna turn pro, like the hard stuff in Harlem.

"Naw, it ain't that big for the racket people to come in," he told me.

"But s'pose it got that big?"

He looked at me for a minute like he was thinking. "I'm gonna tell you a little something, Marcus man, 'cause you blood. It ain't gonna get that big. Not a chance. The Man ain't gonna let it get that big 'cause it's just too fuckin' dangerous."

"For who?"

"For whoever ain't taking it. Listen, baby, this acid ain't like the hard stuff. Society don't care nothin' about the junkies 'cause they ain't no threat, not really. They just got a job like everybody else. Their job is taking junk. They steal and kill sometimes but that gives the po-lice something to do. And everybody's happy, you dig? But acid's a whole other thing. It lets you see what life oughtta be like. It makes you a revolutionary. Not for one stupid fuckin' country over another, that's just a game. But for a whole diff'rent kinda life where there's no power shit at all. You dig?"

I nodded.

"Now society ain't about to let go of the golden apple. Too many power junkies got their teeth in it. And they already gettin' hip to the acid message. Soon they gonna come down and wipe out all the acid freaks like they was some kinda disease, man. And if they don't do that, they'll get some science shit out front to scare everybody off. But whatever they do, they ain't gonna let love take over 'cause that'd be the end of their world."

"What if the people say that's what they want?" I asked him.

"The people?" Super Spade laughed. "You dumb nigger. Who you think I been talkin' about? It's the people who don't

125

want no change. They *like* the setup the way it is. They feel more comf'table with hate than with love. You dig? If they didn't *want* any killing it'd be over just like that."

He was right. The love kids believed the world was gonna get zonked into love and 'stead of that, they got zapped into jail. And nothing really changed. 'Cept Super Spade got hisself knocked off about a year after when I knew him.

Things were gettin' real hairy on the streets 'long about that time. The Black Panthers were starting up in New York and the pigs were beginning to lean hard on 'em. The Panthers were doing good work and everybody was mostly behind them but I couldn' get into that bag. I just stayed stoned in my room most all the time.

Then one day I'm on the street and this pig stops me. He wants to know what I'm doing.

"I'm standing here on the street is all."

"What are you waitin' for?"

"Well, now, I tell you," I say to him, "I just had this big heart attack and I'm waitin' 'round for it to heal up 'fore I move on."

He give me that tight smile they all got. "You live around here?"

"Few blocks over."

"How many blocks?"

"Maybe ten. I didn't count 'em."

"That's the East Village where all the shit lives," he says. Just like that.

I say nothing.

"Where you from?"

"Way uptown." And I pull out papers. But I do it real slow so's he can see I ain't got no fuckin' machine gun under my jacket.

"Maybe you better go back up there," he says to me when he hands over my stuff.

"Where I go is my business," I tell him. Fuck him. I'm stoned anyway.

126

He don't like that. "Are you a member of the Black Panthers?"

I was waitin' for him to ask that. Now I give him my tight smile. "No, I ain't no Black Panther 'cause I still got this hang-up that I talk to chickens and pigs and one thing and another. So they won't let me in."

That did it. I made the top of his shit list. His eyes got hard and his mouth got small. "I'd like to blow your fuckin' nigger head off, only it's still daylight. But if I catch you around here tonight, you're dead. Now get your black stinkin' ass outta here."

"You got the gun and that makes you a man," I said to him. And I walked away.

All the way home I was waitin' for him to shoot me in the back.

I was so mad I was sweating nails. That mothercunt pig-fucker. If I had a machine gun I woulda let the air outta him awright. If I had a sword I woulda cut him into chop meat. I'm walking 'round the room thinking like that. I'm so mad I wanna run down the street busting every whitefucker in the mouth.

Then I get hold of myself. Uh-uh, this just like back in Harlem. No good. I sit down and I start thinking 'bout love. Love everybody. But how can I love that motherfucker that just hit up on me? Yeah, love him too. By time I get my head back on straight I'm stoned on love. I love the whole world and even the things in it.

Next day I moved on up to Columbia. I was still loving everybody, even that pigfucker. But only if I didn't hafta see him.

10.

FROM the outside it didn't look like much. Two small windows with a double door between them, the whole thing raised up a step above the rest of the sidewalk going out to the gutter. Everything was painted that shit brown but it looked good 'cause the whole block looked just as bad. That was the block on Tenth Street and Avenue B. That's where the Annex was. On Avenue B way downtown in the East Village.

The inside was bad as the outside, only much bigger bad. And long as a bowling alley. The bar ran half down one side with sawdust all over the floor and little tables and chairs on the other side. In the back were more tables and the sandbox was in the middle.

The Annex was a night tripper. All kinda heads made the scene there. Sometime the junk was so heavy the whisky'd go to sleep right in your drink. Didn't matter what you drunk. It'd come out the bottle and sniff that crazy air and curl up like a balloon that just farted. Thokk. And you'd be drinkin' something that was nothin'.

Nobody ever got stoned in the Annex from the whisky. One dude sat there seventeen hours one day drinking steady, seventeen hours and he didn't get stoned from the whisky. Didn't feel a thing. Couldn' feel a thing 'cause he got stoned the first five minutes he was in there just from the air 'round him.

The Annex had other things too. A lotta pimps'd stop by, sometimes with their bottom women. And some of the alley cats from the jazz joints uptown would make it there on weekends. Jaspers used it sometimes to score but they were mostly put down. One night two jaspers were at the bar feelin' crotches and this wiseass dude went on over and give this little card to the fem. The butch is sittin' right there staring holes in him but he's cool. The fem reads the card and breaks up. That's too much for the butch, she grabs the card and reads it: "Attention, all faggot females. Your hand on a cock is worth two on a bush. Stay straight." But the butch had no sense of humor. She got up spittin' flame and the dude was already out the door. Good thing too, 'cause she was two of me.

But the big thing at the Annex was the black-white scene. White foxes come from all over just to see what studs were runnin' loose. On a Friday night there'd be so many heavy-hung white fox sittin' 'round dreaming of King Kong, all you needed to score was a dark tan from Coney Island. That's a fact. It got so good you'd get behind a fox and clap your hands over her eyes and she'd say, "Who's that?" and you'd say, "A nigger" and she'd say, "You beautiful." I seen studs so ugly they couldn' make the TEN MOST WANTED posters walk outta the Annex with blond fox a white stud'd sell his kids to get. And the blacker you were, the better you made out. Every day of a black man's life he's trying to be lighter'n the dude next to him. In the Annex it was all upside down. The blacker the better. There was one dude so black no one could find him after the sun went down. And ugly as sin, even scared me. But that ugly black motherfucker could take any fox in the place. All the other studs hated him. Got so bad, one time they were gonna chalk and feather him.

Not too many white dudes hung around there. They'd come in and see all that white stuff laying 'round but when they found out they didn't have what it took, they took off. Some of them almos' seen it too late. Like this one night two of them sat at the bar and one said to the white fox next to him, "Let's fuck." Just then her old man comes back from the sandbox and she tells him and now the white dude is sittin' next to a spade with a blade this long. But the other white boy is cool and he tells her old man he oughtta forget it 'cause whites don't got too much sense anyway. Everybody liked that and them white boys ended up gettin' free drinks.

Another "Let's fuck" story. This friend of mine is in a rest'rant 'round where he works downtown. A lotta white fox go there for lunch. They like his looks and sometimes he gets notes saying things like "I need a *very* dark secret," or "I'm hungry for dark meat." But this one day he sees a creamy fox sitting at the next table and he makes the first move. He passes a note to her that says, "I dig your body. Meet me at the Annex tonight at ten and we'll fuck." She looks at the note, pulls out a pen, writes something at the bottom and passes it back to him. He reads it. "Understood your hint. Will be there at ten."

129

And sonovabitch, she was too.

One time I had this Mary Lou I met in the Annex and I asked her why the white fox all go for the big black bang. Mary Lou looked up at me and she said, "Man, once you see that long black tool moving 'cross your white thighs, you ain't goin' back to no more white-on-white balling, that's for sure." Then she went back to what she liked best.

I was in the Annex least two, three times a week 'fore it closed up. I was living down in the East Village that year, 'long with a lotta other dudes from way uptown. They'd see how easy it was to get the white stuff so they'd move on down there. And besides which, they liked the feel. Everybody there was into something. I knew this one dude, Donald Sharp, he was runnin' a card game every night of the week. Somewhere near the big Con Ed smokestacks they got there, in one of them big houses. You walk in and there'd be eight or ten men sitting 'round a table and another dozen waitin' to get in the game. Donald was the dealer or somebody he'd hire. There'd be a fox serving food and drinks, all free. The high rollers'd come from uptown 'cause it was a safe game, and there was always a fox for them after they blew the roll. They'd just go in the bedroom and knock off a piece. For free. Even after paying everybody off, Donald still made four bills a week and better.

But there was a lotta hate too, just like up here. Just like anywhere. Everybody walked around with blades and guns, and at night it was mostly a jungle. And the Annex was right in the middle of it all.

The night it happened was a Saturday, right at the end of summer. Detroit blew up that summer, so did Newark and plenty of other towns. Harlem started that whole instant urban renewal thing a couple years before, when a white pig murdered a kid from Harlem. But the time I'm talkin' about, people up here were already into other things.

It was a hot week and by the time sell day come 'round everybody was breakin' wind. Me and Tiger were goin' to a gig that night somewhere 'round the Annex. This stud we knew had made a big score for hisself and was holding court. Which was

130

boss with me. Downtown tripping was good most the time and anyway, it was all for free.

When we got there everything was hangin' tough. Man, I never seen so many people in one place. They were laying all over, even on the fire'scape. James Brown was on the box but you couldn' hardly hear him for the noise. Everybody was speed-rapping, that's how high things were. No whisky but all the shit you could handle. Minute I walked in, I spotted a half dozen speed freaks over in a corner. If the pigs ever busted in, they'd think it was some Chinese fuckin' plot to stone the country blind. But there was just too many heads down there so they didn't bother much at the time.

I moved down one wall, watching the action. Into the next room. More asses and crotches. One fox got her whole head on a dude's lap, tight up against him. She was givin' him a suck job right in that chair. Every little bit he'd go uh-uhh-uhh-uh. Sounded just like James Brown doing his number. I didn't wait 'round to see how it all come out.

I copped a stick by the time I made the third room. I dig the weed. I been a grasshopper a long time now, that and a little girl take me a long way. But just snorting, no banging on it. I seen too much of that kinda shit most my life. Too many good men I know gone now 'cause they started bangin' girl and boy into their arms. Girl, what they call coke downtown, is dynamite stuff but only if you stay on top of it. That means no skin popping. And if you on the hard shit, if you shootin' up on boy, then you just a stone heroin junkie and ain't nobody got no use for you. Junkies got nothin' out front, man, they just a stone drag.

Those other tripouts like acid and speed, that's mostly a white's man's goof over the long run. Ain't no other way it can be that I see. All them kids that can go back to the money any time they want, they're heavy into that. Black people way up-town are too busy trying to stay 'live to mess around with head games making out like you crazy. Just being alive being black makes you crazy enough.

"Smoke dope, listen to good music, and fuck as much as you

131

can." I looked to make sure it wasn't just my ear talkin' through the grass. There was this big white boy standing on a bed all by hisself and shoutin' out like a preacher. "Smoke dope, listen to good music, and fuck as much as you can." People all over the room but nobody was paying him no mind. Everybody was too busy smokin' dope, listening to the music, and fucking.

I started moving again and this black-haired fox came on to me and she said, "Hi, I'd like to introduce myself. My name is Lia." Yeah. And her hand was already squeezing hard on my rig. While she was sayin' that, she opened my fly and went right to it like she lived there all her life. A Jew fox. You can always tell 'em 'cause they'd find your rig if it was buried in cement. They love to give head jobs. A Jew fox once said to me, "I'd rather suck than fuck." Meant it too.

So there we was facing each other, with her hand inside my pants. What else could I do? I reached under her dress and introduced *myself*.

We stood there fingerfucking for a while and then she steered the rig over to a chair someone just leave. I followed 'bout a foot behind. The chair was one of them iron things with a cover hung over it, looked like a butterfly. I sat down and it felt like I was on the floor. She stuck her face in my lap and soon I was goin' uh-uhh-uhh-uh. I'm feelin' good and my rig was a giant fuckin' panther running racing roaring in for the kill panting power panther paying back for shit we gotta take yessir nawsir panther pumping white woman wild wonderful white pussy panther shouting take me take me take me and bang shootin' up the inside of warm wet white woman mouth soft yes swallow yes soft . . .

I opened my eyes slow, slow. After a long time she lifted her head up and looked at me and said, "Thank you." There was water in her eyes.

I was still weak and for a minute there I wanted to reach her, to get inside her to see who she was, but then I was in real time again and I was cool. "Anytime," I said to her with my best cat smile. "Anytime at all."

132

The last room was this bedroom just big enough for two small beds. Lots of floor from the door to the wall but too narrow to put anything. On the floor some whites were rolling bones. A fox with a tight little ass was sweet-talkin' them into something, then she let 'em roll. A five and a three. She snorted. Someone said, "What's a matter, he ain't man enough for you?"

Tight Ass looked at him. "More'n you are, lover boy," she purred.

Lover Boy didn't like that. "It's a rim job, Ed to Lorry," he called out roughly. "Your turn, Sal."

I stepped into the room to see what the hell was goin' on. They were rolling the bones on a big board, like one of them TV games. They were playing a game. I looked 'round. The box it come in was over by one of the beds, a big box with a lotta writing on it. I picked it up. First thing I seen was S.E.X. The name of the game was S.E.X. I read more. "This tunnel of fun is a total nonstop adult sex game where two, three or four couples roll the dice to determine who does what to whom. S.E.X. takes over where strip poker leaves off."

Shit. All it is is circus love they talkin' about. You can bet some white dude dreamed this one up. Just like them motherfuckers to need someone to tell 'em where to put it. God*dam*. How'd they beat the Indians anyway?

At the bottom of the box cover was a big red warning. "This sex game is only for mature adults."

Then there's them other kinda adults who don't have the bread to buy this fool thing. They called poor adults.

I walked on outta the room. Nobody asked me to stay and play. One fox looked after me, she could tell I knew where all the holes were.

I saw Tiger up ahead. I boogaloo'd over and he said, "Help me out here, man." He was with this skinny chalk who was rapping on 'bout how dope kills young kids and how they don't need it so why they take it 'cause nobody forces it on them.

Tiger poked me. "I know he's wrong, man, 'bout how they get hooked. But I can't put it down right. You tell him."

I looked at the chalk dude, thinkin' if he don't already know

133

how do I tell him. How can I tell him nobody bangs a kid over the skull and says, "You gotta skin pop, you gotta shoot up?" What happens is the kids look at the young dudes already on the junk and they see 'em with their heads outta the shit they live in. And then they see some of them pushing the stuff and wearing great threads and drivin' big cars. The kids see all that so they start thinkin' it must be boss to be flyin' all the time. And some of them even try out for pusher if they make it that far. That's what I wanna tell this chalk.

And I wanna tell him about Harry. Me and him lived on the same block and we were friends. When Harry was a kid he had this thing that he was gonna be a great explorer. He wanted to travel all over everywhere, finding things. He dreamed about it all the time. But that's all it was. Dreams. He never knew a explorer. He never seen a explorer. There was no explorers on the block, wasn't nothing on the block but junkies and pushers. So Harry got on the junk but he's very together and today he's the supply man for some big names. You see him driving 'round Harlem in his pink hog. One of his big people is a blues singer. Blind. Everybody in the whole world know all about him. Only exploring Harry do now is for new lines somewhere on his body to shoot the junk in.

All that is what I wanted to tell that dumb chalk man standing next to me. I wanted to shove a lifetime of learning up his white asshole so he'd know something about something. But how do you tell anybody what the hell life is all about?

"You wrong," I said to him. And left him and Tiger standing there.

Nobody was on the fire'scape so I sat outside for a while smokin' a cigar somebody give me and watching the street. Down here was almos' as bad as Harlem. Garbage everywhere. The buildings all falling out and full of rats and bugs. Padlocks on the doors, bars on the windows. The sandbox in the hall and everything stinkin' of piss. And everybody sitting outside waiting for tomorrow, which is always same as yesterday. Nothing.

I looked at the little shops full of dust and old people, the bodegas that sell things you can't get in the white world, the dirty

134

offices of drunk doctors and crazy lawyers, the windows with all that spic lang'age on them. And people driftin' in and outta bars and fried chicken joints and pizza places. All of them trying to find something or lose something.

It's enough to make anyone think least twice about killing hisself.

"Hey, man, can you turn me on to a dime?"

I looked down at the voice. Two hippies were hitting on me. I stared at them, trying to flash on what they said.

"Any spare change?"

Spare change. Sure. All my life is spare change. I fished up a quarter and dropped it to them.

"You got any sunshine, man? Or grass?"

I pointed inside. "They got everything in there," I said to them.

"Hey, can we come up?" Their eyes started glowing. "We ain't lames."

No, but you worse'n lames, motherfuckers. You the worse of all 'cause you leave money to live poor and when you see livin' poor ain't livin' easy, you can go back. We got nothin' to go back to. It ain't never no summertime for us. That's what I was thinking.

"Go 'head up," I said. "It ain't my shit."

Two dudes were rapping by the open window. "And this bitch's daddy, he say to me, 'Was yo' the one jumped on mah daughter?' and ah say, 'Not me, boss, t'weren' me,' and he say, 'How yo' know that, nigger, I ain't tole yo' her name yet?' Man, ah almos' shit."

I heard them slapping hands.

"What yo' do, man?"

"Din' do nothin' but wait for him to say her name. When he tell me ah roll mah eyes big and ah say, 'Ah don' even know her.' Ah been jumpin' that wheet woman for weeks, you dig? But ah tole her daddy ah don' know her. That when he come down on me real mean and he say, 'Ah b'lieve yo' lyin' to me, nigger,' and ah jumps up and ah say to him, 'Why yo' say that?' Playin' it cool, yo' know. And he scream out real loud, 'Ah

135

sayin' it 'cause ah done find yo' work hat un'er mah daughter's bed, thas why.' "

"Whooeee."

"Man, ah moved on outta there so fas' he got double 'newmona just from standin' in mah wind. Ah mean ah was on rails headin' north 'fore mah sweat had time to sweat."

"Yo' bes' be careful, man, he gonna shoot yo' ass off he get the chance."

"He gotta find mah black ass firs'. Thas why ah come up to Noo Yo'k. Plen'y black asses up here. He never find me."

"Plen'y white ass 'round here too."

"Ain't nothin' wrong with that, man. Ah ain't one a them racits. Ass is ass. Natch'ly, bein' that ah is a nightfucker ah likes to have as much white 'round me as ah can. People sees yo' better at night ifin yo' wearin' white."

"Ah ain't hear yo' was layin' 'em on the road lately, LeRoi."

"Don' matter, man. Ah always travels white."

"What yo' mean?"

"This boy always goin' firs' ass."

I banged the window down. Them funky niggers always give me a pain in my black second-class ass. All they think 'bout is tricking. You say white to them and they say ass. They don't know whitey got any other parts. We may be gettin' his ass awright but the rest of him is sittin' right the fuck on top of us.

I watched this kid come up the block. He had on a long cape and one of them soldier hats, looked like he 'scaped from a cowboy movie. He talked to some people passing by and then he seen me. "Hey, man, you wan' whip off some pussy? I got it 'round the corner. I bring her for you."

I shook my head no. "Wait a minute." I quick opened the window. Maybe them two assholders want a piece of it, they'd take anything. But they were long gone.

I shook my head again.

"You wan' get rimmed?"

"You got that 'round the corner too?" I asked him.

"How you know?" He laughed. "All the same feel, man. She

136

put on a dildo and she rim you. All the same. How 'bout it, man? I give you cheap."

"Not tonight. Maybe next time, baby."

"Next time never come, man. You don't find nothin' like this again. She waitin' for you, man, all hot and ready to give you that wild sex you not gettin' now."

My turn to laugh. I ripped off a buck and sent it floatin' down to the kid, just for kicks. "That's to keep her warm till next time," I said to him.

He speared the bill with two fingers. "H'okay, man, I be here. My name is Juan and I live 'round the corner."

He waved and moved on, back to his hustle. Just a boy learning all 'bout American business. Buy cheap, sell cheap. But buy cheaper than you sell. Even if it's people.

America? We goin' raise the price for twenty-five million niggers. Way up.

I crawled back in through the window. Still feelin' good. Tiger was on the floor rapping with somebody. "I'm moving," I told him.

He got up quick. "Wait for me, man, I'm goin' with you."

I looked at the dude was with him. He was so spaced out he wasn't even here.

"What's a matter with that dude was with you?" I asked Tiger on the way out.

"He so stoned, man, he is zonked outta this world."

"What he all have to get like that?"

"Just 'bout everything. He told me he took some LSD shit and then some speed. And I seen him with the grass too."

"Man, that is a mother load he carrying there."

"You better believe it," Tiger said. "And besides that, he been drinkin' the wine."

"How you talkin' to him if he that bad?"

"You joking, man. He the one done all the talkin'. Mostly 'bout the white fox 'round here. How he goin' get a taste."

"Plenty 'round awright."

"He know that. He live 'round here with his old lady."

We were out on the street. "He better come down if he just want a taste," I said to Tiger. "He flyin' so high right now he goin' swalla the whole chicken."

It was early still so we headed on over to the Annex. The place was full up with tricks and traps, a reg'lar Saturday night crowd. We eased in and begun a rap to these three cakewalkers from some college. All they knew 'bout was black history and Africa and the slaves and all that jive. A stone drag. I mean, they knew about it and I was living it. But they didn't know nothin' about what was goin' down today 'cause there wasn't any courses in it where they go to school. Yeah, they come right out front with that. How can they know when nobody teaches it? That's what they said.

Shiiit. If I hadda wait for things till somebody give 'em to me, I woulda died in my mama's gunnysack.

On the way back from the sandbox I run into the Marmalade Man. "Hey, man," I said to him, "how'd you and your friends like to dig into some exter prime white meat?"

The Marmalade Man give a quick look over to the cakewalkers. "Marcus, you trying to jive me? Dig, man, they don't do a thing for me 'cause I got two boss bitches waitin' on me. And even if I was bitch light and cock tight, they'd still do nothin' for me, man. That meat is so high on itself, man, you'd need steel balls to weight it down long enough for you to fuck it."

The Marmalade Man is a shooter for Jimmy Dykes uptown. He knows all about weighing things down.

"Awright, man. Just trying to spread it around a little is all." And I moved on back.

We were all sitting at a table right near the door. Other studs come over, and after a while everything got loose and I knew I was on my way to a bad high. The box was playing heavy funk and it made me feel trapped. I was a baby chick inside the egg and I couldn' bust that motherfuckin' shell for nothin'. It was a funky egg and this was a funky place on a bitchy funky October night in the big apple. I remember I was drinking white cadillacs at that time. I was drinking slow, watching the beer-barrel clock over the bar turn 'round and 'round, spilling the hours away down the drain along with the booze.

That's when Juan found me.

He come in the door looking. The kid was maybe fifteen, and very skinny. He still had on the cape and hat. When he saw me he come right over. "C'mon outside, man, I got some'n to show you."

I was stone high and I didn't want him or his dildo bitch. Most likely she was his sister anyway, you never know with these spics. I told him to fuck off.

"C'mon, man." He walked out.

I got up. I was goin' kick ass. Who the hell this kid think he is? I kick his ass for sure.

"You awright, man?"

I turn 'round quick. Tiger. It was Tiger said that.

"Goin' get me some air," I said to him. "I be back."

The kid was already up the street. "C'mon, man. Hurry."

I followed him. The cool air snapped through my head. My eyeballs popped awake and my brain started moving. Where the hell he goin'? I asked myself. I looked all around, nobody on the street. If he don't stop by the corner I'm goin' back. Fuck him.

He stopped before the corner. He stood in front of this ratty building and waited for me. It didn't look no diff'rent from the others 'round here. Stores in front, four or five floors of ratty 'partments on top.

"What you doing, you fool kid?" I yelled at him.

"Easy, man. I goin' show you some'n in the basement."

"What you goin' show me?"

"I show it to you, man. You my fren', man, I like you."

There was something in his voice, something not s'pose be there. Maybe it was a little too tight, like it was all set to break into screams.

I didn't say nothing. Just waved my hand for him to go on in.

He opened the outside door and we walked into this long hallway. The floor was dirty-white tile, those tic tacs of tile you

139

see everywhere in these old dumps. And cracked all over. Toward the back of the hall was stairs goin' up to the next floor. Halfway up, the stairs turned sideways 'cause a wall was there.

Juan stopped, looked to make sure I was behind him, then walked on past the stairs. Way in the back, past a lotta garbage cans up against the wall, were two doors with numbers on them, prob'ly where people lived. But we never got that far 'cause right under the stairs was this door. There was no lock on it. Juan opened it slow, a light was on and I seen stairs goin' down.

"You firs', man."

I shook my head. "It's your show, baby, so you go."

He grabbed my arm. "Please, man" was all he said. But I heard that scream in his voice again. Any other time I woulda said no good but I was still a little high and besides, I was gettin' a feel there was real evil goin' on here somewhere.

When I started down the stairs I seen Juan bless hisself. These PR's don't do that 'less they mean it. Now for sure things were wrong. I walked down them stairs like my asshole was glued together.

I got to the bottom. It was the boiler room. There was the funky old boiler for the whole house and over there was some tools and junk and all the shit you find in a old boiler room and over there was—what the fuck is that over there? I took one step.

Jesus H. Christ!

I aged a hundred years, blew my high, and choked the scream in my throat, all in about one second. I stood there froze, waiting for the cold sweat to hit, for my body to catch up to my eyes. When it did, I shook all over, two, maybe three times, then it was gone.

I moved closer. My legs were just walking sticks, one two one two. I wanted to tear my eyes away from what they were seeing. But no good. I coulda turned my head clear 'round and they still would been seeing it.

Sonovabitch, not like this.

140

I was standing right over them. I looked down, down, it was like a million miles below me. I kept staring at them, my mind racing through all the times I seen things like this, all the things I been through, the killings and pain and death.

Her body was mostly tan from the sun. There was a mark on her thigh and it matched the color of her cat hairs. A band of baby fat went 'round her middle. Pink nipples pointed up the whiteness of her little-girl jugs.

His body was next to hers. His skin was very white and he was too skinny. A few scars stood out in the harsh light.

Their naked bodies were stretched out on the boiler room floor. They were just kids.

They were dead.

Somebody took a brick and busted their heads to catgut, striking again and again, blow after blow. There was blood everywhere. Her short blond hair was drowned in it, his long hair was matted from it.

The blood was still wet.

I seen death, walked around it, faced it, felt its finger on me. I seen many people die, some of them so close to me it was like me dying. Most death I seen was a waste. And that's just what this looked like. A waste. These were just kids.

With all the grass and the drinks and everything, I was feelin' things deep. Water come to my eyes I was so motherfuckin' mad. I never even knew these kids but, goddam, this wasn't no way to go. No way, not like this. I had a kid brother die wasted like this. I had a lotta good friends die wasted like this.

"God*dam*," I shouted.

I turned 'round quick on Juan, I was so fuckin' mad I was gonna kill him on the spot if he done it. I grabbed him by the cape, my hand closed around his neck. "You do this?" I screamed at him.

He was scared shitless. He wanted to say something but he couldn' talk. I looked in his face and I knew he didn't do it. I let go of him.

We stood there catching our breath.

141

"Why'd you bring me?" I asked him when I got myself together.

Juan licked his lips. He was just a kid too. Just a shitass kid trying to stay alive in a shitass world.

"I was scared, man, I din' know what to do. Then I think 'bout you on the fire'scape, that maybe you know what to do 'cause you look it."

"How'd you know where I was?"

"All the spades 'round here end up in the Annex, man."

"What about your people? Why not tell them?"

He looked down at his shoes. "They all out, man, everybody's away for a while. You know."

Yeah, I know. Another alley cat kid all alone, living on his hustle, nobody caring if he live or die. Then I flashed on something else. "You want me to give you some scratch for bringing me here, is that it? Maybe for seein' her cat, eh? Or maybe you think I'm a fag and I'm sizing up his rig. Or maybe I oughtta pay you for letting me see all this blood, right?" I'm all worked up mad again.

Juan was hurt. "No, man, I don't wan' no bread from you. I think of you 'cause I din' know what else to do. That's all."

He was right. He didn't ask for no money. Maybe I was gettin' spaced out again. "How'd you find them?"

"The door's always open. Kids use this place for a lotta things, sometime they crash here for the night. I always check it, you know, see if any business here for me."

"What you do 'sides pimping for your sister?"

Juan balled his hands into fists. "She not my sister, man. You mus' be crazy."

"I'm sorry, man, I know she ain't your sister. I'm just rattled is all." And which was goddam true. "So you come down here and found 'em."

"Then I bless myself and back up the stairs and out the door. I don't wan' stay 'round, maybe whoever done it comes back. I'm thinkin' where to go when I think of you."

"You didn't see nobody here when you found 'em?"

"Nobody. But I tell you some'n, man. 'Nother time when I

142

pass that gig you was at, I see this dude come out he was so
stoned, man, he was floatin'."

"Spade?"

"Yeah."

"I seen him there. You know him?"

"I know him, man. I see him 'round plenty times."

I remember Tiger tellin' me about the dude wanting a taste
of white. "You know where he go?" I asked Juan.

"Sure I know."

I waited. Juan said nothing.

"Well?"

Juan smiled at me. "He go right here, man. Here, in this
building. He live right here with his old lady."

I chewed on that for a minute. The kids were dead, I couldn'
help them even if I wanted to. And it's not my business. "We
gonna get outta here," I said to Juan.

"Then what we do?"

I looked again at the two kids on the floor. They didn't
hardly have no heads left, 'specially her. She couldn' been
more'n eighteen, maybe he was a little more. They were white
but it didn't matter no more, least not to them. Goddam, they
didn't have a chance.

It hurt me to say it. I hadda put my teeth shut tight together.
Even then I hadda spit it out. "I'm gonna call the po-lice."

We backed up the stairs and out the boiler room door that
had no lock, and down the long hallway with the tic tac tile
floor, and past the stairs that turn in the middle, and past the
inside door that was wide open and had no lock, and past the
outside door that had no lock and no door handles. On the
street I told Juan to go on home and forget all about it or the
po-lice'd never let him alone no more. He already knew that, he
was a poor kid living in a shit slum. He knew all about the
po-lice.

"If I ever need anything, man, I find you," I told him.

He liked that. "I be here, man. I live right 'round the
corner."

I walked a block to another bar and called the po-lice. I told

143

them to check the boiler room of the house. Then I banged up the phone. I didn't say nothin' about the dude living in the house. I ain't no stool for nobody.

Tiger was waitin' in the Annex. I needed a drink bad, then another and another. But not there. We went up the street to Stanley's and I told Tiger all what happened. He didn't believe me till I swore on Malcolm X's grave. Then he believed me. He had to.

The next day it was in all the papers. With pictures of her when she was live. She was seventeen and her people lived upstate New York with a lotta money. He was twenty and he had no people and no money. They both were speed freaks and they went 'round and crashed in diff'rent places at night.

The stud who done it was the same one lived in the building. They got him for murder and rape. Him and a friend of his who was in on it.

See what I mean about waste? There was so much white stuff around, all a man had to do was reach out.

Couple days later, a East Village fox was jamming to me about it. "This the worse murder we ever had 'round here," she said. "Except for the next."

11.

COLUMBIA is like a college town. The kids all smoke dope and fuck a lot and hate America. Just like any other college town, I s'pose. First day I moved up there from the East Village I got good vibes from the place. I mean, it's only a little ways from Harlem but I never been there before. There's grass all over and everything smells nice. The college campus ain't so big but you can go anywhere you want, 'cept when the pigs are around or the White Panthers National

Fucking Guard. They don't like any kids being alive so they shoot you on the days when they own all the land.

I got a place near the college and fell in with some of the local heads. They were good people that were into some very outasight tricks. Most of 'em just ate veg'ables and they called all meat their brother and they wouldn' touch it. Real crazy shit like that. And there was this one stud who wanted to fuck till he was a hundred so every time he was on a fox, he stopped right in the middle of his charge. He figured if he kept half of it he'd last twice as long. Over a hundred years. How he was able to do it was every time he pissed, he cut off his piss flow till he got all them muscles strong down there. The more he pissed, the stronger he got.

He was doing great till one day something went wrong. He was bangin' away on this fox and thinkin' about his muscles so he'd only shoot half his load, and he was thinking so hard he musta pressed the piss button by mistake. 'Stead of shootin' up into her, he pissed all over her. That fox nearly drowned is just what happened. There they were swimming in piss.

"That's the worse part of it," he told us the next day. "I was so shook up I forgot to stop halfway and all the piss came out from the last six months."

"What you say to the fox?" somebody asked him.

"What could I say to her? I just looked at her with a lotta passion and said, 'It's the newest sex craze. Dig it.' "

Then there was the speed freak from L.A. She was a real nice kid that was always singing strange songs that nobody ever heard. Very quietlike. But when she was stone stoned, I mean really spaced in between other spaces, she'd talk for hours and nobody knew what she was saying. I listened to her myself. Not one fuckin' word was American or anything else anybody knew. One time a big-shot teacher come over from the college and she blew his mind.

And her best friend was another fox from L.A. that got high one night and just for kicks she balled some pigfucker from one of them L.A. towns and the next day she woke up married to him. He was so ape over her he took her 'cross the border into

145

Mexico that night and tied it up. But she really fixed his ass good. She got a kid by some other stud and then went into court and told the judge, "I have reason to believe my husband is not the father of my child." Yeah. She got the divorce and he got laughed down so hard he hadda quit the pigs.

I was around Columbia about two months when I met Vicki. We started making it right away 'cause it was one of them things that was fuck at first sight. She was a great little Jew fox with big round eyes and dark hair and a body full of smiles. She was goin' to the college and living in some boarding house but after we got together, she stayed with me. We'd take long drives in the afternoon way the hell out to the Palisades in her sports car. It was so small only two people could fit in, I never been in nothin' like that. One time we tried to fuck in that car but there was just no way. "What kind of a girl you think I am," Vicki said to me, "an acrobat?" Best thing we could do was fingerfuck. Then I got so horny I opened the door, threw my jacket on the ground, put her on top the jacket and fucked her right there.

Soon's we got done, about a dozen people cheered us. I forgot we were on one of them lookout points where everybody stops to look out over the Hudson. There we are locked together and I'm feelin' good and all these clowns are clappin' and calling for more. Vicki's under me and she screams, "What'll we *do?*"

What else *was* there to do? I got up and bowed low just like I was on the stage and we knew everybody was there watchin' us fuck. Then I took off my cap and passed it around. One dude threw a buck in and said to me, "Do you always fuck with your hat on?"

"Only when I'm doing the driving," I told him and walked on.

And a little white fox threw in her phone number when her boyfriend wasn't looking.

When I got back to the car Vicki pulled outta there like we were late for the next show. I sat there counting up the money. Over seven dollars. Not bad for a little thing like that. On the way home I was thinking maybe I found me a new hustle. If I could get a big place and tell people ahead of time, I'd make

146

some real money. I even got a name for it. Fuck theater, where the stars come out to fuck for you. Just like years ago with Chris and Girl Girl. Only better.

I told Vicki 'bout my idea.

She was a little mad. "You fucking black ape," she screamed at me, "do you think I'd ever get up on a stage in front of people and just . . . just *fuck?*"

"Well, no," I said to her. "We'd suck some too, and maybe even—"

"Marcus," she shouted, "you are one absolute fucking *idiot.*"

I liked to listen to her talk. Even when she screamed she said every word clear and got every letter in there like it was too important to miss. A lotta people got that hangup when they talk but she made it sound almos' awright.

"Seven dollars," I said to her. "We made seven dollars just from hardly nobody there. Think 'bout all the money we'd make if we had thousands of people watchin' us. We'd be rich."

That shut her up. She had that hangup too. Money. Just like most people.

Her father had plenty. She'd always tell me how he'd make a hundred grand some years, as if that meant anything that meant anything. He was a big-shot lawyer in Connecticut and they had a big house and all that shit. He didn't have no boys, so he made Vicki and her sister grow up like boys that were gonna grow up to be big shot lawyers. I don't know how he done with the sister but he sure pulled the plug on Vicki. She could double think and speedrap like a lawyer with two assholes. And that's what messed her up. She didn't know who she was, there was nobody inside her. She'd try to think everything clear from all sides, using her mind like life was some kinda chess game 'stead of the mix up mirra house it really is.

Another thing was she hated her folks. And hated herself for hating them. Her father treated her like a boy when he knew she was a girl. Her mother treated her like a kid when she was twenty years old enough to smoke drink fuck and make lawyers of her own.

She tried to hang on by thinking that money was the big

147

thing in life and her father was a great man for making so much. I didn't say nothin' 'cause I wasn't gonna blow her mind. I was just passing on by and it wasn't none of my business. But sometimes in bed we'd be balling real fine and she'd call me by her father's name. "Harold," she'd moan. "Harold." With her eyes closed and like she didn't know what she was saying. First few times it shook me up but then I figured, shit, everybody got troubles and if this is how she gets back at him that's okay with me. And besides, sometimes I'd be fucking her and making believe she was somebody else. Maybe the reasons were diff'rent but it was all the same thing.

We been together about three weeks when she got a telegram at the boarding house from her folks. They found out about us 'cause she wasn't sleeping there no more and somebody musta told 'em. She went over one day to pick up books for school and there it was. "Come home. Father very ill in hospital."

I smelled a rat right off. For one thing, it was just too cold. They only lived maybe fifty miles away, somebody coulda come to pick her up if it was all that bad. And I already knew enough 'bout her people to know a white man's trick when I smell one. But I seen they knew enough about her too, 'cause they really hit her where it hurt. If she hated them, she hadda be exter careful to be good to them.

"What should I do, Marcus?" She was crying.

I told her to go on home, wasn't no use to tell her where it was at. She was just a nice little fox who was all fucked up and didn't know how to unfuck herself. But 'fore she left, I said one thing to her. "If your father ain't sick when you get there, don't have no heart attack. Just kick him in the balls."

She looked at me like I was crazy.

Three days later she was back. "The bastards." She walked up and down the room, shaking her head. "The goddam bastards."

I didn't hafta ask her who.

"They tricked me. I got home and . . . and there he was, sitting in his chair like always. He wasn't sick at all. And they

148

weren't even sorry for what they did. They were worried about me."

"So they done what they could to get you back."

"But it was wrong, Marcus."

"What'd you do about it?"

"I told them I was old enough to look after myself."

I laughed. "What else you do?"

"We talked and then I just left."

"After three days."

She blushed. "Once I was there, I had to listen to their side of it and then think about things, didn't I?"

I didn't say no more. I didn't wanna hear what their side was 'cause I knew it already. She was with someone who was diff'rent, strange, not like them. He was, you know, *Schwartze*. Did she think about what all their friends'd say? Suppose she had a baby, God forbid, did she think about that? And what kind of life would it be with one of them? No big job, no big money. Try to understand, we don't want to tell you what to do. You're old enough to know your own mind. But think for a minute. You've always had all the things money could buy. A nice home, lots of clothes, everything clean and neat with your own kind of people. Are you really ready for another kind of life? Where he may beat you, and drink too much, and go with other women? You know how they live. It's a shame but we have to face facts. Can you take it? Can you take doing without things, and living hand to mouth? Is that what we've worked so hard for? Try to think of us. You're so young and you have your whole life ahead of you. Don't ruin it now before it's even begun. Trust us. Try to think of us. Try to think of us.

Yeah, I knew their white fuckin' side of it. And I knew something else too. I knew when she went home and seen what they done and she didn't tell 'em to fuck off and walk on out that front fuckin' door, she lost the ball game. She didn't know that but I did. And so did they. They won and the rest was just waitin' around for the ashes to die out. She was too much like them, and under all that heavy fuck-suck with a nigger she was

149

just a middle-class fox with security stamped on her ass and cash registers in her eyes. Her father done a good job on her.

I asked her just one thing. "Did they promise you like a new car or anything big like that if you just forget this whole thing?"

She looked at me with her big round eyes. "Certainly not. How can you even ask that? Do you think anyone can just buy my feelings?" And then she started to cry.

"No" I said to her, "I don't think anyone in the whole world could buy your feelings." And I meant it too, 'cause you can't buy what ain't there. "C'mon, let's go get some pizza." And we never talked about it no more.

The ashes took another two months to settle. I let Vicki stay with me when she wanted to 'cause she was good enough in bed and that's worth something. But it was never the same as that first three weeks. Soon she got sick for a couple days and went to a doctor. When she come back she was white on white. I didn't need her to tell me what was wrong.

"How'd it happen?" I asked her.

"I forgot to take my pills those days I was home," she whispered. "Marcus, what can we do? I'm scared."

I felt like letting her have the brown skin kid, that'd fix her folks up real fine. But shit, it wasn't her fault she had no guts. She never needed none.

"All you gotta do is get an abortion," I told her.

"But how? Where?"

"Tell your folks."

"No, I won't tell them," she said very quick.

"Your father's a lawyer, ain't he? He can get some doctor 'round here who'd do it quick."

"I don't want them to know. They don't deserve this, can't you understand?"

"I understand plenty," I said to her. "More'n you ever know."

Vicki put her arms around me real tight. "Oh, please, Marcus. Please help me. I need you."

"What you need is an abortion. How long's it been there?"

150

"The doctor said it just started."

"If you got six hundred you could get it done right here in New York. And if you got four fifty you could go to Mexico. How much you got?"

She bit her lip. "Maybe a hundred in the bank."

"Ain't enough. What about your car, you could sell that?"

"No, they'd want to know what I did with the money. I told you, I don't want them to know anything."

That got me mad. "Okay, little Miss Tightass. Then it looks like you gotta do what the nigger women do who ain't got rich daddies."

"What's that?"

"You gonna get rid of it youself."

She looked at me. "You're kidding."

"No, I ain't."

"But how?"

I told her. "It's gonna be the worse fuckin' thing you ever felt but it'll prob'ly do the job."

The next day she done it. Two doses of Epsom salts with quinine and out come the kid. But she was one sick fox for a few days.

A week after that, she got her mother to come to New York to see me. Like it was feedin' time at the zoo. I think Vicki figured if we hit it off, maybe things be awright. She still didn't know the game was over.

Her mother was a nice enough woman for what she was. Still easy on the eyes and soft when she wanted to be. Soon's I seen her, I knew all there was to know. And she knew about me right back. We all talked small stuff but what counted was what we didn't say 'cause there wasn't no need to say it. It'd all been said four hundred years ago.

We drunk coffee in one of the head shops off Broadway. When she got in her car to go, she said goodby to me and I said goodby to her. And all the guns were put away 'cause there wasn't gonna to be no more meetings.

Next day Vicki told me she talked with her mother on the

151

phone. "She likes you, Marcus, she really does. She thinks you're very smart and very nice. And handsome too." And she laughed like a little girl.

That was the only time I ever felt sorry for Vicki. It lasted about two minutes. I was too tough to be sorry for anybody longer'n that.

It was a good spring. The weather was warm, I was gettin' some fine trim from Vicki and laughs from all the heads I was with. Vicki didn't go for the drugs, not even smoke, so she was mostly a drag outta bed but she spent most her time on the books so it worked out awright.

I was feelin' so good I started thinking of Harlem. That's when I knew it was almos' time to move on.

When the end come it was no big thing. The college people were gettin' ready for summer and everybody was thinking of other places. One day Vicki said she was goin' to Europe in the summer. "I want to see new things, places I've never been."

"Sure," I told her. "That's a good idea."

That's what her father paid to buy her off. A trip to Europe. They were worried she'd go with me and that was their big power play. I wanted to tell her she coulda got a lot more. I seen her mother that time, and I knew she was ready to go much higher.

But I didn't tell Vicki nothing. If she was ready to sell herself that cheap, I wasn't gonna tell her the facts of life. But I kept thinkin' the next time they ain't gonna get off so easy. If the kid's got any brains she'll tumble to the key she's holding on the bank. All she gotta do is get a nigger or a long-haired white or a fuckin' Chinaman, prob'ly anything but a Jew lawyer, and they'd pay off just to keep her. Shit. She got it made.

Then my nigger neck told me she already had it figured. And I begun to feel sorry for them.

We walked on the college campus and held hands on what they call Low steps. She was goin' home to her father's house, least till the next somebody come along. And I was goin' home to Harlem, only a few blocks away and a million miles down.

"See you," I said to her. I don't like big scenes.

152

"See you," she said. "Marcus? It was really great, you know." And she walked off.

I stood on them Low steps and I said, "Fuck." But loud as I could. *"Fuck."*

Sonovabitch. Nobody screamed. The pigs didn't bust me. And the White Panthers National Fucking Guard didn't come in.

Nobody cared about the important things no more.

I just said one more weak fuck to myself and walked away. I mean, what good is it if you can say anything you want?

Next day I was back in fuckin' Harlem.

Part Two

I'm the man you think you are. And if it doesn't take legislation to make you a man and get your rights recognized, don't even talk that legislation talk to me. No, if we're both human beings we'll both do the same thing. And if you want to know what I'll do, figure out what you'll do. I'll do the same thing—only more of it.

—Malcolm X

Part Two

12.

THE hotbox room with its walls crawlin' with bugs. Beyond it the jungle streets of Harlem. Dirt everywhere, kids. Everything steaming. Summer. A visitor comes in, Jody from down the hall. "What you got there?" he wants to know. "I'm making a big sign that says FUCK." Jody does not understand, he's only eight. To him it's just a word he uses a million times a day. Everybody uses. It has no meaning.

I take great pains with the sign, finishing it carefully. The bright, flashing Ruby, stopping up for a minute, likes it. His laugh is soft and very high, it's easy to tell he's one of them fox jobs. Ruby, with his blond wig, stacked heels, skintight leather shang skirt and hissing mink scarf, is working the 69 Club downtown. He's done most all the dives between Baltimore and Chicago. Likes Pittsburgh the best, a real transex town is what he calls it. Ruby sometimes uses two queens, pets of his, in the act. Emilio is white, a Frenchie. Crystal's Indian. They do reverse stripping. Coming out with the music, Emilio is a wild fox in full drag. The jokers eat him up with their eyes till he takes off his wig and pasties, then they catcall him 'cause they been suckered. The little queen looks at them and screams, "Motherfuckers." They love it. The Indian, Crystal, opens in a man's suit, looking like he was made for it. He works the crowd with his hands, which seem to float all 'round his body. Little by little he shifts from suit to sari till he ends up a prime fox. It makes a good show and Crystal always gets a lot of suck notes after his number.

Way uptown is where this is, where I am. The hotbox room,

157

my FUCK sign, everything. Way uptown in another world. 128th Street and Park Avenue, my street. Whores and junkies, the crumbly, ratty buildings, sawdust candy stores that sell drugs and dirty books and Bingo bug killer, storefront churches and empty lots filled with a billion broken bricks. And the trains. The big trains tomcatting over everyone's head on Park Avenue. The trains that shake everything to dust and pull you up in a tight sweat when you hear them. And once you hear them, man, once you hear 'em you don't never forget. Ever.

I'm sitting in my room this early evening, lookin' out the one window. Soon the sun will shoot itself full of holes and lay down dead in the west, while Zulu night comes to suck out my eyeballs, leaving me only the soft slurp of black blood to tell me I'm alive. I stand up, trying to see myself in the windowpane but there's no reflection. I'm invisible. I've got shape and mass but I don't cast a reflection. People see me but they don't really see me. I press closer to the raised window, trying to find myself. Something sprawls across my hand, flat on the window sill. A big brown water bug. He don't see me. I wait till he moves off then, shunk, I squash him with my fist. Now he sees nothing.

I look at my watch. Thirty minutes to go. At eight sharp the curfew is on and every motherwhite dude got to have his asshole outta Harlem. Yeah. This gonna be one tight, black camp tonight. I pick up the handbill and read it again. "Effective immediately, an 8 P.M. to 6 A.M. curfew is established for all whites in the black community of Harlem. No whites will be permitted to enter the community—for any reason—during those hours, and all whites inside the community must leave by the 8 P.M. deadline." Sweet Jesusblack. The war's on. This summer. Now.

I go back to the sign I made with a black crayon and a piece of white cardboard, just to kill time. I stare at the one word. FUCK. Not like balling a fox, but like Fuck It. Hate Fuck. Kill Fuck. Goddam right, I say to myself, and my mind goes click and I'm walkin' down the street with a machine gun in my hand bangin' away killin' every white man I see.

Sweat pimples my lip and I wipe it away. Always happens when I think about killing. I lean the sign 'gainst the wall and start walking back and forth on the creaking floorboards. Lookin' around, I try to total up my life. Wobbly table, dresser, fold-up metal bed, three painted chairs, no place to live, everything smelling goodby. TV, radio, pots and pans, a jacket, pants, a few shirts. What's the use? All of it wouldn' bring me fifty bucks. Fuck it.

I sit on the bed with my hands wrapped 'round my ears, my eyes shut tight in anger. I am in the land of the free and home of the rich. My land, my home. But none of it is mine. My land has spread its metal limbs across the gold of the world, and this black block has four thousand people caged in twenty-four firetraps that'll never see the wrecking ball 'cause there's money in misery. My home Harlem, gateway to downtown Disneyland where your skin is your ticket of admission. But only if it's white.

Jody comes back. He looks worried. Wrinkles mark his forehead, play 'round his mouth and lose themselfs in his faded T-shirt and jeans, handouts from Catholic Charities.

"What you got that sign for? You goin' sell it?"

"You want it?" I ask him.

The boy comes over to the bed, sits down. The rickets on his scalp give it a crusty, shiny look. I wonder if he's had anything to eat today.

He scratches the top of his head. "I tell my mother 'bout that sign. She say that sign big trouble. She say they put you in jail."

"Not 'round here. They don't care what goes on up here."

"My mother say theys some things can't be writ down 'cause people don't want hear 'em." He gives me his best cat smile. "Now if I had that ol' sign, I'd hide it in old man Jude cellar so no one ever see it 'cept me and my friends. That's just what I'd do awright."

I pick up the sign. Signs are for marches, and the marching days are over. "Take it," I say to him. He scoops it up quick and runs out the door 'fore I can change my mind.

Eight o'clock. Black time. I shut the window with a screw so

159

nothing gets in and lock the door with a padlock so nothing gets out. Down one two three four flights. When I hit bottom, I hear a noise and I freeze, just like that. I know that sound anywhere. Everybody do. A Harlem cat. I wait a little, my ears open wide, then I move on. When I take that first step, there it come runnin' straight at my leg and I kick it back to hell. It screams goin' away, just to let me know it be back. "Goddam," I shout after the rat. "Goddam your black ratfuckin' ass."

I wait for the rat to answer till I hear nothing.

Nothin' changes, I remember once tellin' Sunny. She asked why the rats in Harlem were big as cats. It couldn' always been like this, could it? She come from downtown, their rats were smaller. When she first come up to Harlem, it blew her mind. "They so big 'cause they eat better'n we do," I told her. "They so big, them rats, they just 'bout wiped out every real cat ever been up here. That's why we call 'em our Harlem cats." She didn't laugh. But she learned to live with them like everybody else 'round here. After a while you get so you forget all 'bout the other kind.

And which is true. You bring a downtown cat up here and half the little kids don't know what the hell it is. All they ever seen is a Harlem cat what got big fangs and a long tail and screams. One time a dude over on Third Avenue put five downtown cats in a empty house next to where he was. Thinking, you know, that the cats'd fight off the rats and maybe he be left alone. That was the last he ever seen of them cats. But he swears the rats that went 'round chomping on his house after that were even bigger. And nobody called him a liar neither.

The street is quiet. Too quiet. Usually this time of night, just when the summer sun is losing itself in the slums to the west, all the street's a carnival. Little kids would open the fire dogs and let the water splash over them, running in the gutters followin' the flow to the clogged sewers on the corner. Junkies would be bobbing and dipping on some nasty scag, their eyelids jerkin' over glazed white balls that see nothing. On the stoops the day trippers would be drinkin' Rheingold outta paper bags, and their women, fat from too many years of too much starch,

160

huffing and puffing like a herd of hippos at a watering hole. Everything would be noise and movement.

Tonight nobody's moving. Everybody's just hangin' out their windows or sitting on stoops or in cars with the doors wide open. Waiting.

Two Mickey Mouse wagons are down the end of the block at Park Avenue, their blood-red eyes turning 'round and 'round. Inside I could see maybe three po-lice in each car, all of them black. I cross the street and walk the other way, up toward Lenox Avenue. Then over a couple blocks to the Lenox Gardens. I swing 'round the corner, my head working this way, that way. People everywhere watching waiting. I get to Sunny's house and the sweat's runnin' down me and it ain't all from the heat. "It's spooky out there," I tell her when I get upstairs. "This goin' be one long motherfuckin' night up here. I got the feel."

Sunny don't listen, she don't give a shit about the streets. Once she's inside her place, with the four locks on the door and iron guards on all the windows, she thinks she's safe. But I tell her tonight is diff'rent, that she better stay home tonight.

"Maybe I stay home, Marcus. 'Specially if you keep me company. Maybe we do some more of them fuck-suck positions from that book I got."

Sunny likes to talk like that. She likes to roll her tongue over the sex words, drawing them out, playing with them. Gives her a nice high. I told her once, I said, "Sunny, you got the greatest tongue I ever felt on a woman." She laughed all the way up my leg.

I remember the first time I met Sunny. She come to a gig at Camel's place, one of those mixmaster things where all the waiters look like Harry Belafonte. When I walked in, there she was, sitting high up on that big round sofa he got. Strobe lights were flashin' all over her body. She was naked by the time I got there, and I figured she was some movie star gettin' her kicks. Her white skin was so white it hurt my eyes. She wore her hair long and loose, honey-blond strands falling over her face. She had bedroom eyes, wide open and soft as sin. All the dudes

161

were jumpin' in their pants, and she knew it. "That Sunny is one swift number," everybody was saying. "She got enough heat goin' 'round here to blow the block."

"I'm going," Sunny had said that night, after we made African love with our eyes. "My tongue is tired and my head is draggin'. What I need is some unusual screwing."

"What you need is a corkscrew," someone suggested.

"Got me one," Sunny said, blowing kisses my way. "He's got the canary for my cat, and it's feeding time at the zoo."

She'd been a dancer in big clubs like the Latin Quarter, and one time she even worked the *Jackie Gleason Show*. Then her legs went on her, so she started hustling. But strictly big time. What they call a industrial call girl, at a hundred a night and up. She did that for a year but all she ever got on the job were white dudes, and for Sunny it's black all the way. She even tried to make believe they were black in bed when she turned out the lights but it didn't work. By the time I met her she'd been through a dozen jobs, and was the hatcheck girl at a big-shot downtown club. The money was good and sometimes she'd go out with a high roller who'd pay her just to be seen with him at all the fancy dives. Everybody liked her and nobody owned her. She was happy.

Our joyride lasted about a week, both of us popping pink pills every day to keep the love juices flowing. By the time I made it home I was out of just about everything. I mean I was cold duck for a couple days. When I opened my eyes there was Sunny standing over me. "Man, I'm ready for some more of that superbang you're holdin' between your legs." It was like a kick in the balls. I was fucked outta my head and this fox is standing there, lookin' down at me with her tongue talkin' love.

Wasn't nothin' else to do. I pulled her down and junked it through best I could. Then I sent her on home and told her I'd stop by later if I was still alive.

When I got there Sunny was crying. She was in the kitchen, on the floor. Dried blood was caked 'round her mouth and one of her eyes was puffed up. And she was ass naked. I washed off

162

the blood while she spit out what happened. She'd moved into Harlem only a month before, comin' from somewhere downtown where she stayed with this dude for a week while she waited to move into her own place. She promised him a throw but on the last day she cut out without givin' him even a smell. Took him a month to find her. When he did, he come up with two friends. They all jumped her, taking turns right there on the kitchen floor. Then they beat up on her.

As she talked, I could see her gettin' mad at the jokers who'd coldcocked her. But mostly at the white dude she stayed with.

"The sonovabitch. I'll kill him."

"Kill him?" I asked. "What'll that do?"

"Kill him," she exploded. "I'll cut his balls off and shove 'em down his rotten gut. I'll fuck him up for good."

"That's jive talk, man."

"The stinkin' bastard. Oh, that miserable cuntsucking faggot."

I handed her a wet rag to put on her eye. "Now you listen to me, Sunny. You go gunnin' for whitey and you gonna get your ass in a sling. He's got this town wired for sound, and if you scream too loud maybe you don't scream no more. You a white woman and that makes you double shit in their eyes. They figure you for a traitor to your own kind 'cause you up here slippin' 'round with us niggers, so you gotta walk soft. You dig? You livin' in two worlds now, livin' like a nigger lives all his life. No use feelin' sorry for youself."

"What you know 'bout how I feel?" she asked me.

" 'Cause I feel the same way. 'Cause everybody up here feel that way. But you learn it ain't worth shit. It don't do no good sittin' in a chair jacking off your hate, don't get you nowhere but down. Like I knew this dude, his boy was walkin' 'round downtown and some white kids japped him. Cut him up bad with a bottle and blinded him. The dude sat home with that boy for two years feedin' his hate till he couldn' stand it no more. He got a gun and shot his own boy right between those dead eyes, then he killed hisself."

"You're making that up."

"Fuck no, that happens all the time 'round here. What do you know anyway? You come up here pullin' a Miss Jones, getting all the wild sex you think you want. Then you scream when whitey bangs your head 'gainst the wall. Shiiit. He's been bangin' mine so long feels like a riot goin' on up there. And I tell you somethin' else, white girl, you got a long way to go 'fore you know what the killin' feeling is all about."

Sunny got real quiet after that and never said another word about it. That was way last year. The next time I come up to see her there were four locks on the door and iron guards on all the windows. And a Judas-hole in the middle of the door to see if it's black or white wantin' to come in.

Tonight my heart just ain't in my rig and we do a little straight balling and let it go at that. About nine thirty she gets a call from some big shot to go nightclubbing downtown. Some Wall Street dude from International this or that. Down there everything's International or General or American. They all have big buildings named after them and carpets in the halls and giant desks with lists of names inside. Sunny's name is on a lotta lists 'cause she knows how to act in public and make a man feel good.

I tell her not to go 'cause she won't get back into Harlem tonight but she don't care, she'll just stay downtown till tomorrow. We share a pipe of hash laced with brandy and I'm back on the street by ten. I get down to the corner and the first thing I hear is someone shoutin', "Get outta Harlem, whitey. You gonna hurt if you don't."

This white dude and his fox are standin' next to a big black hog. The fox is real young and she's crying. The dude's got his arm 'round her, trying to make her feel better.

"What happened? What you crying 'bout, girl?" someone asks.

The dude tells him. "Somebody stole all the things in my car while we were in that house." He points to a brick house with a garage next to it. I look at it and I can guess what happened. That house and garage belong to Morris. Only it ain't no garage, it's where Morris makes all his dirty movies. He's very big in the business, and he's got a steel front door that opens only if he wants you inside. I never been there 'cause mostly he just lets in the people who act in his films, but I seen him around. Very tall with a lotta white hair, looks like one of them saints. The dude musta brung this fox over here to work for Morris.

"What they take, mister?" a little kid asks.

"A small suitcase with the young lady's good clothes."

"And my makeup kit," the fox sobs, "and my other handbag."

"They steal you blind 'round here," an old man says angrily.

The dude asks who he means.

The old man blinks at him, takes a bottle of Gypsy Rose from his back pocket and downs a snort. "You wanna know who *they* are? Just look 'round you, mister, it's a reg'lar sideshow. The pimps, the junkies, the con men. That's who *they* are. And they all 'round you, ready to cut you up and nail you down."

"Shut up, you crazy old fool," a woman says.

But the dude looks 'round like the old man told him, and I could see he don't like things too much. Maybe ten people over by the car now. A few winos are passing a bottle bag around and some mean bloods are standing back at the edge of the crowd.

One of the men asks if there was any money in her things. The fox shakes her head no. The man tells her to write down her name and phone number on a scrap of paper he gives her. "If anything turns up, I'll call you," he says to her. "Now maybe you oughtta get outta here. You dig what I mean? It's a bad night to be in Harlem."

The dude don't want to show fear. He offers a reward for the stuff. The crowd moves in, a half-dozen people ask how much. Ten dollars, he tells them. A kid with one arm asks him to describe the suitcase, but another kid says that won't help 'cause the first thing junkies do is take everything out.

The reward talk puts an edge on the crowd and soon everybody's hustlin' deals to get this and that back. A sawbuck for the suitcase? Too little, with all them clothes in it. How much

165

for the makeup kit? For the handbag? That should be worth more.

I see the crowd gettin' restless. That means things could turn wrong any time now. For some fool reason I feel sorry for these dumbass whites. How fuckin' stupid can you be? 'Stead of just taking the loss and gettin' the hell away from here, they stand in the middle of the fuckin' street hoping for a miracle. The only miracle they'll get, I tell myself, is if they get outta here alive.

I walk on over to the dude and ease up close to his ear. "If I was you, man," I tell him, "if I was you, I'd get my white ass on outta here now." The man who took the fox's name sees the action and gets in closer. "It ain't healthy 'round here for you no more, mister. You better move on while you still can."

The dude looks at both of us real tight. He's stupid but not that stupid. He takes the fox's arm and steers her into the car. Without a word he starts it up and moves on down the block.

Back at the curb the name-and-address man gives me a big smile. He knows I know he just made a killing. Should be worth better'n two hundred to him. He's got the name of a fox who acts in Morris' stag movies, that oughtta be worth a bill to her for him to forget it. And he'll get the dude's name who brung her from the license number he took down, that's another bill. Money in the bank. Plus whatever he gets for the bags he copped. And the fifty he'll get for selling the information to a hot car ring that'll pick up the dude's hog in a couple weeks.

Shit, that whiteface lucky to get outta Harlem with his pants still huggin' his balls.

13.

I LOOK up and down the block. Nothing. Nothing to do, nowhere to go, nobody to see. I take out my chump change. A double sawbuck and twenty-five, thirty, forty cents. Not too much for a twenty-nine-year-old black nigger native American. I take the forty cents and throw it up in the air. Fuck it. Over the weekend I'll pick up a hundred on the job. Who could ask for more?

Yeah. Who?

I don't wanna choke on my own good luck so I head over to 125th Street. Even on the Big Black Way everything's quiet. Not a whiteface in sight, not even the po-lice. But they out there In the wagons all 'round Harlem, sittin' soft without lights. Waiting.

Too early for anything, I tell myself. But I could feel death. It's so heavy I could almos' see it. I pass a store with a big picture of King Martin in the window. I look at it. That's the same feel awright, just like the night King got it. In the spring. A night just like this but in the spring.

That night I was in Keno's over on Lexington Avenue. Me and Tiger and the Lemon Drop Kid and some others. That block is got a lotta bars that give you 2 for 1, even 3 for 1. 'Round here where the money's tight, that's the kinda bar you need. But Keno's is the best.

That night I was in a bad mood 'cause I had this feel something goin' wrong. I'm drinking shooters and badmouthing

167

anyone don't keep up. Then a kid run in the door sayin' King just been shot. I looked all 'round the bar but nobody moved. Everybody figured the kid was just goofing. Couple weeks 'fore that, somebody run in yelling the same thing.

But the kid just stood there. Tiger went over to him and told him to get his ass on outta there. The kid looked at him. "You nigger motherfucker, don't you hear? They got King." And he raced out the door.

Tiger quick threw the door open and everybody heard shoutin' from outside. Then somebody at the bar said real soft, "I'm goin' home for my gun." And the place cleared out like it was a bomb gonna go off.

Outside, people were runnin' all over. Three whites passed, they looked scared shitless. A brother shouted after them, "Man, there's gonna be white blood in the streets tonight."

Then the pigs come. About a million of them. They were all up and down the street, their wagons parked everywhere. They stopped traffic and set up road blocks and moved people around. But I could see their heart wasn't in it. They were scared just like everyone else. Everyone white.

In a while other wagons were on the street with loudspeakers, tellin' the people to keep calm and stay in their homes. But nobody give 'em any mind. Everybody knew this place was gonna blow sky high.

The Lemon Drop Kid wanted to know who'd kill King, he was a good man who didn't have no enemies. I laughed when he said that. Only enemies King had were two hundred million whites, that's all. And it only took one of them to kill him off.

The Kid was a good man and I liked him, but he sure wasn't any too smart in the head.

Standing under the trains on Park Avenue, I could see a couple fires burnin' nearby. It was almos' ten and the streets were full of people. Things were starting to get hot. With Tiger and the Kid I begun movin' up 125th Street. It was shit slow, in some places the pigs were holding everyone up. We hadda go 'round them a half-dozen times on other streets. All the bars were jammed, everybody was trying to get set for what was

168

comin'. Took us least a half hour to get far as Seventh Avenue. By then the looting had started, mostly liquor stores.

Across the street from where we was, somebody broke a supermarket window and the alarm went off. Nobody cared. A big mob raced in and stripped that store bone dry. Two white photographers begun taking pictures and they got jumped but the pigs got 'em outta there.

We kept walkin' up 125th Street, past the movie show and the big rest'rants, huggin' the storefronts so we don't get hit by nothin'. Lotta young kids racing all 'round and the pigs staying mostly in the street. Then the next thing I seen was, sonovabitch, it couldn' be but, goddam, it *was.* Coming down the street, walking our way, was the Head Whiteface and Chief Mother of this town. Tiger seen him and he said, "Man, he sure got womb, that mother."

"You better believe it," I told him. "He's the only one they got can make it up here tonight, that's for certain sure."

We just stand there and here he comes, doing the Lindsay shuffle—left foot out, right hand shake, right foot out, left hand squeeze—only tonight he's doing it with soul. Whole soul. And there's a crowd all 'round him, with some bloods look like football players guarding him.

"He don't need no one guard him," Tiger said. "We ain't animals like the whites."

At the corner the crowd turned up to 126th Street. When I seen that I knew the walk was over 'cause there ain't nothin' much up there but Morris, and this wasn't the time for no stag movies. We left them and went all the way back to Keno's and got ourselfs wasted.

That was some night here in Harlem, the time King Martin got knocked off like that. The crowds and the kids were out most the night, but it didn't blow like everybody figured it would. Fact is, the whole weekend everything up here was one step away from instant urban renewal. And a lot of downtown too, only the motherfuck whites didn't know it. They were too busy feelin' righteous that King, the Commie nigger troublemaker, got what he was asking for. They didn't know most of

169

the black militants felt even better'n them about King's death.

The next night, Friday, everybody was out makin' speeches. I'm still hauling ashes from the night before so I got no eyes for anything. But I went out to check the action and maybe listen a bit. I get to 125th Street and there's Kenyatta, one of the big street leaders up here. He was standing on a sound truck with Jesse Gray and some other people. The crowd was big and they were diggin' his rap.

"When Mayor Lindsay comes up here, how come he's always talking to those bullshit leaders in Frank's? When he comes up here, we want him to talk to the people. Young people who don't own nothing. But he didn't, so you know what you got to do."

"You tell it, brother."

"And don't be snatching no drawers or shoes either—we must have a higher revolution than this. These niggers are crazy. If this city must be flattened, let's do it downtown. And I'm telling all of these leaders to put up or shut up because a revolution don't have no leaders. This country is up for grabs. We gonna move this thing until King's dream turns into a nightmare."

That was enough for me. I had a few quick belts and went on back home and split a joint with Wynona, who was staying over a few days. Soon we tripped into sleep, where my own night-mares were waiting for me.

I'm thinking all that, staring at King Martin's picture in the store window. Shit, that was a long time 'go. Couple years, more'n that even. Plenty of good men gone by since then. Hamilton dead now, shot to hell by the pigs. And Jungle Jim too. Sherlock stabbed by a evil fox. Candy Man blasted down in a bar fight. Gunner dead in jail. Other men too, like John Rose and Zorro and a dozen more I usta know. All long gone for good. And other men that just took off one day and nobody ever see them again. Same as dead.

I quick move on before I get the blues so black I can't move no more.

170

Lenox Avenue is real wide, with a lotta high-stoop houses on both sides. I walked down toward 110th Street, mostly 'cause I wanted to see if the curfew was on all the way down. It was after ten and not a whiteface around. What a beautiful sight. I got so shook up I shouted, "Whitey is a rat's ass." Yeah. Shouted it right on that wide sidewalk walkin' down that wide street. "Whitey is a rat's ass." And three people on a stoop shouted back, "Right on, brother." And two little kids playing in the gutter cheered when I passed 'em. They were only 'bout eight years old but they already knew.

It wasn't gonna last. I knew that, everybody did. But it still was a good feeling. It made me think of the Black Muslim idea that one time there was nobody but blacks in the world. Then about six thousand years 'go, some black shithead named Yakub made another kinda people who were white. They were like devils, these white people, and they were lazy and not too bright and they didn't keep clean or take care of their families. But Allah got mad at Yakub for makin' these bad whites and he fixed it so the whites'd rule for a while. That way black people would suffer and through their suffering they'd see how lucky they were to be black.

I went to a Black Muslim church a few times last year, a mosque they call it, and I read some of them books they got about it. I'm thinkin' of that, goin' down Lenox Avenue with nobody but black people all 'round me. But the best thing the Muslims say that makes everybody listen to 'em is that the white man's day is over. That's what they say. That all the whites gonna die soon. And then everyone else'll be happy.

There's only one trouble. They don't say how it's gonna happen. I mean, I know the motherwhite fuckers gonna die, but only after they kill off everybody else in the world. So it ain't goin' do much for me that they die.

A wagon turned the corner and I looked over. Two Toms in it. I ain't seen a white pig yet. They either so scared they stayed home tonight or they all down there in Central Park with fuckin' tanks and atom bombs ready to blast us. Won't do 'em no good 'cause—

"Fuck job?"

I looked into the darkness by the building. Nothing there. Then I seen a flash of somethin' shiny. I walked over to it.

"Fuck job?"

She was standing way in the back of the stoop, up against the house. She looked about forty so she musta been maybe twenty-five. A little sweater was 'round her shoulders and she wore a scarf on her head. A belt of metal rings hung over her pants.

"How much?" I asked her.

She tried to size me up. If I smelled pig, she'd act mad and say something like "What you talkin' 'bout? I just said it's hot." If I looked sucker, she'd say, "Ten dollars a throw." And if I stared her down, she'd maybe go low as two dollars.

"Five dollars," she said.

I said nothing.

She pressed her lips together. "For that I go all three ways."

She was scared of losing me. Most all of them suck-fuck but a three-way trick is something else, 'less you get a real freak. Rimming hurts a fox and most of 'em don't like it. She must really need a score.

When I still didn't say nothin' she brushed her hand up against my rig. "I give you a hand job for two dollars, lover man. I make you feel good."

I reached in my pocket and took out my chump change and ripped off a five. I held it out to her. "Here, little momma, I don't need nothin' tonight. I give you that just 'cause you is black like me."

She looked at me like I was crazy. Then she looked at the five and quick tucked it in her shirt front. And zzphuk, it was gone 'fore some crazy nigger could take it away from her. Like me.

"But I tell you somethin' else, little momma," I said to her. "Tonight's one bad motherfuckin' night to be out. Whitey goin' kick ass and when he do, best not to be here."

And I walked away.

Didn't even turn around. Didn't need to. I knew what she was doing, thinking and feeling. She was fingerin' the five to make sure it was there, and thinking that the white man is dri-

172

ving all them nigger mens crazy for sure. And she was feelin'
lucky.

I bet that's the only time in her whole life she ever got something just for being black.

Even on the sex stuff, whitey gets the best of it. A fox that got
anything worth something, she's downtown where the money's
at with the wonder-bread man, lappin' up all that white bread.
Down 'round Grand Central and Rockefeller Center and all
them hotels. Only thing left up here are the dogs and the soft
legs. Some of them are so bad you go up to one when you got a
stiff rig and you just look at her and it turns soft as shit on a
stove. Only thing good about it is you save your money. 'Stead
of juicing the fox, you could drink it up or shoot it up or smoke
it up.

There was one whore up here a few years back was so bad she
charged a buck to let you look close at her so you wouldn' be
stiff no more. That's all she ever did, just stood there. Worked
every time. She made so much money she almos' put the other
whores outta bed. She woulda too but some stud georgia'd her
outta the buck one night and she shoved a blade in his throat.
They sent her up and everybody felt better. They didn't like
that strange sex she was dealing out at a buck a no throw.

At 116th Street the junkies were weaving and coasting on the
corner, like always. That's a favorite spot for them, it's wide
and it gets a lotta sun. If there's one thing a junkie don't want,
it's the sun 'cause it hurts their skin. That's why they stand
'round that corner. They get everything fucked up, even that.
A junkie just don't do nothin' right.

Plenty of junk passing hands up here. It's like one of them
sidewalk fruit markets, only this a junk market. But not just
here. All of Harlem the same way, a junk supermarket is what
Harlem is. Motherfuckin' right. When you livin' all your life in
misery and shit, you wanna get away for a while. If you ain't
got a dime to go nowhere, you do what you can. You get on the
junk or the sauce, and if that don't work you burn yourself.
When you can't get spaced out far enough, you just trip out for
good.

173

A black man living in this country is runnin' mad all his life. Angry mad, hate mad. He is so angry hate mad he don't know what he's doing half the time. And it starts ripping him up. He got no heroes, no history, no nothin'. All he knows is that he is a black white man, and that ain't good enough in a white white man's country. He wants to fight but who he gonna fight? Everything's too big, too thinned out. By the time he's growed up he says, "Fuck it." And he tries to hustle his life by the white man's rules, or he turns soft inside and tries to junk it through on horse or wine. No way really works, some just work less'n others.

Whitey is one lucky sonovabitch that most people wanna stay 'live no matter how bad off they are. If it wasn't for that, every black man and his mother'd be grabbing the axe to chop heads. And we'd take a lot of 'em with us 'fore they killed us off.

Yeah, hate, two, three, four.

I'm marching down the block, feeling good feeling hate. Killing off every white man I don't see.

Hate, two, three, four. Keep in step, keep in line, it's Kill Whitey time.

Bang. Zap. Thakk. Sptwangg. I'm fuckin' Superiorman blasting the enemy, knocking 'em off by the thousands. I got twenty hands holdin' machine guns, flame throwers in my mouth, grenades hangin' from my ears and big swords strapped 'round my legs. I'm King Kong come back to kill that fuckin' white Empire State fuckin' building.

"Go get 'em, Superiorman."

"Whup they ass, you mother."

"Kill 'em all, man."

"Kill for peace."

It's all a game. Every black man plays it in his skull a million times. Sometimes it's kill whitey and sometimes it's fuck whitey's woman. But it's all just a head jackoff. The truth is you can't stay live and stay hate 'cause color hate eats up everything inside you. Then you just turn out a stone racist like some of the black nationalists we got up here. The Black Ku Klux Klan. Black or white, same shit.

174

I don't really hate all whites, I got no time for that. I only hate those who try to hurt me. Which is just about all whites. I mean, I wish they were all dead but they ain't, and I ain't goin' waste my time cryin' about it. All my life they banged me over the head, they busted me, and they give me no chance. When I was younger I coulda killed off every last whitefucker goin'. Only the hate was killin' me 'stead of them. Now I just hate all those I meet, it's more easy that way. Like the pigs who beat me upside the head, and judges who let me rot in the slammer 'cause I'm black, and store owners who cheat me to death, and slum lords who squeeze me to death, and politicians who don't care and businessmen who don't care and people who don't care. Which is most white people.

If you hate just the whites you meet, you still got enough time to do your own hustle.

On 113th Street a cab was waiting for a light. A half-dozen brothers swung 'round the corner and saw the cab. They picked up some bottles and garbage. A bottle hit the door, some shit splashed on a window.

I looked close. Two people were in the back, a black stud and this little blond fox. She was chalk white. So was the cab driver.

One of the dudes was on the sidewalk with a brick in his hand.

"Get that mother," someone shouted. "We should 'specially get him."

Two whites were in night town after curfew but the dudes were most mad at the brother stud. Shit. He oughtta know better. This was no time to bring chalk cunt up here. She must have him so sucked he don't know what's goin' on.

The driver saw the brick comin' at him and he zapped that cab through the light so fast the brick didn't even scratch the paint. But not fast enough. A truck slammed into the side, coming crossways at it. The cab spun halfway 'round and jammed up against the truck. The trucker jumped down the other side and started to badmouth the whiteface.

The dudes on the sidewalk split. They had their fun.

175

I walked on over. I was feelin' good-bad and I wanted another look at that chalk cunt. The stud was inside holding her hand when I got there. I stuck my head in the window. "You okay?" I asked her.

She looked up. Blue eyes and long blond hair and a suck mouth that was made for only one thing to go in. She had on one of them tight jump suits and even sitting down I could tell she had a body that curved right down to her toenails. I almos' come just standing there holding that door and looking at her.

"Get yourself lost, nigger."

I heard him but I didn't rip my eyes off her. If she was more'n seventeen I was a white elephant. I coulda stuck my head in her cat and gone to sleep for a hundred years and never feel anything but good.

"I said move on, nigger."

I looked him over. He was hard but not that hard. "You talkin' to youself, motherfuck?"

He kicked the door open and I got pushed back ass over head on the ground. I got up quick. I was gonna take this nigger apart and feed his brains to the rats. Then I seen his hand go inside his jacket and stay there. I stopped. If he's a shooter he's got it in there, and I wouldn' get no second chance to find out.

That's when the pigs come. One wagon, two Toms. They got out, looking bored till they saw Hard Nose. Then they snapped shit.

"Anything wrong, Mr. Delaware?"

Hard Nose smiled. His hand was clear now. "Just a little accident. Some punks throwing things at the cab."

They looked my way. "This one of 'em?"

"No, he was just helping out. He likes to help people."

I was standing there watchin' the play. The pigs went over to rap with the drivers while Hard Nose got Suck Mouth outta the cab. She was curves on curves, that bitch was so boss I woulda knocked off all of 'em 'cluding the drivers and half the block and rode off with her in the pig wagon. But she didn't give me the sign so I just stood there eatin' my rig out.

Everybody stopped talking, they just stared at her.

176

Hard Nose didn't like it. "What about you men taking us over a few blocks?" he asked.

"Sure thing, Mr. Delaware," one Tom said to him. "You and the, uhh, young lady just get in." He turned to his partner. "Andy, I'll take Mr. Delaware. You finish up here." And he walked over to the wagon before Andy could say anything.

"I'll be right back," he shouted as he got in.

"Fuck you," Andy shouted back when they couldn' hear him no more.

He turned on me. "Okay, beat it, man."

I didn't move.

"Get your black ass on down the street, man, 'fore I shove my club up your blow hole. Now move it."

"Who was that dude?" I asked him.

He laughed. "You don't know? Boy, you sure are one dumb nigger. That was Mr. Delaware. He runs things 'round here, a lotta things. You dig?"

I told him about Mr. Delaware reaching into his jacket like that.

He laughed again. "You not only dumb but you lucky dumb is what you are awright. Sure he's holding, but he don't use it on nothin' like you. He just gives the word and one night a couple of his shooters see you, then nobody see you no more."

"He's that big, eh?"

"Big enough. Not the biggest 'round here in the black Mafia, but big enough. You seen that chalk was with him, ain't you? You don't get into nothin' like that just by savin' your Green Stamps."

"She's young enough to be his kid, she's too young for him," I said.

Andy put on the evil face. "Now, you know, man, if she was your kid you'd be fuckin' her. Or trying to. And so would I." He turned away. "Now get your ass rolling."

"Fuck you," I shouted under my breath as I walked away.

I hate those Toms. Most of 'em beat up on their own people. And if it comes to a fight you can't really trust 'em. I'll stare them down and talk them down right in the street if I have to.

177

And gun them down too. But not for nothing so nothing as this. If you gonna get wasted, save your waste for when it ain't wasted.

I made it down to 110th Street and looked into the park. Wasn't no planes or ships or atom bombs I could see, but they could be hiding 'em way behind the trees. Be just like them sneaky whitefuckers to do somethin' like that. But everything was quiet.

I walked along 110th Street. At Fifth Avenue two wagons were parked one behind the other, facing the wrong way. They were full of white po-lice. I could see least four in each. I could see something else too. They all had on their blue riot helmets.

There was a big crowd on Third Avenue. I walked into it. Somebody painted a white line right across Third. Above the line was the words: THE BORDER. Under that it said: PIGS, DO NOT CROSS. On the other side of the line, on the other side of the street, were about ten pigs who could read. They were not crossing the border.

The crowd was mostly young. They were badmouthing the enemy and daring them to come over the line. But they were just runnin' at the mouth 'cause if the pigs ever got word to move in, these kids'd be gone like hell. Everybody would.

"Hey, Marcus."

It was Quint. My man Quint, just the man I wanted to see.

He had on his shades like always. Any time there's anything white near him he whips out the shades. Says he can't stand the glare.

"What the hell's goin' on, man?" I asked him.

"You know same as me, brother."

I pulled him on the arm. "Don't lay that jive on me, man. You one of the leaders put this curfew on. If you ain't behind it, who is?"

He waved his arm over the crowd. "Everybody is, that's who is. Just look at 'em all. Everybody in Harlem is behind it. Behind the Black Curtain. And all the whites are out there, cast into darkness." He laughed.

178

"What if they break in?"

"They ain't gonna break in. We told everyone to cool it so we don't give the motherfuckers no excuse." He slapped his hands together. "This a night to remember, Marcus. This the night Harlem liberated itself. You hear?"

I checked my watch. "Yeah, for three whole hours so far."

Quint give me a stare. "You a pain in the ass sometime."

"It's just I got a bad feel, man. I got the feel things gonna go wrong."

"Things been goin' wrong all your life. My life, everybody's life up here. Maybe now they go right for a change."

I know Quint a long time, seven, eight years now. He was always down on the white man. But I mean doing something about it, not just talk. He went to some college down South and he worked with Snick when they first started up. He was into most of the protest marches and voter drives. When those three workers got themselfs knocked off in Missippi, he was right in that town. I know 'cause I was down there myself, that's where I first met him. I got outta prison the year before that, and some dudes I knew talked me into helping fight the white man in the South. Shit, I couldn' get no good job 'cause of my record and everything so I moved on down. Stayed there almos' a year. It was tough work and I was scared shitless most the time but I glad I done it. I learned a lot, mostly 'bout myself. What all I can take and what I want and things like that, things I never woulda found out no other way.

But Quint, he always knew what he wanted. To get the white man off his back. He didn't think 'bout nothin' else. When one thing didn't work he tried another. From sit-ins and marching to fighting off po-lice dogs and white mobs. He stayed down there least four years and made a big name for hisself.

Then he come up to Harlem. But by now people were picking up the gun. Harlem and Watts and a dozen other towns already blew, and the younger brothers were restless. Quint seen this right off, and what he done was he formed the Revolutionary Armed Movement. It was gonna be the power behind all

179

the black militants in the whole country. They made all kinda plans to bomb gov'ment buildings and kill all the Uncle Tom politicians and things like that.

They even had a plan to take over the motherfuckin' country. A hundred trained shooters were gonna kill off the hundred most important men the whites got, from the President on down. All on the same day at the same time. Black politicians'd be at the right spots ready to take over. And black soldiers and Marines were gonna guard Washington. In a few days all the white leaders'd be dead or in the concentration camps. Detention camps, they were gonna be called. Quint even had ideas about what to do after we took over, like all the whites who wanted to go could go. Those who stayed hadda pay a big tax if they wanted kids, but black people'd get money for every kid they have. He figured in fifty years this'd be a black country 'tween the whites not staying and the whites not fucking.

The idea was good awright. It's easy to knock off anybody if you really want to, even the President. All them men he got 'round him, they don't mean shit. If you really serious, all you need is a roof and the right kinda gun. And if you don't care what happens to you, you don't even need the roof. You could put the gun in a camera or in a sling makin' believe you got a broke arm or in a umbrella or in a book. There's a thousand ways to do it. You could be in the sewer under one of them manhole covers and when his car passes you just blow a ton of dynamite in his face. You go but he go too. Or you could keep a little flute in your pocket that shoots a poison dart. Or a pen with gas or paper with germs. A million things.

Shit. The only reason anybody is alive is 'cause nobody wants them dead enough yet.

Where the idea was no good was the part about the black soldiers and Marines. Most that I seen are nothin' but Uncle Toms. They join the white man's Army and fight his wars, they can't be trusted to fight for black men. Some of 'em still got balls but most is just black crackers.

Quint asked me to join RAM. A couple times he asked me but I was full of big head troubles back that time. Everything

180

was goin' wrong and I was fixin' to move on. And which besides, I didn't go for all that kill shit that Quint and RAM was layin' down. I seen too much of it. I seen killing when I was a kid in Missippi and So'Lina. I seen killing on the Harlem streets, running with the gangs. I even seen killing in school. I seen killing in prison and I seen killing when I come outta prison. I seen killing when I was working in the South. I seen most my own family killed. And I been seein' killing ever since, too. I musta seen more killing than a whole army. And done my share when I had to.

But it's all useless. The more you kill, the more you gotta kill. And if you kill off everybody, it ain't worth it from the other way. I give up on killing when I seen the best thing was to hustle my own life and grab what good feel I can. I don't say I wouldn' kill now but I know it don't do no good. You can't be black 'round here and not think kill all the time. But if it come to that, least I know it don't really help nothin'.

On Third Avenue and 110th Street, with me and Quint standing there, everything looked like what I'd seen a thousand times. The blacks on one side of a line, the pigs on the other side. And everybody noisy and scared and all hot from not knowing what's gonna go.

When something did go, nobody knew what to do. 'Cept for Quint.

A group of young studs was givin' it good to the pigs. The crowd was big enough to give 'em heart and they were really ripping it off out front.

"Pigs eat garbage."

"Pigs eat shit."

"I smells pig feet."

"Oink. Oink."

Then one of them, he just gotta be the dumbest nigger since the late Jesus Christ, crossed the line and started boogalooing down the other side. One pig blew his cool and rapped his pig stick into the kid's gut. Zatt. You could hear the pain 'round the corner. The kid went down and the crowd got real quiet.

That's when Quint stepped across the line and into the street. "Keep your pig paws off him, you pig motherfucker."

It was like a fuckin' atom bomb hit the street. The crowd was one big bloodshot eye, watching. The po-lice was one big shiny gun, waiting. Nobody knew what to do. Everybody froze. There was no sound, no breathing, no nothin'. It was maybe like what death really is.

Then some dumb nigger, even dumber than the jive kid, moved out into the street and stood next to Quint.

It was me.

I had my own hustle. I was livin' inside my skull, trying to survive. Trying to be just me, not black or American or any of that ratshit. But it was all no good when push come to shove. Then you lined up with what you are, who you are. Then all the talk about killing and no killing didn't count no more. Quint was my brother and I stood with him out there in the middle of that street.

"Let him go, motherfuck."

The pig was looking at Quint. He was so shook he didn't move, just kept on wetting his lips with his tongue. The kid got up real slow and limped back across the line.

The other pigs moved closer together. There was about ten of them and only two of us, plus which they had the guns. But the crowd was with us and that made the diff'rence.

"Who you calling names?" one of them asked Quint.

"You. I'm calling all of you racist pigs. You're all pig mother-fuckers."

If we was alone we'd be dead least six times by now.

They were so mad they were turning blue. But they didn't go for their guns. All that pig power and they didn't do nothing 'cause people were watchin' them. And Quint, he was standing them down.

Then a sergeant come from somewhere and he told his po-lice to back off, and it was all over. Me and Quint walked back to the crowd and they cheered us. One old man had water in his eyes. He said he never seen nothin' like it and he was glad he lived to see it, but he still didn't believe it. And some of

182

the kids said it was just like the cowboy stuff they see on the TV, only this was for real. You motherfuckin' right it was for real, I told them when my asshole begun to breathe again.

We got outta there soon's we could. They wanted to hold a block party for their heroes but by then the pigs woulda had their snipers up on the roofs ready to pick us off. We walked away up Third Avenue.

"You sure a dumb nigger for goin' out there like that," I said to him.

"And you even dumber for joining me."

I rolled my eyes. "Join you? Oh, man, listen. I wasn't join' you. I was so scared they were gonna shoot the crowd that I got by you to be safe."

"Shiiit. Why you think I got out there in the first place?" he said. "I seen them motherfuckers shoot."

We both laughed.

"Yeah, but what about if one of them been black?" I asked him. "Then what you do?"

"Makes no diff'rence. I woulda called him a Uncle Tom motherfuck. They all the same. Pig's a pig. It's not your color that counts, it's where your head's at. If you got green skin and you oppressed, suppressed and repressed, then you one of us. And if you got black skin and you playing their game, then you one of them. When it gets down to the gun, color don't count no more."

Quint's a smart man and he's right about color don't count when you pick up the gun. Then the only thing counts is what side of it you on. I know some whites on my side of the gun. Some of them so motherfuck white you can't see 'em 'less they wear clothes, but they live like me and they been put down like me. I met them in jails I been in. Poor whites that never had nothin' and never will have nothin'. Just like blacks. Most of 'em don't give a shit for skin color 'cause they know it's only the money color that does the counting. If you got the bread, you white, don't matter what skin shade you got. And if you ain't got the bread, then you not white and you second class and third class and like that. The more no bread you got, the lower

183

down you go till you so low you turn into a fuckin' sewer snake.

The whites I know are ready to pick up the gun awright. Matter a fact, they been pickin' it up for years. And using it to get themselfs some money so they don't gotta live like the rest of us niggers.

By the time we got up to 125th Street it was after eleven thirty. Quint was sure everything was gonna be smooth. I wasn't sure of nothin'. We walked way the hell over to the Glamour Inn for a drink and Quint started tellin' me how the curfew come about. RAM was finished as a secret outfit, most of its leaders were dead or in jail, and Quint hisself was out on bail. The bombings didn't do much good and the po-lice got most of the guns they hid. Besides which, the Black Panthers and the other militant groups were on the scene. What they needed was for everybody to get their shit together. Quint took the kill outta RAM and made it into a Black Power thing that worked for segregation.

"What you mean, segregation?" I asked him.

"Just what I say. Blacks living all 'lone. Black states, a black nation right here in this motherfuck America."

Quint's idea was to have all the black ghettos be little states by themselfs. Run by black people. And no whites around 'cept when they were needed. That way there'd be least a hundred black states, even more. There'd be black states in all the big cities.

"And you'd have nothin' but black all 'round you," Quint said, banging his fist on the bar.

"Sounds good awright," I told him. But I was thinking 'bout that chalk cunt in the cab. You gotta be crazy not to want that 'round you. And I was wondering what Mr. Delaware gonna say to all this. I got the feeling his shooters be out lookin' for Quint soon's he hear about it.

This curfew was the start of making Harlem into a black state. That's why Quint was so hot on it. If this worked, the next thing they gonna do is get all white business outta Harlem. Take over everything.

"And when we got the power and it's all black, whitey be

184

coming 'round sayin' Mister this and Mister that. You watch, Marcus."

What Quint did was he got together with the militant leaders in Harlem and they worked the thing out. Everybody had a piece of the action. Not the Uncle Toms or the big black-white chitchat clubs, but the real powers who were down with the people. All the local heads, all the Black Power people, all the welfare and rent-strike and school groups, even some of the religion leaders. When they put out the handbills that told 'bout the curfew, RAM was only one of about thirty diff'rent groups that signed it.

It all looked good and sounded even better. I pulled the handbill outta my pocket and read it again right there at the bar. "Effective immediately, an 8 P.M. to 6 A.M. curfew is established for all whites in the black community of Harlem. No whites will be permitted to enter the community—for any reason—during those hours, and all whites inside the community must leave by the 8 P.M. deadline."

I felt sorry for the few whites still living in Harlem. What could they do? But mostly I was thinkin' of Sunny. If she went downtown she's outta Harlem for the night, and if she stayed home she's got all them locks on the door. I didn't want nothin' to happen to Sunny.

It was after midnight. Somebody at the bar had a radio turned on to the news. The pigs were calling the curfew crazy and unlawful, saying it'd lead to riots and sufferin' for black people.

Everybody laughed at that one.

Then the radio said the pigs promised they'd keep on protecting black people like they always done.

That one broke the place up. Even the bartenders hadda laugh, and they didn't like the curfew for nothing 'cause it was cuttin' down their take.

"Man, if they protects me like they always done," someone shouted, "I'm goin' home and get my motherfuckin' gun."

"And you be four steps behind me," somebody else said.

Quint turned to me. "Marcus, I come outta Chicago South

185

Side and I seen a lotta things go down. I been through riots and shoot-outs and bombings and I ain't missed much." He took a quick belt at the drink. "And I'm tellin' you, the black man is at the end of the road in this country. He tried to make hisself white and that didn't work. Now he's trying to make hisself black and they ain't gonna let that work neither. If he can't be white and he can't be black, what can he be?"

"He could just be hisself."

"What the hell you mean, be hisself? He's black, ain't he?"

I held up my palm. "See that? It's black awright. But if I tear off the skin it'd still be my hand. I'm me before I'm black. Same for everybody."

"Won't work, Marcus," he said. "Won't work 'cause the white man don't have a palm. What he got is a fist." He banged the bar again with his fist. "All he got is a fist. We tried everything with him. If nonviolence ain't the answer, and if violence ain't the answer, then there's only one thing left to do."

"What's that?" I asked.

"What else? Go it alone. Black states, a black nation. That's what we got goin' now."

"You think it's gonna work?"

"It gotta work," Quint said. "It just gotta work."

That's when we heard the first shots.

Quint was the first one out the door, me right behind him. We raced to the corner. More shooting. It was coming from up the block. We moved up Seventh Avenue, one block, another.

Quint stopped. "God*dam*. It's Fred's house, I just know it is. The pigs are shootin' up Fred's house."

I knew who he meant. Fred Gordon was a black nationalist, the leader of the New Georgia Nation. They had a big rep in Harlem as very heavy militants. Most everybody walked soft around them.

We got to the corner and sure enough, there was least a dozen po-lice maybe halfway down the block, runnin' behind cars and shooting up at one of the houses. Shots were coming back from the house too.

186

"I knew it," Quint said. "Those motherfuck pigs are startin' a war." He was so mad he was almos' crying.

A black dude come runnin' toward us. Quint grabbed his arm as he passed. "What's goin' on there, man?"

The dude was scared. "I seen the whole thing," he whispered to Quint. "I was sittin' 'cross the street when they pulled up. They called some name and then they just started shootin'."

"Who they call?" Quint asked him. "Was it Fred Gordon?"

"Sounds like it awright."

Quint let him go. "The cuntsuckers. They musta had this planned so's they could bring in their storm troopers and break the curfew. They waited till everybody was off the streets."

"What you goin' do, Quint?"

He looked wild-eyed. "I'm goin' down there, see if I can help Fred."

"You crazy, man. They killin' that house. You never get near there."

"I'm goin' in from 'round the corner." He jabbed me in the arm. "You go on home, Marcus. This ain't your fight." Then he quick went up the street over to the next block.

But I wasn't goin' home, not yet. I didn't know whose fight it was, but I had the idea maybe I was part of it. Anyway, sometimes you wanna do things even if you know it's crazy. Like I wanted to see Fred Gordon don't get killed off by the pigs. And I never even met him. Must be just that I hate pigs so much.

I raced after Quint. "I'm goin' with you."

"That makes you crazy, same as me," he said. But he was smiling.

We got over the next block and I followed Quint in through the cellar of a building and 'cross a backyard, then over a fence and a woodshed. When we jumped down we were in another yard. In front of us was a old wood back porch. Quint run up the stairs and banged on the door. "Fred, open up. It's Quint."

I watched from back by the woodshed.

Quint hit the door again. "It's Quint, man. Lemme in."

"Who's out there?"

"It's me. Quint. Open the door, motherfuck."

"Any pigs out back there?"

"If there was any pigs here, would I still be 'live talkin' to you like this?"

We waited. In a few minutes a voice asked, "Quint, is that you?"

"It's me, Fred. Open up."

The door opened. Quint waved his arm and I shot up the stairs. Bang. The door slammed shut. "Who's this?"

"He's a good man," Quint said. "Name is Marcus."

I looked at Fred Gordon. He was 'bout my size. He wore shades and a Fu Manchu beard. Around his neck was a piece of rope tied to a wood shamen. In his hand was a rifle.

"Only Marcus I ever knew was a teacher I had, and I hated him."

"Yeah, well, Marcus here ain't no teacher," Quint said.

Fred grunted. I wasn't a teacher and I wasn't a pig and I wasn't white so I must be awright. "You sure no one seen you come in like that?" he asked Quint.

"Everybody seen us come in like that. What the fuck you think, with all the shootin' 'round here. But nobody goin' say nothing, if that's what you mean. This a black state up here, ain't it?"

Fred laughed. "If it is then we just been invaded, baby. But least the pigs ain't figured out 'bout this back way, so that's working for us."

"What happened out there?" I asked him.

"The pigs attacked us, that's what happened. They had Toms watchin' us all day from a car. They knew we had guns in here so they waited till real late and then just started blastin' us."

"But didn't they say nothin'?"

"Sure, they asked me to come out peaceful like. Then they'd shoot me full of peace."

"How bad they hit you?" Quint asked.

"Bad enough. Two of my men are dead in there. But we got least one of them I know 'bout."

188

Somebody called him from the front of the house. We followed. "Go upstairs," he said to us. "I be up in a minute."

We got upstairs and I crawled over to a window. Now there was least a dozen pig wagons all over the street, and the guns were poppin' out there like they were firecrackers. "This is no good," Quint said behind me. "If they rush us, everybody be killed off like flies."

Fred come over. "What you think, Quint?"

"No good stayin' here. When they bring up the stoner guns and the gas, you ain't got a chance. They got the block locked up for sure. But what they ain't got is the houses, they scared to go in 'em. How many men you got?"

"Twelve, no, ten."

"Make a running fight of it. They want a shoot-out, give it to 'em. But make it so you the boss. Half your men go over the yards one way, the rest the other way. Then they come outta cellars and doorways all up and down the block. The pigs won't know what hit 'em. Just leave a couple shootin' from here."

"What you gonna do?"

"Me and Marcus goin' get you the hell away from here."

Fred gripped his rifle. "No good, man. I stay and fight."

"Listen to me, Fred. The pigs want you to fight so they can off you. If you stay here you be dead in a hour, and if you go with your men it'll be the same thing. Every motherfuck out there got a shell with your name on it. When your men pick off a few, they can melt into the buildings and hide out with the people. You can't do that, they got your face."

"Quint's right," I said to Fred. "No sense gettin' your ass shot off when it don't mean nothin'. They pulling this number just so's they can get at you. So fuck 'em up."

"Yeah, and they doing it now 'cause they wanna bust the curfew," Quint said bitterly.

"Ain't no use thinkin' about that," I told him. "They already done that."

"There'll be others. And next time we gonna have all the leaders where they can't get to them." Quint said it like he meant it.

189

Fred still didn't like the idea but he'd go with it. The pigs'd been killin' the house for least fifteen minutes and nobody knew what they'd do next. Time to move on.

Fred got his men and told them what to do. Then they went out and done it. We were the last to leave the house, 'cept for the two men that were gonna stay behind.

The night was black dark. We climbed fences and sheds and slowly made our way up the block, yard by yard. Took us maybe twenty minutes to get way up and out the next street over. All that time we heard shooting, the pigs were using machine guns and every other flipfuckin' gun they had. I kept lookin' up in the sky, waitin' to see planes diving down at us. And I knew if I got a drink of water, a fuckin' pig submarine'd come shootin' outta the tap.

We got to the next street. It was empty, no one on the whole block. I crossed first just to make sure. Then Quint and Fred come across. We went into a building and out the back, over some more fences and into more buildings. When we come out we were two streets away from the shooting.

"I know people on this block," Quint said to Fred. "You can't walk the streets to get outta here, too dangerous. So we'll fix it like you been somewhere else for the whole time."

"How you do that?"

"These people we goin' to, you been with them all night. You call from their house and say you just heard 'bout the trouble. By time the pigs get there I'll be gone."

"If Fred calls the pigs, they'll come and gun everybody down," I said to Quint.

"That's right. But Fred ain't calling the pigs. He's gonna call the New York *Times* and the TV stations, let them call the pigs." He turned to Fred. "Did you use the rifle on 'em?"

"Fuckin' right I did."

"They'll check your hand and know you fired a gun. Okay, you still got that gun club you formed?"

"Yeah."

"So you got in a little practice today, that's all. In the back-yard, hitting tin cans. Dig?"

190

"What about me, Quint? What you want me to do?"

He put his arm 'round my shoulder. "You got the hardest job of all, Marcus. You gotta walk outta here and go home like nothin' happened. Right now it don't do nobody good for you to get jammed up so we best save you. You our secret weapon. Now you go on, me and Fred got things to do."

And that's just what I done. I walked outta the biggest shoot-out ever hit Harlem. And then I walked some blocks even the rats left for the night. By the time I got to Lenox Avenue people were movin' around but even from there you could hear the shooting and sirens.

I stopped in the Easy Times for a drink. Everybody was rapping about the action over by Seventh Avenue. Some of 'em were gettin' juiced up 'cause they figured maybe the pigs were gonna close everything down. And some were not drinking at all, just waiting 'round for the looting to start.

Somebody wanted to know how long the shootin' was gonna go on. All night, he was told. Them motherfuckers goin' on a riot, they goin' shoot up everything in sight. But how can they do that, ain't it against the law? Everybody laughed. If they run outta niggers, maybe they'll shoot up on themselfs. Naw, them Uncle Toms they got, most likely. Everybody drunk to that.

"Listen," one brother said, "I hear a couple of them got it in the head. You know what that means. They gonna run wild and kill off everything black in sight. Then when they got their rocks off like that, they gonna call in their White Panthers to hit on anything ain't already shot up. And you know how them White Panthers love to shoot."

"They ain't gonna call in no National Guard," somebody said.

"They'll call 'em in awright. They gotta. Only way they can cover up all the killing they gonna do."

When I got home I turned on the TV. It was after two in the morning but the stations still working kept breakin' into the movies with news about the shoot-out. The curfew was busted, least for one night but prob'ly for good. Hundreds of po-lice

191

were over there, all of them white for sure. I knew my feeling was right 'bout them hiding in Central Park.

But when it come to why they shot their way in, it was like one of them science fuckin' fiction things. They said the black nationalists were gonna have a armed revolt in five or six big cities, and here in New York Fred Gordon's New Georgia Nation was gonna lead it. How they knew this? They got a tip from one of their Toms. So they sent some more Toms to watch Fred's house and they seen his men go in with guns. When the white po-lice come to the house, Fred's men opened up on 'em. So they hadda fire back.

Yeah, all hundreds of them. And they all come in just a few minutes, with machine guns and everything. But it takes all night to find a pig when you in trouble and need one.

Fred was picked up near where I left him and Quint, in them people's house. He was okay but four of his men were dead. So were three of the pigs, and ten of 'em were hurt. They were calling it a plot to kill them. But you'd hafta be stone blind not to see the plot was the other way around.

And that stud in the bar was right. The White Panthers fuckin' National Guard was called in during the night.

Quint's a good man and I like him but he don't got the feel I got. I told him I had a feel that something was gonna go wrong.

And which it sure goddam did.

14.

"NOW listen here, all of us been playing the white man's game long enough," Mustafa Z was saying in his deadliest tone, his eyes snapping left and right like a drill team. Sweat ran down his forehead, trying to escape the hand he wiped across it every few minutes.

192

"Too long!" The muscles in his neck screamed in pain, holding his face tight. "And we been gettin' the ass end of the stick all this time."

The kid in the black leather jacket brung his fist up in a Black Power salute and held it there like he'd never let go. No one noticed. Everyone else was watching Mustafa Z.

"That's right. We been using the white man's words and the white man's laws and the white man's banks. Now when we find out they got everything and we got nothin', we ask how come."

Plastic Man's one good eye looked hard at Mustafa Z. It was blood red and cold as ice. Julian's mouth twisted itself into a sneer and held it. Anger stole across Lazlo's face. Mandrake's jaw fell but the rest of him stayed put. Bobby Small scratched his nose and tried to look smart. The black leather jacket brung his fist up again and caught Mustafa Z's eye. The full face turned slightly and placed its frown on the uplifted arm.

"That don't mean nothin'," he said.

The remark crippled the kid and his arm fell down and got lost somewhere in the leather jacket.

Plastic Man kept his eye open.

All of us were in the meeting hall of the Black Mormons, a religion group that was very tight in Harlem. Mustafa Z was the spirit leader of the Black Mormons. I was there 'cause I knew most the men in the room and I wanted to see what the hell these religion brothers was up to.

Mustafa Z looked around the room, making sure he got everybody's attention.

"Yeah. The black man been sucking wind so long now he ain't got the mother wit to know what to do."

"You people know all 'bout sucking wind." The words come from my left, over against the wall. I looked but I already knew the voice. Eliha Root.

Everybody knew the voice. Nobody said nothing.

"Are we men or are we wind suckers?" asked Mustafa Z, paying no mind to Eliha Root's remark.

The question didn't need a answer. At least a dozen militants

193

were in the room, some of them real wild men. They were all into some kinda black religions and so they hated all the other kinds.

"Working with the white man ain't the way," Mustafa Z said in his deepest voice. "We done tried that and it don't work nohow."

He waited for somebody to talk up, like at a prayer meetin'. Only here there wasn't nothin' to say. Everybody knew the white man can't be trusted.

"There's only one thing to do with the white man," Mustafa Z shouted suddenly, "and I tell you, brothers, I know what that is." Bang. He pounded the table with his flat hand.

No one moved a muscle.

"What we gonna do is become the majority in this country. We gonna be the ninety percent and let the white man be the ten percent. I got the way to make ninety percent of the people soul brothers right here and now. Then we run everything and if the white man don't like it, we wipe him out."

Bang. He pounded the table again.

Plastic Man stuck his finger in his ear, to make sure he was hearing right. Bobby Small popped his eyeballs so loud they screamed in surprise.

Over in the corner Eliha Root was just lighting a cigar. He threw it down in disgust. "Sonovabitch," he shouted. "Sonovamotherfuckingbitch." Everyone looked at him. "We been fightin' on Chuck Chalk for more years'n a cow has tits. And now we givin' him a taste of his own shit. Yeah, and we been whuppin' his ass. Now this closet nigger come along and he say he gonna make people think they black when you gotta be stone blind not to see they is white. He just gonna give 'em a kiss job and blow 'way all that powder they got on. Nothin' to it. And I s'pose listen to that shit? I s'pose listen to him? Man, look out." His eyes grew round and very small and his voice was sharp enough to slice through steel, the words shootin' sparks in the air like fireworks goin' off.

"I listen to him," Plastic Man said evenly, looking straight at Eliha Root with his good eye.

194

Things were gettin' hairy. Heads turned from Eliha Root to Plastic Man in a slow shuffle.

Eliha Root's eyes grew even smaller. "Niggers listen to anything," he said very softly.

Everyone moved back two feet.

Plastic Man choked and that made his blood eye even redder. He was a small, tight man dressed in a dashiki. His face had hair all over it that spilled down into the dashiki, hiding his chin and making him look like a devil in drag. His bad eye, always open and staring straight ahead, didn't help things any. But he was smart and he was tough. And as minister of a local militant religion gang called the Harlem Masai, he wasted no love on Eliha Root who was a power in a national militant black religion movement.

"Eliha," he said slowly, "you best be careful, man. You don't got no say worth spit 'round here. This my terr'tory you is in now."

Eliha Root's eyes disappeared into tiny black diamonds.

"Don't tell me what I best do," he warned.

"I'm gonna make this country black," Mustafa Z boomed out from behind the table. "Ninety percent black, and that's a fact."

"You hear that, you Plastic Man? You hear him say he goin' make this whole motherfuckin' country black—"

"Ninety percent he say."

"Ninety percent black, and then we goin' rule everything 'round here—"

" 'Round everywhere."

"And meanwhile, the whites just be sittin' jacking off in a corner somewhere while we blowin' their brains out."

"Just what we been doing all these years, ain't it, man?"

"Maybe what you been doing. But there's some of us been trying to get what belong to us."

"Everything belong to us."

"Everything?" Eliha Root was shaking. "You dumb nigger, don't you know that's just what the white man wants to hear? Then when he kills you dead he can feel righteous about it."

195

"He just killing hisself when he do that."

Eliha Root looked blank. "What you talkin' 'bout?"

"Ninety percent of him is black."

Eliha Root's face didn't know what to do. It looked like he was having a fit right where he was standing. "God give you balls for brains, that's just what he done with you, man. Don't you know the white man's day almos' over? Don't you know he's trying to save hisself by going 'round saying we all the same? That we all gotta pull together? But we all ain't the same, man. He's white. He's white as the black on your face. You go 'round making ninety percent of them white mother-fucks black, and they gonna 'scape the punishment what God give 'em."

"And then we never goin' be the masters again," Lazlo said in a heavy Chicago drawl, "like we s'pose be."

"This the only way," Mustafa Z said firmly. "Once there's ninety percent of us and only ten percent of them, we got 'em by the balls."

"What we do then?" Mandrake asked.

Mustafa Z lifted his right hand and made a scissors with it.

"Cut 'em off," he answered.

Julian pulled a small plastic case outta his pocket, opened it and put it on the table.

"See that?" he said to no one in particular. "That's what gonna get rid of whitey for us."

Everybody moved closer.

"What's this?" Mustafa Z asked Julian.

"Thunderfuck."

"What the fuck is Thunderfuck?" someone whispered.

"A chemical, that what it is. A chemical that gonna wipe out whitey." He pronounced the last three words like it was some kinda slogan.

"Don't look like much to me," Mandrake said to Julian.

"It'll do the job."

Eliha Root looked at Julian. Plastic Man looked at Julian.

"It's got somethin' in it that makes the white man go crazy," Julian said. "It do somethin' to his head."

196

"Look like it already do somethin' to yours," Eliha Root shouted.

"I tell you it works," Julian shouted back. "It don't affect us 'cause we got diff'rent blood or something. But it make whitey go crazier'n a junkie in the sun."

Mustafa Z put a superior face on.

"Listen, Julian, we don't want them crazier than they already is," Plastic Man explained patiently. "They killin' us off now. If they get any crazier, they gonna wipe us out in a day. Now if that's what you want, you just take this shit and dump it in the white man's cupcake."

Lazlo picked up the case. "Where you get this, man? I mean, you know, who's pushin' it?"

Julian's face turned six shades of black. "Nobody pushin' it," he said in a tight voice. "I got a doctor who help my org'zation to make it up for us."

"This doctor," Lazlo pressed, "what color is he?"

"Don't matter what color he is, he believes in what we doing."

"I know that, man. I know it don't matter but we just interest, that's all. What color is he?"

"White," Julian whispered. "He's white."

"Maybe you oughtta take this back to your white friends," Plastic Man said in disgust, picking up the case and giving it to Julian.

"I think he oughtta be lock up in the nut house," Mandrake said. "And his whole org'zation too."

"Must be soft 'round here," Lazlo said. "In Chicago my Black Nation wouldn' go for this kinda shit."

"Yeah, but you in the big time now, baby."

Mustafa Z grumbled in his throat. "Maybe now we all get back to serious business here, if everybody done talking."

The kid in the black leather jacket didn't say a word.

From a shopping bag on the table Mustafa Z took out a square black box with a little glass tube and some wires inside and a electric cord hangin' from it. On top were two lights, one

197

black and one white. Everybody got up real close to look at the box.

Plastic Man put his face up to the box and ran his good eye all 'round it.

"That's what gonna make white people black?"

"That's what gonna do it."

"Just this one box with some wires and lights?"

"Don't need no more."

"What's that glass thing in the middle?"

"That's where the juice go."

"What juice?"

"The juice that say if you white or black."

Mandrake and Bobby Small started laughin'. Plastic Man turned on them with his one blood-red eye and the other one not moving, just staring at them. They shut up quick.

"Is you sure you know what you talkin' about?" Plastic Man asked.

Mustafa Z smiled. "If I know anything I know that in America one drop of black blood makes you a black man. That the law in this country."

"What about it?"

"What about it is if you can show white people that most all of 'em are really black, then 'stead of black passing for white you gonna get every motherfuckin' white man trying to pass for black. That what about it."

Plastic Man was impressed. "And you gonna do that with just this here little box?"

"That's right."

"How you gonna do that?"

Mustafa Z made his voice like a teacher. "Now listen to what I say. The thing that makes somebody black is the pigment in their skin. If you got enough of this pigment you be black. If you ain't got enough you be white."

"That makes sense."

"That the way it is. But what most people don't know is this pigment comes from when you is a baby. When you born you already got this pigment."

198

"What if you born white?"

"Then you ain't got enough of it you ain't got none."

"And you saying most white people got some of this pigment only they don't know it?"

"That the truth. With all the slippin' 'round been goin' on the last four hundred years, least ninety percent of whites got some of this pigment. That makes 'em black even if they passing for white."

Mustafa Z set his face soft and it kinda glowed from what he was tellin' us. What he done was he built up a good case for somethin' that sounded crazy. Fact is, it sounded so good I was ready to kiss the next nine white niggers I met.

"That may be," Plastic Man said, scratching his hair where his chin musta been, "but how can that box prove it to the whites?"

" 'Cause the pigment is in a man's juice, and ain't no way it can get out. That means every time he on top some bitch bangin' away, he's movin' around some of that pigment."

"What about the woman, she got any?"

"It's in her juice too, same as for a man. You either got it or you don't got it, and if you got it they ain't no way in God's earth you gonna get rid of it. Now the box here is for tellin' if you got it."

Mustafa Z took hold of the box and held it up.

"What the hell that little box goin' do?" Eliha Root demanded.

"What it goin' do is check everybody's juice and if they got the pigment, it'll let 'em know quick enough. That's what these two lights are for. If you got pigment it lights up black, and if you ain't got no pigment it lights up white."

Eliha Root was furious. "You mean you is standing there tellin' us we gotta go out jacking off every white man in America to see if he got pigment in his juice? Is that what you saying? That every white man gotta get his juice in that glass thing so's he can see if he's black?"

"And all the white sisters too," Mustafa Z said cheerfully.

199

" 'Course, that takes more time. Somebody gonna hafta do a lotta diddlin' around fingerfuckin' all of 'em."

"Eliha's people take care of that," Plastic Man snapped. "They real good at diddlin' pussy."

"You dead," Eliha Root said to Plastic Man. His simple words whipped through the room and bounced off the walls of everyone's ear.

The blood rushed to Plastic Man's blood-red eye, drowned it and pushed on to the other one, staring straight ahead. "You the big pussy man," he purred. But the claw was already in his voice.

Mandrake walked over to Plastic Man. "He got no power here, man. Nothin' for you to worry 'bout."

I looked over at Eliha Root and his men and I wasn't so sure of that. There was a lotta bad blood in this room and it was screamin' to spill out.

Behind the table Mustafa Z was still cheerful. "With enough of these boxes around, we goin' check whitey's juice and show him up for what he really is. Just a black man gone white. All we need is enough brothers to do all the checking."

Now it was Eliha Root's turn. "Let Plastic Man handle the dudes. With that fag eye of his, all he's good for is whippin' off some jack."

Plastic Man smiled. "Least it ain't lipsucking pussy like you and your Nation so good at."

The kid in the black leather jacket, silent all night, shot up and yelled, "Pussy Power."

That did it. Eliha Root chopped open his blade and sprung for the kid. Plastic Man shouted to look out. The kid run right under the table. Eliha Root lunged at him, missed and kept right on goin' toward Mustafa Z. Julian grabbed him by the arm but was shrugged off. Mandrake run up and Lazlo hit him from behind. Eliha Root was reaching for Mustafa Z with his blade when Plastic Man shoved a ice pick in his shoulder. Eliha Root turned quick and stabbed Plastic Man in the hair. Plastic Man fell dead. With the ice pick still in him, Eliha Root wheeled 'round and caught Mustafa Z just as he was grabbin'

200

for the black box. Mustafa Z looked up with his hands out-stretched on the table and saw the blade coming down. He opened his mouth to scream but it was too late. His head ripped open at the temple and he was dead before a gouged eyeball fell on top the black box. The blade stayed in his head. Lazlo ran for the door but never made it 'cause Mandrake, blood drippin' from the back of his head where he got hit, punched a hole in him with a .38 that dropped Lazlo like a buff'lo. Bobby Small and Julian and all the others were outta the room already, and I was under the table with the kid in the black leather jacket. Mandrake went for Eliha Root, meaning to shoot him in the balls at close range, but the gun jammed. Eliha Root ripped the ice pick outta his shoulder and plunged it into Mandrake's neck, leaving it there. With blood drippin' down his side, Eliha Root staggered toward the door when Bobby Small come runnin' back into the room and cut him to pieces with a shotgun. He didn't stop shootin' till there wasn't nothin' left. Then he left.

Then I left, leaving the kid in the black leather jacket under the table. I run outta that meetin' hall so fast I was home 'fore my sweat hit the ground.

The po-lice never found out nothin'. When they come nobody was around but the dead. Nobody seen nothing, nobody heard nothing, nobody knew nothing. That's the way it always is, the only way.

I didn't know Eliha Root or any of his people but I knew Plastic Man and Mandrake and I was sorry to see them get it. But that's religion for you. It's a tough racket to get into. Soon's you start talkin' love, everybody hates you.

Papers never said nothing about a square black box with a little glass tube and some wires inside and a electric cord hangin' from it and two lights on the top, one black and one white. The po-lice never found it.

They never found the kid in the black leather jacket either.

15.

SOMETIME late last night Walter Farrell shot hisself full of hop in a hall sandbox and went to sleep for the last time. Which is nothing new for Harlem. Junkies been banging themselfs dead with heroin up here for a long time. One died on the front steps of this hole I'm living in about eight months ago. In the snow. Just sat there the whole freezin' night and by morning he looked like a snowman.

The only thing a little unusual about Walter Farrell's junkie death was his age. He was twelve years old.

I didn't know the kid. He lived down the other end of the block. When Robin come up to tell me about him, I didn't act surprised, I lived too long and seen too much. "You've got no feelings, Marcus," she said to me. "You just don't care about people."

Robin is a welfare worker for the city. She does inside work, moving papers around somewhere downtown. She started two years ago as a caseworker but she couldn' take six months of it. She cared too much. "I had sixty-five cases and two hundred fifty people depending on me," she told me one time, "and all of them lived without hope and I couldn't *do* anything for them." She begun having nightmares and thinking 'bout killing herself and one day she started screaming in the office. The welfare people knew right away what it was. She had overidentified with the poor, is what they call it. So they let her work inside and now she's happy 'cause she's doing her best to help the poor but she don't hafta go 'round and see them.

Whenever Robin visits me she tells me I have no feelings. I say nothing. She comes up from her place in midtown once in a while to see the few friends she got in Harlem. I'm one of them. That's all there is to it.

In the late afternoon we went to a service for Walter Farrell. It was in the Temple of Faith around the corner. The speaker was a young minister who found God and Black Power were the same thing. His voice was smooth and clear. "They tell us God is good, God is just, God is love. That's their God. The white God. Our God is so evil He let a twelve-year-old boy die. He is so unjust He let a twelve-year-old boy die for no reason. And He is so full of hate He let a twelve-year-old boy die for no reason all alone in a stinking bathroom in the dark of night. If our God is all that bad, maybe we oughtta take another look at Him."

His hands moved up and down as he talked, carving and slicing the air. His neck muscles pumped hard. His forehead was shiny and wet with sweat.

"Now this God we got, there's something strange about Him. We been praying to Him for hundreds of years, and we worse off than ever. But the whites pray to Him and He listens. How come? He listens because He is white, same as them. God always listens to His own kind. Then how come He don't listen to us? The answer is clear as that beautiful flat nose on your beautiful black face. He don't listen to us because He is white and we're black. *We been praying to the wrong God.*"

He got a white tissue outta his jacket pocket and wiped his forehead with it. He turned it over and blew his nose. His hand crushed it into a ball and his eyes searched for somewhere to throw it. There wasn't nowhere so he put it back in his pocket.

He wet his big black beautiful lips. "The white man has been running a game on us, tellin' us about his white Jesus and his white God. Now we all know that Jesus was a black man. That's a historical fact. So we know that there's a black God. All we gotta do is start praying to Him rather than to that sissy milk-fed God the whites ripped off for themselves."

203

He was tall and thin and his square face had a small beard. He wore glasses that didn't have no rims. On his black suit jacket was a big button with a picture of Malcolm X.

His hands kept on choppin' the air. "Another historical fact is that about seven eighths of the people in the world are non-white. Always been that way. Now why would a white God make most all the world nonwhite? Don't make sense. The only answer is that there's a nonwhite God up there and we know He's black. And if He gets to make seven eighths of the people, He must be seven times stronger'n that puny white God. *He's the God we gotta start praying to.*"

I looked around. He was reaching the people awright, telling it like it is. Or should be.

"Now you want to know what all this has to do with a twelve-year-old boy dying from drugs? I'll tell you. If we had been praying to the right God all these years, that boy would be alive today. Sure thing. But we been supporting the wrong things. We been praying white, buying white and thinking white. Then when we try to live white, they say hold on. And for once they're right. It ain't the way. But now we're seeing black. Black. Black."

His eyes were on fire. His tongue was a snake. His hands were knives, daggers, swords. His Afro cut stood on end. He rocked on his heels. He juggled his foot.

The words busted out. "If you want God, pray black. If you want money, buy black. If you want peace, think black."

"Amen," someone cried.

"Say it loud," the minister shouted. "Black. Black. Black."

"Black. Black. Black," the crowd shouted back.

"If you want love, love black. If you want power, be black. If you want life, live black."

"You're on the case, Reverend."

"Black. Black. Black."

"Say it again."

"Black. Black. Black."

The crowd was on its feet. Maybe a hundred and fifty people, 'cluding a lotta kids, prob'ly friends of Walter Farrell. If Har-

204

lem's got nothin' else, it's got plenty of people. You can always draw a good crowd by dying.

Robin was one of a half-dozen whites in the place. "He's good, isn't he?" she whispered, her face flush from the heat of the crowd.

"He's good," I agreed, lookin' over at three whites standing on the side. "I wonder who they are."

She turned her head toward them. "I don't know the first two, but the one in back of them is from the welfare."

"What's he doing here?"

"Can't you guess? He's here to make sure the boy's mother spends the funeral money they give her on the funeral."

"Ssssh."

"Again. Black. Black. Black. Say it loud."

"Black. Black. Black."

"Say it proud."

"Black. Black. Black."

"Black is tough. Black is beautiful. Black is together. Integration had its day and it wasn't the way. White America is for white people. White America ain't for black people. The schools don't work for us. The unions don't work for us. The po-lice don't work for us."

"Right on, Reverend," a woman up front shouted.

"Give it to 'em."

"We give them Medgar Evers and they kill him."

"Glory, Jesus."

"We give them King Martin and they kill him."

"Lord, lord."

"We give them our best people to be slaughtered like cattle. But no more. We ain't givin' them nothing."

"Tell it, Reverend."

"Now that we got our blackness together, we going to take care of our own."

"Amen."

That was the signal for the collection basket to be passed around. "This crowd oughtta be good for a couple hundred at least," I said to Robin, and got a jab in the side. I wondered what she'd say if she knew the minister was gettin' least fifty for being here. But all in a good cause. Black to black.

After his take, the rest'd go to the kid's mother. There was always exter things when someone died, things the welfare people never figure on. New clothes, paid mourners, food and drink for a lotta people, a dozen things like that. She'd need the money.

I threw a five in the basket. Why not? Hell, it won't make me rich. Ain't much gonna happen to me one way or the other. I never been anywhere much and prob'ly ain't never gonna be anywhere else. I'm just about staying 'live and that ain't gonna change either.

The basket was filled a few times. Funny thing about us poor black folks. There ain't hardly scratch enough for food and the rent but there's always somethin' for a brother in need. Maybe that's why the con men and grifters got the only real money in Harlem, 'cause they got such a soft touch here. And maybe that's why the motherfuck whites own Harlem.

The minister was still talkin' black but it was just talk till the basket made the rounds. From the looks of it, he was earning his money.

"The black God is a God of love. Remember that it was the white man who kept us in slavery for hundreds of years, who raped our women, who lynched our men. To hate the white man is only natural. To hate the white man is an act of love to our black God."

That made the crowd feel good. It meant they been lovin' this black God most all their lives, only they didn't know it.

God or no God don't mean nothin' to me. But that man's right about hating whitey. You gotta live with them to hate them. I been livin' in this fuckin' city ass to ass with them most my life, and I know there's places I can't go that any stranger come into town can go. Long's they white or half white. Yeah, and things they can do I can't. They more free than I am right where I live. You tell 'em that and they say go somewhere else, go anywhere.

Goddam. Why should I go anywhere? I'm here already.

"Now we're going to pray to our own black God, and I mean *pray*. He's been out in the cold too long and He wants to hear us. He wants to know we love Him. He wants to know we trust Him. He wants to hear it from us. And when He does, then He'll help us."

"Give us the word."

"Black Jesus, there's a mother sitting here that has the misery."

"Hit her with love, Lord."

"Black Jesus, there's a woman crying somewhere 'cause her troubles are too much."

"Take 'em over, Lord."

"Black Jesus, there's a man drinking somewhere 'cause he's all alone."

"Live with him, Lord."

"There's the blind that need to see."

"Do it, Jesus."

"There's the deaf that need to hear."

"Do it, Jesus."

"There's the lame that need to walk."

"Do it, Jesus."

"There's the dumb that need to talk."

"Do it, Jesus."

"There's the sinners that need to be saved."

"Save it, Jesus."

"There's the lives that need to be fixed."

"Fix it, Jesus."

Spit flew outta the minister's mouth. His head danced, his hands shook. He was shouting and the crowd was shouting right back.

"When there are mountains to be climbed, think about the black Jesus. When there are rivers to be swum, think about the black Jesus. When there are deserts to be crossed, think about the black Jesus. Black Jesus is love. Pray to the black Jesus and you'll get nothing but good. I know there are people here who don't believe in prayer. They think the black God has forgot them. But they're wrong. I feel the power of the black God right now, the holy black Spirit is here in this room. Now repeat after me. Black Jesus, love me."

"Black Jesus, love me."

"Black Jesus, save me."

"Black Jesus, save me."

"Black Jesus, help me."

"Black Jesus, help me."

"Again."

"Black Jesus, help me."

"Awright now, one more time 'cause He hears you. Black Jesus, love me."

"Black Jesus, love me."

"Black Jesus, save me."

"Black Jesus, save me."

"Black Jesus, help me."

"Black Jesus, help me."

"Uh-huh. It's awright. Now we're going. Black Jesus hears us. He's tellin' me He hears us. He's tellin' you He hears us. And He's listening close. We got His ear. We got the ear of Jesus. He wants the sick to be healed. He wants the sinner to be saved. He wants the blind to see, the deaf to hear, the lame to walk, the dumb to talk. Now He knows we love Him, now He knows we trust Him, now He knows we want Him."

"Righteous on that."

"Do we love black Jesus?"

"Yeah."

"Black Jesus can't hear you."

"Yeah."

"Do we trust black Jesus?"

"Yeah."

"Do we want black Jesus?"

"Yeah."

"Now the black Jesus is going to give us His blessing. Black Jesus blesses the mother who has the misery. Black Jesus blesses the man who is all alone. Black Jesus blesses everybody who has money troubles. Black Jesus blesses everybody who has mar-

208

riage troubles. Black Jesus blesses everybody who has any troubles."

Sounded to me like that black Jesus wasn't gonna miss nobody, 'cluding the motherfuck whites.

"Keep praying to your own black God and you won't go wrong. Keep praying to your own black God and you can't go wrong. And don't be afraid of him neither. Our black God is stronger than anything the white man's got. Our black God is the strongest. Maybe sometimes He chokes a little but remember this, *He don't strangle.*"

"Glory be to God."

"Black God."

"Glory be to black God."

The service was over. Some people stood 'round crying with the kid's mother. I followed the two whites out to this big black hog, sittin' at the curb with its motor purring. All the windows were closed for the air-condition and the standing lights were flashing in a no-parking zone. At the wheel was a dude in a dark business suit, reading a newspaper. The two whites opened the back door and got in. When it pulled away I found what I was looking for on the rear bumper. It was a city hall staff car. Somebody downtown was on the job awright. Either they wanted to show they cared or didn't want to show they scared.

Shit, I coulda saved them the trip up here. This town ain't gonna blow 'cause a twelve-year-old boy gets shot down on dope. Too many boys been killed that way already. We know all about dying. What we doing now is to learn about living. When we do that, when we learn it's worth living, then this town gonna blow. New York? Man, look out.

Robin was talkin' with the minister standing there on the church steps. I got with them.

"Even one case like this is too much," the minister was saying, "but the fact is at least fifty kids died from drugs in the past year. In one city in one year, fifty kids dead from drugs. We must do something."

"You are doing something," Robin said. "You're getting

your people to believe in blackness, to take pride in themselves. That's what's needed. Once people have a sense of their own worth, they can do anything, overcome anything. They can fight back."

I watched the minister, knowing what he was thinking. Who's this white bitch come up here talkin' about what's needed? What the hell she know 'bout fighting back? She's white, ain't she? Plus, she's got looks and is sittin' on a fancy cat that'd make a lotta scratch for her.

"You're right, of course," the minister said. "But we're still not doing enough. The point is that the white man"—he looked at Robin and decided she was safe—"the white man still got us. He makes what we buy, owns where we live, and controls where we work. That's power."

"Ain't power what you feel inside about yourself?" I asked him.

He shook his head. "Power is what you can get away with. When whitey has it all, he gets away with murder." He took out a used tissue from his jacket pocket and blew his nose into it again, then threw it down the church steps. "It's time we got some of it."

"But they ain't giving."

"Then we gotta take."

"And if they don't like it?"

"Then we fight."

Robin didn't like it. She believed in nonviolence. She marched in the South and was even jailed overnight in Alabama. To her, Martin Luther King was a saint. "There's been too much fighting already," she said firmly. "Violence never solves anything."

The minister looked at her and decided she wasn't safe any more. He tried to back up. "I don't mean bloodshed. The Lord don't approve of killing, like what's going on now in the white man's war in Vietnam." He smiled, knowing he had scored a point. "What I'm talking about is fighting him in the pocket where it hurts. We gotta have more black people owning their own business. We gotta have more products made by black people. Then when the money spreads around, we can have some power. Green Power. That's really what it's all about."

Robin liked that. To her Green Power was nonviolent, not like that Black Power. She didn't know more people been killed for money than anything else. But it wouldn' do no good to tell her. Robin was a social worker who wanted poor people to have what they needed. When they didn't get it, she didn't get mad. She got scared. "I had sixty-five cases and two hundred fifty people depending on me" is what she said, "and I couldn't *do* anything for them." Now she worked inside where it's clean and nonviolent.

The minister went over to comfort the kid's mother. On the way home Robin asked me why he never once said the kid's name in his talk. "He prob'ly don't know it," I told her.

She couldn' believe that. That anyone would hold services and not know the body's name.

"Names don't matter to the dead," I reminded her. "And up here they don't hardly matter to the living. Poor people got no time for the dead. Walter Farrell's mother prob'ly got six other kids she gotta feed and keep alive. How much time you think she got for misery over a dead boy?"

"That doesn't excuse the minister. There's no reason for him not to know the boy's name. Even if he attends five services a day he should know their names."

Later on in bed, Robin asked me if I'd remember her when she was gone. "Would you remember me, Marcus, would you really? I mean, if I'd die tomorrow, would you remember my name and say it sometimes?"

Whites have this thing about death, you know. Even after they dead, they still wanna be around.

211

16.

THE Church of the Spirit World was on 132d Street, sandwiched in between a empty lot and another two-story house with no porch. On a dead tree in the little front yard hung a sign with the church name and some words. The house itself was maybe fifteen feet across, and the two windows on each floor had only an arm's reach between them. All the shades were down. The roof hung out over the front edge and half of it was laying in the yard. A roof gutter dripped down the side of the house at a crazy angle. The front door was missing and in its place somebody nailed together a half-dozen boards. The house looked like nobody lived in it. Which was prob'ly why Salem Smith was living there with his whores.

Madison Wells looked up and down the street while the rest of us stood over by the tree. He was at the curb trying to look innocent, his hands by his side and his jacket smartly buttoned. He looked as guilty as Gov'nor Maddox in a nigger nest.

No one passed, no one was on the other side that we could see. Anybody watching us from the houses 'cross the street was somethin' else. But nobody in Harlem seeing four men huggin' shadows at two in the morning was gonna give it special mind. Outside of taking their gun from under the mattress and putting it under their pillow.

The little sign on the tree got my eye. WE GOT IT—YOU NEED IT. Couldn' be clearer. And so motherfuckin' right for to be up here in Harlem. No matter what you need, somebody else got it. Mostly the white man. And if he ain't got it, it's for sure no-

212

body needs it no more. I stared at the words, thinkin' what it is that Salem Smith got—and who needs it.

Madison walked back from the curb and leaned up 'gainst the tree. "Looks quiet," he said. "Least nobody's shootin' at us."

Vergil took out his flashlight, clicked it to make sure it worked and turned 'round to face the house. Madison put his hand in his jacket pocket and come up with a set of keys that'd open anything. Sweet Willie and me brung up the rear. All of us made big shadows 'cross the yard and up the side of the house. Vergil's shadow was the tallest, its head cut off by the roof. What was left of it.

Madison stepped out from the tree and started walking.

"Let's go," he said.

One two three we followed him. At the basement door Madison used his keys on a old iron gate. It swung back with a lotta noise. "Shut that fucker up," Sweet Willie whispered, "it's waking up the dead."

Vergil grabbed the gate and held it till we all passed, then lifted it closed without a sound. He picked up the flashlight and handed it to Madison. "All yours, man."

The inside door was unlocked. Past that was a short hallway, then steps to the first floor. Madison played the light around the basement. All we could see was a beat-up stove and some broken furniture. A kid's bike was propped up against a wall. Some books and a collection basket were on a small table. Everything was heavy with dust, and spiders owned the corners. "Nothin' here," said Sweet Willie. "Nothin' worth nothin'."

Upstairs was more of the same nothing, at least in the two back rooms. Just a fold-up metal bed and a dresser in each room. Nobody was in the beds. A tiny kitchen was behind the staircase, with a coffeepot on the dead stove.

Madison found the lights for the front room and turned them on. It was bigger'n the other two rooms and was s'pose to be some kinda church room. A lotta wood chairs were in rows facing a small altar set against one wall. The altar was just a long table with a white cloth on it and some candles. In front of

213

it was a long kneeling rug. Next to that against the windows were two big easy chairs and between them was a big wood cross nailed to a beam on the front wall almos' floor to ceiling.

Everybody looked at the cross. It was hard not to look 'cause a white woman was hangin' on it, naked as a cat's ass in a storm. "Jee-sus," Sweet Willie cried out, "what in the flip fuckin' hell is goin' on 'round here?"

The fox was hangin' there peaceful as sin. Her arms were spread out and tied 'round the wrists with heavy sailor rope looped through a hole in the cross. Her feet were tied together the same way. She was young enough, maybe twenty-five, and her small jugs curved under to baby fat around her belly. But it was her cat that made everybody stare. The bush was red brown and tight as a drumhead. Little hairs curled themselfs around the edges. At the bottom, somebody stuck a rose stem all the way up her cat and the red petals blushed tight between her white thighs.

"Is she dead?" Vergil asked in a raspy voice.

I walked up to her and took her jaw in my hand and moved her head side to side. Nothing. But I could see she was breathing. I forced her eyelid open. No pupil. "She's not dead," I told them, "but she's high on smack looks like. A real heavy bang."

"How'd she get up there?" Madison wanted to know.

Sweet Willie smiled. "Maybe that's how she gets her kicks."

"One thing sure," I said to them. "She didn't tie herself up like that."

"Or stick that rose up her own cat," Vergil added.

"Yeah, that too."

The whole thing was spooky. I kept thinking maybe she's what Salem Smith's got that everybody needs. But who the fuck'd need anything like that? Madison and Vergil sat on the little chairs staring up at her and Sweet Willie stood close to the fox with his head right by her flower. I leaned up against the altar, trying to make sense outta things.

None of us heard any movement upstairs.

"Who's down there?" a voice demanded. "Who's downstairs?"

Madison and Vergil jumped up and knocked over their

214

chairs. Sweet Willie wheeled 'round from the hangin' fox so fast his head deflowered her.

"If you don't answer I'll call the po-lice," the voice said. It was a high fox voice. Sounded black.

I stood right where I was. Nobody was goin' call the po-lice, not with that hanging on the wall.

Madison cleared his throat and shouted, "I'm lookin' for Salem. He up there?"

"Ain't home. What you want with him?"

"Know where I can find him?"

"No. What you want with him?"

Madison put his finger up to his lips for us to be quiet. "Just wanna rap with him is all."

Whispering upstairs, then footsteps comin' down. Two people.

Madison and Vergil inched up 'gainst the wall. When the two foxes come in the room they saw me and Sweet Willie. Then they turned 'round and saw Madison and Vergil. One of them went to scream but Vergil stopped her. The other just eased herself into a chair. "What you want?" she asked, cool as ice.

Madison got up close to her. She was a high-yella bitch, very boss in a hard way. "Like I told you, we just wanna talk to Salem."

She shrugged and got out a smoke from her robe and lit up. The other fox was a blonde, looked to be maybe nineteen or twenty. She wore a robe too. When she sat down and crossed her legs, the robe opened at the knees. She folded it over her legs but not before I seen she had nothin' on under it.

Madison pointed to the cross. "What she doing up there like that?" he asked the hightone fox.

No answer.

Madison's eyes got hard. He put his face very close to her. "I said what she doing up there."

Without blinking a eye, the hightone fox opened her mouth and shot a big glob of spit right in Madison's face. He didn't move. He stayed right there, bent over like that, with the spit

215

runnin' down his cheek and his eyes locked into hers. He stayed like that a long time. Then suddenly he backhanded that fox right off her chair. "Don't get up," he said to her.

She heard the knives in his voice. She didn't get up.

"Man, she sure got womb," Sweet Willie whispered.

Madison looked at Sweet Willie. "Yeah" was all he said.

The iron gate outside opened. Nobody moved. The high-tone was still on the floor and the white fox on the chair when Salem Smith come up the stairs and into the room. When he seen us, he froze. I could see from his face that his first idea was to beat it back down the stairs but he shrugged that off. Never make it. Then he looked at each of us while he put the big smile on. By time he got to me his face was humming. "What's shaking, brothers?" he said with great cheer. "What's the word?"

Madison wiped the spit off his face. "Dracula sucks, man. Ain't you heard?"

Salem was fast. Fast and very good. "I heard, baby, I heard but I try to control myself. I'm the dude with the solid gold swipe, the double jackpot with the hips and lips to cream the cat. I'm the ringmaster that runs the circus love, the wet dream artist that can cop a bitch and keep her humping her heart out."

Vergil laughed. "We know you good, Salem."

"I'm the best around."

Madison growled. "Okay, man, you got a tight rep as a pimp. Now what is so important you hadda see me?"

Salem eased hisself into one of the big chairs. He didn't pay no mind to the foxes, they coulda been in China for all he showed. But that's how a pimp gotta act with 'em. When he got all settled the smile left his face and he looked square at Madison. His happy voice suddenly had cracks all over it. "I didn't mean for you to come bustin' in here and scarin' hell outta my whores like you done."

"You send out word you gotta see me," Madison said softly.

"How I know it ain't a trap? I'm the big bad nigger that's al-

216

ways tellin' whitey what shit he is. Whitey don't like that. I mean, there's always some fucker lookin' to get me, right?"

"You know me."

"I know a lotta people, you just one of them. I don't deal in pimps every day so I gotta watch myself."

Salem looked at the rest of us. "Why all the muscle?"

"They ain't muscle, they just with me kinda lookin' out for the edges. Vergil here been with me a long time and Marcus and Sweet Willie are just friends."

Sweet Willie laughed. "I'm just here 'cause I like whores."

"Me too," I said.

Salem didn't like that. "I ain't givin' out no free samples."

"We ain't asking," I told him.

Madison sat down in the other big chair. "I don't got much time, Salem. You wanted to see me and I'm here. Start talking."

Salem didn't like it but wasn't nothin' he could do. He sat still another minute just for show, then his face got soft and smiley again. "I got a idea," he said, "that's gonna mess up whitey's mind real bad. I mean, right at the top with them big gov'ment men in Washington. Gonna shake this fuckin' country apart."

"That's big talk," Madison said, his fisheye watching the pimp. "But big talk got a habit of comin' loose."

Salem acted hurt. "Ain't only big talk," he spit out. "You think I be where I is if I was just some jive artist? I got a four-bitch stable. I got threads they ain't even made yet. I'm driving a hog and holding a poke the size of my fist."

"Come off it, man," Vergil said with a big grin. "We checked you out. You lucky you got chump change. You holding two notes on the Caddy and from what I hear, least half your stable is stuffing on you."

"That's bullshit. My bitches work their ass off for me."

"Uhh-huh." Vergil looked around slowly. "We see that, man, we see how they out there hustlin' for you."

Madison held up his hand. "This gettin' us nowhere. What's your idea, man? I'll listen."

217

Salem shoved the smile back on. "It's like this. We get about two hundred young whores, see? But only high-class stuff, and we set 'em up in Washington. We get them to all the important gigs so they meet the top men. Then they go to work. Each bitch takes on one big shot and plays him along till he grabbin' for her pussy. Then she give it to him. Only we be there taking pictures and tapes when they in the bed. 'Fore we be through, we have that whole motherfuckin' gov'ment in our hands. And we be runnin' the country."

Everybody looked at everybody else.

Salem looked happy.

Madison looked tired. "This is what you hadda see me about? Runnin' whores in Washington?"

"Where we goin' get two hundred whores?" Vergil asked. "The kind you talkin' about anyway."

"I already got one of 'em," the pimp said, looking over at the hightone fox, "and I'll get the rest just as easy."

"How'd you like that?" Sweet Willie asked her. "How'd you like to get that Black Power you got 'tween your legs wrapped 'round one of them big-shot gov'ment men?"

The hightone couldn' care less. "All politicians is a whore," she said. "Besides, what I know about Black Power? I ain't black."

"Bitch, drag your black shiny ass outta here," Salem shouted at her. "Get upstairs and take Shirley with you. Now move it."

"How come I can't stay here?"

When Salem started to get up, she knew how come and she blew out the room fast as the wind.

"She your boss bitch?" Vergil asked.

"Yeah, she my bottom woman awright. Ain't no better."

"What 'bout that Shirley? What she doing here?"

"All my whores is chalk, man. Only black bitch I got is Rona and that's only 'cause she's the momma bitch."

Sweet Willie rolled his eyes. "You mean you got three white whores hustlin' for you?"

"You better believe it, man. Matter a fact, two of 'em is out on the streets right now."

218

"Where they working?"

"Downtown, 'round Lexington Avenue down there."

"Now ain't that too motherfuckin' much," Sweet Willie whispered like he was in a church. "A spade pimp with a chalk stable workin' outta a spook house in Harlem." He turned 'round to the cross. "What about her? You goin' in for rough sex?"

"Naw, that's just my crazy old lady. When she bangs a winner she likes to sleep like that."

Nobody said nothin'. Madison put on a frown, Vergil grunted like he been hit and Sweet Willie didn't know what to do with his face. I looked up at the cross. She was still there.

I had a feeling Salem was just runnin' his mouth off. No pimp's got a old lady, and even if there was such a thing she'd never live with his stable 'cause he'd never be able to hold his whores. "You mean she's your new bottom woman," I said to him.

"No, man, I already told you Rona is boss bitch. That's just my cuntsucking old lady."

"You mean you tied to her?"

Salem grinned like a sheep. "She's a jasper, you dig? I met her in Kansas City and she hadda get tied to stay outta jail on a lesbo charge. She gimme three hundred and we went to some justice of the peace. Then when I head for New York she come along, and she's got this little brat with her. I never split her, see? She's a virgin, least that's what she says. She's got this brat that's hers and she's a virgin. Yeah. Then last year the brat dies and she turns on the heavy shit. Now she bangs all she can get, which is only what I give her."

"Why you keep her?" I asked him.

"I got heart, man. Which besides, she's good luck for me. She don't bother my whores and she cooks and cleans for us."

"But she's a jasper."

"So what? So she don't turn no tricks for me. I don't spend that much on her, and she freaks out with the whores whenever they want her so it all works out. She's like a balloon, you know

219

what I mean? There ain't nothin' you can do with it, but you miss it when it blows away."

Sweet Willie was still standing over by the cross, looking up at her. "What's her name?"

"Mary, her name is Mary."

"Mary," Sweet Willie repeated. "And she's a virgin?"

"That's what she says. The brat was a miracle of God, she tells everybody." Salem smiled. "She sure could be a virgin for all I know."

"The Virgin Mary," Sweet Willie said softly.

"And she's hangin' up on that cross," Vergil said softly.

"Jesus Christ," I said loudly.

"Sonovabitch," Madison shouted. He jumped up from the easy chair. "Are we here for this lesbo bitch doing a junkie number or we here to find out what this pimp got to say?" He turned to Salem. "Now you was on the part where we get two hundred whores to Washington so's they meet all the big shots that run the gov'ment."

Salem's eyes got big. I could see he was really hyped on this thing. It sounded crazy to me. Even if you could get two hundred whores together enough to handle that kinda deal, it'd be too big to keep secret. Another thing, the bankroll to front it would hafta be big enough to fight a war. And who's gonna map out two hundred setups, all with cameras and tape machines and eyeball witnesses. But even if the whole crazy thing was pulled off, it still wouldn' do no good 'cause the CIA or one of them spy outfits'd knock off everybody in it. Nobody was gonna let a black pimp fuck up the country. That was white man's work. And anyway, those big shots in Washington knew more about pimping than Salem'd ever learn. The more I listened to his crazy idea, the more asshole it got.

Madison and Vergil were really leaning on Salem, getting him down to the details. He didn't like it. Sure, he knew where to get the whores. Where? Off the streets, where else? Yeah, he would do the picking. Didn't he think street hustlers'd be too low-down for all them big shots? Naw, the bigger they are, the blacker they like it. Then he was gonna use only black bitches?

Goddam right, that's what those colorless cuntsuckers in Washington need. What did he mean? You know, man, put a little color in your life, fuck a black bitch today. That kinda thing. Did he really think the two hundred top men in the country gonna suck after black ass? Sure, they white, ain't they? What about the bread, where's that gonna come from? From the black people 'cause we gonna sell shares in the gov'ment for when we take over. We'll get millions. You mean all the black people in this whole motherfuckin' country gonna know 'bout this? Not all of 'em, man, just those who buy tickets for the raffle. What raffle? The raffle we goin' run to see who wins General Motors. Awright, never mind that, but where was he gonna get two hundred men to work the cameras and stuff? Ahh, that was the best part of the plan. It'll only take one man. One man? Don't need no more, just one man with everything set up in one place. All the whores get a little card with a day and time stamped on it, and that's when they bring the tricks up. S'pose they can't make it when the card say? Then the whore get another card for a diff'rent time. How long did he figure the whole thing would take? If everything go right and the whores hump quick, ten days'd do it, workin' night and day. 'Course, some of them big-shot peckerwoods maybe can't get it up too fast from all that heavy mindfucking they been doing, so it might take a little more.

Madison and Vergil looked grim as I ever seen them. I didn't blame 'em. But Madison kept at it. Why you wanna pull this off, what's in it for you? Salem opened his eyes wide, trying to look innocent. That's a pigshit question, man, you know I'm always wantin' to help black folks. Madison give him a con smile. Listen, pimp, we all know you look out for yourself. Well, so do everybody. Okay, but why come on now with this crap? What crap? That you lookin' to help your own kind. It ain't crap. The hell it ain't, all you want is to get your paws on a big stable and some ready cash. If that's all I wanted, I'd be out there hustlin' right now. You inside here hustlin' right now and that's the only reason you not out there. That ain't true, man, I'm just trying to make things better for my people. Okay, you

221

straight as a goddam arrow. Why'd you call me in on this? 'Cause you the big Black Power man. Hell, you one of the first to start the whole thing, and you know everybody and can get things we need. What things? I need money so's I can pick the whores I want, and I need org'zation behind me. Then what? Then I train them a few weeks, send them down 'round Wall Street so they can see what the big-shot tricks smell like. What happens to the bread they make while they train? That go for expenses. Whose expenses? Look around you, man. This a big investment I got here and it takes a lotta money to keep it goin'. And when we take over, who's goin' be President? It's my idea, ain't it? A pimp for President? You got better now?

That's when Madison give up. Vergil asked a few more questions just for laughs and got Salem to admit the idea come to him in a dream. Sweet Willie tapped his head and said, "More like a nightmare."

But Salem was a good loser. He seen he couldn' get Madison to go 'long with him and he was prob'ly already thinking 'bout who to try next to suck in on his asshole idea. When we got ready to go, he walked us down and out. Even told us to come 'round whenever we wanted a good piece of ass. "I got it. You need it," he said, slamming the iron gate shut. Ftannng.

The Church of the Spirit World was closed for the night.

"Hot damn!" Madison shouted, walking away. "That shit-smellin' nigger is one crazy animal. He'd cross, double-cross and crisscross his own mother if he got the chance."

"He already done that," Sweet Willie said quietly.

"Done what?"

Sweet Willie lifted his eyes up. "The Virgin Mary."

"She ain't his mother," Vergil said quickly. "She just his old lady."

"And it's not even sure she's a virgin," I added.

Madison looked at us. "You niggers is all crazy. The only spirits he got 'round there is what comes outta the bottle when he has them bad dreams."

222

17.

SUNNY is in love with a preacher. She walked out of her place with the four locks on the door and the Judas-hole in the middle to come over here and tell me that.

"He's beautiful, Marcus. He's the most beautiful man I've ever met."

"And you love him."

"That's what I feel." She curled up on the daybed, fixing a spot for me to sit beside her. "It's like I'm stoned all the time."

"How long you been in love with this preacher?"

"Since I met him yesterday."

Sunny's like that. She falls in love real easy. Which is okay for her 'cause she falls outta love even more easy. Minute she tells a man she loves him for real, he's already on his way out. 'Course it's not love with her, just that she gets carried 'way with her likes and it takes a week or so for her to get calm down. In the year I know her, Sunny been in fake love maybe four, five times. Always the same, like a whisky hangover it don't mean nothin' once it's over.

Sunny never told me she really loves me and I never told her nothing like that. But we got this heavy thing goin' on and I think we know a lot we don't talk about.

But she sure was one great lookin' fox, sitting there with her long legs folded back and her little ass plump in the middle of that beat-up bed. She looked better sitting than most fox do standing. Her long blond hair fell all 'round her face and she kept brushing it back with one hand. She had on this little blue dress that somehow made her skin even whiter than white.

223

I sat there thinking maybe we'd go to the Apollo or something. Anything to get outta the house for a while on a hot summer night.

"Marcus?"

"Umm."

"Would you do me a favor?"

"I might," I said to her, "if I knew what it was."

She squeezed my hand. "Would you go with me to hear him tonight? His name is Bishop Brown and he's really very good."

I didn't answer her right off. She knew I didn't wanna meet any of her one-week loves, it just wasn't none of my business. But every time she was in fake love she asked me the same thing. Would I meet them? And every time I'd tell her no. I think after a while she just asked me outta habit.

But this time I was gonna surprise her. I ain't had a good laugh in a while and a religion grifter was a much better show than anything at the Apollo nine times outta ten.

"Sure, I go with you," I said to Sunny. "Maybe it's 'bout time I was gettin' saved again. Saved from staying here in this oven all night."

She blinked a few times to make sure I wasn't woofin' her, then she threw her arms around me and we fell back on the bed. "Oh, Marcus Black, I just love you to ruin."

"Whose ruin you talkin' about?" I asked her. And we both laughed.

After a while Sunny took off her dress and I got outta my shirt and pants and we just laid there, high on the kick of white and black. She put her leg across mine and it was cool and warm, cold and hot, ice and fire. I was coal black and she was snow white. Dark and light, night and day. And somewhere between we made love, stretching our bodies across a secret world that was turned on only for us.

By the time we come back the earth was dark. I reached out for the lamp by the bed and knocked over a empty wine bottle. Then the lamp fell off the table.

"Goddam."

224

Sunny was laughing.

"What's so funny, little Miss Whiteass?"

"You are, 'cause you're a man and all men are just little boys and all little boys are funny."

"Ain't funny in bed, woman."

"Ain't supposed to be funny in bed. Just the rest of the time."

I picked up the lamp and snapped it on. The light made everything orange. We looked just like any two people again. Funny orange people.

"What time is your preacher goin' on?"

Sunny jumped up. "Help, my preacher. I forgot all about him." She looked at me. "Goddam, Marcus, it's your fault."

It was my turn to laugh.

"I see nothing funny in you keepin' me from my loved one," she said to me.

"I ain't keepin' you," I told her. "It was that little girl diddlin' with that little boy that done it."

Then she started laughing too. "I guess maybe you got a point there. No use crying over spilled juice."

We dressed fast and were on the street in a few minutes. She wanted a cab and she had the money so we got a cab. Sunny never has no trouble gettin' a cab in Harlem. Any blood'd stop for a white fox like that, hoping maybe they could get a taste.

We got there just in time. Just in time to be told by the flunky that it was a full house and he was locking the doors. Then he took off his night shades to wipe his face and he seen that Sunny was a white woman. I watched the wheels in his head. He looked to be a Southern boy and you don't say no to a white woman. 'Specially for something like religion and all that kinda mess.

He let us in. Then he quick banged the doors shut so no more white devils come 'round.

But he was right 'bout it being full up. Looked like most every seat was took. The Central Theater was a small place that usta have live shows long time ago. Maybe five hundred people could squeeze themselfs in and that was it. They were squeezed for Bishop Brown awright, so that meant he must put on a good show.

We walked down one side and got two seats all the way up 'gainst the wall, and a few minutes later Bishop Brown walked out on the stage. He had on looked like a velvet suit with gold on the ends of the sleeves. And more gold on his shirt front and big diamond rings on his fingers. I seen all that and right away I knew he was right to be in a theater 'cause he already give the people a show just by coming out on that motherfuckin' stage like that.

"I could just as easy be somewhere else," he said when everybody got quiet. "I got a big house, a big boat and all good clothes. And I ride around in a big Cadillac." He made the word sound like it was one of them big airplanes. "I come here 'cause God told me I must help them who need help. That means you and you and you. All of you. And I'm gonna stay here long as God tells me to." And he looked at his gold watch.

When he done that I figured God was gonna tell him to get the hell off there in about a hour and a half.

"Wherever I am, I don't let sin in. If you got strife in your life I'll help you. If you got mud in your blood I'll help you. Yeah. And if you got a hole in your soul I'll take care of that too."

He waited for the laughing and shouting to finish.

"I'm gonna get husbands back to their wives. I'm gonna get children back to their homes. I'm gonna firm up your friends and fix your enemies. If any woman needs a man, you'll get one. If any man needs a woman, you'll get one. If you got worms in your head or snakes in your belly, I'm gonna get rid of them for you. If you got worries, I'll set your mind to rest. I'm gonna help the old be young and the crooked be straight."

"That the way, Bishop."

"Now I'm hearing from a lot of you people that you've been here and been there, and you listened to this one and that one, and nothing worked. Nothing worked 'cause wasn't nothing *supposed* to work. Because you didn't go to God. Only God can

226

give you what you need. Only God can take away what you fear. So all these other people you been goin' to couldn' really help you. Those who have been truly doing God's work, who have the *power* from God, are not hanging around. We are out doing business. Just like I'm doing now."

"We hear you, Bishop."

"And the very first business we got is helping God's chosen prophet. God works on love and I work on love but all the people who don't follow God, they don't know about love. They only know about money, and until God shows them the way of love we gotta pay them for all the things we need. So open up your hearts to God, and let God hear them purses and pocketbooks open up too. Fish out all that small change, all them fold-up tiny bills, and let's hear it for God."

Man, I'm ready to pull out fuckin' Fort Knox if I had it in my pocket, just to pay off those moneyfuckers who don't know 'bout God's love. My hand is in my pocket 'fore I catch myself.

"While my assistants walk among you for the collection, we're all gonna sing a song praising the glory of God."

And sure enough, while these three young sisters were scooping up all the loose loot, the Bishop was up there whippin' off a song with everybody join in and a organ playing from somewhere. The singing went on a second time 'cause the collection wasn't done. Minute the collection was over, the singing was over. And so was the organ.

"Ain't he beautiful, Marcus?"

I was so shook up I forgot all about Sunny sittin' there next to me. I put on a big smile for her. "Yeah, he sure is a beautiful something awright," I said to her.

I didn't tell her a beautiful what.

Up on the stage the beautiful what was ready to roll on, now that the small stuff was cleaned up. He mopped his forehead with a little white hank'chief. I didn't see any gold in it.

He hushed the people. "Now I'm gonna begin by telling you a secret. In this life you are supposed to have everything you want. That's right. Regardless what it is, you're supposed to have it. Love, marriage, money, health, whatever you want.

227

Then why don't you got it all? 'Cause you ain't straight. 'Cause you doing wrong. 'Cause you not working with God. Now you ask yourself this: Why is something always happening to me? Why am I all crossed up? Why do I have unnatural sickness? Why are evil spells on me? Why can't I hold money? Why do I have no friends? Why do I have no love? Be honest with yourself. Ask yourself them questions and then think of all the money you spent going one place to another, getting help, getting advice, getting guarantees. But nothing worked. All the getting you got was getting took. You still got love problems. You still got money problems. You still got worry problems. There's only one thing to do. Stop wasting your money! If you don't go to God's Right Hand you won't get results. God works His power in ways of mystery. In secret ways, and God Himself give me the secret power of those mysteries. I got the method. I got the remedy. I got the Right Hand of God. And it's guaranteed!

"You want results and that's why you're here tonight. You know I can succeed where others failed. You know I can uncross you. You know I can set things straight for you. I've been all over the world perfecting my method. The wisdom of Egypt, the mysteries of Africa and India, the secrets of the Deep South. Jamaica and Haiti too. My method works every time 'cause it's God's way. I been chosen by God to be His Right Hand to help thousands of people who need the Spirit of release in them. That's what I been doing and that's what I'm gonna keep doing. I'm gonna work my power to satisfy everyone here tonight. I'm gonna reveal the evil eyes and hidden dangers that could harm you. God wants me to do this and I always do what He wants."

He was good awright, wasn't no way around that. Ain't nothin' but a Southern spiritualist can bring out that old black magic like he was doing. He had them people eating outta God's Right Hand.

"Now you wanna know what my power can do for you. It can make you healthy and wealthy, that's what it can do for you. It can bring back loved ones, remove crossed conditions and stop enemies. Ain't nothing it can't do. Heart pains, head pains, back pains, leg pains. I've helped them all. Bed sores, head sores, white spots, black spots. That too. I can turn bad luck into good luck."

"Do it."

"Stop you from drinking and gambling."

"Do it."

"Remove crazy spells from your body."

"Do it."

"Move evil spirits from your home."

"Do it."

"Bring loved ones back to you."

"Do it."

"Stop that woman from messing 'round your man."

"Do it."

"Stop that man from messing 'round your woman."

"Do it."

"Reduce you if you're too fat."

"Do it."

"Beef you up if you got skinny spots."

"Do it."

"Make your enemies give you up."

"Do it."

"Make your boss give you a raise."

"Do it."

"Give a man back his manpower."

"Do it."

"Give a woman back her juices."

"Do it."

"Yeah, and if all that ain't enough I'll even stop your boy or girl from being a dope addict. Now how you like that?"

Everybody cheered.

"How am I gonna do all this? With God's help, that's how. With the power God give me to help people and see them straight. Divine power is what it is. Jesus Power is what it is. That can bring you peace of mind and make your dreams come true. Jesus wants you to be happy. Ain't nothin' Jesus won't do if you put yourself in His hands. Jesus gonna give you a lucky hand and lots of friends and anything you want. But you gotta work for Jesus Power. You gotta sweat for Jesus Power. You gotta feel Jesus Power all around you. That's what I'm saying. *Feel Jesus.*"

A dozen women screamed. I quick turned all 'round to see what the hell was goin' on. But I already knew. They were outta their seats all over the place, feeling Jesus. They were outta their heads too, 'cause Jesus was in 'em. They moaned, they screamed, they fell on the floor. They bent their legs, they raised their arms, they jerked their bodies. They were feelin' Jesus all over them, on top of them, inside of them. Jesus was coming, Jesus was coming. Do it, do it, do it, Jesus. One woman near me was so into it, she was on the ground jacking Jesus off. That's just what it looked like. Her fists were goin' up and down, faster and faster. Her head was goin' back and forth. Her eyes were closed and she was crying out for Jesus to come to her. Another woman was laying on the ground huffing and puffing like Jesus already come to her. And almos' everybody was howlin' and hummin', shoutin' and singing, stompin' their feet and clappin' their hands.

I looked over at Sunny. She was feeling Jesus too. I know 'cause she put her hand on my rig and it jumped up musta been about a foot. Jesus Power!

After everybody got calm down and things were a little peaceful again, we had more singing and shouting. Then it was testimony time.

"Sure as sin, all things are possible. There was a woman come to me not long ago whose husband was in jail for twenty-two years. I told her I'd get fast results for her. That woman come back to me two weeks later, her husband was outta jail and got himself a good job and they were gonna buy a new car. She was so happy she was in tears, thanking me for what I all done.

"There was another woman whose son was hanging 'round with evil companions and she was worried he'd get in trouble. I told her I'd help her. Inside a month that boy was doing his

230

homework every night and was gonna be a minister when he got outta school. That's right.

"And a man asked me to do something 'bout his wife runnin' around with some other man. When I got done, the only thing that woman was running 'round with was a cold.

"Uh-huh, that's awright. A man wanted me to help him give up the whisky he been on for forty years. I used the power and now all he drinks is skim milk. And somebody else come to me way down on his luck and 'fore I was through with him, he had a job so big he couldn' even tell me about it. That's what happens when I go to work. Things start to move, sometimes fast and sometimes only half fast. No one can hurry God, not even me. But He always listens to His Right Hand.

"A man called me on Wednesday, and Thursday he bought himself a Cadillac. Another man called me about his wife missing for fourteen years, and two hours later she was home. Same day a woman called me she won thirty thousand dollars.

"Here's a letter from a woman who says, 'I want to thank you for what you done for me. Another woman took my husband and told me wasn't nothing I could do. I just knew I was goin' die right there. Then I asked you to uncross me. Now I am happy more than I ever been in my whole life. My husband is home sometimes. You are the one done everything'

"And a letter from a man who writes, 'Keep on with your great work you are doing. Everybody loves you. I had a business I lost through drink, and a wife too. I even took pills all the time to kill myself but they didn't work. That's when I come to you. I don't know what all you did but it sure was powerful. I have not had a pill in months. And even my drinking is better. If anybody need to get straight, you are what they should do.'

"That's just a few of the hundreds of letters I get every day from people who get straight for life when I change their luck. If you have faith you'll be helped. If you have trust you'll be helped. That's God's way."

I listened to him talk about that faith and trust. Sounded to me like he was leaving out the last part. If you have money you'll be took. God's way.

231

Sunny leaned my way. "It's almost over."

"What you mean, almost?"

She didn't like that. "There's the big collection at the end. Bishop Brown has to live, you know."

I wasn't gonna ask her why.

The Bishop held up his hand. "We all have enemies. Even God has an enemy. The devil. But our enemies can't hurt us long as what we got is stronger'n what they got. I know a lot of you are using things like witch's incense and the black candles and cat oil and the dolls and all that mess. Forget 'em. Only thing that works to get rid of your enemies is what I got from God. And that's what I'm tellin' all you people tonight. You give all you can, then God gonna come to you. And your enemies better watch out.

"I want all of you to come up to the front at the end of the service to make your offering. The more you give, the more you get. God's help comes in all sizes. If you give big enough, your enemies gonna head for the moon."

"How 'bout just outta town?" someone shouted.

Everybody laughed.

"God go more places than the Greyhound bus," said the Bishop.

Everybody laughed some more.

Then after the last song singing and word shouting of the night, the service was over.

'Cept for the offering.

I watched the people file up to the front, hundreds of them moving slow, waiting to shuck Bishop Brown's hand or maybe catch a piece of his smile. And to load up on that God's Right Hand. They were mostly women and they were holding their offerings in their hands. It was all green stuff.

Sunny was gonna wait for the Bishop to finish up takin' care of God's business. Looked to me like it was goin' take a spell of time.

"Would you like to meet him?" she asked me.

I told her I wasn't 'specially fixed on meeting with him.

"Why not?"

I didn't rightly know how to answer that. This Bishop Brown was one of the best jive ass niggers I ever heard. And he was as slick a con man as I ever seen, he deserved all the money he was stealing. But there was something wrong about him. Maybe it was all that gold he had on, or maybe just he was so good at it, who could like him?

I looked at Sunny, not wanting to say nothing. Then just like that I knew what was wrong. He was stealing from his own people 'stead of Sunny's people. White people.

Only a mad-dog animal rips off his own.

"I see you later," I said to Sunny. And I quick walked on out, past all the poor brothers and sisters who hadda pay for God to come to them.

18.

BILLY DAVIS come home from Vietnam today. We buried him in Frederick Douglass Cem'tery in the coffin he come home in. It was closed all the time 'cause Billy got all shot up and nobody could see him. His mother was sitting in the funeral parlor next to that strange coffin and she didn't even know for sure if Billy was in it. Nobody knew. And in the cem'tery they couldn' find where we were s'pose to go, and then when they found it some men were still working on the grave and everybody hadda wait till they finished. Billy's mother just sat there with the coffin in front of her like in the funeral parlor. She didn't cry the whole time 'cause she used up all her cries when they told her he was dead. Two soldiers with white hats come to her house. When she opened the door and seen them, she screamed, "I knew it, I knew it," and she fainted dead away. Billy's older brother was home and it took him a long time to get his mother to wake up. Then she sat at the kitchen table and cried all night. "It was awful," he told us later. "She'd sit there calling out Billy's name and wasn't nothin' I could do to help her. Wasn't nothin' nobody could do. He was dead and she didn't even know why. I think that's what got her. Billy was dead and nobody could even tell her why."

Billy Davis was only nineteen years old. Just a kid. When he got drafted he was glad 'cause he figured the Army gives the black man a better deal. He read somewhere that they don't care what color you are long's you can do the job. Some of us asked him how that could be if the Army's full of white men same as in the rest of the country. He didn't know and he didn't care. The Army was gonna give him good food and clothes and teach him a job.

"They teach you to kill too," Kranko told him.

Billy didn't care about that either. Killing ain't nothing new when you been running the Harlem streets all your life. By the time you get nineteen you been 'round it too much to care.

"What you goin' do if they send you to Vietnam?" I asked him once.

"Do just what I gotta do to stay 'live," he said.

Before he left, his brother Mike took him to one of them things where they tell you how to stay outta the Army. Mike was against the war. He'd go around saying things like the Vietnam people were our brothers 'cause they were not white, and that's why America was trying to kill them off. And he was in some org'zation that went around marching and fighting for peace.

But Billy didn't see what Mike was into. He was young and full of piss and ready to take on anybody. When you nineteen you never think you can get wasted, it's always the other dude goin' get it. So at the antidraft place Mike took him to, Billy just listened to them and then he called them all a bunch of faggot punks and he walked out.

But when he got to Vietnam he wrote Mike that a lotta women and kids were gettin' knocked off and he didn't like the Army no more. And one time he said a buddy of his was with a

234

outfit that wiped out a whole town. Killed off everybody, kids, dogs, everything. He told Mike he was goin' be exter careful so's he got out alive.

The last letter Billy sent home he had less'n a month to go in Vietnam, then it was all over for him. His mother got the letter a few days before the two Army men come to her door to tell her Billy was coming home for good and forever.

"Her heart turn to stone 'gainst this country," Mike said to me. "She don't wanna know nothin' about what's goin' on no more. She give up on this country, that's just what she done."

Just like a couple million other blacks already done.

But I don't know one stud who liked it in Vietnam. They all glad to get out. Kranko was over there, he was in and out 'fore Billy was even in. "It's so motherfuckin' bad you wouldn' believe it 'less you see it," he told us when he come back. "Them people are being killed back to the Stone Age, like in this picture I seen where they all live in caves. That's just what it's gonna be like. Everybody living in caves."

Almos' all the American soldiers in Vietnam smoke the weed, Kranko told us. They gotta or they go crazy from all they see and do. And sometimes when they get stoned high, they play this game where they make a big circle, with their arms 'round the shoulders of the men on each side. Then somebody lights a stick of dynamite and puts it in the center of the circle. The first man to pull out is the loser.

Nobody wants to be the loser 'cause you get marked a punk that can't take it. So a lotta heads and faces and arms get blasted off. And then everybody says no more. Till the next time.

The game is called Blast Off.

And the Vietnam soldiers that are on the same side, when they get some of them other Vietnam from the other side, they'd put jars of gasoline on their heads. Then they'd shoot at the jar like they were at Coney Island. But they didn't always hit it. And sometimes when they'd hit it and the gas'd spill over the pris'ner, they'd fire up the gas and burn him alive. Just like what the white man always done to black people in the South, like what they done to my uncle Ben the night I got born.

235

"I'd never go there no more," Kranko told us when he come back. "They'd hafta kill me first, and then I still wouldn' go."

That was 'bout the time I read where this Army dude said they hadda kill some town in order to save it. That's just what he said in the papers. I checked to make sure I wasn't reading the comics but it was right there in the news big as life.

Then I remembered when I was in Florida years 'go I was goin' down to that Key West on the bus and we passed this big Air Force base. Homestead Air Force Base is what it was called. And on the front of it was a great big sign. OUR BUSINESS IS PEACE. I never forget that. OUR BUSINESS IS PEACE.

Somebody's doing a number on somebody awright.

I didn't go in the Army 'cause I was a yardbird and ten years ago they didn't want them. But I sure didn't miss it none. If I was nineteen now and I hadda go in, I wouldn' do it. Not for nobody. And I wouldn't go to no jail neither, I ain't never goin' back to that. I'd get outta the country is what I'd do, go to Canada or somewhere like that. This war don't make no sense to me. I listen to the big shots say we fighting this war so the Vietnam people can live like us. But who the fuck *wants* to live like us? I mean, some of us are ready to fight right here so we can live like other people somewhere else.

What I think it is, is the white man in America is a killer. A born killer. He been killing off the black man for near four hundred years. Now we don't let him kill us so easy no more, so he's gotta get some other people to kill. All they gotta be is not white. The Vietnam people are yella so they okay. After he kills 'em off maybe it'll be brown people or red or even purple people if he can find any. That's what I think this war is all about. Just that the crazy killer white man gotta have somebody to kill off all the time.

Any black man that fights in this white man's war has gotta be so whacked off he don't know he's in a country that's got a army of killers and a po-lice of pigs. Either that or he's really just a white man with a paint job and a burr head.

But there's one good thing about the white man's war. When

236

all the brothers come home there's gonna be a lotta men who know how to kill fast and blow things up and hit and run. Gorilla war. When a pig goes to beat them over the head, it'll be the last thing he ever do. And when they get cheated by some gyp store or fired from a job for no reason or not hired for the same no reason, they be ready to take care of that too. Like Kranko can kill a man with no noise in a few seconds, and he knows how to make bombs that can pull a building down. And I know other brothers who are crack snipers and can drive tanks and lay mines. And they all know about gorilla war 'cause they been in it. When the real war comes they gonna shut down a city just like that. Block by block, street by street, house by house. It'd take a army to go after them, least one in every city. That's a lotta armies. Yeah. Gorilla war.

A few years back there was a picture come out called *The Battle of Algiers*. Every blood in Harlem went to see it. Every blood with balls in the whole country went to see it. It was about gorilla war in this place Algeria and how the people knocked off the French who was like the white man here. King Shit. But they done it. They done it by killing so many French they give up and went home. And the picture showed how the people done it right in the big city.

That picture is the bible of the black man's fight in this country, the blood's bible. *The Battle of Algiers*. The Battle of America.

It showed some of the things to do. Like where the Algiers' women hid bombs under their clothes and took their little kids for a walk so nobody'd think nothing. Then they put the bombs in buildings and stores and like that. 'Course that wouldn' work too good here 'cause the motherfuck whites'd just shoot the women and kids. But the brothers'd find what things work. What the picture showed was it could be done. Somebody done it. Goddam, there's hope. If they done it, we can do it 'cause we gotta be smarter'n they are. We're Americans, ain't we? Don't that make us the best there is?

Somethin' like that is what them Vietcong are doing right

237

now. They trying to get the white man off their back and outta their country. They smiling and bowing, then, zap, they blow you up. Only way to do it. Yassuh them dead.

About three years ago a kid 'cross the street got hisself a five-dollar rifle and went up to the roof and started shootin' at the trains that go through Harlem taking all them whitey big shots home to their plastic houses. Bang. He was hitting 'em as the train pulled into the 125th Street station. Bang. Bang. He musta got least ten 'fore he give up. He didn't have no bullets in the gun, he was just play acting. But it showed what could be done with one gun in the right place. He coulda held off a army. The kid was gonna stay up there all day banging away at Mister Whiteface but his older brother Mike found him and got pissed off. He told the kid to get the hell off the roof with the rifle. "You too young to fool 'round with guns, Billy. The white man see you he goin' blow your fool head off."

Mike was right. Billy Davis hadda wait least another year or two 'fore he was old enough for the white man to give him a gun to get his fool head blowed off.

19.

TIGER is a Black Panther. I know Tiger five, six years now, since before I even lived downtown in that East Village. He's a good man, very strong in the head. He wants everybody to be free but mostly he wants to be free hisself.

Tiger don't think the black man is free in this country. That's what he told me one time, like he was just finding it out. "We ain't got no slack in this motherfuck country 'cause the man still thinks of us as slaves." I just looked at him. "No shit" was all I could think to say. I mean, I was living here same as him. Wasn't that I just come in from the moon or something. Plus which, my skin's much darker'n his.

Last year Tiger joined up with the Panthers. He liked the idea of the guns and all that revolution jive them dudes hand out. He become a member and then he become a big drag.

"Man, how can you listen to all that jive ass talk?" I'd say to him.

"What you talkin' about, you dumb nigger? The Panthers is the only ones picked up the gun 'gainst the cuntsuckers."

"Sure they picked up the gun. So now everybody knows about them. Big fuckin' deal. But what's that doing for the nigger in the street, eh? Tell me that. What they doing to help his ass?" Then I'd really get after him. "I'll tell you what they doing. They talk big about blowin' the white man down but they can't even blow anything up. Their leaders mostly been knocked off or sent up. The only fightin' they do is if a TV camera is there, then they fight to see who gets out front first. They ripping off the money and they ripping off the fox but they couldn' rip off a fuckin' fence."

"You know, man, you know you talk just like the black boogies."

"Black boogies!" Now I'm mad. "Look 'round you, motherfuck. Do it look like I got big things? Do I got a suit job or drive 'round in a big car or own a big house? I come off the streets, you jive nigger, and I still ain't got outta the gutter. I been in the slammers longer'n you been awake. But least with all the nothin' I got somethin' you don't got. I got a head that thinks for itself and knows when it's been fucked, sucked and cold ducked."

"Man, if you were in the Panthers we'd throw you right out on your lily-white ass."

I don't say nothing 'bout the white ass 'cause Tiger know I got the blackest ass clear to Africa. I just smile at him. "If I was in the Panthers, they wouldn' be making a big show outta everything they do. And they wouldn' be fuckin' around in no bullshit revolution neither."

"Bullshit revolution!" Tiger'd scream.

"That's what I say, man. Bullshit fuckin' revolution is where they at, with their plastic jackets and their plastic boots and

239

their plastic heads. They get in trouble and they hide behind white law, they take money from the whites they badmouth, they can't even stay 'way from the white pussy. And every time they get hit, they run to the papers to make sure everyone know about it. 'Stead of waitin' like a real panther'd do, and then striking back."

Tiger'd shake his head in disgust. "You too fuckin' independent is your trouble, man."

"That's right, man. I think for myself. Goddam right. Why you think Malcolm got hisself knocked off like that? 'Cause he wouldn' take the shit a lotta them cop-outs was laying on him. He knew most of the people 'round him were gettin' a rake-off from the man. Anybody dealing with the man is gettin' it from somewhere."

"If Malcolm was around now, he'd be a Panther."

"Paper tigers," I'd say to him.

Then he'd give up. That was too much. "Fuck you," he'd say. And look 'round the bar for stray fox.

"Paper fuckin' tigers is all they are." And I'd take another drink.

That's just the way it'd go every time we talked 'bout them. Tiger was really hyped on 'em and he couldn' see what I was dealing. Sure I liked a lot of what they were into, but there was a lotta big things wrong. Like I told him real revolution people are the ones you never see and don't know nothin' about. They hide and then they strike and then they hide again. That's the only way when you dealing with cities and pigs and all. These people he was with, they were just playing games.

And which is the truth. They go 'round talkin' about killing the country. Like I heard this one Panther big shot. Somebody asked him what they do. "We advocate the very direct overthrow of the government by way of force and violence. By picking up guns and moving against it. We know the only solution to it is armed struggle." That's just what he said. 'Course, there was a lotta reporters and every other goddam thing around or he'd never say it. No sense keeping nothin' secret in a revolution.

240

Then when the pigs kill 'em off, they cry out for law and order. And they want justice. Yeah. Can you beat that? They living here and they call the enemy out, then when he hits them, they cry for justice. If they had any motherwit they'd know ain't no justice for a black man in a white country. Never was, never will be. That shows how fake they are. Long as they look for justice and talk about justice they ain't give up on this country, no matter how much they use the word revolution.

I wouldn' trust any of them with my sister's black cat's fuckin' black tail.

When they first come they had this idea, they followed behind the pig patrols to see they didn't shoot up the black people. And they done a good job too. It got so good some pigs wanted to quit 'cause they wasn't getting to kill all the blacks was promised them when they become a pig.

But then them Panthers started smelling white money. And 'fore you could fuck a duck they were into the whole white-guilt thing. What they found was a motherfucking guilt mine. The whites with the money felt so guilty 'bout it they needed to get they asses kicked. And they'd pay for it too. So the Panthers got after them and hung their asses off the wall. And the white-fuckers loved it. They creamed in their pants behind it all, and they couldn' get enough of it. And the Panthers were riding high.

But then the whites got tired of them and moved on to other things, like them sneaky fuckers always do, and the Panthers got stuck with the whole bag. The word went out that white money ain't behind them no more. The pigs heard the word 'cause they always got their ears open, 'long with everything else. And that's when they picked up the guns for real. It was open season on Panther ass.

Fuck 'em all. I got nothin' for them. NAACP, that Urban League, the Panthers. They all the same. One talks law, one talks jobs, one talks guns. All the same. All talk. I could show them some men right here in Harlem who know what revolution is. They know so much about it they got no time for talk.

I had one stud tell me that things like the Panthers get

241

money from the whites 'cause they use up all the hate in the people that way, and then nobody does nothin'. "But we goin' kill off the whites, anyway," this stud said to me. And he meant it too.

I don't wanna kill all the whites, just those I meet that hate me 'cause I'm black. 'Course, if I live long enough that's gonna be all the whites.

Couple months back, me and Tiger and the Lemon Drop Kid were at this gig and there was some Panthers there. Only they were not in uniform, they had their hats off. One of them was a big shot, a general or something. Everybody was feelin' good, but this general dude was really laying down some heavy shit 'bout how bad things was. But nobody wanted to hear it 'cause we knew it all. I mean, we were living it every day.

Now the Lemon Drop Kid don't know he's black, he just thinks all us niggers are a darker shade of pale. And he went over to the general dude and told him he wanted to join up. He was really stoned out of it by that time. I'm standing there with my ear open 'cause I know the Kid when he gets started on somebody. He don't let loose.

The Panther general looked at the Lemon Drop Kid. "You sure are lemon colored. Your people musta been some of them house niggers."

The Lemon Drop Kid don't like that. "That's right," he said, "so if I join up you can be called the Lemon Panthers."

The general's eyes folded just 'bout when I walked on over. "Been lookin' for you, man. You awright?"

"Sure thing, man. I'm just tellin' this here sergeant—"

"Easy, man."

"—that if I join up with them they could be the Lemon Panthers. Only he don't like my idea."

"Maybe he don't like lemons," I said. Just trying to be playful-like.

"Yeah, that could be." He scratched his head. "Hey, I know. How 'bout we call it the Yella Panthers?"

The general turned to me. "If you don't get this shit-colored motherfuck outta here, his ass goin' be off the wall."

242

I seen he was about ready to pull out his mouth and shoot up the joint so I got the Lemon Drop Kid out fast.

Tiger didn't talk to us for about a week 'cause he said we made him look bad.

"How you make that out?" I asked him. "Just 'cause the Kid was goofing on him don't mean that Panther dude was mad at us."

"What you mean, not mad? He was so mad he left without makin' a speech."

"Tell me this," I said to him, "tell me this. Did he leave without makin' some pussy too?"

Tiger hadda laugh at that. "You coal black niggers all think you King Kong, you know that?"

I looked that Tiger straight in his lemon-colored eyes. "Us bottom niggers are very common, 'part from the fact that we are very special."

Wasn't nothin' he could say to that neither.

20.

Johnny Romero don't burn no coal.

I don't know if he ever had a black piece of ass in his whole life. He's one big chalk eater. All I ever seen him with was white fox, all anyone ever seen him with. He's been through so much chalk, when he walks down the street everybody calls him the blackboard man. Here come the big blackboard man, they all say.

And that's what always got him in trouble too. He been run outta towns and shot at by fathers and beat up by husbands. Then about four years 'go he really hit the big-time trouble. He was runnin' a bar downtown somewhere in the Italian 'hood, and one day in walked this fan-fuckingtastic fox. Long blond hair and soul eyes and suck mouth, she had everything

243

goin' for her. She looked maybe eighteen and Swedish. I seen her a few times, she was tall and heavy hung and just a outasight kid.

She took one look at Johnny Romero and creamed in her crotch. They were suck fucking by midnight. And every noon, night and midnight after that. Every morning too, that the kid could get outta school. There was a little garden in back of the bar and she'd sit out there with him, eating him up with her eyes. It went like that for a month, two months, and a lotta people were hip to it.

Then the shit hit. The kid looked eighteen and Swedish but she was sixteen and Italian. If Johnny knew she was only sixteen it didn't matter none. Only thing counted was her father was a big shot in the Mafia. One Sunday night two shooters walked into the bar and give him a short message. "Get outta town before morning." That's all they said.

They didn't need to say no more. Johnny Romero had been around. By Monday morning he was on a plane for Porto Rico. Later that day his place was busted open and wrecked, if he'd still been there he woulda been wrecked too. The next few weeks everybody asked where he went, but anybody knew the scene didn't hafta ask. They knew a Mafia man said, "No nigger fucks my kid." And sent the word out. Only reason Johnny didn't get hisself killed off right there was 'cause he had friends in the Mafia too.

He stayed outta the country a couple years, till some shooter friends told him it was okay to come back, just stay 'way from downtown. By then the kid was tied up safe to somebody worked for a Mafia front. But it didn't mean nothin' to Johnny Romero, she was just another piece of cake to him. Soon's he hit town he was heavy into white foxhunts again, just like old times.

'Bout the time he come back I was into something outasight myself. Wynona Goodbody. She had a cat that hummed like a canary. A tall dark choc'late-skinned woman with melon jugs and apple ass and a cat that hummed. I'd be stroking that cat and I'd hear this hum. I'd put my ear there to make sure.

244

Hmmm-hmm. Outasight. That was the only woman I ever went down on with my ear. Wynona Goodbody.

We been humming around for five, six months when she met Johnny Romero. We were at one of them circus love things where everybody fucks everybody. Soon's we walk in and take our clothes off, this fox comes up and gives us a little card. I read it. "Please don't exhibit false modesty and pretend not to be looking when a groovy couple are fucking and sucking at your feet. Watching others do it is part of the fun, and we're all voyeurs and exhibitionists both. So let's have fun."

I look down at my feet. There's two people on the floor looking up at me.

I give them the card so they know what they should be doing. When I move away they start reading.

Everybody's after Wynona. She got a great body with smiles all over it. But she don't flash on nobody, she mostly goes just to get a high and maybe have some stud eat on her. And it's good for her job to know what's goin' on in sex 'cause she's a actress.

After a while we get over to the table for a drink and Wynona spots Johnny Romero, lookin' good with some white fox on his rig.

"What's that?" Wynona asks me in that soft scream she got. "He is one gorgeous man."

"That's one gorgeous man you don't wanna deal with," I tell her.

"What you mean?"

"Just what I say. You got nothin' for him. He don't burn no coal."

And what I'm tellin' her is true. But Wynona don't believe that. She don't believe any stud can stay outta her cat once they see her. So we go over and I introduce her and we stand there rapping and laughing and feeling good and Wynona is lookin' at Johnny Romero with soulfuck eyes and her ass is smiling and her cat is humming and nothing is happening.

To Johnny Romero she was just a choc'late bar and he eats nothing but cheesecake.

245

She done everything but stick his rig inside her. No good. He wanted no part of her. She told him she'd get a skin bleach. He told her she's too dark. She told him she'd wear goose feathers all over her body. He told her he's not a birdfucker. She told him to keep his eyes closed around her. He told her they already were closed.

She told him to fuck off.

He told her to let go of his rig.

After he hit her after she called him a fag, we were told to leave. On the way out I told somebody nobody fucked at my feet.

"Maybe your toes were dirty."

When we got home Wynona was so mad her cat was barking. She kept walking up and down.

"That nigger goin' be one sorry nigger. Oh, how could he be so black blind? Didn't he see what all I got?"

"He seen you."

"Well?"

"Well, what?"

"Well, why didn't he grab me?"

"He didn't grab you 'cause he don't go for the dark meat. He's strictly a light-meat man. I told you that."

Now there's one thing about Wynona. She hates white. She just don't have nothin' to do with white, least when I knew her. She never let any white studs near her that I ever seen. So it hit her double hard that Johnny Romero who was hisself deep black would pass her by for anything white. She just couldn' get over it.

I'm a switch fucker myself so I couldn' see what all the nigger noise was about. But I didn't say nothin'.

"I'm gonna even him up if it's the last thing I do. Goddam, I just hate a man who'd stoop so low he'd fuck an animal. Ain't there some kinda law 'gainst that? Ain't that like fucking a sheep? Well, ain't it?"

There wasn't nothin' I wanted to say to that.

"Goddam it, Marcus. You hear me? Ain't he doing something wrong?"

246

I just kept on cleaning my toes. And keeping my nose clean.

The next couple months Wynona tried a dozen tricks to get Johnny Romero to juice her. She sent him presents, followed him around, even got some crazy doctor to sign a paper saying her blackness was just a skin condition and she was really white.

Nothing worked.

She finally give up after she sent him a painting someone done of her all naked. And he sent it back without the frame, which was white.

When she got him busted on the rape charge, he was out in three hours and the po-lice said she oughtta be in a hospital for wishful thinking.

"I'm wore out" was all she said.

And the big black war was over.

Which was too bad, 'cause Wynona and Johnny Romero woulda made a good two. If they could only made it with each other.

That's just what I told her one time. "You and Johnny Romero were made for each other," I said to her.

"Me and who?"

"Johnny Romero."

"I don't know nobody with that name. You must be getting me mix up with someone else."

That's another thing 'bout Wynona. She got one of them trick memories that she don't remember nothin' she forgets. And she forgets everything she don't wanna remember.

'Cept when she don't remember to forget.

Like when I met Sunny.

It was months after the Johnny Romero thing and me and Wynona were still having a black ball. We'd get together whenever we felt like it, which was most all the time. Her cat'd be humming and my rig'd be coming and everything was outasight just like always. I was gettin' ass on ass and it was all good. I didn't have no big reason for moving on down the line, and I wasn't looking for no reason.

Then the ass broke. She got a job in some picture they were

doing somewheres far away, and she hadda leave town for a while. I sure was sorry to see that fox go and I told her so.

"I be back."

"By then my rig's gonna dry up and fall off."

She patted its head like it was a pup. "You just keep it wet, it'll be awright."

"What 'bout your cat? How you gonna make it hum?"

Wynona looked at me. "I'll keep it wet too" was all she said.

A week later she wet her way outta town and my rig was left standing all by itself.

Then I met Sunny.

It was at Camel's place and first minute I seen her, I knew she was for me. Soft white. Her body was the most beautiful thing I ever seen. Her face too. I kept lookin' her all over and then she turned my way and looked at me and we both knew everything was gonna be awright. We were made.

By time Wynona come back to town me and Sunny were heavy together. Wynona didn't like it much 'cause she always gotta be the star whatever bed she's in. But there it was and wasn't nothin' nobody could do.

"Get rid of her, why don't you?"

" 'Cause I don't, that's why. And I don't 'cause I don't wanna 'cause I'm tight with her."

That got Wynona mad. "What you mean you tight with her? Has she got a body like I got? And a cat like I got? Has she got that? How can you be tight with some little black bitch when I'm around again?"

That's when I told her Sunny was white.

I waited on the countdown. Ten nine eight seven six five four three two one. Boooom.

"Get out! Get out, you chickenfuckin' fag black fuckin' ape! Get out my house!"

She was a little upset. And a little upmix too.

"I can't get out. This my house you in, woman."

She begun throwing things. "What's that gotta do with anything? How dare you go with white? Ain't your own kind good enough for you no more? Ain't I good enough for you no more?" She sat down. "Oh you mis'ble motherfucker, you sis-terfucker . . ."

"Watch you mouth, girl."

"You . . . you *Johnny Romero!*"

She really screamed it out too.

That's when I knew we was through, me and Wynona. She had a great body and a cat that hummed. And she didn't like anything white. Or anything that went with anything white.

I was sorry to see her go like that. I asked her if she wanted to have one last fuck. "You know, like one for the road."

All I wanted was to hear that cat of hers hum one more time. But I wasn't gonna hear it.

Wynona smiled all teeth. "Take your motherfuckin' black stick," she said to me, "and shove it in your motherfuckin' black ear."

And she picked up her cat and walked out my white front door.

21.

"THE time is coming when I'm gonna drag your ass out there in the streets, motherfucker."

It was the Turk.

"I was a gang leader at fifteen, a cop killer at sixteen and in prison before I was eighteen. I hate whites and I hate Jews. Before the year is up, Whitey Jewboy, I'm prob'ly gonna come in here to kill you."

The white man just stood there. Turk's words broke his face apart and he didn't know what to do. I saw the word nigger in his eyes but he couldn't get his mouth to say it. He kept wetting his lips and shifting his eyes 'round the store. It was empty. Just him and us. Then the door opened and a woman walked in and his whole body shook from being so glad.

249

It was Mother's Day in Harlem. Which is the day the welfare checks come in the mail. On Mother's Day and for a couple days after, all the food prices 'round here go up in the stores the whites own. Which is most all of them. Soup that's two for thirty-five cents is two for thirty-nine all of a sudden. Beans that's two for twenty-nine cents is two for thirty-three. Milk is higher, bread is higher. So is soap powder and baloney and kidneys and spaghetti and toilet paper. And mostly everything that kids eat.

Maybe it don't seem like nothin' much, just pennies and nickels and dimes. But most people on welfare get just sixty-six cents a day for food so them pennies mean a lot. Which is why me and Turk were in the food store. He was gonna do something about it and I wanted to hear what he was gonna do.

"Ain't nothin' nobody can do," I told him. "They charge what they want. It's the American way."

"It's them fucking Jews," Turk said.

I hadda laugh. "All you niggers is the same. It's them fucking Jews. That's all you know."

"Look what's talkin' about niggers."

"Least I don't blame being a nigger on them fucking Jews."

"You too black to blame it on anybody but a fucking coal burner." And it was his turn to laugh.

Turk really hated the Jews. Mostly 'cause they own most of the shops in Harlem and they cheat the people. I told him they cheated us 'cause they were white, not 'cause they were Jews. "Hate Jews 'cause you hate white," I said to him one time. "That way it makes sense."

But it didn't make no sense to him. Like a lotta the brothers, Turk got a kick from hating the Jews double. If he was a nigger to the white man, then the Jews were like niggers to him. That made him feel better 'cause everybody needs somebody they can depend on to hate no matter what come up. And Turk had the Jews.

"That Jew bastard's gonna be the first one we put outta business," he said when we left the store.

I told him that won't do nothing 'cause it's the big chain

250

stores that do all the business. "They the ones you gotta get. But it ain't easy 'cause they could let one lose money and still keep it goin'."

"Not if it burns down, they can't."

Turk's idea was to start what they call food co-ops where poor people buy the food a lot at one time and sell it for what it cost plus a little to pay for store rent and like that. But they sell it only to other poor people.

"If we had one of them in every poor 'hood, we'd get rid of them fucking Jews just like that."

"No, you wouldn', man."

"What you mean?"

"They'd open a store next door and sell things you'd buy with the money you saved on the food. That's just what they'd do, and you know it."

He run his hand over his head. "You right about that. What we gotta do is put the food stores between two empty lots."

"Or a couple old buildings nobody lives in no more."

"Yeah. Them too."

"Plenty of 'em around," I said.

"And the fucking Jews own 'em all." He shook his head. "Someday we gonna blow up every stinkin' Jew building in Harlem. Boom. And they all be gone."

"Harlem be gone too, man. Wouldn' be a building left. Nothin' but smoke."

"Yeah, and them fucking Jews'd be selling it in bottles as holy smoke from when they burned that Jesus."

I smiled at Turk 'cause I was smarter'n he was. "They didn't burn Jesus. They nailed him to a cross."

"So they'd be selling it from when they made the nails. Smoke is smoke." And he give me his smart smile.

We were walking up 125th Street. It was early and the stores were just open. Turk wanted to tell all the fucking Jew food-store owners that the black people were gonna do something 'bout always being cheated. Only he made it sound like what we were gonna do was kill off all the fucking Jew food-store owners.

251

We went into this one store and he told that to the man. "We know that every month on Mother's Day you raise your prices. You keep that up, man, and someday you gonna get killed. You know what I mean?"

The man said nothing.

"And we gonna open a co-op right around here and run you outta Harlem."

The man still said nothing.

"I could be starving to dead and I wouldn' buy nothin' in this fucking Jew store."

"I don't like that kinda talk," the man said.

"What kinda talk?"

"That you are here in my store and from me you buy nothing. You come in a store you should buy something."

That's what they hate the most, if you don't buy nothing. 'Cause it hits them in the pocket where it hurts. But they listen to you talk if they can make money on you. They heard it all a thousand times anyway.

Back on the street Turk asked me how come the Jews don't have a place of their own. "I mean, like we got here in Harlem. You know."

"They got a place, man. It's called Israel."

"Israel, yeah. How many blacks you think are over there?"

I laughed. "I don't think they got no blacks over there. Least none I ever heard 'bout."

"That's what I figure," Turk said. "We ain't where they are, but they come up here and share Harlem with us, the greedy motherfucks."

"They ain't sharing it with us, man. They just using it is all."

"That's even worse." He hit his fist into his palm. "I wish them Arabs'd kill 'em all off. What 'bout you?"

"Fuck, no. I don't got a big thing for the Arabs."

"They better'n them fucking Jews, ain't they?"

I seen a quarter on the sidewalk and beat a little kid to it by half a step. He started crying, the little punk. He don't know this is America where everyone is equal. I just got longer legs than him is all.

252

"Well, ain't they?"

"Ain't they what?"

Turk worked his eyes like he was talking to someone stupid. "Ain't the Arabs better'n them fucking Jews?"

I put the quarter in my pocket. "That depends," I said.

"On what?"

"On where you are. Like right here they better 'cause they don't cheat us, right?"

Turk shook his head.

"But why don't they cheat us?" I asked. "I'll tell you why they don't cheat us. 'Cause there ain't enough of them 'round here. That's all."

"Balls."

"That's the truth. If they owned all the stores you'd be calling them the fucking Arabs."

"But they don't own the stores," he said.

"So that makes them our brothers. But what about over there in Africa? The Arabs always been the big slave traders. Yeah. They been making slaves of your real brothers for like a thousand years. And your pappy and grandpappy goin' all the way back."

"Who says?"

This Turk sure was stupid. "What you mean who says? Everybody knows that. Everybody knows the Arabs still runnin' a big slave thing over there right now today. They selling black men right now as slaves."

"Balls."

"Man, you are one dumb ass nigger you don't know that. Not only are them fucking Arabs still buying black people for a bunch of beads, but in one of them countries over there they already killed about a million of 'em in some war."

"How you know that?"

"I read it, that's how I know. In some country called the Sudan they musta knocked off least a million already. Them's my real brothers gettin' wasted. Yours too, 'less you turned into a Arab."

"Shit. I be a Arab when you turn into a Jew."

253

The two of us coal black niggers walked down the street ripping off hate.

"Fucking Jews."

"Fucking Arabs."

But the only thing we turned into was another food store.

After a couple hours and a dozen million stores I was tired and hungry so we stopped in a soul food place run by a brother. I asked Turk when he was gonna start the co-ops.

"Soon's we get about two hundred people and a storefront we open. Then when we get a few of them goin', people can see how much cheaper the food is."

"Where you gonna get everything?"

"Up in the Bronx there's this Terminal Wholesale Market. They sell you anything if you buy big enough, and with a couple co-ops working we'll be big enough."

"And you really think you can force the whites outta business and make 'em leave Harlem?"

He looked serious at me. "It's either force them out or blow them up. But they leave one way or the other."

"What 'bout the big supermarkets like A & P? You can't force them out."

"If they put in a black manager and all black help we let 'em stay for now, till we get real big. But if they don't, we blow them up or burn them down. Don't matter which to me."

Turk meant it. When he was sixteen he told a pig not to reach for his gun and when he did, Turk killed him with a knife right in the throat. He did fourteen years for it. While he was in the slammer he become a Black Muslim and then a big follower of Malcolm X. When he got out two years 'go he joined the Black Panthers but quit 'cause they spent all the time defending themselfs and gettin' in the papers. "All talk, no action to help the poor," he said.

Now he was doing something to help the poor. Inside a year he figured he'd have food co-ops all over Harlem to drive out the white man. If he lived that long.

"What you think of the idea?" he asked me.

"It's gonna take a lot to get the whites out," I told him.

254

"They been making money jumpin' on black bones for a long time. And they ain't about to stop just 'cause you say so."

"That's right, they ain't about to stop. So we stop 'em."

"Ain't that easy."

"We hit 'em in the only place they hurt. In the money."

"They gonna try to hurt you back."

"When they don't make nothin' they got no reason to stay."

"They gonna be real mad at you."

"First the little stores go and we put in our own people."

"They gonna kill you, Turk."

"Then we go after the big supermarkets."

"You remember Malcolm?"

That stopped him. Malcolm's name stops anybody. That's 'cause he is Saint Malcolm, every black man knows that. It was Malcolm give us back our balls. He was the first and the best and the only real saint the black man's had in this country. The motherfuck whites don't know what he's all about 'cause they never been where we were. And never will be neither.

"What about Malcolm?" he asked.

"There's some people think he was knocked off 'cause he was trying to crimp the drug thing here in Harlem. That'd hurt a lotta very big people. White people."

"So?"

"So you wanna do the same thing with the food. There's a pile of money goin' 'round here for food and some of it comes off the top for protection. Once you move in, somebody's gonna get hurt."

"Won't be me," Turk said. "I got the people on my side." . . .

"So did Malcolm. That's why they got black shooters to hit him. But he's dead all the same."

Turk put his pork chop sandwich down. "Listen to me, Marcus, I goin' tell you somethin' here. Malcolm was killed in some other age. Sure, he begun everything for us but that was a long time ago. We got our shit together now, anybody hits us we give 'em double back. There's more fire power up here than the white Mafia boys ever seen."

"Not if the po-lice join up with them."

"You think they'd do that?"

I shook my head. "I think they already done it."

"How you make that?"

" 'Cause they don't really care nothin' about the rackets. To them the drugs and the numbers and the whores is just niggers gettin' their kicks. Anything go long's they get their share and nobody rocks the boat. But all the Black Panther talk, that kinda shit is dangerous for them. So the po-lice gonna lean on anybody that talks change. They want the same thing the white racket people want. Business like always. Maybe they don't work together but they sure as hell ain't gonna get in each other's way."

Turk smiled big. "You right about all that. But don't forget I know something 'bout the rackets too. One thing I know is that the white boys are finished up here. They gonna fight but their day is just about over." He started chompin' on the collards. "You see what I mean? When the shoot-out comes it's gonna be white shooters 'gainst black. But on black turf. And the po-lice will stay out of it 'cause they don't know the winner." He leaned over to me and whispered. "But I tell you a secret, Marcus. We gonna win. The black Mafia is taking over Harlem and everything in it. We gonna drive the white racket boys out. We gonna drive the Jews out. Then we gonna run Harlem just for black people. That's the way it's gonna be."

"Will it be any better?"

"Can't be no worse, can it?"

I sat there thinkin' about that. The rackets will always be goin' on 'cause it's what people want. So if blacks handle it, that's gotta be better'n if the whites do it. Black Racket Power. It's what we been fighting for. If we gonna have home rule, may as well be in everything.

"You really think you can beat them, eh?"

He picked up the plastic coffee cup and squeezed it in his fist till it broke. "Just like that," he said.

"And the brothers are ready for them?"

"Sure thing. Look, the food co-ops are just one of a hundred diff'rent ways to help our own people. If we can help and still make a buck, we gonna do it. Simple as that. It's what they call free enterprise."

I hadda laugh at that. If it was just free enterprise I'd put my money on the brothers any time. In the rackets, in the straight world and everything in between. We were better hustlers than the whites could ever be. But I was a little worried 'bout them Jews. They hadda do some fancy hustlin' of their own over the years.

When I left Turk he was still feeding his three hundred pounds, dipping into a big batch of fried chicken asses and some turnip stumps. Looked to me like he did right by gettin' into the food end of the black Mafia.

Outside I was thinking maybe after we took over the world we should split it with the Jews, just so there'd be no more trouble. The black Mafia and the Jew Mafia. Who could beat that? And if the Jews didn't have no Mafia, all they hadda do was get that Israel gov'ment they got over there.

That was good as anybody's Mafia in taking things over.
Better.

On the way home I passed the Rat Man. He was carrying his sign, same as always. Nobody hardly paid him no mind 'cause he been doing the same thing so many years. Long's I can remember he been walking up and down 125th Street with that big sign, which wasn't nothin' but two sticks of wood in the shape of a cross and a piece of cardboard or something nailed to the wood. Rat Man was walking my way. I musta seen that sign a thousand times but it was hard not to look at the big home-made words. I DO NOT BELIEVE IN HUMAN BEINGS.

Years 'go a rat crawled into his kid's crib. He was living in some old dumpy building somewhere 'round here. The rat bit the kid, a little girl 'bout two years old. She died a couple days later. Rat Man went crazy. She was the only thing he had 'cause his woman die when the baby was born.

Everybody around here knows the story of Rat Man. A lotta mothers when they put the little kids to bed, they tell 'em the story of the Rat Man, just like little white kids get told 'bout that Jack and Jill and Humpy Dumpy. Everybody feels sorry

257

for him but there's nothin' nobody can do. Plenty of kids get bit by rats all the time up here. Most of 'em live but sometimes they die from the bites. That's just the way it is till we get rid of all the rats. After we get rid of all the whites.

There's some people think when one goes, the other'll go too.

But that Rat Man is crazy. He's dirty and wears old rags and talks to hisself and never talks to nobody else. If you try to talk to him, he walks away. And ever since his kid die like that, he been carrying around a sign with just one thing on it. I DO NOT BELIEVE IN HUMAN BEINGS.

I kept thinkin' about the Rat Man all the way home. Maybe after Turk gets all set with the food co-ops he could begin getting the black Mafia into the houses up here. They all so bad they need to be tore down and start over. And if they gotta make money on it, there's plenty ways to do that. Everybody could bring their guns and pay a dollar to shoot the rats coming outta the houses when they get tore down. And the winner of the biggest rat gets a free turn at the next house to shoot the rats outta.

And if that don't work, free enterprise can take care of the whole thing. All Harlem gotta do is say it's a country by itself and not pay taxes no more. Inside a day the motherfuckin' white Army be in here blasting 'way at every building above ground. There wouldn' be a rat left standing 'cause there wouldn' be a house left standing.

That's called instant urban renewal. It takes a lot less time than the old ways which took forever.

And it's free enterprise. The American way.

22.

SUMMERTIME, and the livin' is easy. If your daddy's rich and your mama's good lookin'. And both of 'em was white. Mine wasn't none of that so I'm livin' in Harlem and it ain't easy any time of the year. But it's exter bad in the summer. That's when the sun throws up all over the dirty buildings and the dirty streets, spitting a film of fire on everything. The dark halls and small rooms get so hot the rats go screaming in the walls and the roaches leave for downtown. Then all the garbage that never gets picked up comes to life and after a while people run to the roofs to get away from the stink, only they can't get away 'cause it's already there everywhere. And Harlem is one big garbage dump, rotting in the center of fun city. It's hot as a bitch and everything you touch melts off your fingers and if you go to sit down you stay cemented till they dynamite your ass off. You wanna jump in the river and never come up till December. And a lot of us do.

When the sun goes mad and blows itself up in the west and darkness comes, you just know that if it be back tomorrow like it was today you goin' get your gun and start shootin' at something. And if that don't do it, then you might just burn the whole stinkin' town down.

Friday night I was on a Harlem bus hot enough to fry fatback. The bus was crowded and people were waitin' in line to faint. One big fat woman kept saying, "When they goin' aircondition these bus?" Somebody told her it already got the black man's air condition. "Just open the windows." She asked

259

the driver and he said if she wants air condition she gotta ride the buses downtown. "Whitetown got all the air condition so they don't get hot in their white skin." She told him she don't work downtown. "Don't look at me, momma," he said. "I just drives this animal, I don't feed it."

I'm sitting in the back, sweating machine oil I'm so hot. And I'm lookin' at this bus card that tells you how to stay cool. It's called Myrna Loy's Summer Soup. All about this woman, whoever she is, how she travels 'round the country and needs a quick summer dish which is a cold soup. Then I read how to make her cold soup. And I read it again 'cause I can't believe what I see. I close my eyes to make sure I'm where I was, then I read it out loud just so my ear hears it. My ear don't lie. You take two pints of Jellied Madrilene, whatever the fuck that is, and you put it into four soup dishes. Then you add one tablespoon red caviar and a pint of sour cream and chopped fresh parsley.

I'm sittin' there staring at the bus card and the more I stare, the more mad I get. Sonovabitch. Now I know the motherfuck whites flipped out sure as shit. They just gotta be crazy. This here is Harlem, where there's people living on greens and beans and tomcat stew. Where little kids sit on the streets eating sugar tits in a rag. Where lunch is a piece of bread with a little sugar on it and some water and you eat it slow so's you think it's a full meal. Where mothers buy shit soda for their kids 'stead of milk 'cause it's much cheaper. Where almos' everybody eats shit candy bars 'cause they make you feel full. Where half the people are too fat 'cause they never ate nothin' but fat, and the other half are too skinny 'cause they never even had the money for the fat foods. Where kids got arms and legs so thin the bones stick out, and their bellies are big as they are.

And this dipshit motherfuck card is riding on a bus in Harlem talkin' about caviar and sour cream and parsley and that other fag thing nobody ever heard of. *Caviar*. I'm so mad I go over and I rip that card right off the wall. Just stand there and tear it into pieces and throw 'em on the floor. Then I go back to my seat and someone's sitting there. But I feel so good I just smile. I see mostly everybody else is smiling too. And one stud comes up to me and says, "I was gonna do it if you didn't."

If the white fuckheads wanna know why the blacks are talkin' about starting World War III right here in this country, all they gotta do is spend a day in Harlem. Yeah, and ride the buses too. We'll start it and we won't finish it and we *still* don't care.

I was smiling all the way down on the subway goin' to work. What I'm working is weekends as a bartender in this place 'round by Union Square downtown. Few years back I give up the fast hustles. Now I just work for what I need. Nobody ever give me a big job in the straight world and I sure ain't no part of this money society. No, and I don't wanna be neither. It's awright for the black boogies that wanna be like the white man but it ain't for me. I don't need none of them, and I ain't gonna be like none of 'em.

This place where I got the weekend gig is called Bentley's. It's a white bar but a lotta brothers stop 'round. The whisky is good, none of that cheap 2 for 1 shit. And they got live jazz on weekends. Bentley is the dude that owns it, him and some English Chinaman named Jerry Chang. They don't give me no bother 'cause I do my job and they do their job. Which is mostly standing at the bar drinking and watching me do my job. But I mean them white motherfucks can drink. 'Specially that Bentley. He drinks all night, slow sipping his glass to death. And he drinks 'bout twenty diff'rent things so you never know what the fuck he wants. But you never see him drunk. Nobody ever seen that man drunk. All he gets is even more strange than he already is.

One time I said to him, "You must be a profess'nal drinker. You know, like there's profess'nal junkies and profess'nal whores. You the first of the profess'nal drinkers."

He liked that. "Most people don't know how to drink," he said to me. "There's only one way, the right way. You just keep chipping away at it." And he picked up his glass and took a chip.

I told him once I was gonna bet him a hundred dollars that I

261

could drink him under the bar. He just laughed 'cause he seen I don't drink much no more. But if I really wanted to I could do it awright. There's a trick to it. You get a little bottle of olive oil just before you start and you drink the whole thing down. Yeah. All of it. Then if you still alive you can drink anybody into the dirt.

I seen a dude cop five hundred dollars that way in a bar I was working. He was drinking shooters, same as what I drink now. But I never seen nobody drink 'em like that. After he had about fifteen and he was still standing, I knew he was doing some kinda number. A shooter is the toughest fuckin' drink in the world and he was rapping 'em down like soda pop. The sucker was on scotch and then he was on the floor.

After it was all over the dude ordered drinks for everybody. I poured a round and set him up with a shooter.

"What's this?" he asked me.

"What you been drinkin' all night, man."

"That was work. Now I'm thirsty."

"What'll it be?"

He looked me right in the eye and he said, "Gimme straight club soda. I don't drink when I'm off duty."

That's when I found out about the olive oil trick. "Bartenders gotta know these things," he said to me.

"You a bartender?"

"Fourteen years. But no more."

"What happened?"

"I was making more in front of the bar than behind it. So I asked myself, Why should I stay? and I couldn' come up with no answer."

But I never tried that con myself. I took one taste of that olive oil and I knew there wasn't enough money around to get me to drink a whole bottle.

Bentley got some fine-lookin' fox working for him at the bar. They serve the food and the people who sit down at the tables. There's this one white fox, Astrid, that got a little-girl body and long hair and short skirts. Every stud comes in the place wants to ball her. They just sit there all night watching her then they

262

go out and come back the next day and sit there all night watching her. 'Stead of just goin' up to her and asking her if she wants to fuck. I mean the white man got some real kinky ideas about fox. Like they something special and you can't let them know you horny till after you get them in bed. Some studs prob'ly try to stick it in without the fox even knowing 'bout it. I don't know what's the matter with them, they don't make no sense. A fox is just the other side of the glass. They need you just as much as you need them 'cause there ain't nothin' else to fuck for real. There's nothin' special about nobody. Every fox opens their legs the same way, only thing is some know how to close 'em better.

Astrid told me about this one dude come in every night for a week just to watch her. Then one day he went up and offered her a hundred dollars if she'd undress for him.

"That's all he wanted, just to watch me undress. He swore he wouldn' touch me."

"Easy hundred."

"Fuck, no," she said. "Any man who saw me nude with the body I got and he didn't touch me and fuck me all over, there's gotta be something wrong with him."

I told her any fox that wouldn' undress for a hundred dollars, there's gotta be something wrong with *her*.

A week later Astrid come up to me. "I made that hundred."

"Easy money," I said to her.

"I took him over my place for coffee and we went into the bedroom and I stripped down. He just sat there looking at me, and he was squeezin' and smelling my panties and bra. Then he asked me if I wanted to make another hundred and I'm saying to myself, I knew it, you just can't trust nobody these days."

"So you got your hundred and threw him out."

"No, but wait. All he wanted was for me to watch him jack off. Honest. He was gonna give me that if I just sat on the bed watching him. So I said sure. I figured I went this far I may as well go all the way with my eyes."

"And make youself two hundred."

"Yeah, but it's a funny thing. I'm sitting there on that damn

263

bed watching him and he's really having a hard time. He hadda stop and rest his hand about ten times. And I'm thinking for fifty bucks more I'd jack him off. C'mon, just another fifty and I'll do it for you, just to get it over. But then he came and I went."

"Went where?"

"After he left I was so horny I couldn' stand it so I went over to my boyfriend's place and we made love." Astrid flashed her two-hundred-dollar smile. "You know, taking your clothes off for a man and then watching him jack off is a very sexy thing for a girl." And I saw her thinkin' about a whole new sex life she just found.

I wanted to tell her about the olive oil man. They'd make a good pair. But I didn't say a word.

Most of the blood that comes into Bentley's is middle class and shucking for the white man. But some great jazz sidemen play there sometimes and they bring the blood with balls in 'em. I get along fine with all of them 'cause I been down the same road. We all look around us at Mister and Miss Whiteass and we know how the blues was born. Yeah, and the blacks, browns, greens and purples too. And out of it all come jazz and they go back to playing it and I go back to living it. And Bentley and Jerry Chang and Astrid and all the other hip hype diddly bop finger pop white fuckheads are feeling the pull of the music, feeling what they never suffered, tasting what they never threw up, hearing what they never screamed out. What the fuck do they know about anything?

But then I catch myself. Hold on, man. Real music is about suffering, and everybody suffers. Don't matter what color skin you got. If you born, you already got the misery. White people know about pain and hate and death just like we do And I think they know more about being lonely than anybody do.

Being black don't give you a ticket to all the suffering, just a whole lot of it.

On this hot Friday night I was busy right up till it was time to close. The music kept sending waves up and down everyone's skull, laughing, shouting. I was feelin' good. 'Bout a half hour before closing, this great-looking white fox come in all by herself. Young and warm and wonderful is just what she was too. And dressed outasight. Every stud in the place got turned on to her but she wasn't having nothin' but a screwdriver. I served her and walked away. Ten minutes later she ordered another.

On the third drink she asked me to light her smoke. "I hope you're not one of those West Indians," she said, smiling behind her eyes. "I don't like West Indians."

Do I tell her I been here almos' four hundred years or to just fuck off?

"I'm as American as cherry pie," I said to her with a Southern twist to my voice.

She smiled for real this time. "That's nice. Then we can be good friends."

I got her a drink at last call. "This one's on me."

She thanked me. "I'd like to wait for you if you're not busy tonight."

"I'm not busy."

It took me another half hour to check out the money and clean up. She just sat there, not saying a word to anybody. One stud went up to her but she brushed him off quick. Nobody else tried.

By the time I was done nobody was left but me and her and Bentley.

"I'll lock up," he said. "You go on."

"See you tomorrow," I told him. And I went on out with her.

Right in front of the bar was this big dark-blue car, looked like a million dollars. She unlocked the door and we got in. "What kinda car is this?" I asked her.

"It's a Rolls-Royce" was all she said.

As we pulled away I was humming to myself. Can you beat that? I walk out of Bentley's and into a Rolls. Can you beat that?

23.

A LOTTA whites know about Madison Wells. They see his face in the newspapers and hear his growl on the TV when something happens around here like a riot or another pig murder. They know he's big in the Black Power thing in Harlem. What they don't know is how big he really is.

Madison Wells is the leader of the Black Brotherhood.

They are getting ready for gorilla war. Black against white. Right here in this country, in the cities. When they ready, look out. Right now they making the things they need. Making, stealing, buying, getting. They got home factories and basement workshops. They got org'zation. What they ain't got is a lotta talk that don't mean nothin'.

The Black Brotherhood ain't simple shit. They are made up of teams, diff'rent teams in every big-city blacktown in the country. Each team works on its own, in some cities there could be dozens of teams. The teams got blowup artists, snipers, gas men and soldiers. They hit and run. If a team gets knocked off, there's others. They got no orders. Their only job is to kill, burn, destroy, wipe out.

Gorilla war.

Someday soon they gonna push the button and go all the way.

I know Madison Wells a long time. I even been to a couple of the bomb factories he put together in Harlem. One was in the back of this garage where there's always a lotta tools laying

266

around. We went down some steps and into a workshop in the basement.

Madison picked up something off a workbench. "Ever see one of these?"

It was a big double nail, shaped like a X. But all the edges were sharp as a razor. Hurt to even hold it.

"That's a gorilla nail," he said. "Throw a bunch of 'em on any highway and you got a traffic jam in less'n three minutes. Don't matter how it lands, it comes up sharp."

I juggled the nail in my hand.

"Be nice to have a whole mess of these."

"We got thousands. Now s'pose you tied up city traffic like that. And then hit them with bottle bombs from the roofs, and had snipers in the houses."

I looked at him. "You'd have war."

"Gorilla war."

Against a wall were a lotta cases, looked like maybe twenty cases of something. "What's in them?" I asked him.

"Dynamite."

"Twenty cases of it?"

"Twenty-three cases of it," he said with a big smile. "And it's a bitch. Every couple weeks somebody gotta turn all them cases upside down so the nitro don't settle."

"What happens then?"

"If a stick starts to sweat, you in bad trouble. You get rid of it very fucking fast."

I walked away very fucking fast. Just in case. "How 'bout other cities, they got anything like this?"

"Some do, most of 'em do. Some gotta make their own gunpowder."

"In places like this?"

He took a jar off a shelf. "See this? It's sulphur. All you need is this and charcoal and saltpeter, and you got yourself gunpowder. 'Course, you need a gas man to work out the mixing," he said, putting the sulphur back, "but we got 'em."

I picked up a sheet of paper with some typing on it. At the top it said, *How to Make a Fire Bomb.*

"What's this for?" I asked him.

"When I get enough of that kinda information typed up, I'm gonna make it into a handbook on gorilla war in the city."

"You make youself a bundle sellin' a book like that."

"Can't sell it, Marcus. But I'll get it to all the other cities so they can use it."

I read the paper. Never know when I gotta make a fast fire bomb. "Fill a whisky or soda bottle with one-fifth sulphuric acid and the other four-fifths gasoline. Cork the bottle. Dip a strip of cloth in a mixture of water, sugar and potassium chlorate and let dry. When fully dry, wrap tightly around the bottle and fasten with cord or wire. When bottle breaks, the acid and chlorate instantly ignite the gasoline."

At the bottom of the paper it said, "Be extra careful. When this goes, it *go*."

"Man, this is dangerous stuff you dealing here. How many papers like this you got laying around?"

"About fifty so far. Everything from putting ground glass in food to knockin' out whole electric power systems like that California team did a couple years back." He took a bunch of papers from a drawer. "See these? All the blueprints for the city's electric lines under the streets. We know where everything is and exactly where to hit them. Three teams could knock everything out for weeks. It's fantastic how easy it is to kill a city." He wiped his glasses off. "Just picture New York all dark and then a half-dozen magnesium bombs go off, blowing all the tunnels and bridges. See what I mean? Boom. The city'd die."

"How you make them magnesium bombs?"

"My gas men can do it. And they'll have the stuff to make 'em when the time comes. Till then I got plastic bombs here and I got suitcase bombs."

I laughed. "Ain't you got no atom bombs?"

Madison Wells don't laugh much. "If I knew where to get me some I'd get 'em." He walked over to some other cases piled up and opened one and took out a hand grenade. "Here, catch." And he threw it at me.

268

The hair 'round my balls stood straight out and my voice went five miles high. "Yiiiiii." Then I got it. And held it like it was a goddam baby.

Now he laughed. "Wouldn' done nothing if you dropped it. The firing pin is still in."

"How I know that, motherfuck? You took ten years off my life doing that." And I give it back to him, gentlelike.

"If this thing was live, it woulda took all the rest of them years off your life, starting with right now."

He put it back in the case.

"What they good for?"

"Good for most anything. But what they'll be used for is to blow all the TV and radio towers and knock out all the electronic shit in the airports and train stations. Nothing broadcasts, nothing moves. No lights, no way to get out. Then we poison the city water and blow up the sewer system so all the shit backs up. And we send teams out to plant bombs, stab people, throw acid on them, put sugar in gas tanks. We jap the pigs and the fire dogs. You dig? It's a battlefield."

Sounded more like he was talkin' about the end of the world.

"You really think you goin' be able to do all that?" I asked him.

Madison didn't say nothin' for a long time. I'm sitting there with dynamite and bombs and guns and grenades all around me and I'm thinkin' if only the whitefuckers knew how much the black man really hated them, they'd kill off every nigger they could find. Only reason we don't kill them is 'cause we know we can't. Too motherfuckin' many of 'em.

Madison looked at me like he knew what I was thinking. "I'm gonna tell you, Marcus. I don't know what we be able to do. Sure, we can do all I said. We can turn this city upside down and kill off half the people before they get all of us. And we can do that in every big city in the country. But that ain't goin' make no revolution."

"But how 'bout what all them dudes say that we in a revolution right now?"

269

"They all suckin' shit, man. They just jacking off in the head. We ain't in no real revolution now and we ain't goin' be in no revolution. Least not here anyways."

"How you make that out?" I asked him.

" 'Cause to have a real revolution you need the people to be on your side. They gotta hate the gov'ment, they gotta hate it so much they wanna do 'way with it. But in this country most people like the gov'ment they got. Now how you goin' revolt when four outta five people don't want revolt?"

"You sure 'bout that?"

"Goddam right I'm sure. This ain't Cuba or Algeria. The motherfuck system works in this country good enough to give most people a lotta toys and shit. What they care if they sucking it off the poor? Long as they get theirs." He brushed a spider off the table. It fell on the ground and he smashed it with his boot. "All you got here to fight the system is the poor and some of the kids, and that just ain't enough."

The more I listened to him the more I begun to see one thing for sure. If Madison Wells don't think a gorilla war gonna bring on the revolution every black man with balls is waitin' for, then maybe we gotta go some other way.

"What you gonna do, man?"

He sat there holding some of the papers for the gorilla handbook. "There's only three ways to go, Marcus," he said very soft. "You could cop outta the country into one of them back-to-Africa things or get with something like the Muslims that want a black country right here. Or you could stay and try to make it best you can in the enemy land." His voice got to a whisper. "Or you could stay and just blow everything up, 'cluding yourself." He waved his hand 'round at all the stuff in the workshop. "Some of us are gonna blow everything up. We ain't got a choice no more."

On the way home somebody shoved a handbill at me, passing 'em out on a corner. On the top was a big question mark and under it was some big print. "Why is a Senator of Mississippi receiving $13,000 a *month* in federal crop-control subsidies for not growing food on his plantation while the government pays a starving child in Mississippi only $9 a month? What are you going to do about it?"

I knew what the Black Brotherhood was gonna do about it 'cause they didn't have a choice no more. And I kept wondering if I still did.

"When the time comes," Madison Wells once said to me, "if you're not up here with a gun, we don't want no part of you."

What he meant was which side of the gun was you gonna be on when you picked it up.

24.

SUNNY'S lived about a thousand years, same as me. But she's only twenty-four. She thinks rock music is where it's all coming together. She wants to get everybody hyped on it 'cause it's salvation. I'm very special to her and so I must be saved.

"Just let it soak into your skull, don't fight it. Dylan *knows*. Goddam, Marcus, he's laying it down for all of us."

Sunny cries sometime when she listens to Dylan. She feels it so much she gets stoned right outta her mind. It's a religion is just what it is, but it's not like the hootin' and howlin' I seen in church when I was a kid. Inside is where it happens to you, behind your mind where everything real is hiding. I feel it myself sometime when I listen to rock. For a few seconds I know what it's all about but before I can get a handle on it, ZAP, I lose it and I'm back in the game of life.

"It's for us, Marcus, and for everybody on the outside. For all the outlaws and down people."

Sunny goes to hear rock whenever she can and sometimes I go with her. Acid rock does the most for me. And groups like the Grateful Dead and the Jefferson Airplane. Only the groups

271

"I lived down here a few years back," I told him, "and I met some of them groupies. They were into some very boss things."

He shook his head. "They were the best for a long time. Very great. Only now the kids here think it's still the whole apple, but the show's been moving to a lotta places these last few years. L.A. and London are getting a lot of the action."

I don't know nothin' about that but when I was living down here in the East Village, it was one big boom town for balls. There was so much free cat you hadda leave town every month to rest up your rig. And there was a free clap clinic, whenever you went the line'd be up the block and 'round the corner. Mostly all fox and they looked to be about sixteen.

The groupies I met were all into the dope thing. What they'd do is they'd get the shit for whatever rock studs they were gonna fuck that night. Nobody wanted to travel all over holding the shit 'cause it was too risky so they counted on the groupies to get it for them. That and the sex were the two big things the groupies had to give 'em.

One time this groupie told me she was in bed with some English cock star for three days straight without stopping. "We musta hit on every drug there was just to keep goin'. It was in-*sane*."

A lotta them use amyl nitrate when they fuck. I use it myself sometime. You pop one just when you gonna come, and it blows the whole thing up king-size. It's just a little thing, poppers they call 'em. You sniff it deep a few times and bang, when you come you feel like you shootin' for the moon.

But all them studs in the rock groups, they got it made for gettin' laid. They could fuck fifty a night if they could fuck fifty a night. Somebody told me a few of them got so much cat they turned fag 'cause there was just nothin' new. I believe it too. I mean, after you fuck a thousand fox and shove pickles and soda bottles up their cat just for kicks and have them beat you and take yogurt baths with them and come in their ear and plug up every hole in their body till they turn blue, what is there left to do?

One thing left is to get your rig cast in plaster so that after

274

you go, people can see you were a stud with balls. Yeah. There's a groupie doing that right now. She calls her outfit the Plaster Casters. Cynthia is her name and what she does is she goes 'round to the rock groups and puts their rigs and balls in a mess of plaster that she mixes up. After a couple minutes the stuff is hard and when the stud takes his rig out, there's this plaster thing that looks like it. 'Course, if he can't get it out he's got the hardest-on of all time. But from what I hear, Cynthia knows what to do and ain't nobody been shot down yet.

All the stud needs is a hard-on to start the ball casting.

I been through all the other things with fox but I ain't never had myself casted, not yet. But I ain't in one of them rock groups and she's just casting them now. When she goes on to bigger things, I'm gonna get her to do me. Then maybe someday I could be in one of them big art museums, hanging by the balls.

And people'd ask themselfs, What kinda elephant was this?

I never met Cynthia Plaster Caster but when I see her I know she's gonna do me. I could tell she ain't just one of them star-casters 'cause she is a artist. Plus which, if she wants to get what's goin' down today, she gotta go past the rock thing into the whole revolution bag. Most of it is black and that makes me what's happening.

Once I told Sunny about that I'm gonna get my rig plastered when Cynthia gets down to it. We were in bed at the time and she ran her tongue all over it. "Can't be done," she said. "There ain't that much plaster."

She was only woofing. But I wonder if Cynthia could make black plaster for it. All them white rigs'd look faggy next to my big black tool.

When we got home from Aretha Franklin, I asked Sunny who she'd like to meet the most if she could have anybody in the whole rockin' world.

"Frank Zappa," she said. "He knows where it's all hid."

Sunny falls in and outta fake love real easy. But she's got this thing for Frank Zappa for a long time. She thinks he's from some other world come down here just to open things up. "It's

275

his music and how he lives," she says. "He's free, like nobody ever been free."

I like to be free myself so one day I asked Mollie Girl about Zappa. Mollie Girl been on the music scene all her life, her daddy was one of the Duke's sidemen and he played with Bird and Monk and like that. And she been into rock since way back and lived with dozens of groups. "What's this Zappa?" I said to her.

Mollie Girl smiled like she was feelin' good. "He's the man."

"What man?"

"The man that's putting it all together for the rest of us. He's the guru, the whacked-out piper that's leading the only real revolution goin' on." She was quiet for a minute. "That's 'cause he's got pthokk."

"What the fuck's pthokk?" I asked her.

Mollie Girl laughed. "Pthokk is what's left after you get rid of all the plastic bullshit in your head. The more you get rid of, the more pthokk you got. Zappa's pure pthokk. He's the only one been able to crash all the way over to the other side. He's pure spirit."

Zappa runs with some rock groups like the Mothers out there in L.A. I told Mollie Girl if I ever get there I'm gonna go see Frank Zappa. "Gonna get me some of that pthokk so I can be a spirit too."

Be just my luck to come out a black spirit. Then everybody could still see me and all the whites'd say, "Look at that nigger spirit over there." And nothing'd be diff'rent.

But I meant what I told Mollie Girl 'bout seeing Frank Zappa. He's a white stud but it sounds like he's hip to everything goin' down. And I could pick up on that pthokk he's got. I'm always trying to free myself, every black man living here is goin' through the same changes. And if this pthokk can do it then I'm gonna get me a head full.

Just a big pthokk sucker is what I am.

25.

"COCKSUCKERS. Faggots. All of you. Sucking the blood of poor people. This country stinks. It's the enemy. I know that. You know that. It's a prison and an insane asylum. You can't do anything to make it better. Revolt. It's too late for anything else. The schools are prisons. The churches are prisons. Your fuckin' jobs are prisons. Smash everything. Burn the schools. Wreck the churches. Destroy the office buildings. Revolt. Free yourself. Nobody can own you if you don't let them. Drop out of this stupid fuckin' system. Free your mind. Free your body. Don't work. Don't fight other people. Do your thing. Whatever it is, do it. Let the system run down. Let it die. This country is killing the world. Vietnam is only one place. You fuckin' people make me sick. Look at you. You sit there cursing the system but you're living off it. Most of you are crazy already. You can't live in this country and be sane. Drop out. Don't go to meetings and talk politics. They're all shit, left and right. They all want to own you. Be your own leader. Be your own party. Do your thing. Drop out of everything and be yourself. Don't let anyone tell you what to do. Get out. Fuck the system. It's killing you. Live in your head. Blow your mind. Other people are doing it. There's a whole Dropout Party. Don't let them kill you. Drop out. Drop out."

There was maybe two hundred people in the hall. Most of them were trying to listen to the speaker up at the mike but you couldn' hardly hear him 'cause the dude from the Dropout Party was shouting so loud. He had on a shirt that looked like a flag and pants that looked like a shirt, and he just stood on a chair in the last row and rapped on.

It was a meeting of the New York people in what they call the New Left, and I was there 'cause I been reading some of the mosquito newspapers they put out and they were really laying down some heavy shit on their brother whites. Sonovabitch, if a blood ever said some of them things he'd be shot dead like Malcolm X.

I was sitting with Johnny Pick. And Carter Smith was there too, up on the stage. Carter was a big shot in the New Left. In the black part of it. A few years back at their first big meet in Chicago, he was the one got power for the blacks. He run them white fuckers right into the ground. And made them love it. Now he was a big name in the movement and everybody listened to him. Everybody white anyway. They trusted him 'cause he didn't talk 'bout killing off every white man. He talked politics and doing things legal and all that shit.

Some whites even talked about him like maybe someday he'd get real power. "Julian Bond is gonna be the first black President," they'd say. "And Carter Smith is gonna be in his Cabinet."

But way uptown, the bloods like Madison Wells were thinking Carter don't need to be in no black Cabinet 'cause he's already in the white man's pocket. Madison Wells' people just didn't trust any black man who worked with whites ever at any time anywhere.

And other bloods like Fred Gordon, who didn't trust bloods like Madison Wells, believed there wasn't nothing for any black man to even *talk* to any white man about ever at any time anywhere.

And other bloods like Ben Pride, who didn't trust nobody, believed that any black man who even talked to any other *black* man was already in a white trick bag.

And then there was Johnny Pick.

He got a rash every time he was near white. He'd get this big rash on his chin. You'd see him on the street with his rash and you'd know he been near white. Somebody'd see him and they'd say to him, "Been fuckin' around white again, eh?" He couldn' hide it. One time he went to a doctor for it, a black doctor, and this doctor told him it was a skin condition. Like he didn't already know that. Then the doctor told him the trouble was with his nerves 'cause he didn't trust whites. So he just hadda stay 'way from them best he could.

That's when he started hating whites. He hated them so much he'd even get a rash from another black who'd been near white. Only trouble was he liked the white fox. Couldn' stay 'way from them. He tried fucking them with a mask on, he tried fucking them with his eyes closed. He even tried it for a while only with white fox who had heavy suntans. Nothing worked.

It got so bad he decided to junk it through. He moved downtown and went 'round with nothing but white. Wouldn' even talk to anything black. Then he didn't keep getting the rash, he just had one big rash all the time. After a while nobody paid it any mind 'cause it was part of him.

That's when he started liking whites. He balled the fox and hustled the dudes and everything was awright. His rash was just like the nose on his face, they were only skin-deep. He didn't even think about it any more. It was just there on one side of his chin.

He figured he had it beat. So he moved back to Harlem to be near his own kind.

The next week he got this rash on the other side of his chin.

When they let him outta Bellevue he was a changed man. They musta got him to see that color is only skin-deep. Just like a rash. Now he handles white, black, green, blue. Don't matter none to him. And he ain't had a rash on his face since then.

Only thing is he ain't balled any fox at all since then, and nobody seems to know why.

"Do your own thing. Don't buy and sell people. You don't need money. You don't need possessions. You don't need property. Fuck the system. Get out while you still can. Stay away from politics. What the fuck are all you people doing here right now? Politics makes slaves of people. Don't be a slave.

279

Drop out. You've got to learn to survive. Get back to nature. Learn to take care of yourself. Don't work for someone else. Be your own man. Don't be a faggot. Drop out. Drop out while there's still time."

The flagman was still rapping on.

Then somebody went over and pulled him off the chair and punched him in the mouth. A few of flagman's friends started swinging and some studs from the New Left jumped in. Me and Johnny Pick were sittin' there watching the whole thing and I'm thinkin' that if the rest of the New Left is anything like this New York New Left, the power people sure ain't got much to worry about.

A half dozen of them were in one corner mixing it up and the dude on the stage was banging for order and everybody else was just sitting in their seats. All of a sudden I heard this whistle and these two whites got up and walked over to the stage. Two more from the other side went to the back. They all had old sweaters and long hair and looked just like everybody else in the New Left trying to look like poor people.

They got on the stage and one of them went over to the mike. I figured maybe they were big shots in the New Left and they were gonna tell those studs in the back to cool it. But there was somethin' real familiar about that whistle I heard.

"We're police officers. There is a riot going on here and we are arresting everybody in this hall for incitement to riot and rioting. Please remain calmly in your seats as you are doing."

And he blew the whistle.

Everybody was sure it was a joke. Some fools even laughed. But I knew it wasn't no joke. They didn't know the po-lice but I did. Right away I knew what they were up to. They wanted to find out everybody who was here and this was a good way to do it. They'd book everybody and get all the names and pictures and prints. Then most everybody'd be let out on a nothing bail. The charge wouldn' hold up in court but that wasn't what they cared about. By then they'd already have what they wanted.

All that was goin' through my mind without even thinkin'

280

about it. And I knew there wasn't no way I could get out now, they'd have men all around the building. I looked over at Johnny Pick. He knew it too. We just sat there and waited.

"How long you give 'em?" I asked him.

"Three, maybe four minutes," he said.

He hit it right. First thing we heard was bangin' on the doors, then 'bout a thousand po-lice rushed in. They musta been waiting right around the corner for the sign.

They took us down to the head po-lice station in buses they just happened to have right there. Some of us were kept till the next day; I was one 'cause I had a record. And they kept some of the leaders sitting on the stage, 'cluding Carter Smith. And the flagman, they got him too. The one I was watching for was the dude who started it all by sandbaggin' the flagman like that. But I didn't think I'd see him 'cause he was a pig fink.

Some big-shot lawyer come in 'round midnight to get somebody out that was on the stage, and he asked how the po-lice could make out there was a riot. And this big-shot po-lice said to him, "Whenever two or more people get together and break a law, that's a riot."

I could see the lawyer wanting to laugh in his face. But he didn't do nothin' 'cause he was a lawyer. He just walked away shaking his head.

Everybody was mad at the flagman 'cause they figured he done it all. Like they were blaming him. They were just nice, stupid white people that didn't know the first thing 'bout how the po-lice work.

But that flagman had a lotta balls. He did something I never seen nobody do. We were all standing in line when they were taking our names and he just walked up to the records desk and jumped up on it. And 'fore anybody could stop him, he dropped his pants and shit right on that motherfuckin' desk with all the papers about us on it. Then he picked up some of the papers and wiped his ass with them.

Everybody there seen him do it but nobody could believe it. Not even the po-lice. When they checked their eyes with their head they hadda believe it. By then they could smell it. A couple of them rushed over and pulled him off the desk but he already had his pants back up.

I was the first one to clap my hands for him. It was one of the greatest things I ever seen in my life. After I started it all the people from the New Left cheered him, even the foxes.

I just knew the po-lice were gonna try to stick him with everything they could. Maybe even something like incitement to shit.

By the next day when they got who everybody was, the charge for most of us was dropped to disorderly conduct. Which just meant a fine.

Soon's I got out, I called up Carter Smith. He was so mad he was spittin' steel. "They had the whole thing planned," he said to me. "Not only they had it planned but they treated us like we was from some enemy country."

"Well, ain't we?"

"Hell, no. We just tryin' to get the country *back* from the enemy is all."

"Listen, man," I told him, "you lucky you was with the whites 'cause if that thing was all black, some of us big shots'd be dead now."

"Why you think we work through the whites like we do? 'Cause we love the motherfucks? Shiiit. We just using 'em 'cause we gotta right now. When the time come that we don't gotta, we ain't gonna. Goddam. We ain't gonna work with no whites. And we ain't gonna talk to no whites. We ain't even gonna talk to no other blacks. Man, look out. I don't trust *nobody*."

I was gonna tell him to watch out he don't get a rash on his chin.

So that's how come I didn't learn too much about them whites that feel like they living in a enemy country. But it don't matter none 'cause they just feel what every black man's felt all his life. Nothing new there. Plus which, I don't know what a black man who wants to fight can talk about to that New Left. They just wanna change some things in what's been goin' on for a long time, like in the gov'ment.

282

We wanna blow the whole fuckin' shootin' match up and start all over.

But that Dropout Party the flagman is in. That's outasight. They not only don't trust nobody, they don't even *like* nobody. They don't like nobody so much they don't even wanna be around.

I think maybe they got the right idea. If things are so motherfuckin' bad, it don't hardly pay to try and change a little here and a little there. And if you ain't got no power, it don't make no sense to fight. This ain't no little country where you can go up into the mountains and everybody's waitin' for you to come and save them. Shit. You gotta always look out for number one.

Black people know all about dropping out. Every junkie is a dropout. And every wino. And everybody who can't get a job and so they leave their family. And most everybody who's not let in is a dropout too. There's a whole fuckin' nation of dropouts right here in this country. A black nation.

After that night when I heard the flagman, I figured I'd see what that Dropout Party is up to. I sent my name in and a week later I got a answer from them. It was on a small piece of paper.

"Dear Sir: The Dropout Party is not a party and there are no members since everyone is a dropout. If you are interested in joining the Dropout Party, forget it. You're not qualified."

The letter was unsigned.

And I hadda pay the post office the six cents 'cause there wasn't no stamp on it.

26.

THE Man come into Harlem in a crazy way this morning. As part of the mayor's thing to cool the streets this summer, top po-lice were goin' around to talk to poor people where they live. The Harlem team had four men. The deputy chief inspector was white. The captain was white. The lieutenant was black and the sergeant was black. That made it two and two. Nothin' racey about the New York Po-lice Department. Us niggers got a black looey. More'n one too. Yeah. Fanfuckingtastic.

Last week another team was down the Lower East Side. Jew, Italian, and a Pollack, something for everybody. And somebody was smart enough to take along a Spanish-speaking sergeant. That was the highest they could find in thirty thousand po-lice. Now the Lower East Side is dirt poor, man. And the dirt poorest is the Porto Ricans. But they got a lotta color and they dig music you can flash on, and when they start rapping in that crazy spic lang'age, it sounds like fuckin' machine guns goin' off. They fight a lot too, like everybody poor. They fight mostly with other spics who are Cubans. The PR's and Cubans don't like each other, something like the blacks and whites.

When the po-lice team went down there they run up against all kinda heavy shit. Everybody poor got problems with the po-lice, but the PR's got the most 'cause they don't talk American. The Jews and all them other people down there can talk to the po-lice but the PR's can't even do that. So they go that day and tell the Man all 'bout what's wrong. Like everything. They doing it through this Spanish-speaking sergeant. But the Man's just there to listen. I mean, they ain't there to *do* nothin'. So the PR's gettin' mad.

Then one PR dude got up and he said, "The Cubans are stealing us blind." And everybody waited for the Spanish-speaking sergeant to say it in American so's the po-lice could hear it.

But his face got all mad. "That's a lie," he said. In Spanish. And the machine guns opened up. That's when the PR's found out he was a Cuban. Only reason there wasn't no riot was 'cause the Man said they'd make a PR sergeant soon. That made everybody feel good, everybody PR anyway. And it made the Cuban sergeant feel even better 'cause he knew he was gonna make lieutenant soon.

This PR friend of mine told me about it. Angel lives down there. He come to this country three years ago and first thing he done was learn to talk American, thinkin' he'd get a good job. But he couldn' get shit. Nothin' that paid enough for him and his family, so he's gotta work two jobs plus be a janitor in his building. I told him my people been here four hundred years and we still couldn' get good jobs.

I don't like them pushy people.

The Harlem po-lice team talked to us in the YMCA on 125th Street. There's a meetin' room on the first floor that holds maybe a hundred. It was filled up, mostly young brothers and older women. What happens is the young sisters are out playing whitey's game. They wanna be Negro, not nigger. So they dressing white, talking white, trying white. The brothers already know the score and they don't waste no time on that shit. They wanna fight, not fade.

But when everybody gets older, things change. The sisters been through the misery and they know they can't slip and slide into whitey world. Now they ready to fight 'cause they mad and mean as a blackass queen. They fat from too much no-good food, they got broke families and dead kids. But now they got womb. The brothers been through the misery too. They tried to fight but you can't beat something with nothing. By the time they old they been pushed down so much the spirit is all gone. They got no balls left, so they hang 'round and do nothin'. 'Cause there ain't nothin' no more to do.

I'm sitting in that meetin' room with the brothers and sisters waiting to hear Mister Chuck and Uncle Tom tell us what good lil' chillun we is, yassuh. There's least a dozen halls 'round here much bigger'n the YMCA room, and enough people to fill them all. People mad enough to bite the beast's head off. But Mister Chuck been to college and he knows all 'bout crowds, so he gets a room that holds maybe a hundred and he puts a lotta space between the rows and he sits the other side of a long table at the head of the room and now we all back in school and the teacher is up there and we down here.

Reg'lar suburb PTA meeting, you know. Like trying to de-

285

cide what to do with the million dollars from the last cookie sale.

But we fucked 'em up. Some hairy dudes moved the front rows way up close to the table. Now they not only goin' see us, they goin' smell us. That oughta shake 'em up. Maybe we get somethin' big outta them, like pickin' up the garbage every week 'stead of every month.

When the po-lice walked into the room a few people stood up. They forgot to remember they ain't in school no more. Everybody laughed. 'Cept the po-lice. They walked quick from the door at the back of the room to the front, then they quick sat down. The two whites in the middle, the blacks on the outside. To protect the whites just in case us gorillas go wild 'cause all they got on 'em is clubs, guns, blackjacks and maybe some hand grenades in their pockets and blades in their shoes.

The captain got up and told us his name and then he named the others. I looked at the deputy chief inspector, his face was hard as stone. Easy to see he took no shit from nobody but hisself. The captain was softer, like Santa Claus. When he talked his mouth was dancing and his hands were moving and his belly was shaking. He was all rhythm.

The two Toms were black. They looked just like any two handkerchief heads. Nothin' special 'bout them. They didn't even have rhythm.

The captain was saying how glad they were to be up here. How glad these whitey big shots were to be in Harlem. So right away everybody knew it was gonna be the same shit as always.

Then he talked about how the mayor was doing his best for the poor people. Everybody listened 'cause Lindsay is a big man up here. You ask little girls 'round here you say, "Who you wanna make when you grow up?" And they all say the same thing. "Lindsay, I want make Lindsay." And they mean it too.

If he keep on blow their mind, they gonna suck his soul right into the White House someday.

When the captain done with his talk, the looey give us this long rap 'bout how they run the po-lice and what a hard job it is and how nobody likes them and what you need to be a

286

po-lice. Like white skin or a fade job. Nobody said nothin'. Everybody been through this kinda shit a million times with these Oreo cookies, their choc'late outside don't fool us. When he was all through he said if anybody got troubles, they'd listen. Yeah, and he said it with a straight face. Like maybe nobody in Harlem got troubles. One slick brother jumped up and shouted, "You got nothin' we wanna hear, Knee-grow, so you just sit down. We got business with your white masters there." Least six people shouted, "Right on." And the bag was open.

All eyes were on the white masters. Mouths opened, tongues sharpened, gold teeth flashed. Voices were pulled up from somewhere deep in the gut. The first to make it out told the message.

"Why you beat up on us all the time?"

The captain put on a big face. "A police officer's job sometimes involves the use of force."

"You tellin' us."

Reaching into his pocket, the captain took out a sheet of paper. He held it up. On one side in big red print was the word "Confidential."

"What's that?" someone asked.

"A piece of paper, you clown," someone else answered.

"I see that, mainly 'cause I got eyes. But what it do?"

"Yeah, what that paper mean?"

"It's a breakdown of all reported cases of so-called police brutality for last year," the captain said brightly.

"Who did the breakin' down?"

The captain didn't answer.

A woman spoke sharply. "What you mean *so-called* po-lice brutality? Is you saying we crazy?"

"Some of that so-called stuff broke three my ribs last year," a brother called out, "and year 'fore that I got a cracked head from it."

"Time you was seein' the po-lice again, ain't it, man?"

"No use lettin' no grass grow under your head."

"Only thing grow under his head is balls."

"Then he go get them busted."

"You people hush up," a woman demanded. "We here to get things done and you carrying on somethin' foolish."

The two white po-lice just sat there with their hands crossed on the table and silly grins on their faces.

"I think the captain has some figures on this question," the black looey said. He sounded tired already.

"We don't need no figures," a brother yelled. "We got plenty of them. What we needs is some answers."

"Which we ain't gettin'," said a dude right behind me.

"The answer is they ain't got no answers."

"Right on there, man."

"There has always been a certain amount of police brutality," the deputy chief inspector said, "especially in poorer neighborhoods." His voice had a quiet to it, like it could put you to sleep while you was gettin' beat up.

"We know that, man." The voice had anger all over it. "We been living with it and we tired of it."

"But it's always the same few who are guilty of it," the deputy chief inspector explained.

"Then get rid of 'em."

"We do our best but people don't file complaints against them. So there's nothing we can do."

"Why can't you police your own police?" a woman asked.

"The law says a man's innocent until proved guilty. We can't file charges against a man until we investigate, and we usually don't investigate unless a complaint is filed." The deputy chief inspector looked very wise sitting there with his white hair.

"Oh, man, you expect us to believe that shit? What about the pig that—"

The captain jumped up. "Now wait a minute here. We won't stand for that kinda talk."

"*You* won't stand for it?" The voice was drippin' anger. "What about what *we* been standing? Your pigs go 'round knocking off our kids even when they off duty. You been holding a kill-a-kid week up here for years. And those who do it are always back on the job or else they get to retire with a lotta money. That's what *we* gotta stand."

288

"Yeah. And what 'bout all them Black Panthers you been offing?" someone else yelled. "You commit murder and you get a promotion, we do the same thing and we get the chair."

The captain was whiter'n white. The deputy chief inspector was quiet. The two Toms looked like they wished they were dead.

"What you say to that, pig?" somebody asked loudly.

The captain shook his fist. "The next man who uses the word 'pig' will be arrested on the spot."

Everybody howled. We'd broken this white motherfucker pig.

"Cool it, man," somebody said to the brother who was pigging 'em on. "You gonna get your ass hung up off the wall."

"Yeah," another voice added, "like this a big crime wave you doing here, man, and it goin' on your record. Then you ain't gonna get none of them big-shot jobs they got waitin' for us. Shiiit, man, you ain't got good sense."

Everybody laughed again.

"Maybe we should go on to something else," the deputy chief inspector said softly. Easy to see he been around and nobody was gonna run a game on him.

"Hey, man, how do we get jobs?"

"Yeah, ain't nothin' in the schools but shop toys, man. We can't get no good jobs with that kinda shit."

"You don't give us no slack, man. What you gotta do is give us some slack."

The deputy chief inspector looked real sorry. "Unfortunately, the police department has very little to do with finding employment. Except, of course, for the department itself."

"You got plenty to do with it," someone cried out. "You make sure to bust almos' all of us, then we got po-lice records and we can't get any good jobs or nothin'."

The deputy chief inspector looked real hurt. "We arrest only those who break the law."

"Everybody breaks the law," the voice boomed back. "Everybody everywhere. Only up here we get busted for it every minute. A black man walkin' down the street, if he's under fifty he'll get picked up 'fore he gets three blocks. You can always find something to lay on him. He spends months in your stinkin' slam 'cause he ain't got the money for bail. Then even if he walks outta court free it don't mean nothin' and he can kiss off the good jobs. And if he had a job, he's lost that too."

"That happen to my boy," a woman said. "He got pick up right off the street for doing nothin'. He spend five months lock up 'fore they see he is inn'cent as a lamb but it's too late. He done lost his job, a good job he had. The welfare people say why he lose his job, they act like they don't understand. Now he's shinin' shoes."

"That's another thing," a second woman said. "The welfare give us sixty-six cents a day for food. You try feedin' your kids on sixty-six cents a day, see what happen to 'em."

"Righteous on that, sister," a young voice called out. "All we got in my house is rats and roaches. No food. I'm hungry."

The captain was beginning to get his color back. He made a deep sigh like he cared. "We'd like to help with these problems but they are out of our hands entirely."

A young sister jumped up. "What the hell you mean, outta your hands? Your hands are in everything goin' wrong up here. You let the dope pushers work right out in the open where my kids can see them. You let the whores do the same. You let the stores charge whatever they want. You let the rapers and murderers walk the streets. The only thing you don't do is let us honest folks alone."

The captain lost his color again, which he never had much anyway. His hands shook. "I don't think that's fair," he said in a raspy voice. "This is a high crime area and we're doing our best."

"Then maybe your best ain't good enough," another woman shouted. "Maybe what we needs 'round here is po-lice that live here and know everybody."

"Hallelujah."

"And why you people always comin' 'round bugging us 'bout how we live when it's all your fault? I'm sick to death of turnin' on the TV and seeing all everything and knowing I can't have nothin' what I see. No, and never goin' get nothin' either."

"Get it out front, sister."

"Sock soul to 'em."

"I live in a three-room 'partment that's so bad it wasn't good enough to have its picture took for the worst building in New York. Only reason it's three rooms is 'cause somebody got tired of it being one room and chopped it up. I don't got no heat and hot water, and the light so weak all I could put on is the TV. And when the welfare ask me is I livin' alone, I tell 'em, 'No, I'm livin' with rats.' They in the walls in the day and in the house at night. Tell you God's truth, I'm tired of livin' with rats."

"Amen," someone said.

"That the truth."

Another woman spoke up. "What 'bout what we eat up here? It ain't hardly enough to say grace over. Pinto beans and greens and fatback. Keep eatin' on that long enough and you eat youself right outta life. But nobody got no money to eat better. We need milk and meat, 'specially for the young 'uns. But we ain't got the money. Where the hell the money at?"

"Yeah. How come we don't get none of them federal funds?"

"And why we gotta pay more for things up here that cost less downtown?"

"What about all them free clinics we was promised?"

"Who goin' give us good jobs?"

"Why we gotta fight in Vietnam?"

"What you goin' do about the po-lice knockin' off all them Black Panthers?"

The brothers and sisters were really giving it to them. I almos' felt sorry for 'em but shit, they deserve it. All of it and more. Whoever got the idea for them comin' up here to be targets for people is one crazyass fool. Or else he's so smart he knows if people got somebody to lay all their mad on, they don't do nothin' about it. Like fight.

The head po-lice was smooth and he seen us gettin' all

worked up so he give a sign to the head nigger. The looey quick got up and thanked everybody for their interest. That's just what he said. "Thank you for your interest."

And it was over.

Everybody was steaming mad 'cause they saw the white man was just doing another number on them. They didn't solve anything and didn't get anything. The young brothers were the maddest of all. They didn't expect nothin' but they were hoping to maybe get a lead on some jobs. And they wanted to string it out so's they could really give it to the po-lice.

The white masters left right away. The black Toms shuffled their asses slow so they could make time with their people. But nobody was buying it.

Outside the room the looey was tellin' us why we all got to stick together. "Man, I'm with y'all but I'm over there watchin' on whitey to make sure he don't pull the plug on all of us." And he give a short laugh.

One dude put acid eyes straight on the Tom. "Cool it, my man. I know who you are, what you are, where you been and where you goin'. Nothin' you could say would make a power of diff'rence to me. I got your past banged on my head and your future hangin' on my balls. Since I first clapped eyes on you, I know you for a white man who come out the wrong color. Only reason I'm still standing here is to see the whites in your eyes. You got something to say, go kiss white ass. You so square you not even there. Your day is over, man. You wanna play that black-white skin game you been laying down here, go 'cross the river to New Georgia or out to Wrong Island. Don't come up here jacking off your jib about how you a black man. I look at you, I don't see black, I don't see nothin'. You just chalk-colorless white. You the albino nigger is what you are. And 'round here, my man, that's just shit."

Sonovabitch, that Tom just 'bout died. His eyes were popping and his mouth was hanging and he was having big trouble with his hands.

And the dude what said all that? Mister Cool. I just turned around and . . . *walked away.*

27.

I READ a lot. It's a habit I picked up in prison when I worked in that asshole library. I never opened a book in school but locked up like that, you found yourself something to do or you went crazy. Some men played cards all the time or collected things or made plans to bust out. I got turned on to books 'cause I seen the more you know, the better you can hustle. After a while I even got to where I liked it.

One thing I like to read is about Africa. How black people live in all them black countries they run themselfs, and how there ain't no whites around to fuck things up. Reading them books started me thinking that maybe the Black Muslims and the Republic of New Africa got a good idea when they say we should all live by ourselfs in our own nation. 'Course we ain't gonna get any of the United States 'cause this is white man's land now and they ain't gonna give a inch. All that shit about gettin' them Southern states for us is just crazy talk. The Indians had *all* the states and look what happened to them.

But the real Africa is something else. Maybe all them Africans got nothin' to do with me now 'cause there's four hundred years between us and that's just too long. But it's still good to know that when everything blows up here in America, there's a place to go. If any of us niggers is left to go.

With all the dudes I know, I'm a big Africa man. They see me and they say, "Here comes King Africa." That's what they call me sometimes. "There's that Marcus Garvey Black, the big Africa man." And shit like that, just sounding me. But I keep my cool. The more you know, the better you can hustle. And if I know Africa, I can hustle it. Like everybody do.

Yesterday I went over to see Oginga Kush open his new Africa bookstore over on Lenox Avenue. Oginga is a big power in this Africa thing. He's not a black man and he's not a nigger. What he is is a Afro-American. You call him black and he turns all 'round to see who you talkin' to. "The black man is in South Africa," he tells everybody. "Over here we're Afro-Americans. We're the product of two cultures and that makes us twice as good."

And he means it too. He hates the white man almos' more'n anybody I know. Only it's not really hate, more like he thinks the white man is just shit. He don't even like to be 'round them. "All lower forms of life make me uncomf'table," he says. Only trouble is he says the same thing about the blacks in Africa. And sometimes even about a lotta us black nigger Afro-Americans right around here. "You are some big snob," I once told him.

He liked that. "I'm a snob," he said, "because I got a lot to be snob about. If you got it, why not snob it?" Wasn't nothin' I could say to that. I'd be a slob not to be a snob if I had all he had.

Oginga been to Africa a lotta times and he even lived over there. First time he went, he was just Clive Jackson, the nigger born and raised in Harlem. When he come back, he was Oginga Kush, the Afro-American. He found his hustle and he worked hard at it. He learned that Swahili they talk over there and he started the whole natural-look thing all the brothers got into. And he was the first I know 'bout to call us Afro-Americans.

Then Oginga was ready. He opened a Africa clothes store and he made money selling dashikis to all the new Afro-Americans. Then he opened a Africa arts store where he sold things like a piece of a tree he called Heart of Darkness and wood drums that could send messages 'cross hundreds of miles of New York jungle. He made money there too. Then he opened

294

a Africa bowling alley where all the pins were white wood carved in the shape of a man. And all the bowling balls were solid black. More money. Then he opened a Africa bar where live monkeys were runnin' around pissing on people drinking things like rhino on the rocks and elephant highballs. Still more money.

Then he lost it all.

He got the politics bug and run on his own ticket 'gainst Acey Powell for Congress. Everybody told him he was right outta his head. Then he spent everything he had trying to prove Powell wasn't a true Afro-American. Everybody laughed him right outta his money.

When it was over Powell got a hundred percent of the vote.

"How could that be?" Oginga wanted to know. Some people tried to tell him. Acey Powell's been giving it to the white man for a whole lotta years, and he's been doing it with style. Whenever he does a number on the whites, he makes every man in Harlem feel a little better. They love him. He's a great showman and a great folk hero.

And there's something else. This is a war between blacks and whites. The black man on the Harlem street knows he's black. When he sees white skin coming down the block he knows that's white. When he looks at Powell, he sees black beating white and that's good enough for him. He don't need none of that Afro-American shit. To him that's just so much color in a black and white world.

But it does got a nice sound to it. And outside of politics it's still worth money and Oginga still got the best hustle in it. Which is what he's doing with the new bookstore.

"You think it can make money?" I asked him when I got to the store.

"You bet your Afro-American ass," he said. "Not only make money but help the struggle."

"How you make that out?"

Oginga set hisself behind the cash register. "Seven eighths of the world is nonwhite. Right?"

"Sounds about right," I told him.

"It is right. And that means the struggle is goin' on in Africa and Asia same as here."

"What about it?"

"And in Latin America too."

"So what?"

"So it's really a world war that's goin' on, you see what I mean? Not just black against white like here, but nonwhites against whites. Some places it's hot, other places it's cold. But everywhere it's on. That means there's a movement that's much bigger'n just here in this country. This thing's so big everybody's in on it." He put on his best money smile. "Now maybe an army fights on its stomach but nobody's gonna start throwin' atom bombs around, so most of the fighting in this war is gonna be in the head. It's gonna be mostly a paper war." He looked at me.

"I still don't get it."

"A paper war," he said softly, "fights on paper. Lots and lots of paper. Newspapers, magazines, books, pamphlets, even records and tapes. I'm gonna have all the best stuff from all over the world. This store gonna have nothin' but revolutionary writings. That's where the money's at today."

I think of the name. The Revolution Bookstore. Goddam, that Oginga sure got mother wit. And he's right about where the money is too. All them Kill America blacks are in the big bag making money. Not only things like the Panthers and all the poverty groups and them black fag playwriters. Which is super fine with me, I don't care what they steal long as they black. But even the motherfuck whites like them crazy yippies are into it. They use the struggle to make a name for themself and then they go into the movies and fuck everybody. Always been like that too. Fuck 'em all. I don't like none of them. Anybody ask me why I stay by myself and go it alone, they must be crazy to ask me that.

"You think enough people goin' come around?" I say to Oginga.

296

He don't look worried. Matter a fact, he don't look worried so much he don't even answer me. That's 'cause the store is full with people. It's the first day and there's free drinks and fag food so everybody's here. Mostly writers and Black Power people. Some whites too. I talk to this one dude and the first thing he says is "I love Africa."

"How long you there?" I ask him.

"Oh, I've never been there."

I look at him close. He could be young or old, it's hard to tell with these motherfuck whites. "How you know you like it?" I ask him.

He didn't know. But he wrote a book about Africa. All 'bout the animals they got there, with pictures of lions and stuff like that. "How'd you get the pictures if you never been there?" I say to him. "Did somebody take 'em for you?"

"Naturally. How else could I have done the book?"

I didn't know. But I knew enough to get the hell away from him 'fore he wanted to write about me. But there wasn't much chance of that, I s'pose. No use writing about what you already seen.

Madison Wells was over in a corner and I rapped to him for a while. He wasn't too happy with Oginga's store. "It ain't Africa," he said. "The man calls himself an Afro-American but he's got shit from everywhere else."

"But it's s'pose to be a revolution place," I told him.

"Fuck the revolution. I ain't interested in people I don't know nothin' about. Only thing counts with me is what's goin' down right here."

"This ain't Africa, man."

"Same thing," Madison said. "We're black and so are they. That makes us brothers. Only diff'rence is they own everything where they live and we don't got spit 'round here."

"Some diff'rence," I told him.

His eyes got hard. "Yeah. That's 'cause they all black in Africa. If this country was most black we'd have everything."

We stood there thinkin' about everything.

297

"First thing I'd do is kill off every last motherfucking white."
"Only the men," I said to him. "No use to kill the golden goose."

"Yeah."

"Yeah."

We stood there thinkin' about white women.

Over by the underground newspapers some people were laughing like crazy. When I got close, I seen they all were holding diff'rent papers. I asked a dude what they were playing.

"Fuck It. You know the game?"

I shook my head.

"Really very simple. Everybody gets a copy of one of these papers and then whoever is up just reads one of the classified sex ads. The others have to try to find ads that are even wilder. Whoever gets a good one first is next up."

"How you win?"

"If you read an ad that nobody can top, you're the winner."

"That all?"

He laughed. "I've been playing the damn game for three years and I've never seen anybody win yet, I don't think anyone *can* win. Whatever you find, somebody can beat it. That's why it's called Fuck It."

I listened once when he was up.

"Nineteen-year-old wants to find out if she's a lesbian or not. Anyone who can help and is experienced and attractive. Please hurry."

Everybody quick looked in their papers.

"I got one that beats it," someone said. "Just listen to this: Black male, thirty, tactful, will make love to your wife while you watch. Prefer white women only. Husbands can be any color."

The dude I was talking to leaned over to me. "You see what I mean? You just can't win."

"Why you play?"

"Because the others can't win either. That makes me feel good."

298

I walked away. Fuck it. No sense hanging 'round somebody who feels bad 'cause he can't win and good 'cause nobody else can win. He's just a loser is what he is. No winners, all losers.

Shit, that game oughtta be called Black and White.

On the walls are big signs that Oginga put up in all the diff'rent book sections. EAT. DRINK. TALK. FUCK. BUT DON'T TOUCH THE BOOKS.

Everybody's eating, drinking, talking and touching the books. Nobody's fucking. Then I see Wynona Goodbody and I get stiff just thinkin' about her, thinkin' maybe I can get the balls rolling in the fuck section. Me and Wynona usta be tight 'fore I met up with Sunny but then we just fell apart. Wynona didn't like Sunny no way and no how. Mostly 'cause she was white. Wynona's darker'n shark shit. The whitest thing she smiles at is black, and it gets darker from there.

I'm watching her twitch and I know her cat is humming down there like a black canary. I remember it, all soft and wet. Been more'n a year but, shit, that was a long time ago. I figure she be glad to see me 'cause she never was the kind to remember nothing. I put on my best cat smile and I walk on over. The big fuck section at Oginga's is about to open.

"You lookin' real boss today, Wynona."

Her eyes get wide and she turns on a smile that's sweet as sin. Her lips begin to move and I'm purring to myself. I'm the big cat man.

"You talkin' to me, you shit-colored nigger that hangs out with white women?"

And the big fuck section at Oginga's closes faster'n a turtle in a tornado.

After that I got stoned best I could. I remember there was a horse in the store and I wanted to paint it with white stripes so's it'd look like a zebra. Then 'stead of Black Power and White Power we'd just have Zebra Power and everybody'd be happy. 'Cept the blacks who wanted Black Power and the whites who wanted White Power. Which was everybody.

I was all set to paint the horse when somebody asked me

299

what I was doing with a sand pail full of cigarette butts. I told him it was a bucket of white paint that I was gonna use to paint the horse.

"What horse?"

"The horse that's standing right there."

"There ain't no horse standing there."

I didn't think he should lie about a thing like that so I threw the bucket of paint on him and burnt a half-dozen holes in his suit.

That's when the cannon went off.

Some joker had tied the horse 'cross the mouth of this big motherfuck cannon while I wasn't looking. And then they fired it. Now I didn't have a horse no more but least I had the cannon, so I went over to it and this big fat momma screamed 'cause I had my hand up her ass. Some devil had turned my cannon into somebody's ass.

I got my hand out just in time to see the floor crack open from the earthquake. It was gettin' wider and wider and it looked just like a long snake slippin' 'cross the floor. I yelled for everybody to watch out but people kept falling into the crack and then I was the only one left and Oginga Kush come up behind me and chopped off my head and took it into a back room where there was no earthquake and the rest of my body followed my head.

I was on a real bummer.

By time I got home on a flying book that looked like a coffee cup I was awright again. I took off my clothes and hung 'em on the trees that were growin' outta my ceiling and I went to bed.

That's when I had the dream.

Only it wasn't just a dream. It really happened, I know that. But maybe it was at some other time or in some other life, something like that. All I know is I wasn't really asleep and I wasn't just dreaming 'cause I said and did things I didn't know nothin' about. And besides which, everything was in all kinda colors just like real life.

I was the president of Africa. Me, Marcus Garvey Black. What I did was I started a Afro-American Improvement Association. All the black people joined it 'cause I was gonna go there to Africa and take it over and arm everybody and make it the big mother country for blacks all over the world. I was the biggest big shot in the whole Home Is Africa Movement. I went all 'round America talkin' about how black is beautiful and everybody should learn about Africa history. All my followers wore Africa clothes and buttons that were red and black and green. Everybody liked me 'cause I told 'em that the black man was better'n the white man. I didn't let no whites in the Afro-American Improvement Association and I didn't take no money from them. When I set up all kinda business they couldn' even buy stock. I told the whites they were devils and Satan was white but God was black.

There was branches of the AAIA in every big city in the country. But New York was the biggest 'cause that's where I lived. I started a new black religion and called it the Africa Black Church. It had a black Jesus and his black Virgin Mother and a black Ghost and all the saints and angels were black too. Only thing white in that whole church was the white phones 'cause they cost more'n the black ones. I started a Black Cross that had doctors and nurses and sent food to people that needed it. And I had my own black army, the Africa Legion. They wore black uniforms and black boots. Even their shorts was black. And they had tanks and ships and planes. All painted black.

Another thing I started was clubs for young people, like the Brother Scouts and the Sister Scouts. And the Marcus Garvey Black College, where black kids went to school to learn about me. I done a lotta business too. There was a black toothpaste company and a black soap-powder factory and I even had a black transportation thing. The Black Circle Steamship Line. It took black people all around Manhattan.

Whenever I talked to people I wore a uniform that was black and red and green with gold drippin' all over and a big helmet with a lotta black feathers. Once a year I'd have a big meetin' in New York and a million people'd march down Lenox Avenue and I'd be riding in a big black car with the top down so's everybody could see me in my uniform. When we got to Madison Square Garden I'd step outta my car and they'd throw black flowers in front of my feet all the way inside. Then I'd tell 'em how black is beautiful and Africa is home and the black God is good 'cause He gives black people what they want. And which they could see was true just lookin' at me 'cause I was sure gettin' mine awright. And after I'd tell 'em how great everything was gonna be in Africa, they'd make me president of Africa all over again.

It was a good life.

Too good to last.

Just when I had everything set for all us Afro-Americans to go to Africa, the brothers over there sent a message. It was very short and very clear.

"Niggers, Stay Home."